ONCE BURNED

A JACK McMORROW MYSTERY

GERRY BOYLE

ISLANDPORT PRESS

Lyrics to "A Hard Rain's A-Gonna Fall" (Copyright © 1963 by Warner Bros. Inc.; renewed 1991 by Special Rider Music) reprinted with permission.

ONCE BURNED
A Jack McMorrow Mystery

First Islandport Edition/ March 2015

All Rights Reserved.

Copyright © 2015 by Gerry Boyle

ISBN: 978-1-939017-60-4
Library of Congress Control Number: 2014911176

Islandport Press
P.O. Box 10
Yarmouth, Maine 04096
www.islandportpress.com
books@islandportpress.com

Publisher: Dean Lunt
Cover Design: Tom Morgan, Blue Design
Interior Book Design: Teresa Lagrange, Islandport Press
Cover image courtesy of Rynio Productions

Printed in the USA

For Vic. We sail on.

ACKNOWLEDGMENTS

ONCE BURNED could not have been written without the generous assistance of several people in the Maine law enforcement community, especially Sgt. Ken Grimes of the Office of the State Fire Marshal, and investigators under his supervision, including Ken MacMaster. The villain in ONCE BURNED would have been hard-pressed to evade Maine's real-life professionals. I also want to thank John Morris, Maine commissioner of public safety and inveterate reader, for his readiness to hook me up with the right people.

I'm also grateful to Genevieve Morgan, senior editor at Islandport Press, for her perceptive reading of the manuscript for ONCE BURNED and contagious enthusiasm for all things McMorrow, and to Dean Lunt, Islandport publisher, for reissuing the McMorrow novels and introducing Jack and friends to a new audience.

Oh, who did you meet, my blue-eyed son
Who did you meet, my darling young one?
I met a young child beside a dead pony
I met a white man who walked a black dog
I met a young woman whose body was burning
I met a young girl, she gave me a rainbow
I met one man who was wounded in love
I met another man who was wounded in hatred
And it's a hard, it's a hard, it's a hard, it's a hard
And it's a hard rain's a-gonna fall.

—BOB DYLAN, "A HARD RAIN'S A-GONNA FALL"

ONCE BURNED

A JACK McMORROW MYSTERY

PREFACE

He bought the wick online from a candle-supply shop in Houston, calling the people up first to ask which type of wick burned the hottest. The woman said to go with the paper core, as it burned much hotter than the zinc, but only to go with paper if he would be using it with very large containers. He said, Yes, as a matter of fact, he was. Very large containers.

The idea was that he'd lay out six feet or so of wick so he'd be outside watching before the fire started. He'd timed it and found that six feet gave him twelve to fifteen minutes, the wick burning faster with no wax to slow it down. Fifteen minutes was plenty. He had time to get away but the gasoline hadn't dissipated too much. He didn't want an explosion—too quick—but he didn't want a smoldering fire, either.

He'd tried it first on a couple of abandoned outbuildings. They were half-collapsed sheds, tinder-dry, at the back of an overgrown lot behind a beatdown strip mall. The first one went up in minutes, snapping and crackling, embers floating into the sky like orange stars. The second, a bigger garage sort of thing, was filled with trash, and it burned slowly, with billowing clouds of gray smoke. That was when he noticed the colors.

Sometimes he wanted to tell somebody, you know, you think flames are just yellow and orange, but they're more than that. When the fire was just getting going there was red and orange, with flares of yellow and white. Later the flames would turn blue and green. He looked it up online and it had to do with the amount of soot. All this knowledge he couldn't ever share.

So there was always tension, whether to stay or go. It seemed a shame to miss the fire entirely, the wick burning down, the gas igniting, the flames hesitating, darting, pausing again, racing ahead. And that moment where the gas has almost burned off, a few seconds where you think maybe the fire is going out. And then a wisp of flame, a crackle of burning wood, and the flames reaching upward, uncoiling like some living thing.

When they died in the fires, when he stood and listened to their screams, it was like their lives were carried upward with the smoke, the screams a cry for forgiveness that would never ever come. Because this was punishment for what they'd done, but it was a sacrifice, too. His offering to her. His way of showing that she would never be forgotten. He remembered. And they would remember.

Because it was the last thing they felt. The heat. The flames. Skin and hair igniting like they were made of paper. The excruciating pain. The suffocating smoke. The searing hot gases sucked into their lungs until the last agonizing breath.

It was hell on earth.

1

"You know we're in the red," Roxanne said.

"Uh-huh," I said.

I kissed her bare shoulder. Then again.

"As in, we're spending more money than we're taking in."

I pulled the sheet down and kissed the top of her breast.

"Jack," Roxanne said, pulling the sheet back up.

"I never made love with an accountant before," I said.

"You just did. Now we need to talk about money."

"You know you're sexy when you get all financial."

"When I think about money, I don't feel sexy," she said. "I feel stressed."

"You weren't feeling stressed a little while ago."

"That was then. This is now."

"Can't we bask a little longer in the afterglow?" I said.

Roxanne reached for her wine. Sipped and put the glass down on the bedside table. Lay back and tucked the sheet under her chin.

"Last month we were thirteen hundred in the hole. That's coming out of savings. Which is just about gone."

She sighed.

"I've got checks coming in," I said. "Twelve hundred from the *Globe* for the Trenton murder and the high-school bullying piece. Eight-fifty from the *Times* for the Hillyard trial."

"That's all spent," Roxanne said. "The house insurance and my car."

"The car was a one-time thing. It's not like the transmission will go next month, too."

"It'll be something else."

"Clair and I ought to see the next payment from the Martins pretty soon."

"Last time you cut wood for them it took weeks."

"They're slow but reliable."

"Jack," Roxanne said. "Sophie starts school soon. I'm thinking it's time for me to go back to work."

"I could just write more."

"You say that, but you do the same amount of stories."

"The papers are shrinking," I said. "They can only take so much."

"What happened to the ninety-three-year-old lobsterman?"

I frowned.

"I'll wait 'til he's a hundred. Better hook."

"Just because there's no crime in it—"

"No, I just have a better idea: This whack job down in Sanctuary has torched three old barns in three weeks. It was in the *Press Herald*. Just a brief. I'll head down there and check it out."

Roxanne looked skeptical.

"Sanctuary? The town in *American Living*? What was it? Top places to retire?"

"No, it was 'Hidden Treasures.' The magazine's big cover story. Subhead was something like, 'Twenty American towns where it really is a beautiful day in the neighborhood.' Ha. If you don't mind the arsonist."

"Whoops," Roxanne said.

"Really. Like the Man of the Year turning out to be a child molester. The perfect community turns out to have some sicko out in the woods with a gas can and a lighter. A lot of times there's a sexual thing connected to it. Some sort of twisted pyro/sexual perversion."

I smiled.

"Wouldn't you rather read about that than some crotchety old fisherman?" I said.

Roxanne looked over at me, her beautiful eyes narrowed. She shook her head.

"There's something wrong with you, Jack McMorrow," she said.

I leaned over and kissed her shoulder.

"I've never made love with a psychologist before."

It was six-thirty. Sophie had been up for an hour, rising with the sun.

I'd given her breakfast—waffles and fresh strawberries, a glass of juice that she drank with two hands. She slipped down from her chair, ran to the back door, and sat to put on her boots. Little riding boots that Clair and Mary had given her. They'd come with a brown-and-white dappled pony, just two weeks before.

"I have to go see Pokey," Sophie said, struggling to get the boot on. I walked over and bent down and gave it a yank.

"You sure Clair is up?"

"Clair's always up," she said.

"He must sleep sometimes," I said, pushing her foot into the other boot.

"No," Sophie said. "He doesn't have to sleep. He was in the Marines."

"Really," I said. "Marines don't have to sleep?"

"Not Clair, 'cause he was a 'mando. I want to be a 'mando when I grow up."

As if on cue, there was a tap at the sliding-glass door.

"Clair," Sophie said, scrambling to her feet. She ran to the door and tugged. Clair slid the door open and stepped in. He was wearing a tan barn jacket and jeans. His cap was orange-yellow with STIHL and a chain saw on the front.

"Is Pokey awake?" Sophie said.

"Waiting for you, pumpkin," Clair said.

"I bet he's hungry," she said.

"I bet you're right."

Sophie ran to the table, dragged a chair to the counter, climbed up, and took an apple from the bowl.

"Just hearing about my daughter's career plans," I said. "She wants to be a commando."

"Expanding role for women in the military," Clair said.

"Good to hear," I said.

Sophie trotted past us, boots clattering on the pine floor.

"Let's go," she said to Clair, and was out the door, across the deck, down to the lawn.

"Officer material," Clair said. "Could be," I said.

"Supposed to rain pretty heavy later this morning."

"Yeah. Right call to stay out of the woods."

"You always say that," Clair said. "Gonna do something constructive? Or just tippy-type one of your little stories?"

"I don't know. Maybe I'll iron some doilies first."

"Attaboy," he said.

Sophie was back at the door.

"Come on, Clair. Pokey's starving."

"I'm coming, biscuit," he said.

He turned to me and smiled.

"I'll bring her back."

"Happy trails," I said, and he was out the door, crossing the deck and the lawn in his long strides, Sophie trotting in front of him like a tumbling cub. I watched them until they disappeared down the trail through the trees, felt the bubbling over she gave me. I'd look at her, in mid-Sophie conversation, and lose track of what we were saying. Just look at her and grin. "Daddy," she'd say. "You're being silly."

So I was, yet again, and then I walked to the side door and outside to the drive. There were morning birds calling, and I stopped for a moment and listened: cardinal, hairy woodpecker, phoebe, chickadee, the usual crows. I kept going to the road, slipped the newspapers out of their boxes: *Portland Press Herald, Bangor Daily News*, and, this being Thursday, the *Waldo County News*.

On the way back up the drive, I paused again and listened. Red-eyed vireo. Tufted titmouse. Flicker. Chestnut-sided warbler. A distant raven. To the east the sky was darkening and the air was heavy.

I went inside and Roxanne was up, putting coffee in the machine. She was barefoot, wearing one of my flannel shirts. I patted her backside.

"I've never made love with a barista before," I said.

She ignored me, started the drip, took her laptop from the counter.

I went to the study and ran a finger down the bookshelf, past the homicide investigation and firearms manuals, and pulled out a textbook. Guide for Fire and Explosion Investigations. It was the 2001 edition, picked up years back for another arson story, but I figured fire starters couldn't have changed that much.

I flipped the book open, skimmed. The general arson categories: excitement, vandalism, revenge, crime concealment, profit, terrorism. Subcategories of retaliation under revenge: personal, societal, institutional, group. Under excitement: thrill seeking, attention seeking, recognition, sexual gratification or perversion. Spree arson versus serial arson. (A cooling-off period between fires marks serial arson, like a serial killer.)

I smiled. "Ready to rock and roll," I said, setting the book on the desk and going back to the kitchen.

We sat. I sipped my lukewarm tea and started on the papers. Roxanne flipped her laptop open and started reading. She began with the previous day's *New York Times*, which I'd picked up for her in Belfast. I had the Waldo County News police blotter.

"Break-ins over on the Hidden Valley Road," I said. "They're coming in during the day."

"Huh," she said. "Syria is a nightmare."

"Huh," I said.

Roxanne got up, fixed her coffee, came back and sat, legs crossed. Very pretty legs. We sipped. The papers rustled. She tapped at the keys. I moved on to the *Bangor Daily News*. A big drug bust in Woodland, some guy with a meth lab in a parked woodchip trailer. A stabbing in Bangor proper, a melee outside a bar. Victim was stable. Fight was over a woman.

I rustled the pages. Roxanne tapped the keys.

"This budget goes through, I may not have an agency to go back to," she said.

"Here we go," I said. "Another arson in Sanctuary."

"Oh, my God," Roxanne said. "Oh, my God."

2

Roxanne's face was gray, her mouth open. She closed it and swallowed. Her finger touched a single key.

"What's the matter?" I said.

"It's Ratchet," she said. "He's dead."

"Ratchet the kid?"

"Oh, my God," she said again.

"What?"

"It's under investigation. They're interviewing Sandy."

A long pause as she read, her mouth hanging open.

"Who's Sandy?" I said again.

"Ratchet's foster mom," Roxanne said, peering at the screen. "Oh, I can't believe this."

"This is the kid with the junkie parents?"

"Beth."

"And the boyfriend who gave him the weird name."

"Alphonse," Roxanne said.

"So what happened?"

"Cause of death appears to be blunt force trauma. Oh, God."

"The foster mom? Would she do that? Aren't they trained?"

"She called 911. He wasn't breathing."

Roxanne was shaking her head.

"You knew this person, right?"

"Sandy? For years. She was fine. A little rough around the edges."

"Are they saying she did it?"

"It's under investigation."

Roxanne started to take deep breaths. Her faced turned from gray to a sickly white.

"Oh, Jack," she said. "I feel sick."

I got up, put my arm around her shoulder.

"It's okay."

"But I pulled him," Roxanne said.

"You didn't know."

"I helped place him."

"Nobody could have known that—"

"He was three, Jack," Roxanne said, tears spilling down her cheeks. "Just this skinny little boy. He'd hang onto my legs."

She reached for the keyboard, touched a key, pressed her clenched fist to her mouth.

"Oh, no."

"What?"

"Beth."

"What about her?"

"She's out of jail."

"For the robbery? The credit union?"

"Oh, my God, I'm in here, Jack."

"What?"

Roxanne fell back in the chair, swallowed hard. I turned the laptop and read:

> *Contacted Wednesday, the child's mother, Beth Leserve, 22, of Portland, said the State Department of Health and Human Services (DHHS) was responsible for the child's death. In addition to Sandra St. John, the foster parent, Leserve faulted DHHS caseworker Roxanne Masterson for removing the boy from Leserve's home and placing him in State custody.*

"They said I wasn't a fit mother," Leserve said. "And they give my son to a murderer?"

She said she was following an action plan, devised by Masterson. "I was trying," Leserve said. "Working real hard at it. Then one day they just freakin' pull the plug."

After her child was taken into State custody, she was so distraught that she had a relapse, she said, returning to her abuse of prescription medications, which led to heroin use. She ended up in prison for robbing a credit union in an attempt to get drug money. Leserve said she was released from prison three weeks ago, had gotten off drugs, and was trying to regain custody of her son when news came of his death.

"I know I'm not perfect," she said. "But the State killed my son. They killed him. They took my baby and gave him to this murderer. My baby's blood is on their [expletive] hands."

According to DHHS spokesperson Anthony Shea, Masterson had worked as a child protective caseworker for nine years. She resigned from her position with the agency last November for personal reasons. Masterson could not be reached for comment Wednesday.

"She was just totally strung out," Roxanne said, to me, to herself, to nobody. "She'd forget to feed him. Change his diaper. And the people in the house, my God, they were all addicts, substance abusers, junkies. I mean, he would have died if he'd stayed there. Malnutrition, getting stepped on, something. What choice did I have? We tried working with her for a year. More than a year. I mean, you remember."

"It's okay. She's just feeling guilty, taking it out on everyone else."

I put my hand over Roxanne's and squeezed.

"We did have a plan. An action plan. She'd promise she'd get clean, but she could never pull it together. Three or four days, right back to it, needle in her arm."

"I remember."

I looked at the story, scrolled down.

There was a photo of Beth, the mom. Dark hair, attractive in a tough, I-could-kick-your-ass sort of way. But what struck me was her eyes: hollow, tired, sunken in shadows. Eyes that spoke of years of drama, and tumult, and disappointment. And now this. She was clutching a teddy bear to her chest and staring mournfully into the camera. Next to that was a Facebook-looking photo of Sandy St. John, the foster mom. She was smiling brightly, with perky, pointed features, hair still in high-school bangs.

I tapped the keys.

And there was Roxanne, a newspaper file photo. It was winter, the collar of her black leather jacket turned up, angry eyes, mouth curled in a snarl.

"I look like a criminal," she said.

"From when you were outside court in Galway."

"We were coming out, after the Eddy trial. I was telling the photographers they couldn't take pictures of the kids. And that one jerk wouldn't stop."

"I remember."

She reached for the keyboard, looked at the screen.

"Damn."

"What?"

"Beth says she's going to get a lawyer," Roxanne said. "How can she afford that? She doesn't have ten cents."

"They'll take thirty percent, if they think they can force a settlement."

"From us? But I didn't do anything wrong."

"Wrong's got nothing to do with it," I said. "Wrong is in the eyes of the jury."

"Jury?" Roxanne said, burying her face in her hands, shaking her head. "Oh, Jack."

The phone rang.

"Don't answer it," I said.

We sat and waited for the answering machine to click on. It did. A woman's voice—young, earnest, and sympathetic. "Hi. This is Caitlin Carpenter. I'm a reporter for the Portland Advertiser? I'm trying to reach Roxanne Masterson, formerly a child protective worker for DHHS? Roxanne, could you call me back on my cell? My number is—"

Roxanne picked up a pen. I reached over and took it away.

The phone rang most of the morning. Caitlin Carpenter called four times. A reporter for the *Bangor Record*, Sam something, rang up twice. Two TV reporters called, one breathless young guy saying he was preparing a report for the six o'clock news and on a tight deadline.

"Tell somebody who cares," I said.

The phone stopped ringing only when Roxanne was on it. She talked to her former supervisor, David, and a DHHS lawyer named Sylvia, Roxanne alternating between defending herself and beating herself up. I went out on the deck and stood under the overhang of the roof and watched the rain. It was falling steadily, noisy on the trees at the edge of the grass, the smell of summer welling up from the woods. Ordinarily I loved days like this, the hush that fell over the green-walled woods, everything softened by the gauze of rain. But not today. The woods seemed dismal and dark, like the sadness in the house had spilled out, the melancholy spreading.

And then Roxanne was off the phone. I slid the door open and went back in. She came toward me, phone in her hand, looking slightly relieved.

"Dave says I shouldn't worry; it'll sort itself out."

"That's good," I said. "I'm sure it will."

"He says Sandy thinks Ratchet tried to climb up on the kitchen counter while she was in the bathroom. She heard the noise and found him on the floor. He must've fallen and landed wrong."

"So it was a freak accident?"

"She was out of the room for three minutes."

"Climbed up to get a cookie or something?"

"Maybe," she said. "He didn't say."

"Huh," I said.

"Dave and the lawyer say they don't think Beth has much of a case. I mean, it's tragic, but it's not negligence. You can't tie a four-year-old down every time you leave the room."

"Or they get you for that," I said.

Roxanne walked over and stood beside me. We looked out at the rain, the grass, the green wall of the sad woods.

"I love you," I said.

"I know," she said.

"I'm sorry for your troubles."

"Yes. I'm sorry, too."

She took a long breath and exhaled and it came out a trembling sigh.

"He was so sweet. This sweet little boy, in spite of it all."

"I remember you saying that," I said. "How he was a bit of light in that mess of a house."

"Trusting. I mean, with all that had happened to him, he still would look at you and just smile. That was his first reaction to people. Me. His mom's junkie friends. His dad, that piece of garbage."

She wiped her tears. My eyes started to well.

"He never got any breaks," I said.

"And now this," Roxanne said. "He didn't deserve this."

"He didn't deserve any of it."

"And Beth didn't deserve whatever it was that made her. She had some awful story, being molested by her uncle or somebody."

"Evil begets evil," I said. "Passed down like a gene."

She turned to me, her cheeks glistening.

"But you know what was funny, Jack? It was Ratchet, this skinny little kid with a weird do-it-yourself haircut and too-small clothes, he was the one who seemed to break the cycle. He just loved everybody."

"Like Sophie," I said.

"Yes," Roxanne said. "Like Sophie."

"Who's gotten all the breaks."

"Yes."

"And this little guy," I said. "He got no breaks at all."

She bit her lip, and the tears squeezed out. "Maybe if I'd left him there. Maybe if I'd let Beth try a little longer. Maybe—"

"Stop," I said, and I took her in my arms and she sobbed and shook.

After a while, we separated and Roxanne sighed and I said, "Wonder how Clair's doing with our cowgirl?"

"We should get her home for lunch," she said.

"They won't call if you don't. And she'll stay with Pokey for days."

"Yeah."

A long pause, the rain coming down, the leaves trembling like they were about to burst into tears.

I broke the silence. "You don't think . . . I don't know . . . that Sandy could have lost it or something?"

It had to be said.

"I can't imagine. I mean, I know Ratchet was pretty hyper, ADD and who knows what else. Beth was using so much when she was pregnant—he was born addicted—and then he was on meds. And it could get to you, how he could never get enough attention, how he just never settled down. But hit him? I don't think so."

"What if Sandy just pushed him and he fell? Hit his head on the side of a table or something?"

I could feel Roxanne deflate.

"Sorry," I said. "I just never quite believe the party line. And your bosses have reason to circle the wagons."

Roxanne turned to me.

"Jack, they're not liars."

I shrugged. She turned away again.

"You think we need a lawyer, then?" she said.

"Wouldn't hurt to talk to somebody," I said. "In case she pushes it."

"Where are we going to get the money for that?"

"I'll get to work," I said.

"It'll take you two days to make what a lawyer makes in two hours," Roxanne said.

"Then maybe I'd better get started."

3

I pulled into Clair's on my way out. There were lights on in the barn, and as I approached the door I could hear Vivaldi playing. The Four Seasons. "Summer."

"Hey," I called. "Where are you cowpokes?"

"Daddy," Sophie called, from the back of the barn. "In here."

I walked through the shop, slid the wooden door aside, and started for the box stalls. Halfway down on the left a door was open. I stepped into the stall, saw Clair brushing Pokey, Sophie standing by the pony's head, holding the halter and stroking his nose.

"We're making Pokey beautiful," she said.

He was stumpy and swaybacked, with a shaggy mane, doleful eyes.

"He's looking great," I said.

"One fine piece of horseflesh," Clair said.

I gave him the look.

He said, "Honey, I think Pokey's earned a carrot."

"I'll get it," Sophie said, and she handed me the halter and slipped out of the stall, her boot steps echoing down the wooden walkway.

Clair kept brushing as I told him about Roxanne and Ratchet and Sandy.

"Little guy never had a chance," he said. "In the war, the kids were what tore at me. Didn't deserve any of it. Parents gone, eating garbage in the streets. You wanted to pick them up, as many as you could carry, and take them home."

"To a place like this," I said.

"Yes," Clair said. "I even looked into it. They threw up all kinds of road-blocks. Maybe should have tried harder."

"I'm sure you did what you could."

He was quiet, mind racing into the past.

"You know, for a little while there I used to keep a count. Number of enemy I killed. Number of kids I should have saved."

"Wipe the slate clean?"

"Cleaner, maybe. Nobody comes out of war clean."

We stood for a minute. Pokey looked over at me and snorted.

"I've got to go do some work," I said.

Clair said, "I'll shore her up."

"I doubt any reporters would make it this far."

"If they do, I'll shoo them along," Clair said.

"I mean, Roxanne. Really. Of all the people to get caught up in something like this," I said.

"Of all the people."

"Not fair," I said.

"Fairness is an abstraction, a human invention," Clair said. "Justice is elusive, random, and accidental."

"Who said that?"

"I did," he said.

I smiled.

"Should've taught college instead of wasting your time crawling around in the jungle."

"They wouldn't like my research methods."

"Or your penchant for firearms," I said.

"So here we are," Clair said.

"Yes," I said. "Here we are."

Boots clattered and Sophie slipped back into the stall with a long, thick carrot clutched in her fist. Pokey stirred and snorted. She held it out and he bit the end off and chewed. She held out the carrot again.

"I've got to go do some work, honey," I said.

"Okay, Daddy," she said. "I'll just be here, making sure Pokey's all set."

Another chomp, Sophie yanking her little fingers back with the remnant of the carrot. Pokey chewed. I bent and gave Sophie a kiss on the cheek and left. Vivaldi escorted me out.

Sanctuary is west of Rockland, on the banks of the Sanctuary River, which runs eight miles south to the sea. I'd been through it, in my meandering, remembered a town square surrounded by black-shuttered colonial houses and marked by monuments to Sanctuary's war dead. I had stopped one rainy fall afternoon and checked out the monuments. I remembered being impressed that somebody in the town had made sure to include the dead from recent wars that had never quite been declared: Iraq, times two, Afghanistan, a war without end.

I took the overland route from Prosperity, driving back roads through Knox and Morrill, slogging the pickup down muddy tracks through Searsmont and Appleton. The roads were marked by four corners named for settlers who had died off and, in many of these deserted tracts, had never been replaced. Their houses stood empty, paint scoured away by wind and rain, barns collapsed like a tornado had spun through, when really it was just the twister of time.

But not in Sanctuary, which was close enough to the allure of the coast to keep people and money in good supply. The magazine story had listed it as one of twenty "Hidden Treasures," coming in at number seven, between Black Mountain, North Carolina, and Prescott Valley, Arizona. A town where you can have your boat out back, motor to the sea in a half-hour. A town where the general store sells live bait and the Wall Street Journal. A town where a horse farm goes for the price of a mobile home in bluegrass country. A town where your neighbor's family may have lived in Sanctuary for five generations, or she may have just retired from a Foreign Service post in Oman.

Or she may be an arsonist—but not likely. Most arsonists are male.

The treasure remained hidden as I crossed Route 17 and continued south past scruffy ranch houses and a gun shop. Then after a few miles, the town emerged—first a few farmhouses perched on roadside knolls, and then bigger houses, the square, the store and post office.

The fire station.

It was a big, brick building with four bays, a paved parking lot, and a sign with a painted thermometer that said the fire danger was moderate. I wondered if that meant forest fires or arson. I pulled in and looked for someone to ask.

There were two big pickups parked by the side door: a jacked-up Chevy painted flat black, a NASCAR #88 plate in the back window, and a gleaming red Tahoe with SANCTUARY VFD on the door and CHIEF in an embossed tag above the license plate.

I eased my Toyota truck between them, grabbed my notebook, got out, and walked to the door. I opened it and stepped inside.

The firehouse was cool and dimly lit, smelling of soap and wax and rubber hoses. A teenage guy in jeans and work boots and a dark-blue T-shirt was crouched next to the wheel of the closest truck. He was polishing a big chrome valve sort of thing. I walked up behind him and could hear him grunting along with whatever music was streaming from his iPod.

"Hi, there," I said.

He kept polishing. I tapped him on the shoulder and he whirled, reached reflexively for the knife in the sheath on his belt, next to the fireman's pager.

"Easy," I said

He was wiry, muscled, with a tan that ended above the elbow like he'd dipped his forearms in stain. His hair was a grown-out buzz cut, and his face was long with a mouth set in a stoic frown.

He yanked one earbud out, said, "Shouldn't sneak up on a man like that."

"Shouldn't listen to music that loud. You'll make yourself deaf."

He ignored the advice, said, "You need something?"

"Chief here?"

"Chief's my dad."

He said it like it gave him clout.

"Good for you," I said. "He around?"

He looked at me more closely.

"Who's asking?" he said.

"I'm Jack McMorrow. I'm a reporter."

His eyes narrowed with distaste.

"Chief's in his office."

"Where's that?"

He jerked his thumb toward the rear of the building.

"Carry on," I said, and headed that way, walking past the red pumper. Its chrome was polished like the brass on a yacht, and the floor was damp in places, freshly washed. When I looked to my left I saw two more young guys polishing a red-and-white rescue truck. Behind the trucks was an office with windows facing the truck bays. A man seated at a desk. The sign on the door said CHIEF FREDERICK.

I knocked and he said, "Yeah."

I opened the door and stepped in and smiled. He was fiftyish. Cropped gray hair and ruddy drinker's cheeks. Thin lips. The same blue outfit as his kid. Handsome, in a beer-commercial sort of way. He didn't get up.

"Chief Frederick," I said. "I'm Jack McMorrow. Newspaper reporter."

He continued shuffling through papers covered with columns and numbers. He didn't look up. Or reply. I kept going.

"I live up in Prosperity. I saw the news briefs about the arson fires."

A flicker in the eyebrows. His version of dialogue.

"So I'm interested in knowing more about that."

He didn't answer. This time I didn't help him out. He stared up at me and I thought of the kids' game where you stare at each other until one of you breaks down and laughs.

The chief took a long breath, through his nose, mouth still clenched.

"What'd you say your name is?"

I told him.

"What paper you from?"

"I'm a freelancer. A stringer. I write for different papers."

"Like what?"

"*New York Times. Boston Globe.*"

He finally looked up.

"Don't they have their own fires down in New York?"

"I'm sure they do. But I write about Maine."

"What do they care about Maine in New York?" the chief said.

"Some stories are just interesting," I said.

"Somebody burning down an old woodshed?"

"You'd be surprised."

He gave me a long look.

"I guess I would," he said.

There was a sound behind me, his son standing in the door, rag in his hand.

"I finished the pumper, Chief," he said. He didn't address him as Dad.

"Got the hoses laid out?"

"Yessir."

"Casey and Ray-Ray done with Rescue One?"

"Finishing the wax."

"Well, Paulie, then get over there and help them, 'stead of just standing here jibber-jabbering."

"Yessir," Paulie said, and he was gone.

Ah, I thought. The chief was the king and this was his fiefdom. His son polishing the truck, hoping for a morsel of approval.

I turned back to Frederick.

"So, the arson fires; like I said, I saw the news briefs."

"Uh-huh."

"I'm just wondering. Is there a pattern? Seems like the buildings are getting bigger. What was the last one—a poultry barn?"

"Falling down. Probably shoulda had a controlled burn ourselves, keep some kid from falling through the floor."

"But that's not a small fire."

He shrugged. I was encouraged.

"So have you seen this sort of thing in town before?"

"Fires? We have 'em once in a while. That's why we have all this equipment."

"Arson," I said. "Three fires in what, three weeks? I mean, are people in town getting concerned? It's been fallen-down barns. Next week, it could be one with animals in it, right?"

Frederick stood up. He was a big slab of a man, probably had lost a little muscle to age, but not much.

He rubbed his chin, seemed about to say something but thought better of it. He sat back down again. The chair creaked. He picked up a yellow pencil.

"Been chief long?" I said, trying a new tack.

He looked at me closely, like he was deciding whether to answer or have me flogged for impertinence.

"Twenty-five years. My father was chief for twenty-two years before that."

"So you've been with the department since you were a kid?" I said.

"Right," he said.

The three guys walked by carrying buckets. I heard water pouring into a sink.

"Any idea who's doing this?"

"Oh, we're looking into it."

"You worried one of your guys will get hurt? Barns really go up fast."

He didn't answer, started scratching more figures on his notepad. I'd been dismissed. I felt a burble of annoyance. This morning, Ratchet, Roxanne, all piling on.

"So you must know about firefighter arson," I said.

He looked up like I had a rope on his chin and had jerked it. Then he was up from his seat, around the desk. A big finger in my face, a gold ring flashing on his fist.

"You saying one of my boys is burning these places?" he shouted.

A sound behind me. One of the boys in question.

" 'Cause I'll tell you, mister, I run one of the tightest departments in the state of Maine. And no flatlander reporter is gonna come in here and say that my firefighters are arsonists."

"That's fuckin' crazy," Paulie said, behind me. "You gonna put that in the paper?"

"Shut up," the chief said.

"Them's fightin' words," Paulie said. "Let's settle this outside."

"No, he's not gonna put that in the paper in New York or Boston or any-where else, because it's a lie, and I'll tell you right now, you print any bullshit like that and I'll sue you for slander."

"Libel," I said, ignoring the theatrics.

"What?"

"When you print something, it's libel. Slander is speech."

"I don't give a goddamn—"

"I'm just talking about the phenomenon, a known predilection that some people associated with fire departments are known to have. That's why they're drawn to fire departments to begin with. It's a minuscule minority. Like some pedophiles get involved with kids' groups."

"Now he's saying we're molesting kids?" Paulie said.

He stepped up behind me and gave me a shove. I staggered and he said, "Come on, asshole. Outta here."

I looked at Paulie, his arms at his sides, fists clenched. I took out my notebook and said, "Seems like we got off on the wrong foot."

"Dude, you can't come in here—"

"So you have any theories about who is setting fires in your town?" I said.

"A fuckin' whack job," Paulie said.

I wrote that down in my notebook, in big letters.

"These fires are under investigation by the office of the state fire marshal," the chief said. "There's no indication whatsoever that anyone in the Sanctuary Volunteer Fire Department is connected to these fires."

Huh, I thought. No dope.

"I'm sure," I said.

He pulled the papers toward him.

"Got work to do, sir," he said. "Budget season."

Paulie waited at the door, Casey and Ray behind him. Frederick looked up, like he was surprised I was still there.

"You're sure that's all you'll say?" I pushed. "What about the way the fires were started. The same MO? Any tracks leading to or from? Would it have to be somebody local? Could you see the buildings from a road?"

He stared, then heaved himself back up, came around the desk, boots squeaking on the cement floor. We stood nose to nose. I was looking up.

"Listen, Mr.—"

"McMorrow."

"Right. I'm gonna tell you something. And this is off the record. Agreed?"

I hesitated.

"Agreed," I said.

"Okay. Here's the deal: People who do this, they just want attention. Picture it. You're some nobody. Total loser. You light a building on fire, get the fire trucks, the lights, the firefighters running all around. Well, now you're somebody."

"Right."

"So the bigger deal you make of it, the more they want to do it. And you're right. Maybe next time they want something bigger. Maybe next time they do an empty house. Maybe the time after that, it's a house that's not empty. You see where this is going?"

"No, you tell me," I said.

"The more attention they get from the media, the more likely somebody's gonna get hurt."

"Well, Chief, I respect your opinion, but—"

"You want a story about small-town life or whatever, how 'bout you write about the pumpkin festival. Second week in October. People come from miles around. Lotsa tourists. Got your Pumpkin Princess. Your pumpkin pie contest. That's a nice story for the people down there in New York."

"Thanks for the tip."

"Not a problem," Frederick said.

"But I'm still going to do something on these fires," I said.

"I got no comment."

"Okay."

"Except for this: Somebody gets hurt, you're gonna have blood on your hands."

The jacked-up Dodge was idling beside my truck, the three firefighters— Ray-Ray, Paulie, and Casey—seated in a row. Paulie was on the passenger side, closest to me. We looked at each other and nodded. I started to open my door, stopped and turned. They stared. Paulie pushed a pinch of tobacco between his bottom lip and gums.

"Gentlemen," I said. "What's your theory about these arson fires?"

The one in the middle, said, "It's all 'cause Woodrow's a douche bag."

"Ray-Ray, shut up," Paulie said, and he smacked him in the shoulder.

"Woodrow?" I said. "Who's that?"

Casey, behind the wheel, revved the motor and said, "Woodrow the Freak Show." He backed out, stopped, and pulled into a turn. The door slammed behind me and the chief poked his head out. "You boys talking to him?"

They clapped their mouths shut. As the truck pulled away, Paulie, facing straight ahead, said, "I'll be seeing you, dude."

"Looking forward to it," I said.

The truck motor roared, the back tires spun in the gravel, and they squealed off down the road.

I turned back to the chief, smiled, and said, "Nice guys. They were a huge help."

He looked at me, scowled, and pulled his head back and shut the door.

4

The Sanctuary General Store was on the far side of the common, taking up the first floor of an old brick building, an open porch on the front like the Old West. There was red, white, and blue bunting draped across the storefront and window boxes with red geraniums blooming on the porch floor.

I parked and headed for the door just as a woman was climbing out of a red Jeep, the top down. I waited and held the door for her to let her pass. She gave me a quick glance and I did the same: dark hair in long ringlets, beaded earrings, gauzy hippie skirt. A wildness in her dark, intense eyes. A boundlessness to her, like there was way more to her than showed. Very attractive.

I followed her into the store, heard the guy behind the counter say, "How's Lasha today?"

"Okay, Harold," she said. "How you doin'?"

"Hangin' in, dear," Harold said. "Hangin' in."

He nodded at me, said, "Good morning—or is it afternoon?"

I looked at him—glasses, ball cap, hair cropped or nonexistent—and checked my watch.

"Twenty more minutes," I said.

"Time's flying, I'm having so much fun," he said.

I circled the store once, past the groceries, the fishing supplies, the beer cooler, the meat counter. Next to the meat counter was a small deli, and I stepped up and ordered a ham-and-cheese sandwich from a high school girl in a Red Sox jersey. Number fifteen. Dustin Pedroia. She turned and went to work and I stood by the counter and waited. And listened.

A police scanner on the wall behind the meat counter bleated scratchy chatter, a common sound in small towns where the fire department was volunteer. Two men in khaki shorts and polo shirts (one maroon, one pale blue) were standing to the side of the counter.

A third—same uniform in lime green, reading glasses slung around his neck—stepped up and ordered boneless chicken breast. He turned to the pair and moved closer and I drifted over toward them, eyed the hams, the blocks of cheese.

"You know he's got problems," Maroon Shirt was saying.

"Totally antisocial," Blue Shirt said.

"They come back from that war and they're never the same," Green Shirt said.

"People blown apart," Maroon Shirt said.

"Never even see the enemy, these goddamn IEDs," Blue Shirt said.

"But you don't think he would act out like this?" asked Green Shirt.

"Heard he stopped going to counseling at the VA," Maroon Shirt said. "Just stays out at the cabin, twenty-four/seven."

"Or not," Blue Shirt said. He looked up, noticing me, and nodded.

I smiled, turned back to the deli counter.

The high school girl handed me my sandwich and I thanked her.

When I turned back, only Maroon Shirt was left. He ordered a pound of smoked turkey, sliced thin. A pound of Swiss, the imported, not the domestic.

I headed for the front of the store.

There was a line at the checkout and I lingered, made sure I was at the back.

From the chatter I learned that the woman in the hippie skirt was Lasha; Green Shirt was Russell, a summer person from away; and the guy behind the counter was Harold, and he was in the fire department.

"Just like they're made of kindling," he was saying.

"Wood's been drying for a hundred and fifty years," Russell said. He put a copy of the *Times* on the counter by the chicken.

"Scary fast, way they burn," Harold said.

"Well, I hope somebody's doing something about it," Lasha said.

"Oh, they're working on it," Harold said.

"Question is, will they do something about it in time," Russell said.

"But it's just these old sheds, right?" Lasha said, as Harold put fruit and yogurt into her cloth sack, pushed a six-pack of Geary's summer lager toward her.

"For now," Harold said. "Who knows what's next."

"Exactly," Russell said, his accent unfamiliar; maybe Maryland?

"I'm telling people, check the batteries in your smoke alarms," Harold said.

"By that time it's too late," Russell said.

"You don't think this freak'll do houses, do you?" Lasha said.

Shrugs all around. Harold handed her the sack and beer. Lasha turned and glanced at me, and she and Russell started for the door. I put my sandwich and juice down on the counter, waited as Harold rang them up. I gave him a twenty and watched out the window, Russell and Lasha standing by her convertible Jeep, still talking. Then she was getting in and he was headed for his car, a big blue Audi. Harold was counting out my change.

"Be right back," I said.

Russell was backing out by the time I got outside onto the porch. Lasha was in the Jeep, the motor running, but she was digging in the sack. By the time I got to her, she'd come up with an apple

"Hi, there," I said.

She looked up, not startled.

"Jack McMorrow," I said. "I'm a reporter."

"Lasha Cabral," she said, and added, "I'm an artist."

She held out her hand and I clasped it. Her grip was strong, her skin rough.

"Could I talk to you for a minute?" I said, smiling. She held my gaze.

"About what?" Lasha said, tentatively smiling back.

She was older up close, nearer fifty than thirty-five. Pretty face, her dark eyes lined with mascara, a hint of fortune-teller. She smelled of soap and cigarettes. Her shirt was open at the neck and a gold cross dangled in her cleavage like an arrow.

"The fires," I said.

"Oh, God."

"Sorry—eavesdropping. It's a professional pastime."

"Oh, it's okay," Lasha said. "I mean, I don't know why it's getting to me. Probably just some kids."

"Yeah," I said.

"But when you live alone."

She glanced away, then back.

"In a big old house. I mean, there's the shed and my studio, and this building that used to be the sap house; now I just keep a kayak in there. And another shed behind all of that."

"Cedar shingles?"

"Not the house. That has clapboards. But the rest, that's shingles. Flammable as hell. My ex—well, he wasn't my ex then—he used old shingles to start fires in the woodstove. Just a little newspaper, a few pieces of shingle, and—"

"Whoosh?"

"Goes right up," Lasha said.

She adjusted her skirt, up and then down. For my benefit? Her legs were muscular and tanned, her toenails painted red There was a tiny gold band on her left little toe.

"So I've been telling myself I shouldn't worry. But if the *New York Times* sends somebody, this must be a big deal, right?"

"I live up here, actually. Ten miles away."

"Oh," Lasha said. "So I shouldn't worry?"

I smiled.

"Listen. I've got to get my sandwich from inside," I said. "Will you wait? Do you have a few minutes?"

Lasha looked at me. I counted the small gold hoops in her left ear. Six. She ran a hand through her hair, which was held back by her sunglasses.

"Okay, Mr. Jack," Lasha said. "I'll take my fifteen minutes of fame."

Lasha didn't want to talk in the store parking lot with Harold watching through the window, so I climbed in the passenger seat and she backed out, her tanned legs working the clutch and the gas.

We rounded the common, passed the war monuments, more geraniums in pots. She kept driving east, down a long hill, past big restored colonial houses, long gravel drives leading between century-old maples. She saw me looking them over, said, "Old money. Not from here."

I nodded, saw the Audi parked by the barn at the next place.

"Russell?" I said.

"He has some connection to Harvard, some diplomat thing. Some people say he was CIA but who knows. There's a little group of them retired here. We call them 'The Think Tank.' "

"Huh. How'd they find Sanctuary?"

"One bought a place, summer house. The rest followed. Kind of like immigrants, the way they follow each other to a place, you know? Like my grandparents, my mother's parents. Came here from Portugal. First one, then another. Before you knew it, the whole village had transplanted to Fairhaven, Massachusetts."

"Where you grew up?" I said.

"Until I escaped," she said. "Hated being in a place where everybody knew my business."

"And now Sanctuary?" I said.

She looked at me, shook her head. "I know. Into the fire."

Partway up a ridge the road ended at a T and Lasha took a right. Then she slowed, pulled off the road and onto a dirt lane, a mailbox at the end, no number. The Jeep bumped and heaved over the ruts as the lane swung left through clumps of trees, small ash and poplar. The road snaked right, then left again, and we emerged into a clearing.

There was a white clapboard Cape Cod house, the outbuildings stretching beyond it. A porch on the front, two Adirondack chairs, one occupied by a black-and-white cat. Lasha skidded the Jeep to a stop by a shed door and shut off the motor.

"Nice spot," I said.

"My ex bought it for me, as a surprise. Our summer retreat. Surprise number two was when he left."

"Sorry."

"What can you do?" she said, reaching for the six-pack on the floor by my feet, the cross dangling free. "Guys always want the newer model."

Lasha slid out. I followed her to the porch, my recorder and notebook in hand. She walked to the far chair and put the beer on the table. Taking two out, she twisted the top off of one bottle and held it out. I took it and she opened another, motioned with the bottle to the other chair and sat. I picked up the beer.

"Often invite strangers in for a drink?" I said, smiling.

"Not often," Lasha said. "I go with my gut, and my gut says you're good people."

She held up the bottle and I did, too. We clinked.

"Sláinte," I said.

Lasha took a long swallow of ale. Then another. The beer was half gone and I could see a calm pass through her like she'd just shot up. It was 11:55. I wondered if that explained the rush to get home, even with a reporter in tow.

I took a sip and I looked out at the ridgetop view: the tree-green valley, the storybook village, the river meandering through it.

"Pretty," I said.

"Especially from a distance," she said.

5

It was pretty, the pale green of the distant forest canopy, white clouds tacked to blue sky. We drank, the beer cool and sweet. The cat hopped up on my lap and purred.

"So does it make me nervous?" Lasha said. "Sure. Up here all by myself. Kip took the dogs."

She'd kicked off her sandals and tucked her feet underneath her, like a little kid. She fiddled with the gold cross, fishing it from her shirt, poking it in her mouth.

"You could get another one," I said.

"Yeah, but I don't know. The puppy thing, pooping all over the place, chewing stuff. I have a gun instead."

"What sort of gun?"

"A shotgun. Kip bought it, actually. Was going to go up partridge hunting with the guys in town, be a real Mainer. Ha. Couldn't shoot a pigeon in Central Park. Anyway, he was packing up the shotgun. I said, 'You may be leaving me alone, you lying, cheating bastard, but you're not leaving me defenseless.' "

"You know how to use it?"

"I do now. I've been practicing out back."

"Pump?"

"No, you just pull the trigger."

"Semiautomatic," I said.

"Right. I'd have a machine gun if it was legal."

I opened the notebook on my lap, rested my pen on the page.

"You'd use it?"

"Hell, yes."

She raised the beer, drained it. I wrote the two words on the page. Hell and yes.

"We starting the interview?"

"If you want."

Lasha reached for another beer and opened it, put one on the armrest of my chair.

"Shoot," she said.

"How have the fires affected your life here?"

"Let's see. Well, I don't sleep much. I get up and grab the gun and take a walk around."

"Outside in the dark?"

"Right. I have my spots. I just sit and listen. Me and the owls."

"Scary calls, huh?"

"Oh, yeah. There's one, sounds like somebody's being murdered."

"Barn owl," I said. "So what's your biggest fear?"

"The smoke. That I won't wake up. And—"

Lasha drank and got up.

"And what?" I said.

"I'll show you," she said.

She slipped her sandals on and, carrying the beer, started down the drive, past the Jeep, toward the rear and the outbuildings. There were pieces of rusty farm equipment propped here and there, the smaller ones set on chunks of granite like cemetery monuments. Lasha led the way to a long shingled shed, big windows set into the south side, shades drawn.

She unlocked a padlock, slid a wooden door aside. We stepped in and she reached to the wall and flipped a switch. Lights blazed on and giant wooden creatures stared.

They were nearly life-size, like something from a crazed carousel. A dragon with bared teeth; a flying horse, eyes bulging, front hooves threatening; a snarling lion, his torso pierced with arrows. The figures seethed with an almost explosive energy, their eyes deep and expressive, muscles taut.

"Wow," I said. "You're the real deal."

"A blurb for the next show," Lasha said.

"I can't believe you can create this out of a block of wood."

"Actually, many blocks. Clamped and glued and then shaped. Rock maple, mostly."

"Amazing. You've got an amazing talent."

"Talent and three bucks will get you coffee at Starbucks," Lasha said, looking over the collection. "This is ninety percent hard work."

I moved between the sculptures. They were cool to the touch, sanded and polished. One was in progress. A wild boar, cornered, back on its haunches, mouth fixed in a toothy snarl. The snout was rough with chisel cuts, the floor beneath it sprinkled with pale wood chips. On the far side of the studio was a workbench. On the bench and the wall were sanders, chisels, clamps.

Lasha's muscles. Her rough hands.

"So you worry your work would go up in smoke."

She grinned. "Knew I shoulda sprung for the marble."

"You can't move it all? To a safe place?"

"Weighs tons. And then the next day they'd catch the guy."

I turned back, ran my fingers over the horse, his bulging eyes. I thought of Pokey, a very distant relative.

"Who do you think it is?" I said.

She hesitated. "The arsonist?"

"Yeah."

"I don't know. I mean, we all have our theories."

"Like who?"

"I can't say. I'd get sued."

"Off the record, then."

Lasha hesitated, raised her beer and drank. Wiped her mouth with the back of her hand.

"You know a kid named Woodrow?" I said.

"Woodrow Harvey?"

"Another kid at the firehouse said it was Woodrow's fault. Woodrow the Freak Show."

Lasha hesitated. Took a quick sip.

"Well, you could say he's the type."

"The arsonist type?"

"Or something. I heard that he's autistic or has Asperger's or one of those things. Whatever it is, it's made him kind of an outcast. The kind of kid who would do some weird thing in the middle of the night. Peek in windows or something. Black clothes, sort of Goth for around here. You see him walking around town in this long coat."

"Columbine."

"Right."

"Parents?"

"Split up. He lives with his mom. Shirley. She works in the elementary school. In the kitchen. There's a sister, too. Father's a truck driver. What I heard is he met a woman online. Moved to Lewiston."

"And left the family behind?"

"Guess so. Never see him around. Now my Kip, he met his new chickie the old-fashioned way. At an opening. She works for a gallery. Old enough to be his daughter. Almost."

She smiled.

"He collects art?"

"And women, it turns out."

"Huh."

I ran my hand down the horse's neck. Looking down, I saw that it was a gelding.

"Anybody else?"

"Anybody else what?" Lasha said.

"On the list of suspects."

"I don't know. There's this guy, Louis. He was in the army in Afghanistan or Iraq or someplace, and he came back all messed up. In the head, I mean. What do they call it?"

"PTSD?"

"Right. He lives in this cabin he built out in the woods. Grandfather left him land here or something. Some people think it could be him, but I don't want to spread rumors."

"It's not rumors. It's the speculation that's going on in town. You're just relating what's actually happening."

"You are relentless."

"Aren't you, when you're working on one of these?"

She looked at me as she put a finger to her mouth, let it open her lips and slip off. It trailed along the thin gold chain of her necklace, came to rest on the cross between her breasts.

"Married?" she asked.

"Yes."

"Happily?"

"Yeah."

"How happily?"

"Blissfully so."

"Shit."

Then she smiled and I smiled back. With a little snorting chuckle, she lifted her beer and drank, drained it and swallowed.

"Story of my life. The good ones are all taken."

"Kip wasn't a good one?"

"Only from a certain angle. In a certain light. Just like the two before him. Over time they reveal their inner asshole."

"Huh."

"Besides, for Kip I was a phase. Like the house in Maine."

"I'm sorry."

"Hey, that's life. It doesn't always work out according to plan."

Her expression shifted from rueful to bitter. I looked over the wild and angry menagerie.

"Must be hard to be alone here," I said.

"In the middle of the night? Yeah," Lasha said.

"With somebody out there burning stuff down."

"That, too," she said.

6

Lasha drove me back to the store, her third beer in the cup holder of the Jeep. She was quiet, her alcohol mood shifting from chatty to flirty to morose. We drove down the hill, past Russell's house, across a small bridge, and climbed to the town center. Lasha whipped the Jeep around the common, rolled up behind my truck.

"Thanks for the beer and the conversation," I said.

"Anytime," she said. "When's this gonna be in the *Times*?"

"Not sure. Maybe I'll write it tomorrow. Depends on who else I can find."

"Fast worker."

"This isn't *The New Yorker*, as one of my editors used to say."

She half-smiled, looked away. I got out and she hit the gas, spinning the wheels in the gravel. Lonely, I thought. Fairy-tale life up in smoke.

But not literally. Not yet.

The store was quiet so I went back inside, heard Harold talking in the back. I went to the line of hot drink canisters and picked a flavor of coffee. Breakfast Blend in the afternoon. I added milk, stirred. Lingered and waited. Harold came back to the front counter, saw me, and said, "You finding everything?"

"Yeah," I said. "Coffee for the ride home."

I approached the counter, put the cup down.

"Two dollars, sir," Harold said. "Pay cash money and we'll throw in a stale doughnut."

He grinned. A round face, bristly salt-and-pepper mustache, round glasses to match.

I handed him two bucks. He took a piece of paper from a box, reached in another carton, and took out a plain doughnut.

"Might want to dunk it first," he said. "Save your dentures."

I took the doughnut, held out my other hand.

"Jack McMorrow," I said.

"The newspaper reporter," Harold said, shaking my hand.

"Word travels fast."

" 'Round here, doesn't have far to go."

"You're Harold."

"That's my name. Don't wear it out."

"Can I talk to you for a minute?"

"You can talk," Harold said. "Don't know what I can say gonna be of any interest to folks down in New York."

He sat down on a stool behind the counter and pushed back his cap. It said SANCTUARY GENERAL STORE, in case you were disoriented.

"The fires."

"Yeah."

"Have the town on edge?"

"Well, I'd say they've got people talking."

"Ever had anything like this before? Somebody burning buildings?"

"Oh, once or twice, kids drinking and smoking."

"This is more than that," I said.

"I suppose. But the places weren't worth a whole lot. Sinking into the ground. This just speeded things up."

"But still," I said. "It makes people nervous when someone's out there torching buildings."

"When it isn't the fire department," Harold said.

"So, Harold, you in the fire department?"

"Oh, yeah," he said, like in Sanctuary it was a given, if you were male and ambulatory.

"Even if the sheds and barns aren't worth anything, there's a risk here, right? I mean, you guys are out there putting the fires out."

"Well, mister, you hit that nail right on the head. You fall off a ladder during a fire at an old barn, your leg's just as broke as if you'd fallen off the roof of a mansion."

I scribbled in my notebook. It made Harold uneasy.

A white-haired woman came in and he said, "Hello, Ada, honey," and she said, "Hi, Harold," and headed for the meat counter.

"So are the firefighters concerned, then?"

"Well, I can't speak for the fire department. That's up to the chief."

"Chief Frederick."

"Right."

"Spoke to him."

"That so?"

"He didn't think this was much of a story," I said.

"Well, it's not like we're calling in all the surrounding departments. Time we get there, these places are pretty much burned flat."

A young woman pushed through the door, a little boy in tow. Harold was off the stool, a lollipop produced from somewhere.

"It's all right, Samantha?" he said. She smiled, and the boy took the lollipop. The mom said, "What do you say?"

The kid said nothing and Harold came back to the counter but didn't sit. I said I had one more question, and he seemed relieved that it wasn't two.

"Any idea who it is? I mean, you must know everyone in town."

"Most everybody. Might be somebody new, hasn't come in yet."

"So—"

"Really can't imagine why anybody would do something like this," Harold said.

"Do people in town have their suspicions?"

"Oh, you know how people are."

"No," I said. "How are they?"

"Oh, it's natural to wonder," Harold said.

"Are you worried? As a firefighter and a business owner?"

"Ada, dear," he said, looking past me. "Did you see the ground chuck? Real nice, and it's on sale."

Ada had. She stepped up to the counter. The woman with the little boy was behind her. "How's Ralph?" Harold said.

I put my notebook away and stepped aside.

The sun had slipped behind banks of clouds and the wind had picked up out of the southeast. It felt like rain again. I wondered if the arsonist checked the weather, staying home on nights when a downpour might spoil the fun.

I was back in the truck, considering what I had. Chief Fred, telling me it was a nonstory. Lasha, sucking beers, lamenting her cheating ex, and toting a shotgun in the middle of the night. Not bad, but not enough to hang the story on; not for the *Times*. Harold saying little and probably wishing he hadn't said anything at all.

Ada came out and kept her eyes on the pavement as she walked past my truck. I looked out at the deserted town common, the road leading away. I had one trip invested, now might have to make two. The mom and kid came out of the store and I reached for the door handle but she hurried by, looking the other way. She hoisted the little boy into a car seat in a big pickup and then climbed in herself.

I watched them, wondered if this little boy was Ratchet's age. I pictured him lying dead on a kitchen floor, and all of Roxanne's distress came flooding back. It was time to go home.

On cue, my phone buzzed. I picked it up off the truck seat and read the text. It was Roxanne:

YOU GONNA BE LONG? XOXO

I replied: ON MY WAY OUT RIGHT NOW. YOU OKAY?

Roxanne: YEAH, WOULD BE GOOD TO SEE YOU, THO.

Me: 40 MINUTES.

Roxanne: I'LL PUT IN A COUPLE BEERS.

A couple of beers with my loving wife. Sure beats a lonely six-pack in an empty house. I pictured Lasha wandering from room to room, beer to beer. Ending up in the studio with the banshees.

I shook off the image and started the truck.

Out of the store lot, I took a right, north and east. The road passed some big colonial houses set up high, overlooking the road. One had a very big sailboat in the driveway on stands. Another had a motor home with little hoods on the tires.

At that house a guy was mowing the lawn on a red tractor. A woman sat on the front porch with a couple of little kids, who looked like they were playing some sort of game.

Maine: The Way Life Should Be.

I passed them and continued on, past more big houses. The houses looked out toward the river, and a short commercial stretch that looked like it dated to the mid-nineteenth century. A café with chairs and tables outside. A hardware store with rakes and shovels standing in wooden barrels. An entrance that led to the Sanctuary Opera House, "Home of the Sanctuary Players."

I could see why people were drawn to this gentrified part of rural Maine. On the surface it all seemed so simple, so wholesome. Community theater. A café where you could buy a decent $10 lunch. A store owner who knew your name.

And in the rearview mirror, a kid in a long black coat.

I slowed the truck, watched him. He'd walked out from beyond the café and was headed down the road away from me. I pulled off the road and turned around, drove slowly back.

He was walking slowly but deliberately, like he was in no hurry and had no particular place to go. With the black coat he looked like he was from a

Western, the marshal on patrol. I drove past him and he glanced over. Shaggy hair pulled down over a pale, expressionless face. Black jeans, T-shirt and biker boots under the black coat. Johnny Depp meets Johnny Cash. In small-town Sanctuary it was no wonder he was a target.

I pulled onto the shoulder fifty feet past him and stopped, shut the truck off. In the mirror I could see that he was still coming and I got out, slipping my notebook into the back pocket of my jeans. I leaned against the side of the truck and waited. He watched me until he was thirty feet away, then shifted his gaze to his boots. When he was ten feet away, I stepped away from the truck.

"Woodrow?" I said.

He looked up, startled, but kept walking. I stepped into his path and he stopped. Still no expression, except in the eyes, which were dark and intense. There was a gold ring in his left nostril. A bar through his right eyebrow. A circular disk sort of thing in the lobe of his right ear.

"I'm Jack McMorrow. I'm a reporter. Can I talk to you?"

He stared.

"How do you know my name?"

"I've been talking to people in town. Somebody mentioned you."

"Who?"

"Just some guys."

"What guys?"

"At the firehouse."

Woodrow scowled, the eyebrow bar moving.

"Fire jocks," Woodrow said. "Fuck 'em."

He stepped around me and I fell in. We walked ten paces in silence, both of us looking straight ahead. Finally I said, "Why don't you like those guys?"

"They're assholes."

"Oh, yeah? Why's that?"

"I don't know," Woodrow said. "Ask them."

"What'd they do? I mean, did they do something to you? You don't hang out with the fire jocks?"

"I don't hang out with anybody in this hick town. This shithole."

We walked. He was holding it together. Tough on the outside, crying at the center.

"So you don't like it here."

"I'm outta here, soon as I'm sixteen."

"When's that?"

"Three weeks."

"Where you going?"

"Portland. Where we lived before."

"You have friends there?"

A moment of hesitation, and then the lie.

"Lots of 'em."

"Why'd you move here?"

"I didn't. My parents did."

"From Portland."

"And then my dad left. Traded for a younger model. What's your name again?"

"Jack."

"Jack what?"

"McMorrow."

From his pocket he slipped out an iPhone. He stopped walking and twiddled at the phone with his thumbs. He peered at the screen, shielding it from the sun.

"Okay, you're legit."

"You found my stories."

"Yeah. *New York Times*. What the hell you doing up here?"

"It's a perennial question."

"What?"

"Everybody asks me that."

"What do you tell 'em?"

"I got sick of the city. Moved to the woods."

He looked at me sideways, started walking again.

"That's messed up, dude."

"So I've been told," I said.

We walked, his black boots matching my running shoes, step for step.

"How long you lived here, Woodrow?"

"A fucking eternity."

"How long's that in years?"

"One. Seems like a friggin' lifetime."

"Really don't like it, huh?"

"Buncha redneck assholes."

We were walking away from the town center, the river down the hill and through the woods to our right. It was a pale shimmer through the trees. Woodrow didn't seem to notice. His boots made a scrunching sound in the sand and his mouth was set in a scowl.

"Didn't mean to upset you, man," I said.

He shrugged, shoulders moving the coat up and down. "I'm fine."

Another lie. The scowl stayed in place. We kept walking.

"You go to the high school?"

"If you want to call it that. Freakin' dump."

"Must be some good kids there," I said.

"Buncha shitkickers."

"What about the girls?"

"Bitches," Woodrow said. And then, "So what do you want?"

"What do I want?"

"Yeah. What's your story about?"

I hesitated for three steps.

"The fires," I said.

Woodrow stopped short and turned to me. I could see his hands clench into fists in his pockets. We were eye to eye, him in my face. "What'd they say?"

"One of them said the fires were your fault."

He snorted, started to pant. The hands came out, fists clenched. I was ready to block him if he started swinging.

"Those—"

Then all of sudden he was swallowing, breathing hard, grunting. His face turned red, as if trying to get the words out was choking him. Like a toddler having a tantrum. The Asperger's? Some autism thing?

He made a sound like a frightened animal and the hard shell broke apart. He started to cry. "I hate them, those fucking—"

"It's okay, Woodrow. Don't get upset."

"I'm gonna kill them. I'm gonna kill everybody in this fucking town."

He swiped at his face, smeared the tears.

"They're gonna be the ones crying when I . . . when I get done. They're gonna be the ones, gonna be so afraid they're gonna be shaking."

He held his clenched hands in front of him. They were trembling. I reached out and took his wrists.

"Easy. I'm sorry. I didn't mean to get you all—"

He yanked his fists back, shouting, "Get your hands off me." He started walking fast and I hurried to keep up, the two of us like a squabbling couple.

"Woodrow," I said, "I'm sorry. It's okay."

"I hate those assholes. I hate this town. You put that in the newspaper. I'm gonna fucking kill those motherfuckers so bad."

Spittle flew from his lips and he was walking with his arms swinging.

"You don't mean that, Woodrow. You're not gonna kill anybody, are you?"

"Gonna kill 'em all. You put that in there. Tell 'em I'm coming. I'm gonna burn them up. Burn this place to the fucking ground."

He broke into a trot. I kept up and then he started to run, boots thudding. I let him go, watched as he turned off the road and skidded down the embankment into the woods. I stood and listened and heard him crashing through the brush and then heard him yell, no words, just a long and anguished bellow.

Nice going, McMorrow, I thought. Which of the downtrodden will you torment next?

7

"So you called?" Roxanne said.

"Yeah. They said they'd pass the message to the fire investigator handling the case."

"Who's that?"

"Investigator Reynolds."

"He didn't call you back?"

"She," I said.

We were sitting on the steps of the deck, Roxanne holding a glass of Chardonnay and me a can of Ballantine Ale. From somewhere behind the trees, we could hear Sophie's laughter, Clair egging her on. Smoke drifted from the Varneys' backyard.

The rain had held off, the clouds scudding over, hurrying east.

"But you don't think he's the one," Roxanne said.

"No. I don't think he'd go off threatening to burn the town down if he was already doing it."

"But would he do it now?"

I drank some ale, shrugged.

"You know more about messed-up kids than I do, but I don't think so. He was just venting. Like a little kid having a tantrum, someone who might be—how do they put it?— on the spectrum? This woman Lasha said it was something like that."

She considered it. Sipped. A vireo sang from the top of the big oak, the same six notes, over and over. No worries. Must be nice.

"Those sorts of rages in autism are usually short-lived," Roxanne said. "Frustration with a rule or a social situation."

"How 'bout a newspaper reporter comes along and accuses you of arson."

"You didn't know, Jack," she said. "You were just doing your job."

I raised the can and drank, put it back on the step. "I was pushing things because I didn't have a story yet. Thought I'd shake the tree, see what fell out. I pushed the fire chief, too. The guy just rubbed me the wrong way—one of these who runs the place like his little fiefdom. I just—"

I hesitated.

"What?"

"The whole thing with Ratchet. I don't know. The poor little guy, odds stacked against him right from the start. It's just wrong. Like this cosmic evil or something just picked him out."

Roxanne watched me. Waited.

"So I just went down there, mad at the world, looking to take it out on somebody. Not very professional."

"You had no idea that the boy might be autistic."

"Could have gone easier all around," I said.

"Yeah, well," Roxanne said, "you know what they say about hindsight."

She sipped, rested her hand on her crossed legs. Above us, the vireo sang on. In the distance Sophie laughed. A bubble of contentment.

"Dave called from the office," Roxanne said.

"What'd he say?"

"He said Beth called him. She was drunk."

"Going around," I said, thinking of Lasha. "What did she say?"

"She said she wants to meet with me. She said she thinks it might bring closure."

"Beth said that?"

"She's had counseling. And she's smart. Underneath. Another one who could have made it. Maybe."

"What'd Dave think?"

"He seemed to think it might be worth it. To talk to her, I mean. Could save a lot of legal costs."

"Beth's lawyer know she's conducting her own negotiations?"

"I doubt it."

"Well, he'll put the kibosh on that. Thirty percent of nothing is nothing."

She was mulling it over, her expression serious and sad.

"I don't know. It might be good. I can tell her nobody meant for her son to die. I was trying to help him. We all were."

"And she says what?"

"Maybe she'd understand."

A long pause. I sipped. Put the can down on the step.

"Nothing against healing and reconciliation and all that," I said, "but I'd search her on the way in. It's not just her. People are crazy when it comes to their kids. Just think how you'd feel if something happened to—"

I caught myself, but not in time. Roxanne bit her lip and closed her eyes and the tears started to flow. I leaned over and held her, said I was sorry. We leaned against each other for a moment and then Roxanne pulled away, dabbed at her eyes. Woodrow, and now my wife. I was getting good at this.

"We've got to go," she said. "They're making dinner."

The fire was ringed by rocks, a cast-iron saucepan hanging on a metal tripod. Clair prodded the coals, said it was about time us cowpokes had some grub.

"There's beans," Sophie said, hopping up and down and pointing at the pot. "And potatoes. Those are the silver things right in the fire part. We wrapped them up. And there's hot dogs on sticks. Daddy, you can have two."

Mary came out of the house with a salad in a wooden bowl and a pitcher of lemonade. Clair walked to the table and picked up paper plates. He ladled beans onto each one and I added a potato and hot dog and carried them back to the picnic table, one by one.

We sat, Roxanne and I on one side, and Sophie between Clair and Mary on the other. Mary poured lemonade for herself and Sophie and we raised our cups, glasses, and bottles for a toast.

"To a home on the range," Clair said.

"Git along, little doggies," Sophie said.

I smiled. The line was "dogies," or motherless calves. Doggies was good enough. "Cowboys had it pretty good," I said.

"Because they had cowgirls," Roxanne said.

"Right," Mary said. "It was the cowgirls did all the work, don't forget."

I smiled, sipped my beer. Felt my phone buzz in my pocket. I got up from the table, walked toward the drive. By Clair's pickup I answered it.

Road noise and police-radio chatter.

"Mr. McMorrow."

A woman's voice. All business.

"This is Davida Reynolds. State Fire Marshal's Office."

"Hi."

"We need to talk. Where are you now?"

"Home, in Prosperity. Dump Road."

"Landmarks?"

"Blue Toyota truck. Green Subaru. From the Knox end, a little over a mile in."

"Half-hour," she said.

She didn't ask if it was a convenient time.

Roxanne read my expression as I approached, took my hand after I sat. Clair caught it, too, the pair of them knowing me better than I know myself.

Sophie came over with a second hot dog for Clair, smothered in ketchup. She asked if I wanted the next one, and I said yes.

"We worked up an appetite, didn't we, Clair?" Sophie said.

He winked at me.

"Sure did, pumpkin," Clair said.

"Now it's Daddy's turn."

She turned and scuffed back to the fire in her boots.

"Fire investigator is coming," I said. "From Sanctuary."

I gave Clair the thirty-second version, too, pausing as Sophie approached. She stumbled and dropped the hot dog on the lawn and frowned. She stooped, picked grass off of it with small fingers, and put it back in the roll. She handed it to me. I thanked her and took a bite.

"Delicious," I said. "You're a good cook."

She nodded and turned and ran back to Mary.

"Must've been looking at this kid already," Clair said.

"If it took me just twenty minutes to have his name come up," I said.

"So the whole town is talking about him," Clair said. "If he has nothing to do with it—"

"Probably all over Facebook and who knows what else," Roxanne said.

"Well, people are cruel," Clair said.

"And the ones who think they aren't," I said, "are kidding themselves."

After hot dogs and beans came vanilla ice cream and coffee. Sophie asked how the cowboys kept their ice cream cold. Clair said they had freezers in their chuck wagons, with blocks of ice covered in sawdust. Sophie looked skeptical and then sleepy, and Roxanne said it was bedtime for cowgirls.

She and Sophie started down the path through the trees to our house. As they disappeared I saw a maroon Suburban drive by slowly.

"The truth and nothing but the truth," Clair said.

"So help me God," I said, and got up and walked out.

The Suburban was parked across the end of the drive. A dark-haired woman was in the driver's seat, head down, writing. I walked to my truck, got a notebook and pen off the seat. When I turned back, Investigator Reynolds was walking toward me.

She was small, not much over five feet, short, dark hair, stocky, but it might have been the jumpsuit. Mid-thirties, maybe, round face with ruddy cheeks and an upturned nose. She had a confident stride that said she wasn't going to be intimidated and you'd better know it up front.

"Mr. McMorrow," Reynolds said.

She held out her hand and we shook and her grip was strong, her gaze direct. "Thanks for seeing me."

I hadn't thought that saying no was an option.

She went to my truck, put a legal pad down on the hood. I followed and stood beside her. We leaned.

"So tell me what happened," she said.

I did. She scribbled a few notes.

"So he flipped right out. Like he'd heard this before," Reynolds said.

"I'd say so."

"When he made these threats, do you think he could have meant them?"

"I don't know. I didn't know the kid. If I'd known he wasn't quite right—"

"It's not that he isn't right," she said. "It's that he has an illness. Diagnosed. We inquired."

I looked at her, waited.

"My nephew is nine and he has autism," Reynolds said.

"I see."

"When you say 'not right,' it implies that they've done something wrong."

"I didn't mean that. I liked him. I feel sorry for him, stuck in this place, everybody picking on him."

"Did he really say he was going to kill these other kids?"

"Yes. And everyone else in town. 'Kill those motherfuckers so bad,' was the way he put it."

She wrote that down.

"He was suddenly, explosively angry. I don't know if that translates to hurting somebody tomorrow or next week, or just spouting off. I'd lean toward spouting."

"Did you feel threatened?"

"No. But I'm not from Sanctuary."

"But you still took it seriously enough to report it to us."

"If I didn't and something happened . . ."

"Right. And it was the guys at the fire station who first mentioned Woodrow to you."

"More to each other. And it was just one of them. Paulie and Casey and Ray were in the truck. I think it was Ray who said it. They told him to shut up. I don't think the chief wants them talking to the press."

There was a flicker of reaction. She scribbled, then reached for the recorder and turned it off. She straightened and turned toward me.

"Mr. McMorrow," Reynolds said. "A question—off the record?"

"Sure," I said.

"What sort of story are you planning to write?"

"I don't know," I said. "I won't know until I've done the reporting."

"Who do you have left to talk to?"

I considered it. "The victims of the fires. You. That veteran I heard about, the one who lives out in the woods."

"Louis."

"Right."

I slipped my notebook from my pocket. Took out my pen.

"You know his last name?"

"Longfellow," Reynolds said. "Like the poet."

I looked up from the notebook.

"I went to Bowdoin College, Mr. McMorrow; Longfellow's alma mater."

"Have you talked to Longfellow? Louis, I mean?"

"I can't tell you that."

"What can you tell me?"

"For the record? That the investigation is ongoing. We're interviewing residents of Sanctuary in an effort to apprehend the perpetrator, or perpetrators, of these fires."

"Same MO each time?"

"Can't say."

"Use an accelerant?"

"Can't say."

"Buildings targeted are getting bigger with each fire. Is that part of the pattern for an arsonist?"

I knew the answer from the book, but I needed Reynolds to say it for the story. She hesitated.

"We're talking generally?"

"Right."

"For a thrill arsonist, it can be."

"What other kinds are there?"

"Insurance fraud. Revenge. Cover up another crime. Extremist."

"Like somebody burns down churches because they don't believe in God?"

"Right."

"But a series of arson fires like this. That isn't insurance."

"It would appear not. But maybe it's a setup for the bigger fire, the one with the big insurance payout. Make it seem like a thrill arsonist to cover up the real motive, which is profit."

"Devious," I said.

"It happens."

"But not often," I said.

"No."

"So in this pattern, if you have a fire every week for three weeks, do you expect another one soon?"

Reynolds paused, then said, "Hypothetically."

"Right."

"The thrill arsonist gets a release out of it. Like a serial killer."

"The sexual thing?"

"Small minority get off sexually. Some like the excitement. Some like to be the hero—report the fire, help put it out. It can be like that. It makes them feel good. But for the real thrill arsonist, the same type of fire over and over loses its effect. They need to get bigger. Riskier. More dramatic. Like drugs. You need more to get the same effect."

I was writing it down. She looked away for a minute like somebody out in the woods might be listening. She looked back.

"Off the record, I made some inquiries," Reynolds said. "I heard things about you."

"You left out the word 'good,' " I said.

"Guys at State Police in Augusta say you sure know how to stir up the shit. Direct quote."

"Oh, they say that about all the reporters."

"No," Reynolds said. "Actually, they don't."

A pause, the two of us looking each other over.

"Detective I talked to did say you're a man of your word, though."

"Keeps things simple."

"And you throw yourself into a case and you don't let go," she said.

"Why throw yourself in if you're going to let go anyway?"

She looked around: the funky house with the cozy dormers, the woods out back, just the tops of the trees showing. The leaves were a delicate shade of yellow-green, the setting sun illuminating them from the west. From the house we heard Sophie's cackling laugh.

"Yours?"

"Yeah. She's almost five."

"Country life, huh?"

"That's the idea," I said.

"I grew up in a town called Milo. Milo, Maine."

"Milo—A Friendly Town."

"You've seen the sign."

"Yeah. Is it true?"

"Was for me, but I was from there."

I smiled. A red-tailed hawk passed over, scanning the woods. We both glanced upward, then back down, our gazes coming to rest on each other.

"So you were in Sanctuary for what, two hours?" Reynolds said.

"Maybe a little more."

"You talked to a bunch of people, succeeded in getting at least one resident all wound up."

"That was unintentional," I said.

She looked away.

"Listen, I know I can't keep you from asking questions."

"Nope."

"But I need to have people comfortable with me, maybe confide things they've been keeping secret, or maybe things they didn't think were important. They give me a call because they like that fire investigator lady. And they trust me. Small town, Mr. McMorrow. Sometimes people don't want to be the ones ratting out their neighbors."

"And sometimes they can't wait," I said.

"So the problem is, when somebody like you shows up, asking the same people the same questions, it can scare them off. They see their name in the paper, the rest of the press starts calling."

"Can't be the first time you've had this situation."

"No," Reynolds said. "But I haven't had a reporter so much like—"

She paused, hand on her hip, the one without the gun.

"Like what?"

"Like me," she said.

"Huh."

A pause, the two of us.

"Play sports at Bowdoin College?"

"Basketball."

"Point guard?"

"You saying I'm short?"

She smiled. I was starting to like her.

"So you don't like to lose," I said.

"No. And I don't give up, either. So, Mr. McMorrow—"

"Jack."

"So, Mr. McMorrow, how are we gonna keep from stepping all over each other's toes?"

I thought for a moment, two.

"I don't know," I said. "Small dance floor, Sanctuary. It may be unavoidable."

"But we have the same objective, right?" Reynolds said. "To see that this person is caught before someone gets hurt."

"That's your objective. I just write stories."

Her expression hardened. She picked up the pad and put it in the pocket of her cargo pants.

"Be a lot easier if I knew we were on the same team," Reynolds said.

"Easier for whom?" I said.

"For both of us, Mr. McMorrow," she said, and then she was past me, walking to the Suburban. She hoisted herself in, started the motor, and pulled away, leaving a faint plume of dust that from a distance looked like smoke.

8

Roxanne was reading to Sophie, the sound of their muffled voices coming from Sophie's room above me. I got a can of Ballantine from the refrigerator, went to the study. Flipping the laptop open, I sipped the beer, then sat and started typing.

I started with the fire station and the chief, typed everything I could remember about him, the conversation, the building, his office. The guys in the truck outside, what they said, did, looked like. Then I did the same for Harold at the store, the guys at the meat counter, Lasha up on the hill. I was just a phase, like the house in Maine.

I paused. Typed two words, uppercase. ALONE. LONELY.

A lot of that going around, I thought. Beth. Ratchet—who could have been more alone than him? Lasha and this Louis guy, probably. Hiding in the woods. All the lonely people, the Beatles sang. Where do they all belong? The Maine woods.

Back to work. I typed in my recollection of my conversation with Woodrow. I did the same for Davida Reynolds, paraphrasing the conversation. When we went off the record, I noted that. But it was all recorded. You never knew where the story might lead, when and if there would be another fire. Or where.

I drank some beer, got up and went to the kitchen to the wine rack on the counter. I took out a bottle of Malbec, found the corkscrew, and opened the wine. Then I got a glass from the cupboard and went back to the study with the bottle and the glass and waited.

I heard the bedsprings squeak—Roxanne getting up—and then her footsteps in the hall. I started for the stairs, met her as she was coming down.

"She wants to know who the police lady was, talking to Daddy," Roxanne said.

"Davida Reynolds, investigator, Fire Marshal's Office."

"She says she wants to be a police lady if she doesn't grow up to be a cowgirl."

"She didn't say social worker?" I said.

"God forbid," Roxanne said, and she brushed by me and down the steps.

I went up to Sophie's room, on the back side of the house overlooking the yard and the woods. She had gotten out of bed and was sitting on her toy box, looking out the window.

"Hey, doll," I said. "You're supposed to be in bed."

"I'm worried about Pokey," Sophie said.

"Pokey's fine," I said. "He's sleeping in his cozy stall."

I picked her up, carried her to the bed, and laid her down. Then I pushed her stuffed animals up beside her pillow: Mittens the Kitten, Teddy the Bear, Rocky Raccoon.

"That police lady had a big car," Sophie said.

"Yes," I said. "She carries around all sorts of stuff. For fires."

"So she's a fire lady?"

"No, she's a police lady. She tries to figure out how fires start."

"Matches," Sophie said.

"That's right. And we don't play with them."

"No," Sophie said. "Or we get in trouble."

"Yes," I said. "People who play with matches get in trouble. But you need to go to sleep. You were yawning at the picnic table."

Sophie was looking away, her eyes narrowing. She looked at me.

"What if there was a fire in the barn? How would Pokey get out?"

"Oh, there won't be a fire. But if there was, we'd go get him."

"What if we weren't home? What if me and Mommy went for a walk?"

"Well, Clair would get him."

"What if Clair's way out in the woods? What if you're with him?"

"Mary would be home."

"What if Mary—"

I put my finger on her lips.

"There's nothing to worry about," I said.

She looked up at me, pulled my finger aside.

"How do you know?"

"I just do, honey. Daddy knows these things."

She looked at me harder.

"Then why did the fire lady come here?"

"It's for a story I'm writing," I said. "It's for a story about a town far, far away."

Sophie didn't answer.

"And now you and your friends here have to go to sleep so you can get up early and go give Pokey his breakfast."

"He'll be hungry," she said, and I kissed her cheek and it was soft and smelled of soap. Her dark curls held the faintest whiff of hay.

"Good night, darlin'," I said.

"Good night, Daddy," she said.

I reached for the lamp and turned it off. The room filled with twilight and she was a shadowy face in the bed. I got up and went to the door and said "Good night" again, and Sophie whispered something. I closed the door—and heard the knock.

It was downstairs, the side door through the kitchen that led to the mud-room. It was three knocks, then nothing. As I started for the stairs I heard three more. If it had been Clair, he'd have let himself in by now. So who? Davida Reynolds, back to ask more questions?

I was halfway down the stairs when I heard Roxanne's footsteps. She was crossing the kitchen. I was in the hallway when I heard the door creak open.

"Oh," she said.

There was a muffled response, a woman's voice. Not Reynolds. Not Mary.

I was in the kitchen. I heard Roxanne say, "Oh, let me get my husband, Jack. He'll want to meet you."

And then I was at the door, Roxanne with her back to me, a young woman standing on the landing outside the door.

Beth, in the flesh.

She was taller than Roxanne, thin, wearing a hoodie.

I stepped up, stood beside Roxanne.

Beth looked at me. She smelled of cigarettes. Her skin was pale, her eyes deep and sunken like in the newspaper photo, but now framed in crude mascara. The rest of her was lost under the sweatshirt, black yoga pants, dirty white running shoes.

"So this is your husband," she said, like I wasn't what she'd pictured.

"Yes," Roxanne said.

"And you have children?"

Roxanne nodded, hesitated. "Yes. One."

"Boy or girl?" the woman said. I smelled alcohol.

"Girl," I said. "And you are?"

"Oh, I'm sorry, Jack," Roxanne said. "I should have introduced you."

She turned back to the woman.

"Jack," she said, "this is Beth. Beth, this is my husband Jack."

Beth held out her hand and I glimpsed a scrawled jail tattoo, scars, and scratches. I took her hand and she held on, kept her eyes fixed to mine.

"Good to meet you," I said. "I'm very sorry for your loss."

She sat at the table in the kitchen and I sat across from her. Her hood was still up and her hands were in her pockets and her eyes—dark, wary, predacious—darted all around. The counter and cabinets. The den and my desk. Sophie's drawings on the refrigerator door.

Roxanne offered Beth coffee but she said no, that's okay. Roxanne put the kettle on anyway.

Then Beth started to take something out of her pocket and I half-rose from my chair. She caught it and smiled. Took out a can of Budweiser and put it on the table. Sixteen ounces.

"May I?" she said.

I nodded.

Beth opened the beer. Her fingernails were dirty and unpainted. The tattoo on the top of her left hand said RATCHET. Beside the name someone had written in pen, RIP.

Roxanne was at the counter, spooning coffee into two mugs. Beth took a long pull on the beer, her throat undulating as she gulped. The kettle hissed. Beth put the beer down, rotated it with two fingers.

"We need to talk," she said. She looked up at Roxanne. "You and me. But Jack, can he stay? Sure. Why not."

It was like she was having a conversation with herself.

"Thanks," I said.

Beth smiled. I saw that she was missing a tooth, bottom right. I wondered if Alphonse had punched it out. I wondered how many beers she'd had when she'd set out to find us.

The kettle started to whistle and Roxanne took it off the burner. I heard the water pour, kept my eyes on Beth, her left hand still in her pocket. Roxanne went to the refrigerator, took out milk, added it to the coffee. She brought the mugs to the table and set them down. She sat beside me.

"You know, Beth," Roxanne said, "I couldn't feel any worse about this. I—"

"Stop," Beth snapped.

Roxanne did. I tensed. Beth held up her hands like she was calming us.

"Sorry. But please don't tell me you know how I feel."

"I wasn't going—"

"Because you don't. Your little girl is here? Where is she—sleeping? In some nice little room?"

She looked to me. I didn't reply.

"My baby's fucking dead," Beth said. "He's fucking gone. I'll never see him again. Not ever."

"I'm sorry," Roxanne said.

"That bitch foster lady killed my little boy. That bitch, she . . ." Beth stopped. Closed her eyes. Took a deep breath, exhaled slowly. Again.

"I can't do that. They told me. In anger management. They said think about your breathing. Concentrate on that. Let the fucking anger fall away."

She kept her eyes closed, did the breathing thing a couple of more times. Opened her eyes.

"You all right?" I said.

"Yeah. I mean, I'm okay. Except—"

She started to cry, a melting, sagging wail that began deep inside her and bubbled over.

"Beth," Roxanne said. She put her hand on Beth's sweatshirted arm. "Easy now."

Beth started to sob.

"I was trying. I was trying to be a mom. You remember? You remember how I went three days?"

"I know, but then you relapsed," Roxanne said. "It was one step forward and two steps back. And it was dangerous for Ratchet to be there. Something could have—"

"Dangerous," Beth said, snapping upright. "Dangerous like what? Like one time I forgot to get his supper? Yeah, well, look at what this bitch did. I wasn't fit to be his mom and then this bitch who kills little kids—how fit was she, huh? This fucking baby killer, this motherfucking piece of—"

"Beth," I said.

She paused, out of breath.

"Please don't use that language here."

Roxanne looked at me, her eyes saying Don't go there.

"So we can talk," I said, "but if you keep that up, you're going to have to leave."

Beth's mouth hung open, the gap showing. And then she closed her eyes and did the breathing thing. It was a moment of silence, but not in Ratchet's memory.

Beth's hands were over her mouth, scratches and scrawling and the blue jailhouse tattoo. On the left hand, across from RATCHET, was ALPHONSE. The "o" was a crude heart.

Beth dropped her hands. Looked at Roxanne.

"Alphonse is getting out," she said.

"I thought he had two more years."

Roxanne looked at me. "Alphonse is Ratchet's father, Jack. He's in prison for aggravated assault and drug trafficking. He beat Beth with a chair leg. Broke her collarbone, bruised her lungs, and—"

"And lacerated my liver, too," Beth said. "He was wicked messed-up on crank."

She drank. We waited.

"They're letting him out to go to the funeral. It's tomorrow morning. Ten o'clock."

"I see," Roxanne said.

"You think I'm pissed."

"You have every reason to be," Roxanne said, "and so does Alphonse. But what you have to try to understand—"

"But I coulda cleaned up. I coulda gotten my shit together. I coulda been a good mom, all loving and everything. Look at me now. I'm fine."

We did. She lifted the can and drank, a long swallow. Put the can down.

"I'm totally clean. I coulda done it, you gave me more of a chance. Coulda had a nice place like this for my little boy, pictures on the refrigerator and—"

There was a noise. A shuffle. We turned.

Sophie was standing at the end of the hallway, her blanket in one hand, a stuffed animal in the other. Mittens the Kitten.

"Honey," Roxanne said, and she went and scooped her up and held her.

"I woke up," Sophie said.

"Oh, I'm sorry we were so loud," Roxanne said, kissing her on the cheek.

I watched Beth watching the two of them. She was smiling, her mouth slightly open, the predatory look again. The teeth. She got up and came around the table and stood, pushed the hood off. Held out her hand and Sophie, hesitating, took it. Beth held on.

"Hello, honey," she said, her voice soft and gentle. "I'm Beth. What's your name?"

"Sophie. And this is Mittens."

Beth let Sophie's hand go but the stare was fixed.

"Sophie is a real pretty name for a pretty little girl," she said.

"I have a pony," Sophie said. "His name is Pokey. But he doesn't live here."

"Oh," Beth said. "Where does Pokey live?"

"He lives in Clair's barn. There's a path that goes there. Clair gave him to me. He's my friend."

"Well, aren't you lucky, Sophie. To have such a nice friend, and a nice mommy and daddy, and a pony. I'm sorry we woke you."

"We were just talking," Roxanne said.

"You were talking loud," Sophie said, leaning her head against Roxanne's shoulder. Her bare feet dangled. "And somebody was crying."

Beth said, "You know, I never had a little girl, but I used to have a little boy."

"That's enough," I said.

"His name was Ratchet," she said.

"That's a funny name," Sophie said. "Rhymes with 'catch it.'"

"Yes," Beth said, taking a step toward her. "Aren't you smart."

"You could say, 'Catch it, Ratchet,'" Sophie said.

Beth smiled at Sophie and Sophie said, "You have writing on you."

"Yeah," Beth said. "I write things there that I have to remember. Like Ratchet." She held up the other hand and said, "And Alphonse."

"Who's that?" Sophie said.

"He's my boyfriend."

"Why do you have to put his name there?"

"He went away."

Beth turned to me.

"But he's coming home."

She turned back to Sophie and Roxanne.

"Well, sweetie," Beth said, "it was wicked nice to meet you."

"I have a jacket that has a hood," Sophie said.

"You have a lot of nice things," Beth said. "But now you have to go to bed."

"Are you staying at our house tonight?" Sophie said.

"No, I've got to go. But you know what?" Beth smiled at Sophie, then looked at Roxanne, then at me, where her gaze rested. "I'm gonna come back," Beth said.

She blew Sophie a kiss and walked across the kitchen and out the door.

I glanced at Roxanne, then followed outside to the drive. Beth was standing by the car, an old Ford Taurus, blue and primer black. She was lighting a cigarette, flicking again and again at a pink lighter. I came up beside her and could see her hands shaking, the flame wavering. The cigarette glowed and she took a long drag. Exhaled. Another drag, this time the smoke billowing out of her nostrils.

I said, "I really am very sorry for what happened to your son."

Another drag, smoke forming a cloud above her head like she was smoldering.

"Yeah, well," Beth said, turning to me, her black eyes glowing with anger. "All the fucking sorry in the world don't change nothin'. Everybody else is living the dream and I'm stuck in this fucking goddamn nightmare."

"I'm sorry," I said.

"You and a lot of other people. And if they're not, they will be."

She put the cigarette in the side of her mouth and held it there. Opened the car door. It creaked and she got in the car. I glimpsed beer cans and a cigarette carton on the passenger seat. She slammed the door, started the motor with a rough snarl. Looked at me and flashed a carnivorous smile and put the car in gear. She pulled away and the car, with a taillight out, disappeared over the rise. After a minute, the sound of the motor faded, too.

I looked back at the house, the lights glowing in the deepening darkness, like lanterns hung to guide someone right to our door.

Starting up the drive, I was alongside my truck when a voice came from my left, in the cedars.

"Who was that?"

9

Clair stepped out. He was holding a shotgun in the crook of his arm like it was a baby.

"Name's Beth," I said. "The mom. The boy who died."

"I figured. Got a little heated."

"Yeah. She started to vent."

"Can't blame her," Clair said. "Horrible thing, losing a child."

"No. If that was the end of it."

I told him what Beth had said to Sophie, about the dad, Alphonse, getting sprung for the funeral.

"What is he in for?"

"Aggravated assault. Meth head with a serious mean streak, Roxanne says."

"He'll be shackled," Clair said.

"Yeah, he's nasty, but I think she's the one we have to worry about. Her moods swing all over the place. She's drinking, angry."

"To be expected. You going to report her? That she came here?"

"Roxanne will, I'm sure."

"You know," Clair said, "it's her only chance to do right for her son."

"Screwed things up so bad when he was alive," I said.

"Now she has to prove to the world and to herself that she really loved him. One last shot."

We stood there in the dark. A nighthawk swooped low over the house, zigging and zagging like a giant bat. It was cutting through the light from the windows, feeding on the moths and bugs swarming there.

"Hungry babies back at the nest," Clair said.

"All that parental instinct," I said. "Why do you think it doesn't work right for humans?"

"Modeling," Clair said. "We turn into what we see."

"Sometimes," I said.

"And then there's old-fashioned evil. Plenty of that to go around, too."

The bird swooped. The bugs swarmed.

"Thanks," I said. "I feel better now."

"Anytime," Clair said. He shifted the shotgun from one arm to the other. "This girl carrying, you think?"

"I doubt it. I see her more as the box-knife type."

"But brazen, come right out here, plunk herself down."

"She and Roxanne, they did talk a lot. Back then," I said. "But still. There's something nutty about her. From sorrow to rage, just like that. And the way she looked at Sophie."

"I'll make sure I'm here," Clair said. "She won't walk in again."

"Counting on it," I said.

Roxanne was upstairs when I came in. I stopped at the closet by the side door, pressed the hanging coats and jackets to the side. There was a shelf in the back and I reached up, moved a stack of blankets, and took out a gun case. I brought it out to the shed and laid it on the workbench and worked the combination lock. It clicked open and I flipped the lid.

There were two long guns inside: a Remington 700 deer rifle and a Remington 870 pump-action shotgun. I went to the cupboard on the end of the bench and unlocked the lock, took out a carton of double-aught shells, and then went to the gun case and lifted the shotgun out. I slid five shells into the tube, put the gun back in the case, put the lock through the hasp. I didn't clasp it.

I walked back in the house, put the case on the shelf above the jackets, then closed the door. When I turned Roxanne was standing there.

"She got to you, too," Roxanne said.

We spoke softly.

"I'm sorry for her, I really am. But she's cracking," I said. "Losing her son, and all the drugs and alcohol."

"I thought she'd be angry," Roxanne said. "Maybe violent, even. But this—this was creepy. It scared me."

She opened her arms and we embraced. We held each other tightly and when I started to let go, Roxanne didn't.

"It's like part of her is reaching out, wants me to forgive her," she said.

"And the other part is ready to lash out," I said.

"I never saw the anger before," Roxanne said. "She was high, mostly. I never really saw her in touch with reality."

"And this reality would set anybody off. The guilt—the grief."

"Now that she's straight. Sort of."

"So what we need," I said, "is to get her some heroin."

We fell away from each other.

"You think she'll really come back?" I said.

"I don't know. She knows where we are now."

"Did you call and report it?"

"Not yet," she said. "It took a while to get Sophie back to sleep."

"Was she frightened?"

"A little. I think she just wanted me to explain it all."

"And could you?"

"To a five-year-old? Yes. To myself? Not really."

Roxanne called Dave at home. While she talked I went around and closed the windows on the first floor and locked them. I made sure the front door was locked, and the shed doors, and the side door. When I came back to the kitchen, Roxanne was off the phone.

"What did he say?"

"He said I should keep the lines of communication open."

"Like what? Invite her for coffee?"

"No, just don't shut her down."

"Let her go over to his house," I said. "They can have their own heart-to-heart."

"Jack, we're doing damage control. We're better off if we're not adversaries."

"Seems like an awful lot to expect when—"

I caught myself. Again.

"When I'm responsible for her child's death?"

She had picked up a cloth and was swirling it around the already-clean countertop like she wanted to rub through the rock maple. I reached out and took her arm and stopped her. She sagged and her head fell forward into her hands. I held her, felt her shoulders shake as she started to sob.

"Jack," she said. "It's all my fault."

"But baby," I said, "it isn't. You did the right thing. No one could have known."

"They paid me to know," Roxanne said, holding back sobs. "They paid me to protect children."

I held her until the shaking had subsided. She sniffled and I got her a tissue from the box on the counter. She blew her nose and said, "I'm very tired."

So we turned the lights off and went upstairs and I pulled the comforter down, shucked off my jeans and shirt. When I turned, Roxanne was coming into the room with Sophie, still sleeping, in her arms. Roxanne put Sophie in the middle and went to the closet and slipped her clothes off, dropped a nightshirt over her head. She came to the bed and climbed in. I turned off the light and went to the window and looked out. I stood there for a time, until they'd fallen asleep.

The windows were on the gable end of the house, facing east, the direction Beth had taken when she'd left. The window was open, and for a long while I listened. A hum of insects. A bullfrog croaking out in the marsh. The hoot of a barred owl, Lasha's screaming woman, like a deranged person calling out in the woods. Rustling in the leaves and grass.

I looked over. Roxanne and Sophie were on their backs, their soft throats exposed. I listened a minute more and went to bed.

It was 5:03 a.m., the first glow of morning light. A phoebe had just started calling behind the shed, repeated and insistent. I looked to my left, saw Sophie asleep with Mittens, Sophie's mouth open, snoring softly. On the other side of her, Roxanne's back was to me. She was asleep, too. I lay there, ran through the night in my head. Even in the dim light of dawn it seemed some of the threat had faded.

Had Beth been that threatening, or just understandably upset? Had she come to reconnoiter or to find some closure? Would she ever come all the way out to Prosperity again, or had she done what she'd set out to do—to see Roxanne face-to-face?

Was it just my imagination running wild?

I eased into the bed, lay back, and stared at the ceiling. As I listened to Sophie's small, soft breaths my cell phone rang in the study. I slipped from the room, down the stairs. Picked up the phone.

"Yes."

"Jack. Jack McMorrow?"

A woman's voice. Husky.

"Lasha?" I said.

"Yeah. Listen, sorry to bother you."

"No, no bother. I was up."

"You said to call if there was anything."

"Did you think of something?"

"No, I didn't. But I thought you'd need to know."

"Know what?" I said.

ONCE BURNED · 73

"The fires," Lasha said. "There's another one."

"When?"

"Right now. It's still burning."

Clair was in the barn. He had a book on the workbench, a biography of Mozart, and he was fiddling with his iPod. He held up one finger, clicked the iPod, and stuck it in the docking station in the stereo. Music filled the space, all the way to the rafters, a soft building of violins.

"To understand the book you have to know the music," he said.

"I've got to go," I said. "Another arson fire in Sanctuary. Right now."

"I'll take over here."

"Sorry. I'll be three hours or so. Back by nine."

"Not a problem. Our little girl ought to be up pretty soon."

"I told Roxanne to bring her over."

"I'll head over, sit on the deck."

"Okay."

"Then Roxanne and Sophie can come back here with me," Clair said. "Mary'll make coffee."

"Thanks," I said, and started for the door. Stopped. The violins had given way to cellos, more ominous, foreboding. A soundtrack for our conversation.

"Loaded the shotgun last night," I said. "Probably overreacting."

"Handgun's better at very close quarters," Clair said.

"Yeah, well, hard to tell Roxanne that's for hunting."

"There's guns for hunting and there's guns for the hunted," he said. He held up his hand again, started to conduct. The strings were joined by trumpets, a crescendo that rolled through the barn.

"Allegro," Clair said. "You go."

The Sanctuary firehouse was empty, bay doors open, trucks gone, a few pickups parked helter-skelter to one side. Lasha had said the fire was off South

Sanctuary Road, beyond her house, a dirt road on the left, a couple of miles out. She couldn't remember the name. She thought the place was owned by a guy named Don.

I drove out beyond the school, took a right, and headed south. The road followed a ridge, the river a silver ribbon beyond the woods to my right. It was a little after 6:30, the morning mist clinging to the roadside brush. I drove slowly, not wanting to miss the turn, but then a pickup came up from behind, red light flashing on the dash. I pulled over, then followed my escort, a latecomer in an old rust-white pickup who didn't want to miss the party.

It was 1.8 miles from Lasha's driveway, a single-lane dirt road that disappeared into the woods. I followed my man, bouncing the Toyota over ruts and bumps until he swerved into the brush. I did the same and a tanker truck came out of the trees and eased past us. We crashed out of the brush and continued on and I could smell smoke.

Then the road broke out of the woods and into a clearing with a shingled farmhouse at the near edge of an overgrown field. At the far edge a barn was burning.

I parked alongside the Ford and, while the driver wrestled his gear on, gathered up my notebook and phone and ran along the rutted path that the fire trucks had made through the grass. There were trucks parked around the barn and a stream of water cascaded onto the half-collapsed frame. Smoke billowed into the sky, sending embers aloft like tiny flaming balloons.

I saw Chief Frederick in a yellow jacket and helmet directing Ray-Ray and Paulie, manning a hose. Other firemen were walking the perimeter with shiny water tanks on their backs, extinguishing fires in the field. Harold from the store drove up at the wheel of a tanker truck.

To my right was a small crowd, some holding paper coffee cups. I approached, saw Davida Reynolds in a dark blue jumpsuit, taking notes as she talked to a tall guy at the edge of the crowd.

Ten feet away, I stopped and listened.

The tall guy—lanky, tanned, blond curly hair—was saying something about gasoline. "Some kerosene, too. A bunch of old paint. Haven't had a chance to go in and clean the place out. I mean, it was filled with the old man's—"

There was a whoosh from the barn, blue and yellow flames leaping skyward. The crowd flinched. Across the clearing the reflection of the flames danced on the side of the house.

Reynolds turned and Chief Frederick started shouting, "Back up, back up." The guys on the hose staggered backwards, like the feet of a dragon in a Chinatown parade. There was another explosion and Reynolds left the tall guy, started for the fire.

I raised my phone and snapped a few pictures. Then I eased into her place. I told him my name, said I was from the paper. I didn't say which one.

"Don Barbier," he said, shaking my hand. Big hands, strong arms, broad shoulders under his dungaree jacket.

"You're the owner of the barn," I said.

"Was," he said. He mustered a smile.

"What was in there?"

"Not entirely sure. The old guy's farming equipment, some antique tools. Just bought the place in February. Moved up six weeks ago."

"From where?"

"Down south. Atlanta area."

"Your family here?" I looked toward the house.

"Single. Divorced."

I scribbled in my notebook. He didn't seem to mind.

"Glad it's just the barn?"

"Jesus, yes," he said.

"What brought you up here, Don?"

"I flip houses," he said. "Me and Tory and Rita, we're kinda teaming up."

"Who's that?"

"They own the real estate place."

He looked in the direction of a fortyish couple, nice-looking, like actors on a daytime soap. They were wearing matching blue fleece vests.

"They buy them, you do the work?"

"Yeah. They picked some up just before the "Hidden Treasure" article. This one I bought myself. Used to build new houses, but that went to hell."

"So you're fixing this place up?"

He looked to the barn, where white smoke billowed and the fire crackled but the flames were down.

"Not this part of it."

"Insurance?"

"Yeah. But not enough to rebuild. Mortise-and-tenon, oak pegs, massive beams."

He looked toward Davida Reynolds, talking to Chief Frederick. They both looked my way. Frederick shook his head. I hurried.

"So how'd you know—that it was burning?"

"Got up around four. Heard something howling. You all have wolves up here?"

"Just coyotes," I said. "But big ones."

"Well, it was pretty cool, howling back and forth. I stepped out back and I was listening to 'em. Kinda like the Old West, you know? And then I see this glow."

"Was it going pretty good?"

"Oh, yeah. Back wall was all flames. I ran back up and called 911, but by the time they got out here . . . I mean, they did the best they could."

Reynolds had broken away from Frederick and was starting over.

"Any electricity?" I said.

"No. It was all rusted and rotted. I disconnected it. Figured it was a fire hazard."

"So what could have started it, then?" I said.

He looked at me.

"You know what's going on around here, right?" he said.

I nodded.

"So it isn't a what," he said. "It's a who."

Reynolds was taking photos of the crowd, snapping as she panned the camera. She slipped it into the pocket of her jumpsuit and approached. Time for one more question.

"So who do you think?" I said. "Any theories?"

He shook his head, watched the smoke billowing skyward.

"You tell me," Barbier said. "Figured it was one of those nice quiet New England towns. Said so in the magazine, right?"

Reynolds stepped between me and Barbier, and led him off. I turned around, saw the bystanders behind me. They were mostly women, the menfolk busy fighting the fire.

I scoped out the closest woman, maybe thirty, pretty in a big-boned, farmer's wife sort of way. She had a toddler in her arms, an older kid standing next to her, his arm around her thighs. I walked over and stood beside them.

The little boy, maybe six, looked up at me and said, "Are you a policeman"

"No," I said. "I'm a reporter."

Nobody ran away.

"I'm Jack," I said.

"I'm Elias," the boy said. "She's my mom. My sister, her name is Abigail, but we call her Abbie."

I smiled at the woman. "Hello, Mom," I said.

"Hi there," she said. "I'm Eve Johnson."

"Everybody's up early," I said.

"Peter, my husband, he's in the fire department. We only have the one pickup right now, so we said we'd drop him off. Then Elias wanted to stay."

"I'm sure," I said. "To watch his dad."

"And the fire," Elias said. "I like fires."

"Good thing your dad is here to put it out," I said.

Abbie watched me, her thumb in her mouth, her arm wrapped in a threadbare green blanket.

"So," I said, "do you live nearby?"

"Four miles," Eve said. "Other side of town, toward the river. Know where Overlook Lane is?"

"No," I said.

"It's a great spot, looking out over the river. I mean, it's a great little town. Nice people. We moved here from the Bangor area. Bucksport, really. I grew up there and it's fine, but this is really beautiful. Nice and quiet. Well, not lately. But a lot of people are coming here for that. Retired folks, people with families, even Don here. He owns this place."

"Right."

"Mom," Elias said, "Mrs. Hubble is here. Can I go see her?"

"Yes. But stay right there."

The boy ran toward the parked cars where a gray-haired woman leaned down and gave him a hug.

"His first-grade teacher," Eve said.

"Small-town life," I said.

Smoke billowed from the rubble. We stood and watched like villagers who'd just been pillaged.

"Don," I said.

"Right. He came here all the way from California or someplace. At first I thought I knew him from school or something, but then it turned out not to be him. But he heard about the town. Some people are from Washington, all kinds of places. But everybody gets along. I mean, the old-timers, the new folks."

She was a chatterer, probably eager to talk after being cooped up with the kids.

I slipped my notebook out, took a pen from my pocket, gave her some direction. "This fire stuff making you nervous?"

Eve glanced at my notebook. "Is this for a story?" she said.

"Yes. It's what I do."

"What paper? *Bangor Daily?*"

"I write mostly for the *New York Times.*"

"Oh," Eve said. She seemed relieved.

"So are you worried?"

The little girl stared, her big blue eyes fixed on mine.

"My husband," Eve said. "He drives a truck. Like, a tractor-trailer?"

"So he's often away?"

"Yeah," she said. "Usually it's like, three days on, two days off."

"So you're alone."

"Yes, but please don't put that in the paper," Eve said.

I hesitated.

"Okay. Do you think the arsonist might see it?"

"I don't know."

"Do you think he reads the *New York Times?*" I said.

"What makes you think it's a he? Do they know who it is?"

"No," I said. "But almost all serial arsonists are male."

"Serial. That means they do it over and over again, right?"

"Yes."

"This makes four," Eve said. "Right here in Sanctuary."

"I think that would qualify, but I'm not the expert."

"Who is?"

I pointed to Reynolds, talking to Don Barbier and Chief Frederick. "Fire Marshal's Office," I said.

"Well, I hope she catches him soon," Eve said. "Because . . ." She paused. I waited. Abbie watched. "Because, I mean, it's terrible seeing this. They're just barns and stuff, but you never know what might be next. And what if there are animals in the barn? I mean, do you think he checks to see if there are cows or a horse or whatever?"

"I don't know," I said.

I scrawled, trying to keep up.

"Another thing," she said. "Do you think somebody would come from far away and just pick out our town for this?"

"I don't know."

"I mean, I can't imagine somebody just picking us off the map. And then you have to be able to find these places. He can't just drive up and do this. So if he's walking around the woods—"

Eve stopped. I waited. Smoke billowed and embers hissed as the firemen trained the hose on a new spot.

"If he's walking around," I prompted.

"Well, I mean, you'd have to really know your way," she said. "There's woods and puckerbrush and swamps. There's some ATV trails, but it's not like they go everywhere. And in the dark."

She trailed off.

"So that means?" I said.

Eve held her blue-eyed daughter closer. She turned and looked at her neighbors, friends, people she saw at the general store.

"It means," she said, "that it's one of us."

Eve called to her son—"Elias, let Mrs. Hubble be"—hiked Abbie up on her hip, and hurried off.

I finished my notes, underlined that last quote. I was close to having enough material to file it today. SMALL TOWN WORRIES AS ARSONIST PROWLS. I made a note of the photo possibilities for Kerry at the *Times*, in case she sent a real photographer. Don with the ruins of his barn behind him. Eve and the kids. Chief Frederick outside the firehouse, if he'd go for it.

Frederick was climbing into a pumper truck, moving it closer to the barn, now a Stonehenge of charred beams. I could see the frame of a tractor, tires melted off. Some people were leaving, the exciting part of the fire over. I wasn't ready to go, but I fell in with Don's friends, the couple in matching blue fleece vests.

I turned and gave them my pitch, read the logo on the vests: SANCTUARY BROKERS, the "S" and the "B" in red. Matching polo shirts, crisp jeans, and new hikers rounded out their outfits. Both in their forties, fit and tanned and ready to do business.

They smiled, showing luminescent teeth.

"I'm Rita."

"I'm Tory."

"Stevens," they said in unison.

"We sell real estate here in town," Rita said.

"You from around here?" her husband said.

I felt like their next question would be about my price range. Instead, I stopped and they stopped, too. He had a half-smile set permanently, like it had been Botoxed on. At an early-morning fire scene her hair and makeup were perfect. And their focus on sales wouldn't allow them to walk away from a conversation.

"These fires," I said. "Are they beginning to have an effect on business?"

Tory was ready. "You mean, is Sanctuary, Maine, 'the arson town'?" he said, making air quotes with his fingers.

"Yeah," I said.

"Jack, this will be old news in a couple of weeks."

"Some firebug kid will get counseling and do some community service," Rita said. "End of story. You know, there's a lot of troubled youth. I blame the Internet and all that."

"*New York Times*, huh," Tory said.

"We sell a lot of property to New Yorkers, Jack," Rita said. "Just last week we closed on a lovely nineteenth-century colonial. Full restoration, modern appliances but hidden behind a pumpkin-pine facade. A very tasteful update."

"Water view and an apple orchard," Tory said. "We showed it when the blossoms were out and didn't they just have to have it."

"They're both doctors," Rita said. "Retiring soon. He wants to use the barn for his car collection."

"And she wants to get back into horses," Tory said. "Build a new stable."

"Nice," I said.

Tory was handing me his card.

"Oh, yeah. I mean, this is the perfect small-town community. Upscale, but still has those authentic touches. Like Harold at the general store. Have you met him?"

"Just a wonderful character," Rita said. "You can go in just a couple of times and he knows your name."

"And the authentic old Maine accent," Tory said.

He said it like Sanctuary was Plimoth Plantation. See the people in period dress.

"Listen, Jack," Tory said. "Any of your friends down in New York want a country place, now's the time to buy. I mean, interest rates are at rock bottom. Prices are down. And we get all the prime listings in this area."

"For the boaters, twenty minutes down the river and you're out in the bay," Rita said.

"Or horse people," Tory said. "We have a listing right now. Two hundred acres, sixty in pasture. Connecticut, Westchester County, it would be millions. I mean, mega. Riding trails through your own woods. House would probably be a tear-down, but—"

"The fires," I said.

They paused for a breath.

"Does it bother you that someone in your own community may be doing this? You know the arson people say that these things tend to escalate. First it's sheds and barns, then vacant homes. For an arsonist, after a while an old barn doesn't do it. It's like drugs. You need more and more."

Rita and Tory looked at each other, then at me.

"They won't continue," Rita said.

"You can count on it," Tory said.

"How's that?"

They started walking down the dirt road. I could see a silver Mercedes SUV parked up ahead, the Sanctuary Brokers logo on the driver's door.

"We're working on it," Rita said. "That's all I can say."

"We take care of our community, Jack," Tory said. "It's a Maine thing."

Suddenly a local, he said it like I wouldn't understand.

"What sort of Maine thing?" I said.

Rita had the keys out. She pressed the button and the Mercedes beeped and flashed. She veered slightly, leaving us guys alone.

"Jack," Tory said. "Somebody is threatening your property, even your family. What do you do?"

"Call the police?" I said.

"Sure, but what if the police are a half-hour away? What if by the time you see the fire, it's been burning for at least that long? What if the person doing this has free run of the town because at three a.m., everyone is asleep?"

"I don't know," I said. "You tell me."

"In a situation like this you have to take back the night, Jack," Tory said. I looked at him.

"What? Some sort neighborhood watch?"

He pointed his index finger at me.

"Bingo, my friend," Tory said.

Rita started the car. Tory had his hand on the door. I fished in my jeans for a card and handed it to him. He looked at it, stuck it in his vest pocket.

"One more question," I said.

"Shoot," he said.

"It's a big town. In square miles, I mean. How do you know where to patrol? What if you're on the east side when something's happening on the west side?"

Tory tapped his temple as he opened the car door.

"Intelligence, Jack," he said. "It's the same in the real estate business. You want to be successful, you have to do your homework."

10

The spectators left in dribs and drabs, the stragglers driven out when it started to rain, a little before eight.

I went to the truck and got a rain jacket, came back. As I walked up the dirt road fire trucks approached and I stood at the edge of the brush to let them pass. Casey, riding on the side of a pumper, gave me a little wave. I continued walking up to the house, heard a car approaching, and stepped aside again. A sheriff's department cruiser passed, blue lights flashing against the green of the woods.

By the time I reached the clearing, the deputy—a short, stocky guy with a shaved head—was walking around to the rear of the barn. Through the burned beams, I could see Reynolds and the fire chief standing close, staring at the ground. Barbier was standing by the house under the overhang by the side door, talking on a cell phone.

I skirted the smoldering rubble, rain pattering on the smoking beams. It smelled of burned building, a very different odor from a campfire or wood-stove smoke. It was caustic and clingy. Like the odor of decay.

When I reached the back of the barn, the deputy was standing. Frederick and Reynolds were crouched, staring at the ground. Reynolds had a pen in her hand and she was tracing something in the grass. She turned away from the rubble and scooched along for ten feet, still peering at the ground.

"Oh, yeah," she said. She smiled, reached into the pocket of her jumpsuit for a plastic bag. She opened it with the pen, reached down, and flicked something into the bag, flicked some more and zipped the bag shut.

"Used something for a fuse," Reynolds said, and she looked up. "Mr. McMorrow, I didn't know—"

"This is a goddamn crime scene," the chief said. "No press."

The deputy advanced, hand by the Taser on his belt.

"Sir, you're gonna have to—"

"What sort of fuse?" I said. "Can you tell by the ashes?"

"You can't be snooping around here," Frederick said.

"I wasn't snooping; I was just standing here. I need to talk to Investigator Reynolds."

"I'm asking you to leave this vicinity," the deputy said.

"You can't print that," Frederick said. "It'll jeopardize the crime investigation."

"So this is the fourth arson," I said.

"I didn't say that," the chief said.

"Sir, I've asked you politely," the deputy said.

"I'll go," I said. "No problem."

I turned away, slipped my notebook from my pocket, pulled out a pen. As I walked, I started to write. After five steps and two words—fuse, arson—Reynolds called.

"Mr. McMorrow."

I stopped and turned.

"I'll talk to you," she said.

"Great," I said.

"If you could wait by my truck."

"Okay," I said.

Frederick glared at me, said, "You don't have to tell him—"

Reynolds held up a hand. "Chief, it's okay."

"But he—"

The deputy watched me, hands on his hips, like he thought he still might have to subdue me and stuff me in the cruiser. I started for the Suburban, heard Reynolds say, "We can work with the press, Chief."

Frederick muttered, the words unintelligible but for one. "Trouble."

I watched from the truck. Barbier was still on the phone, reading from a document, probably talking insurance. The deputy strung crime-scene tape from a stake at the front of the barn to a stake all the way to the rear. The scene extended into the back field where it crossed behind the barn and stopped.

Birds called from the woods—a veery, a redstart, a cardinal—oblivious to the human mayhem. I waited in the rain, a steady and heavy drizzle. After five minutes I called Roxanne but she didn't answer. I called Clair but he didn't pick up, either. There wasn't much reception in Pokey's stall.

Reynolds was pointing to the woods, asking Frederick questions. They talked for a few more minutes, then Reynolds took out an iPhone, flicked her fingers across the screen, and held it up for the other two. They squinted at the screen, then looked back across the field.

"Google Earth," I said aloud. Reynolds slipped the phone into her breast pocket and they started in my direction. Reynolds kept pausing to look at the charred beams, stepping closer. She lifted a camera and started taking pictures like an archaeologist sifting through the ruins of an ancient civilization.

I wrote that down. Frederick and the deputy approached, the deputy giving me a hard look, like I'd dodged him this time. Frederick said, "We're gonna have to talk."

"Anytime," I said, but he kept walking to his truck, the red Tahoe still gleaming, the gold lettering glittering even at a fire scene. The radio blared chatter and static. The deputy put his cruiser in gear and sprayed gravel as he pulled away. Frederick followed. The birds called. Davida Reynolds walked up, her boots crunching in the gravel. She stood in front of me for a moment, then turned to look back at the burned barn.

"Like a giant puzzle?" I said.

"Oh, this is just part of it. In fact, in some ways this is the easy part."

"The how?"

"Right. Now we need the who and the why."

Her dark hair was wet where it protruded from her blue cap, the curls stuck to her neck. Her boots and the bottoms of her trousers were covered with black grime and soot, and she smelled of the rubble. But her eyes were bright.

"You love your job, don't you?" I said.

She looked at me.

"You ask weird questions, Mr. McMorrow," she said.

"More an observation than a question," I said.

She glanced at me, turned back to the barn.

"Yeah, I do. Each investigation is unique. A new case."

"So you solve the puzzle—and you get the satisfaction of putting a bad guy away."

"That's the goal," Reynolds said.

"And in the process maybe you're saving somebody's life."

"If you stop somebody before they burn a house down with somebody in it," she said.

"I can see why you'd like it," I said.

"Most of the time."

I waited a beat, then said, "What's with the fuse? Is that unusual? I thought most arsonists just poured gas on the place and lit it."

"Splash and dash," Reynolds said. "Problem is, it's almost impossible not to get gasoline on your shoes, your clothes, your hands."

"So this one is smarter."

She looked at me.

"Is this how you do it?"

"Do what?"

"Get people to talk. You get them chatting, figure out what interests them, what gets them revved up. And once the conversation is rolling along, you slip in the question you really want answered."

I smiled.

"Don't you do the same thing? With witnesses, I mean."

She eyed me.

"Yeah. And I'm pretty good at it," Reynolds said. "But I think maybe I can learn a trick or two from you."

"I don't think of it as tricks," I said. "I think of it as putting people at ease. And I'm generally curious about people, what makes them tick. Aren't you?"

"You're doing it right now."

I shrugged.

"The fuse," I said.

"That's information we're not releasing at this time. It would jeopardize the investigation, if the suspect knows we know."

"Right. But I know."

"So here's where we come to some sort of arrangement," Reynolds said.

I waited.

"How 'bout you leave that off the record until we make an arrest."

"What if that takes months?" I said.

"What if I keep you abreast of my progress in the meantime?"

"I don't like to withhold things from the readers."

"But you'll have a lot more to tell them if you wait," Reynolds said. "In the long run, the readers benefit."

I thought about it. The smoke rose. The birds called. In the house, a pan clanged. Barbier putting on coffee?

"You talking to anybody else? Reporters?" I said.

"I will be later. They'll be calling."

"They get the bare-minimum official line, I get the real stuff. But I don't pull the trigger until you arrest somebody, or you decide you want something out there."

"Competitive, aren't you?"

"Yes."

"What do I get out of it?" Reynolds said.

"I'll be talking to people," I said.

"Like who?"

"Like the people in town starting a citizen patrol."

"A what?" Reynolds said. "Oh, shit."

"They have suspects, you know. The Goth kid, the army vet out in the woods."

"I heard about them. Didn't know about the patrol."

"The fuse," I said.

"Our agreement?"

She peeled a latex glove off of her right hand and held it out. I took it and we shook.

"Okay."

"The fuse buys the arsonist time. He—or she, but they're almost always a he—can melt back into the crowd, be sitting at home, in the office when the place goes up."

"Unusual?"

"Yeah."

"The Goth kid and the army vet don't have offices," I said.

"No," Reynolds said. "They don't."

"So your list of suspects—"

"More like a list of all of the people who live around here," she said. "Now we start crossing them off."

Reynolds threw me my bone. She took me back to the barn and showed me how she figured out the fire's point of origin. It looked like stinking rubble to me, but she pointed to ways the fire had burned. There was talk of movement patterns and intensity, depth of char on the standing beams.

"So you consider all of that and come up with the footprint of the fire," she said. "In this case it's relatively simple: The fire started at the base of the back wall. It climbed the wall, moved up the cedar shingles, and into the ceiling. Then it worked its way to the front."

We moved to the front of the building and she pointed to a charred beam, the back side more intact. "Fire went up and over," she said, "then worked its way back down."

"All this old wood," I said. "Must really go up."

"Not really," Reynolds said. "People think that, but wood just absorbs ambient moisture. Once it's dry, doesn't matter if it's from 1800 or if it's kiln-dried stuff you bought last week."

I scrawled.

"That'll make some people feel better," I said.

"When you get to houses, modern construction makes a big difference," she said. "Fire stops, drywall."

She kept moving, pointing at the mess with a pen. I stepped back and took her photo and she flinched but didn't object.

"So you've got your secondary heat sources. Here, it was stored paint and gasoline. But the paint cans are more burned closer to the rear of the barn. The gas was in the front half of the building, and that didn't blow until the building was fully involved."

"Which all tells you what?" I said.

"Point of origin."

"Plain English?"

"Somebody set the back of the barn on fire."

"No accelerant?"

"We'll get the dog in, but I don't think so."

We rounded what would have been the corner of the building, had it been standing.

"I think it might have been a bunch of twigs and sticks piled up against the back wall," Reynolds said. She bent and stared at a scattering of light-gray cinders. "Maybe some broken-up cedar shingles on top of that."

She picked with the pen, turned up a charred nail. "Shingle nails. From the burning wall? Maybe, but these are a foot back, may have toppled from the pile of combustibles."

"Light the fuse and—"

"But we're not saying that."

"Yet," I said.

"Yet," she said.

"But you're ruling this a set fire?"

Reynolds hesitated, composing her statement. "All indications are the fire was of human origin," she said.

We were back in the dooryard. Reynolds took off her cap and pushed her hair back. I had a flash of a girl who had grown up playing with older brothers.

"So what do you think?" I said.

"About what?"

"Is this a thrill arson, or whatever it is you call it?"

Reynolds thought for a moment, scanned the mess.

"Same time of day, three to four a.m. Similar buildings. Another common denominator is that they're out of the way, easily approachable from the woods. Arsonists tend to stick to their comfort zone."

"But getting closer," I said.

She glanced at the house.

"Yes, we're getting closer. So if it's a serial arsonist, he may be looking for a bigger thrill. Lighting it up with someone sleeping in the house right over there."

"The risk."

"Oh, yeah," Reynolds said. "Half the fun of doing something wrong is getting away with it."

"And then having your secret," I said.

"Why most arsonists can't resist watching. Stand back and watch the BRTs."

"BRTs?"

"Big red trucks," she said.

I pictured the crowd. Eve and her kids. The real estate couple, Tory and Rita. Barbier—but it was his barn. Random others drawn to the most exciting thing happening in Sanctuary that morning.

"The Goth kid, Woodrow, wasn't here. The crazy vet."

"I never said they were suspects," Reynolds said.

"But the people here—"

"—aren't investigating these fires," she said. "I am."

"They're going to be doing their own patrols," I said.

Reynolds frowned.

"Yeah, well . . . we'd rather leave law enforcement to law enforcement," she said.

I smiled.

"Good luck with that," I said.

I drove out to the road, headed north. There were cars moving slowly in front of me and I eased back, slipped my phone out, tried Roxanne.

The phone beeped. No service. I tried twice more on the way back to the center of town, finally connected as I approached the common.

No answer.

I tried her cell. It went to voice mail. I said I was checking in, to call when she had a chance. I pulled into the lot in front of the general store and parked. Tried Clair's house. No one picked up. I tried Clair's cell, left a message.

I sat for a minute, then took out my notebook and flipped through the pages. I found the best quotes, filled in the places where my shorthand hadn't kept up. Some quotes got stars. Some were underlined. Some were both.

I considered what I had: Reynolds confirming the arson. Barbier saying he thought Sanctuary was a nice New England town, Eve saying she was worried about being home alone, Tory talking about the community patrol.

I tried to anticipate Kerry's questions: They're going to just drive around all night? Will they be armed? How do they know where to go? Who are these suspects? Can we get someone to say that they have some? At some point, we should talk to this veteran guy. You went off the record with this investigator person? Oh, Jack, I wish you hadn't told me that. You know how I feel about withholding information from the readers.

I frowned, looked out at the store. A few people were coming and going, stopping for coffee, a newspaper. The first two or three I didn't recognize. Tradesmen types getting into pickups. And then the blue Audi rolled up and Russell from the Think Tank got out.

I cut him off at the door.

"Russell," I said.

He turned and stopped, looked at me and said, "*New York Times.*"

"Yes. Jack McMorrow."

"Must be a slow news day," Russell said, "the *Times* covering Sanctuary, Maine."

"No, I think it's a good story," I said.

"The pumpkin festival?" he said, with a patronizing grin. He was a smug sort of fellow, in his pink Brooks Brothers polo shirt, iron-gray hair combed straight back.

"The arson fires," I said. "The citizen patrol."

The grin fell away. A guy came out of the door with a coffee and we stepped aside. Russell kept stepping and I stayed with him. He looked around the parking lot like we were exchanging classified information.

"Yeah, well, we'd like to keep that on the down low," he said.

"Why's that?"

"You don't divulge your field strategy to the enemy," he said.

"Is that the way you think of it? A military campaign?"

"Is this off the record?" Russell said.

Here we go again, I thought.

"Do you want it to be?"

"I try to keep a low profile," he said. "Google, you know."

"You don't want your past coming back to haunt you?"

"In a word, no," Russell said. "And I'm not the one running the operation."

"Who is?"

"I'm not in a position to reveal that."

"Who is in a position?"

"I can't say. Maybe I could take your number and pass it on. No promises."

"What is this? Pakistan? Covert ops?"

He shrugged, gave me a knowing smile.

"Okay," I said. "How 'bout if I just attribute this to someone familiar with the patrol planning?"

Russell took a couple of steps, turned away from the store entrance. I did the same.

"I just want to get it right, Russell," I said. "If it's not you, I may have to use a less-reliable source."

He took a deep breath, looked left and right.

"I'm writing the story either way," I said.

Another breath. Another sideways glance. When he spoke it was out of the side of his mouth, like someone might read his lips.

"Okay, Mr. McMorrow," Russell said. "Ask your questions."

"There are patrols planned?"

"Yes."

"How many people involved?"

"On the ground, a dozen. Maybe more."

I paused and scrawled, getting it down verbatim.

"When do you begin?"

"Soon."

"Will you be armed?"

"No comment."

"Will you be targeting any particular individuals?"

"No comment."

"Why not leave it to the police?"

"This country was founded by people who protected their own rights. We're just doing the same. And law enforcement in this area is terribly overburdened."

"So is this a militia?"

"That's a loaded word. This is just a group of concerned citizens trying to protect lives and property."

"So what will you do if you come upon a suspect?"

"There are protocols," Russell said.

"Hold the person for the police?"

"That's a situational decision."

"What's that mean in English?"

"There are protocols," he said, "but they have to be flexible. For the safety of the patrol personnel."

"So your guys are prepared to defend themselves."

"To not do so would be irresponsible."

I wrote that down. He waited, eyes darting all around like he was Jason Bourne. The spy come in from the cold? These ex-CIA types were slippery.

"One last question, Russell," I said.

He gave me a quick nod.

"What's your last name?"

"I'd rather not say, if you don't mind."

"Not for print. I just need to know who I'm talking to," I said.

"Then just Russell is fine," he said, and he turned and walked to the door and went into the store.

I waited a minute and followed him. Inside, I could see him at the back of the aisle, by the meat counter. There was a teenage girl at the register and I turned to her and smiled. She was leaning against the counter in her green Sanctuary General Store apron. She smiled back.

"You know Russell, right?" I said.

"Sure."

"You know his last name?"

"Yeah—Witkin."

"Thanks," I said. And I turned and walked out the door.

11

—ᵐ—

"Ten to one he was a pencil pusher," Clair said.

"He and his buddies are going to be pistol pushers now," I said.

"Just what you need, middle of the night—civilians with firearms rousting an Iraq vet with PTSD."

"I'm not betting on this Witkin guy surviving that firefight."

"No," Clair said. "That wouldn't be smart money."

I had just rolled in and we were leaning against the fence of the paddock out behind his barn. Roxanne was standing in the center of the ring and had Pokey on a long tether. Pokey was plodding along like he was pulling a plow. Sophie, crouched on Pokey's back, hung on like it was the Preakness.

"Faster, Pokey," she said. "Do your gallop."

Pokey hadn't galloped since President Bush. The first one.

"This is fine for now, honey," Roxanne said. "We don't want Pokey to wear himself out."

Little chance of that, but we erred on the side of caution.

"No calls?" I said.

"Don't know," Clair said. "Been out here most of the morning. Take her mind off sad things."

"Working?"

"Hard to be sad when the little one's so darned happy," Clair said.

"Luck of the draw," I said.

"Yes," Clair said. "In the grand scheme, Sophie hit the jackpot."

He looked at me.

"With Roxanne for a mom, I mean."

"Right," I said.

Pokey walked on in his circular path, like he was attached to a winch and hauling up an anchor. Sophie leaned back in her saddle, held the reins in front of her. Roxanne said, "That's right. Just relax."

I looked at my watch.

"It should be long over," I said. "The memorial service."

"Right. Where was it?"

"Gardiner."

"Poor kid," Clair said.

"No jackpot for him," I said.

"No," he said. "In the random crapshoot, he lost. Not right. Not right at all. And no way to fix it."

We paused. I waved off a deerfly. Clair had a radio on his belt and it squawked. Mary's voice came over, saying, "You all want lunch?"

Clair unclipped the radio, said to me, "Pony'll be ready for a break."

"Let's go to our house," I said. "You've done enough."

"Tell that to the boss," Clair said. He handed the radio over and I had lifted it to my mouth to speak when the car rolled up to the front of the barn.

A blue cruiser. State police. I lowered the radio. We watched as the trooper got out of the car, put on his wide-brimmed hat, and closed the door. He walked toward the house. Jutting chin, military posture, stern expression.

"Uh-oh," I said.

Roxanne turned and watched. Pokey stopped. Sophie said, "Giddyup. Giddyup." The trooper started for the side door, then saw us out back. He marched toward us, like he was delivering a telegram and it had bad news.

"I'm Trooper Foley," he said.

"Yes," Roxanne said, still holding the end of the line, Pokey and Sophie waiting.

"We tried calling the house."

"We've been out here," Roxanne said, nodding toward the pony.

He looked toward Pokey, back at Roxanne.

"I've got some bad news."

"What?" she said.

"There was a memorial service this morning. For the little boy who died."

Roxanne nodded. Clair moved to the gate, started across the paddock. "And?"

Clair lifted Sophie off of Pokey and, carrying her in his big arms, started for the house. The trooper waited. Roxanne walked over to him, Pokey trailing behind her.

"The child's father, Alphonse Celine, is an inmate at the Maine Correctional Center."

"I know that," Roxanne said. "What happened? Just tell me what happened."

"Mr. Celine was allowed to attend the service in the custody of corrections officers. When he—"

He paused, looked at me, back at Roxanne.

"When he what?" she said.

"He escaped from custody, ma'am," Trooper Foley said.

"You have got to be shitting me," I said.

"No, sir," the trooper said. "Unfortunately I'm not. Went out through the restroom window."

It took a moment to sink in. A violent psycho meth head whose son had just died. He blamed my wife and he was loose.

"I'll shoot him on sight," I said.

We stood, the three of us. The radio squawked in the cruiser. Pokey swished his tail and looked up at us with his bottomless brown eyes. Roxanne turned away, looked past me at the wall of trees at the far side of the field. A hawk passed just above us, slipped into the line of woods, and disappeared.

Anything could hide in the second-growth ash and maple. Anyone. We had no way of knowing what was lurking in the woods in the dark.

Clair came out of the house, started toward us. We did have one way of knowing, I thought. We stood, quiet. Clair walked up and I introduced him. Foley and Clair shook hands and there was recognition between soldiers.

"Military?" Foley said.

"Marine Corps, a long time ago," Clair said.

"Army," the trooper said. "Five years out. Vietnam?"

"Yessir," Clair said. "Afghanistan?"

"Yessir," Foley said. "Rangers. Seventy-fifth."

Clair didn't reply.

Foley gave him an assessing look. I'd seen it before. People, good and bad, took in Clair's muscled arms and shoulders, the Semper Fi tattoo. But mostly it was the hardness in the eyes.

"You live here, sir?" the trooper said.

"Yes," Clair said. "I can help keep an eye on things."

"So here's the question," Roxanne said, like she was bringing the meeting back into focus. "Alphonse didn't care about Ratchet when he was alive. Why would he care about him now that he's dead?"

"Maybe he feels like he was dissed when his son died," I said. "He was still his son."

"He was the biggest reason we pulled him," Roxanne said. "Alphonse is a total piece of crap. Irresponsible, mean, a total narcissist. He used to beat Beth. I mean, once he beat her up and then urinated all over her. Horrible person. Doesn't care about anyone but himself."

"Could he have developed a conscience in prison?" Clair said.

"I've seen it," Foley said. "They get counseling. Get off the drugs. Sometimes they grow up."

"So he gets a sense of responsibility," Clair said.

"And comes after the social worker who took his kid," I said.

"Or he's already out of state," Roxanne said. "The Alphonse I knew would use his son's death as a way to get out of prison, and once he was out, he'd be long gone."

"So we're hoping for the old Alphonse," I said. "The one who didn't care if his son lived or died."

Pokey swished at the deerflies. Foley adjusted his hat.

"Well, either way, you folks ought to be alert," he said. "If you see Celine, just call 911. We'll be in the area. We consider him dangerous, and if he's at large for any length of time, he may be armed. He's facing a substantial prison sentence when he's recaptured, so he may not go quietly."

The trooper looked at Clair. Clair didn't answer. I knew him well enough to know what he was thinking: If Alphonse Celine came here and he was armed, 911 wouldn't be the first response. Foley read it, too.

"What did you do in Vietnam, Mr. Varney?" he said.

"Oh, crawled around in the jungle," Clair said.

"Force Recon," I said.

I could see it all coming together for Foley—that Clair was the real deal, that with him on duty we would not be sitting ducks.

"Guys like this, sometimes they don't come at you directly," he said.

"Backshooters," Clair said.

"Beat up kids and women," Roxanne said.

"Cowards," I said.

Foley looked toward Pokey, the paddock, the big barn.

"The kind of guys who don't necessarily say anything to your face," the trooper said. "Just come around in the middle of the night and set your house on fire."

He tipped his hat and walked away.

12

There was a pot of tea on the desk, organic Earl Grey. I was on my second cup, writing my story about Sanctuary, Maine. The patrol angle had elevated it, and Kerry had given me 1,500 more words, a featured blurb on the *Times* home page, a tentative slot on the New England section front in print.

It was seven o'clock, almost Sophie's bedtime. She was lying on the floor near my desk, drawing pictures of Pokey. She talked to herself as she worked, her legs waggling in the air. Crayons were strewn around her like spent cartridges around a machine-gun nest.

In the kitchen, Roxanne was on the phone.

She'd been talking to Dave at DHHS on and off all afternoon, into the evening. He'd been talking to the State Police patrol supervisor. The cops wanted to know what she knew about Alphonse Celine, his associates at the time she pulled Ratchet, the relationship between Alphonse and Beth. From what I could overhear, they were trying to figure out whether Alphonse would blame Beth for the child's death or whether they would be in this together against the agency.

"He'd beat her up and an hour later they'd be having sex," I heard Roxanne say. "The relationship was utterly dysfunctional. I mean, Beth's self-esteem was nonexistent."

From the floor, Sophie said, "Daddy, is Mommy going to keep talking all night?"

I said I was sure she'd be done soon, though I wasn't. When she wasn't talking to Dave, she was getting calls from her former colleagues at the department. They were offering their support. There but for the grace of God . . . .

I had notebook pages spread on the desk. Davida Reynolds, Lasha the sculptor, Harold at the store. Russell from the Think Tank, Chief Frederick and the boys in the truck at the fire department, Tory and Rita at the fire scene doing PR damage control. Eve Johnson with her kids and concerns, Don Barbier watching his barn smolder.

Reading through Don's quotes, I paused. The only direct victim in the story. How to describe his reaction? Philosophical? Resigned? The guy was Mr. Cool, like nothing rattled him, not even somebody sneaking onto his property in the middle of the night and setting his barn on fire. I made a note to talk to him again for the follow-up.

What do you think of Sanctuary, Maine, now, Don? Sleeping okay?

Last but not least, Woodrow. I had his best quotes underlined, but was trying to decide what to include. I didn't want him to seem like a raving lunatic—not when the kid had been minding his own business when I confronted him with the accusations. Also, I'd be doing more stories on the Sanctuary fires and I didn't want to burn bridges.

I flipped through the pages. "Gotta get Louis the army vet next time," I muttered to myself. On the floor, Sophie was whispering. A couple of mutterers, we were. I smiled at her just as she said, "Mommy's off the phone."

Sophie was on her feet, running to the kitchen. I looked back at my notes, the laptop screen.

> Someone is putting a match to the town of Sanctuary, Maine. Four arson fires in as many weeks have destroyed farm sheds and a barn in this seemingly idyllic rural enclave—and rattled residents who suspect the arsonist is in their midst. Now the townspeople are fighting back.
>
> "We take responsibility for our own community," said local real estate broker Tory Stevens, who planned to join other Sanctuary residents on nighttime citizen patrols of the town's back roads. "It's a Maine thing."

A decent lead, and the rest of the story followed pretty easily. I got everyone in with the exception of Woodrow. I figured I'd do a follow-up on the suspects, see if I could get Louis Longfellow to talk to me. IN COZY SANCTUARY, MAINE, RESIDENTS EYE NEIGHBORS AS SUSPECTS IN ARSON SPREE—or something like that.

I reread it three times, tightening it up. I cut it from 1,703 words to 1,508. I took a deep breath and sent it off, that die cast.

Now to wait for the reaction, see how I was received next time I walked into the Sanctuary General Store. Hey, Harold. How goes the—

Sophie's barefoot steps coming from the kitchen.

"Daddy," she said, "Mommy says to come quick."

"Why?" I said, but Sophie had slid to a halt, delivered her message, and run from the room. I went to the kitchen where Roxanne was saying, "Listen, Dave, I've got to go."

Sophie was headed for the door. "State police," Roxanne said. "They're here."

I caught up to Sophie at the door, slung her up, and turned to Roxanne, passed Sophie over.

Then I went out to the driveway, saw the blue cruiser parked in the road. Trooper Foley was in the driver's seat, talking on the radio. There was someone in the backseat, a hoodie on.

"So he did come up here," I said. "That son of a bitch."

I walked slowly down the drive, heard the police radio chattering as Foley got out. He glanced at the figure in the car, waited until we were close. The person was turned away, fumbling with something on the seat.

"Tried to call, but the line was busy," he said. "She was pretty upset. She says she needs to talk to your wife."

I looked to the car. From the backseat, Beth Leserve peered out.

Beth's car had run out of gas on Route 137 in Freedom, five miles away. She'd waved the trooper down, said she needed to get to Prosperity. She told him she was the mother of the little boy who had died. She said she didn't know where Alphonse was. She said he was a piece of crap and never cared about his own son, his flesh and blood. She said she had to talk to Roxanne. Roxanne was the only one who would understand.

I took Sophie back to the house when Roxanne went out to the cruiser. We watched from the mudroom door, Sophie in my arms with one hand on the back of my neck.

They stayed by the cruiser, Roxanne listening as Beth smoked and talked, Foley standing five feet away, arms folded across his chest. Beth started to cry and Roxanne reached out and touched her shoulder. Beth put her arm on Roxanne's shoulder and then drew her into a hug.

"Beth is very sad," Sophie said.

"Yes," I said. "Her little boy died."

"Was he sick?" Sophie said.

"I don't know," I said.

Clair came around the corner of the shed and I put Sophie down.

"You can go say good night to Pokey," I said, and Clair lifted her onto his shoulders and headed back toward the barn. I walked down the driveway and joined Beth and Roxanne and the trooper.

"You're the only one who knows me," Beth was saying, wiping tears from her cheeks. "You know it was the crack. I mean, if it wasn't for the dope, I could have been a good mom, right?"

"I think that's true," Roxanne said. "Without the drugs."

"I mean, people look at me, I can tell what they're thinking. Like at the thing today. These people work in the funeral place, all dressed up in their suits. This one lady, fucking high heels and stockings."

Beth was wearing a tight striped top and a short faded denim skirt. Pink flip-flops.

"This lady looks at me like, look at that drug addict—she's in jail when she should be with her kid. What a horrible person. And then Alphonse takes off out the bathroom window. I told them not to let him come."

"You can't worry about what people think," Roxanne said. "That's what started you down this path."

"My dad, he always told me how stupid I was. Numb as a fence post. Numb as a pounded thumb. Number than a hake. He said Ma shouldn't've drank when she was carrying me."

"I know, Beth. We've gone all through this."

"Well, how do you think that makes you feel? When even your own friggin' dad thinks you're a total loser."

"He's gone, Beth. You've got to move forward. Like we said before, you've got to get unstuck."

Beth was sniffing, wiping at her nose with her fingers. Foley reached into the cruiser and took out a box of tissues. She took one, said, "Thanks."

She wiped her nose, her mouth.

"And now look. Everything's totally turned to shit."

It was hard to disagree.

"I was at the thing today. And the minister guy, he's saying Ratchet is in a better place. He's in Heaven with the angels—they'll hold him in their arms."

She blew her nose. Held the balled-up tissue in one hand, cigarette in the other.

"Do you believe that?" Beth said.

"I believe we live on," Roxanne said.

"But the angels. Do you believe in angels?"

I waited. Foley looked to Roxanne, like we were discussing theology.

"Yes," Roxanne said. "I believe in angels."

Beth mustered a smile.

"Good. I think I do, too. And Ratchet up there. Maybe they're playing with him. Do you think angels would play with a little kid?"

"Sure," Roxanne said. "Of course, they would."

"Because you don't see them playing—in pictures, I mean. They're usually just floating around. But I was thinking: They can't do that all day. They have to do things. I mean, they run Heaven, right?"

"Yes," Roxanne said. "I suppose they do."

"I was thinking," Beth said, starting to cry. "You know the Eric Clapton song? The one after his son died? It goes, like, Would you know my name? If I saw you in Heaven?"

She sang it, not badly.

"Yes," Roxanne said. "It's a beautiful song."

"Well, I heard it on the radio in the car on the way here. This oldies station. I mean, I cried so hard I had to pull over. And then I was thinking, Well, if I'm gonna have a chance to see Ratchet in Heaven, I'm gonna have to get my shit together, you know what I'm saying? I mean, they're not gonna let me in just 'cause he's there already. It's like, 'I'm here to see my son Ratchet. Could you tell him his mom's at the gate.' "

Beth grinned, wiped at the tears with the tissue, mascara smearing across her cheekbone. Roxanne smiled. Foley and I listened. The police radio hissed and popped.

"So here I am," Beth said.

"So here you are, what?" Roxanne said.

"To get my shit together. Like you always wanted me to."

There was a pause.

"Beth," Roxanne said, "that's great. But I don't work there anymore."

Beth looked crestfallen. "But I thought we could just keep talking. Like we used to. It's not really work, is it? I mean, we don't have to talk every day. Just every coupla days, have coffee or whatever. I can tell you how I'm doing, staying off the dope. Gettin' a job. Maybe I'll volunteer in a homeless shelter or whatever. Really rack up some points."

"Beth," Roxanne said.

"I don't want to go back to the way I was. Not now. Not with Ratchet up there all by himself."

"Beth, listen."

"Because for a while, when he first died, I mean, I was just so angry, I was ready to go down and take everybody else with me. This Sandy bitch."

She slapped a hand over her mouth.

"Oops. There I go. But it was like, screw it, you know? You kill my baby? Well, here's a taste of your own—"

I could see Foley tense. Around the eyes.

"Okay," Beth said. "But now I'm seeing that the only way I'll see him again is to go the other way. And when I was at the service today, I'm thinking about Eric Clapton and the song, and I'm looking at the people who showed up—my cousin and her friends and some of my homies from before I went away—and I'm thinking, these people aren't gonna get me into Heaven. These people are gonna drag me the fuck down."

"Beth," Roxanne said.

"And I'm thinking of the people who can help me be a better person. And I know I didn't always do what you said. Maybe I almost never did what you said. But you were the one who said I could do it. I mean, of all the people. So I thought maybe now we could kinda start again."

Roxanne started to reply, stopped. Looked at me, then said, "Maybe we could talk. On the phone or something."

Beth smiled. She'd just won.

"Great," she said. "I'll just keep checking in."

"Sure," Roxanne said.

"Hear about your beautiful little girl," Beth said.

"We'll see," Roxanne said.

"With her pretty curls and her pony. And the pictures on the refrigerator. Maybe I could have a picture of her. I'll put it on my fridge. Maybe the three of us could go out for ice cream or something. The playground at McDonald's."

Roxanne didn't answer.

"Well," Beth said. "I should get going. The nice trooper here said he'd drive me to get some gas."

"We'll get you back on the road, ma'am," Foley said.

Beth turned toward the cruiser.

"I have a question," I said.

Beth turned back.

"Yeah, Jack?" she said.

She said my name like we were old friends.

"Where's Alphonse?" I said.

"I have no idea," she said. "Halfway to Florida? Like I told the trooper here, we didn't keep up after he went away."

"Should we be worried?" I said.

"Probably not," Beth said. "But on the other hand, you're the only ones I know with anything to lose."

13

Sophie was asleep. It had taken all of her stuffed-animal friends, much reassurance that Pokey wasn't lonely, a glass of water, an exhaustive search for a painful splinter in her left big toe. Or was it the right?

Roxanne came downstairs, found me on the deck. I was watching the bats silhouetted against gray clouds, darkening from the west.

"Storm coming," I said.

"Up there or down here?" Roxanne said.

"I don't think you should let her back in," I said.

"I know, but it's hard. I spent a year telling her how to make a better life."

"They paid you to do that. They're not paying you now."

"I was the only one who cared."

We stood, close but not touching. There was a rumble of thunder in the distance, so faint you thought you might have imagined it.

"I know you think you can still fix her. But I worry that she's just worming her way in," I said.

"An occasional phone call," Roxanne said. "That's not worming."

"It opens the door."

"I won't let that happen."

"I don't trust her," I said.

"Jack, she just lost her son. And . . ." She paused.

"And if you're nice to her, she won't sue you?" I said.

"Maybe."

"I'd rather see her in court."

"Than me talking to her on the phone once a week?"

"It won't be once a week, Roxanne," I said. "It won't be once a day."

"I can control that. I don't have to answer the phone."

"So then she shows up."

"She won't."

"She already has. Twice."

"But she's trying to get better," Roxanne said. "You heard her. So she can see her son again."

"I know, and my heart goes out to her. It really does. But she's nuts. Or at least manipulative. It's a junkie's survival skill."

"You don't have to tell me. I spent ten years working with these people."

Another rumble, this one closer, black clouds billowing up from behind the tree line to the west.

"I think Dave's strategy—disarm and conquer, or whatever the hell it is—is too risky. For you. For Sophie."

"You don't want to make enemies of these people, Jack," Roxanne said.

"Why not? Tell her you can't see her. You're not allowed to. If she comes back, get a protection order."

"Jack, she just lost her little boy. She's got a lot of problems, but underneath it all she's still a mom."

"And three days ago she was blaming you for it. Now she wants to come over and have tea?"

"She's always been erratic."

"No shit," I said.

"Jack, please."

"I'm sorry. But I don't trust her."

"You don't know her."

"And that's just fine. It's your thing, playing shrink to these lowlifes."

I regretted the words as soon as they left my mouth.

Roxanne didn't answer. I could feel her tense. There was a flicker of lightning in the distance, blue light reflecting off the clouds.

"I wasn't playing anything."

"I know. I'm sorry. I didn't mean that."

"A lawsuit could absolutely sink us, Jack," Roxanne said. "Win or lose. I mean, we're barely making it as it is."

"I know, honey. I just don't like it."

"I don't either. But if a few phone conversations can save us from financial ruin . . ."

We were quiet for a moment. The bats had disappeared into the darkness. The thunder was moving closer, rolling east like an approaching army. Lightning, a shimmering flash. A two-count and a peal of thunder.

"And her boyfriend—"

"He's long gone."

"If he comes around here I'll blow his head off."

Roxanne was quiet. A puff of wind ruffled her hair.

"You or Clair," she said.

"Me or Clair," I said.

I reached out and took her hand and squeezed. I waited, and finally Roxanne squeezed back.

We woke to see that Sophie had joined us, chased into our bed when the storm blew through.

It was a little after six, the night's rain still dripping from the trees but sunlight filling the room. Roxanne reached over Sophie and touched my shoulder. We lay there and listened. The birds: redstarts, a veery, then a loon calling as it flew over, chased from one of the ponds by the storm. The loon's call faded into the distance and then I could hear Sophie breathing—quick, shallow breaths. A delicate creature.

I touched my hand to Roxanne's and eased out of bed. I was halfway down the stairs when the phone rang. I trotted to the kitchen and answered it.

"Mr. McMorrow."

"Yes."

"Trooper Foley. Hope I didn't wake you."

"No," I said. "I was up."

"I thought you might be."

"So," I said.

"So I thought you'd like to know. Alphonse."

"You got him?"

"No, sir. But we think we know where he's headed."

"Here?"

I heard Roxanne start down the stairs.

"No, sir," Foley said. "It seems Alphonse made arrangements to be picked up."

"By whom?"

"What, Jack?" Roxanne said.

"Where do you think he is?"

"Sister of one of his cellmates. Young woman from Lawrence, Massachu-setts. It appears she picked him up on Route 201 in Gardiner, Maine."

"And went where?"

"We have video of them going through the Kittery tolls. Headed south."

I turned to Roxanne, wide-eyed beside me, covered the receiver. "He hooked up with some woman, last seen headed south in Kittery."

I took my hand off the receiver, returned to Foley. "When?"

"Three a.m.," Foley said.

"Headed for Lawrence?"

"That's our best guess. PD there is looking for her car. Of course, she may just drop him off. He'll go to ground."

"A lot of rat holes in Lawrence to hide in," I said.

"They'll pick him up," Foley said.

"Or they could just shoot him," I said.

There was no reply and then the trooper said, "I understand you're upset, Mr. McMorrow, but be careful what you say."

"I'm not upset," I said.

Another pause. I could hear traffic in the background, a truck horn blasting.

"Well," Foley said. "I thought you'd like to know. You and Ms. Masterson and your friend."

"Clair. Alphonse shows up here, he'll . . ." I held it back.

Another long pause, and then Foley said he'd keep us posted. I told him I appreciated that. He hung up and I put the phone down.

Roxanne, arms folded across her chest, said, "Lawrence, Massachusetts?"

"Yeah," I said. "And you said he's got a big mouth. He'll blab to somebody and then he'll be back inside, doing another three to five."

"Don't say that just to make me feel better," Roxanne said. "Give me the honest answer."

"They haven't caught him, so he could be anywhere."

"Don't patronize me," Jack," she said. "Not about this."

"Okay," I said.

"And keep the rifle loaded."

Sophie was out of our bed at seven. I made her blueberry waffles, her favorite. She was chopping the waffle into quarter-inch cubes when the phone rang again. Roxanne looked at me, went to the phone, and picked it up from the holder. She went through the room to the doors to the deck, slid them open, and stepped outside. Sophie was lining up the waffle cubes in the shape of an S. Roxanne walked back in, held out the phone.

"For you," she said.

"Who?" I said.

Roxanne shrugged, an odd look on her face.

I took the phone, said hello.

"Jack."

A woman's voice, husky and sultry. A little slurry.

"Yes."

"It's Lasha, Jack."

"Hey," I said. "How are you?"

"Not so good. Tired. Been up all night."

"Can't sleep?"

Roxanne was watching me, brow furrowed.

"No. Serious stress levels." A pause. "Was that your wife?"

"Yes," I said.

"She sounded suspicious. Like she thinks you're screwing around."

A swallow, the clunk of a bottle being set down. Lasha was drunk.

"No," I said. "She wouldn't think that."

"Why not?" Lasha said.

"Because I don't."

"Must be nice," Lasha said, "to be so virtuous."

Another pause, another clunk.

"The reason I called you," she said.

"Yes," I said.

"This town."

"What about it?"

"This hick town. This fucking pretentious place. How can a hick town be pretentious? This one has managed to do it."

I waited.

"This town is fucking imploding," Lasha said.

"The fires."

"The fires. The whole place turning on itself. We're eating our young, Jack."

I waited a moment while she drank.

"How so?"

"I'll be your Deep Throat, Jack," Lasha said. "Not like the porn movie; your little wifey doesn't have to worry. I'll just feed you the scoops. Like . . . like whatever it was."

"Watergate," I said. "Listen, Lasha, I've got to go."

"But I haven't told you," she said.

"Told me what?" I said.

"About the kid. Woodrow. The Goth kid."

"What about him?"

"They beat the crap out of him, Jack."

"When?"

"Last night sometime. But they just found him. My friend, Maggie. She heard it on the scanner. "

"Where?"

"Horseback Road. In the woods."

"How bad?"

"My friend said it sounded really bad. Like he might die, even."

"They still there?"

"I think so. I just heard a siren go by."

A pause for Lasha to drink. Roxanne was listening from the kitchen, the sun streaming in.

"So you coming to town?" Lasha said.

"Maybe," I said.

"Stop by, Jack," she said. "I'll stay up."

When I left, Clair was having coffee in the kitchen while Roxanne helped Sophie pull on her riding boots. Sophie was chattering away, telling her mom not to forget the carrots, did horses only eat sugar in cubes, why didn't ponies grow up to be horses, did Pokey know all of our names? Clair was wearing a denim shirt, untucked, the bulge of a Glock at the small of his back.

I gathered up my recorder, police scanner, notebooks, and phone, stuffed them in a small backpack. Turned as Roxanne stood up, Sophie headed for the door, Clair behind her.

"So you'll be there with her," I said.

"Yeah. I'll bring my phone," she said.

"Three hours," I said. "Kerry will want this followed up."

"Go," Roxanne said. "Come home before we wear out our welcome."

"Can't be done," Clair said.

Our eyes met. He nodded.

"We'll hold down the fort," Clair said.

He would.

I banged the truck down the back roads, speeding through Montville and Liberty, passing guys in pickups moseying their way to the dump. The sky was pure blue, the blurring tree line a shimmering green. It was a beautiful day in the neighborhood, and I found myself mouthing the words to Fred Rogers' ditty, picturing Sophie kneeling on the floor in front of the TV. In Mr. Rogers' neighborhood, nobody was beaten into a coma.

I crossed Route 17, wound my way south past Cape Cod houses and organic farms, signs hand-painted with pictures of flowers and goats. The scanner was on, a trooper calling someone in CID, asking for their ETA.

So Lasha's info had been good. CID was homicide. Woodrow had either died, or there was a good chance he wasn't going to make it. I pictured the angry kid, a frustrated child in a man's body, exploding when I'd told him what people had said, his emotions amplified by Asperger's or whatever it was that was his burden. I tried not to picture him on the ground, kicked and stomped, but I couldn't help it. I scowled and drove, trying to outrun the guilt.

Horseback Road was west of the river, a couple of miles from where I'd talked to Woodrow. The road was several miles long and I'd come in at an intersection, after the bridge. I was wondering whether to turn north or south when I saw the Life Flight helicopter crossing ahead and to my right, just above the trees, headed west. My guess was the trauma center in Lewiston.

"Hang in there, Woodrow," I said.

I crossed the river, saw kayakers from the bridge, their boats red, yellow, and blue. They were paddling gracefully, riding the current to the bay. I slid through the stop sign at the far end of the bridge, took a left, sped on.

A mile down the road, a dark Chevy sedan appeared in my rearview, blue lights flashing in the grille. I eased over and a detective passed, a guy wearing sunglasses, a baseball cap. I pulled back out, let him lead me to the scene.

There was a sheriff's office cruiser on the side of the road, blue strobes flashing, a deputy standing alongside. The deputy pointed to a dirt road leading into the trees and the detective turned in. An oncoming car slowed and stopped and the deputy walked across the road to talk to the driver.

As he turned away, I took the right, followed the detective in, the truck bumping over the ruts. The road crested a rise, then veered to the left and down. I could see flashing lights through the trees to the right, then cars and trucks parked alongside in the brush. I pulled in behind the last truck and parked. The pickup had a Sanctuary Fire Department placard above its license plate, the next one the same.

Different scene, same cast.

I walked up and into a wood yard, an open area cut for loggers to stack and load wood. The ground was torn, littered with bark slash and crushed spruce branches, like some gigantic monster had stomped through. At the far side there was an ambulance and a State Police cruiser parked and running, and beyond them yellow crime-scene tape stretched across the far end of the yard. Past the tape was a muddied pickup with a fuel tank in the back, the name of a logging company on the side. A yellow log skidder with big chained tires. One side of the metal engine housing was scorched black.

Just inside the tape was the detective—a short, chunky guy with dark thinning hair thick with product. Blue polo shirt, hand next to the gun on his hip. He was talking to two cops, one state, one county. The trooper was a tall, slim woman with red hair pushing out from beneath her broad-brimmed hat. The deputy was the same guy from the fire at Don Barbier's barn, the one with the iPhone. In their midst was Chief Frederick.

I stopped, raised the phone, fired off a few shots.

Frederick looked up and saw me. Shook his head.

Then the detective was talking and Frederick turned to him. I moved closer, shot a few more: the cops, the logging equipment, the yellow tape. I tucked the phone back into my pocket, eased up to the group, stopped six feet away. Listened.

"So the loggers get here to start work, find the kid on the ground," the detective was saying.

"Right," the trooper said. "Called it in. Covered him with a blanket, checked his pulse. One of them was ex-military. Knew not to move him."

"Kid hasn't regained consciousness yet?" the detective said.

"No," the deputy said. "Serious head trauma."

"And you were the first responder, Chief?"

"Just on the other side of the bridge when I heard the call. I knew where they meant, 'cause I'd seen where these boys was cutting."

"And you knew the victim?"

"Knew who he was. Small town. He kinda stands out."

He paused.

"Actually went by the clothes, mostly. His face was pretty stove up."

Frederick looked up at me again, took a step toward me and held up his hand.

"This is a crime scene. No press."

"What paper?" the detective said.

"*New York Times.*"

"Word travels far and fast," he said.

"I live twenty miles from here," I said. "When I heard it was Woodrow I drove right over."

The detective ducked under the yellow tape and stepped up. He had a red fleshy nose with distended pores, a scar on his forehead shaped in a V. His eyes were small and close-set. He held out his hand and we shook. It was a small hand. No macho death grip.

"Scalabrini," he said. "CID."

"Jack McMorrow," I said. "NYT."

He smiled, an air of confidence to him, a pudgy sort of wisdom.

"So you knew the victim?"

"Met him once. A couple of days ago, just up the road. Asked him a couple of questions and he freaked out, went storming off. I told Investigator Reynolds this. From the Fire Marshal's Office."

"So you won't mind telling me," Scalabrini said. "What sort of questions?"

"About the fires. I've heard some people in town think he's the arsonist."

"What people?"

"A kid I met. At the firehouse. He was working there."

Chief Frederick was under the tape and on me, finger in my face. "My firefighters would never do anything like this. And anyone who says so, he can answer to me."

"Chief," I said, "I think we got off on the wrong foot. The thing about firefighters and arson—that was uncalled for. I'm sure your boys there are good firemen. So I'm—"

"You got that right, McMorrow, And if you think you can come into this town—"

"Chief," Scalabrini said.

"—and spread lies and—"

"Chief," the detective said again.

Frederick paused, looked at him.

"Please back off," Scalabrini said.

Frederick scowled. "But . . ."

Scalabrini looked at him, unblinking eyes hard as glass.

"I'm just telling you," Frederick said, retreating. "Doesn't do us any good to start barking up the wrong trees."

And then he was under the tape, back with Foley and the deputy.

"What'd the kid say?" Scalabrini asked, undistracted.

I told him the story. The douche bag, the whack on the arm.

"So you tracked this Woodrow kid down, asked him about it?"

"Didn't really track him. Just saw him walking down the road."

"And you confronted him with this?"

"Started to, and he got all upset. He has some sort of spectrum disorder—autism or Asperger's."

The detective looked away. An evidence tech had arrived in a State Police box truck and was talking to the cops and the fire chief. They led her closer to the skidder and pointed at the ground.

"Not shy, are you, Mr. McMorrow?" Scalabrini said.

"Wouldn't be the best thing for my job," I said. "Or yours."

"No," he said.

The evidence tech was crouching, pointing at something with a pencil. She stood up and started walking toward her truck, the three men watching her backside.

"You think this kid was the fire starter?" the detective said.

"I don't know. I guess you could ask Investigator Reynolds."

"Oh, I will. But what's your gut?"

"I don't think his denial was rehearsed. He just went crazy."

"How so?"

I recounted it. He slipped a notebook from his trouser pocket, a pen attached. I waited for him to get the pen out and start to scribble, felt the tables turn.

"What else?" he said.

"He said he was going to kill them. He was going to kill them all."

"Did you take that threat seriously?"

"Not really. It was more like a kid having a temper tantrum, maybe out of control because of his condition."

"Were you going to put this in the newspaper?"

I hesitated.

"I don't know."

Scalabrini looked up from his notebook, eyed me curiously.

"Speaking of which, I have a couple questions," I said.

"Ask away."

"On the record," I said.

"Yessir," the detective said.

"Someone tried to light that skidder on fire?"

"Yeah, but it didn't catch. Reynolds will be here soon, I think."

"Do you think this assault was connected to the fires?"

"No comment."

"Loggers found him. Chief Frederick was first responder on the scene."

"That's correct."

"What are his injuries—that you can tell?"

"I would describe his injuries as very serious, compounded by the amount of time he was lying out here."

"How long?"

"I'd say several hours. A lot of blood loss. Head injuries bleed a lot. Loss of body temperature."

"Multiple assailants?"

"Hard to say. We're assessing the evidence at the scene. This was not a fistfight. It appears that someone intended to do serious damage."

"Boot marks, that sort of thing?"

"Just evidence."

"Okay," I said. "For now."

Scalabrini raised his eyebrows, lowered them.

"I'm going to talk to these kids, Ray and Paulie," he said. "Tell 'em what you've told me."

"Go for it," I said.

"Just so you know."

"Whatever," I said.

He gave me the look again. "Play a little rough for a reporter, don't you, Mr. McMorrow," he said.

I shrugged.

"The truth can be a hard thing," I said. "As we both know."

He watched the evidence tech pouring the white goo onto the ground from a plastic tub. I slipped my phone out, snapped a few shots. Scalabrini didn't seem to have noticed. Still looking away, he said, "Maybe somebody could've intervened. Warned both sides to go easy. If we'd known."

"Not my job," I said. "I just write stories. I don't get involved."

"Who you kidding, Mr. McMorrow? I've heard about you, read your stuff. Really know how to stir the pot."

"Thanks," I said. "Speaking of which, you know about the citizen patrol, right?"

"Oh, yeah."

He reached into his back trouser pocket, took out a small case, fished out his card. I did the same, taking one from my wallet.

"So our paths will be crossing again," I said.

"No doubt," he said, and he turned away.

Chief Frederick, watching, fell away from the group and started for his truck. I headed for mine and our paths did cross, at the edge of the clearing. He was getting into his truck and he didn't look at me as he hoisted his big frame up into the seat.

"What goes around comes around," he said.

The door slammed shut. I stopped, stepped to the open window. "You talking to me, Chief?" I said.

He didn't look at me, just started the motor, revved it once, put the truck in reverse, and roared backward. I had to jump aside.

14

It was ten o'clock and the general store was busy, the parking spaces full out front, the white-painted benches, too. One bench was taken up by a mother and kids, and as I got out of the truck I saw that it was Eve from the barn fire, Abbie and Elias beside her. They were eating strawberries, and as I approached Elias held up the green cardboard carton.

Eve said, "Hi there."

I stopped, took a strawberry, and said thank you. Elias said, "You're welcome," and I saw that both he and his sister had strawberry juice running down their chins and onto their white T-shirts. Eve dabbed at them with a paper towel.

"Having a strawberry party?" I said.

"It's not a party," Elias said.

"They were hungry," Eve said. "Want another?"

I demurred, and she held the box out and each child took one. They were chomping them down when a bearded, shaggy-haired guy came out of the store with a bag. He looked like a homesteader from another century.

"Daddy," the kids said. "Drinks."

He was very tall and rail-thin, and I pictured him folding himself into a truck cab. He looked at me, then at his wife, and she said, "Honey, this is—"

"Jack McMorrow," I said, holding out my hand.

"Jack is the newspaper reporter we met at the fire. I told you."

"Peter Johnson," he said. He reached over the bench and shook my hand, then took a jug of fruit punch from the bag and a stack of plastic cups. Each of the kids got a drink. Abbie spilled hers on her shirt, and for a moment it looked like blood, dripping down her chin.

"Honey," Eve Johnson said, "be careful," and she got up and crouched in front of her daughter, wiping with the paper towel. Her husband came around and stood beside me.

"So you're a trucker," I said.

"Mostly," he said, watching the kids. "A little carpentry in between. Whatever it takes."

"And a firefighter."

"Oh, yeah. We all try to pitch in."

"Been busy lately, huh?"

A pause this time, wariness creeping in, the chief's no-press edict.

"Hasn't been slow," Johnson said.

"You heard about what happened last night?"

A longer pause, Johnson staring straight ahead, rocking slightly on his running shoes.

"I guess I heard something," he said.

"Sad business," I said.

He took a step back and turned away from his family. I turned, too, and we looked across the common and down the hill, the fields on the far side dotted with hay bales.

"Very," he said.

I waited.

"Not for any story or anything," Johnson said. "I mean, what do you call it?"

"Off the record?"

"Yeah. I mean, between us, I don't like to see nobody get hurt."

"No," I said.

"And I don't approve of violence, generally."

"Right."

"But this guy had to be stopped," Johnson said.

"Woodrow."

"Right. I mean, I'm on the road, three or four days at a time. I can't have some crazy running around town setting fires."

"No," I said.

"Bought a couple of those rope ladders, the ones that hook on the windowsill."

"Because of this?" I said.

"Yeah. But hey, can you see her trying to get those kids down a rope ladder? In the dark. The house on fire?"

"It would be difficult."

"These houses go up fast."

"Yes."

"And we live kind of out in the boonies. So it's not like the fire department is around the corner."

"No."

"So what if she dropped one of 'em? What if she got one out and couldn't get back in for the other one? I can't even think about it."

"I'm sure you can't."

"So like I said, I don't like seeing anybody get hurt."

"So you think it was this kid? Woodrow?"

Johnson waved to a passing pickup, the Sanctuary Fire Department tag on the back license plate. The driver waved back.

"Well, that's what they were saying around town."

He turned and glanced back at his kids, Eve gathering up Abbie, with her red-stained shirt, Elias stomping his plastic cup flat on the pavement.

"Thing about a case like this," Johnson said.

"What's that?"

He looked at me.

"Time will tell," he said, and he reached for his son and turned away.

The family headed for their old pickup and I went into the store. The place was bustling, a line at the counter and Harold running the register, the high school girl from the previous day bagging. I made a loop through the store, didn't see Russell or Lasha or any of the people I knew. I considered getting a cup of tea but the line was too long, so I walked back outside into the sunshine. I stood for a minute and called Roxanne. Waited. She didn't answer and I felt a stomach flip of panic, pushed it away, but still started for the truck.

And the phone buzzed.

I answered it, heard Roxanne's voice. In a millisecond I knew from her tone that she was fine. "We're good," she said. "Sophie is playing with Mary. They're having a tea party. Clair and I brushed Pokey. You know he's getting ticks?"

"Yuck," I said.

"We're picking them off him but his mane is so thick."

"And what about Alphonse. Foley call again?"

"Yes. Said they're concentrating on Massachusetts. New Bedford area. I guess that's where his prison buddy is from. He told the police that Alphonse had been writing to people down there, setting up sort of a safe-house thing."

"Good. Sounds like they'll be picking him up."

"And putting him back in jail," Roxanne said.

"Great," I said. "So you okay if I make one more stop here before I head home?"

"Sure. How's the boy?"

"Not good. Beaten unconscious and left on the ground all night."

"Awful," Roxanne said.

"Not if you live here," I said.

I wanted Woodrow's parents, but they'd be at the hospital in Lewiston. Maybe tomorrow. That left my next question: Was the citizen patrol still going forward? Did the patrollers think the vigilantes had gotten the right guy? Or maybe the two groups were one and the same.

I walked across the common, past the war monuments and the cannons and, now, a memorial for Woodrow Harvey. There was a hand-painted sympathy sign on cardboard that read WOODROW—WE LOVE YOU.

I stopped and looked at the display. There were flowers spread on the grass in front of the sign, a piece of paper with a song lyric, something about souls and scars, by a band I'd never heard of. It was hard to say whether it was all enough to assuage their guilt.

I crossed the street to the block of storefronts. Sanctuary Brokers was on the corner, flowering plants hanging from under the blue awning with the big SB. The silver Mercedes SUV was parked out front.

I pushed the door open, heard the bell jangle above my head. I crossed to the center of the outer office, heard elevator jazz and voices from somewhere out back. I went to a big board that had the latest listings, lovely homes photographed from the precise angle that would make them look lovelier. There were big colonials, cozy Capes, sprawling lawns and colorful perennial gardens. I was reading about a waterfront place with a pool, tennis court, and newly renovated stables when there was a rattle from behind the scenes.

Tory came into the office, wiping his hands, a toilet running somewhere. "Jack," he said, the broad smile flashing on like a light. "Good to see you."

He marched toward me with his hand out like I'd saved his life. His grip was firm and the handshake was long and he was grinning and beaming like he could send some sort of X-rays into my head that would make me buy the first house he showed me.

We finally broke apart and he saw the listing I'd been reading, said, "Handsome place. The Montagues, the sellers—breaks their hearts to give it up, but they're getting older, and their only daughter lives in Boca Raton. And they want to be near the grandchildren, as you can expect. Still, you talk to Kip Montague—the attorney? Montague, Lewis, and Dorchester?—and he tears right up at the prospect of leaving Sanctuary."

Tory paused, started back in.

"Rita is showing some property. She's going to be so sorry she missed you."

"I'm sure," I said, "but I actually have a question for you."

The grin again, the belief that there is no problem that can't be solved with a positive attitude.

"Question away, Jack. Hey, can I get you a cup of coffee?"

"No," I said. "Thanks. Listen, I just got back from Horseback Road."

Tory folded his tanned arms across his blue SB polo shirt.

"A sad business."

"I guess so."

"I don't like to see any young person hurt for any reason. Rita and I, we don't have children of our own, but we run the Key Club at the high school. I mean, I just love the kids, their energy. It's just so contagious. We have a Key Club Facebook page and the kids are just so funny and smart. The things that—"

"Woodrow Harvey."

"The young man who was hurt."

"Beaten unconscious, actually."

"Horrible. My heart goes out to his parents. I mean, what they must be going through."

"He is a suspect in the arson fires."

"I had heard that, Jack. I mean, I have no way of knowing whether it's true. I mean, that's up to the police and the fire marshal's office to determine."

"But you're organizing a citizen patrol of the town."

"To aid the investigators. They can't be everywhere. I mean, a couple of patrols out every night, that could make a huge difference. Eyes on the ground, you know? Did you know there are only two arson dogs in Maine? Some of us are talking about starting a fund-raising project to buy a third dog. I mean, the training is very expensive. It's something like—"

"So my question, Tory," I said.

"Yes."

"If the suspect is incapacitated, will you still have the patrol?"

"Well, that's a good question, Jack."

"What's the answer?"

He hesitated, for the first time.

"This is for your story in the *New York Times*?"

"Yes. I'd like it to be."

Tory held his forefinger up to his mouth and pursed his lips.

"I want to get this right," he said.

"Take your time," I said. I slipped my notebook from the back pocket of my jeans, pen from the front. Waited.

"The short answer is yes, Jack. I don't know that this young man has perpetrated any of these crimes. If he didn't, somebody else did, and they're still out there."

"Right," I said, taking notes.

"Well, until we know, we can't take a chance."

"When do the patrols begin?"

"Soon."

"As in tonight?"

"Possibly. Off the record, we're trying not to tip our hand."

"Are your people going to be armed?"

"My goodness, you do go for the jugular."

The smile. I waited.

"Well, I know that many people in town do have permits to carry firearms. I don't know whether they will or will not be carrying firearms in their capacity as patrol members."

"You're not going to frisk them," I said.

"No. We have no right to do that."

"Do you carry a gun?"

"Well, Jack, I really can't say. Off the record?"

I didn't answer.

"In this business you're often in empty houses, miles from anyone, with complete strangers. Sometimes it seems prudent to take certain precautions. Women are especially vulnerable."

"Huh. So your local real estate agent might be packing?"

"Can we just sort of dance around that one?"

"I guess so, for now. So the patrols are getting under way and the assault on this young man hasn't changed that."

"Not in the least, Jack," Tory said, smiling as he felt the interview coming to an end. "We will protect our community until it is absolutely clear that this threat has been eradicated, with the perpetrator behind bars."

"Are you surprised that you have to be doing this in little Sanctuary, Maine?"

"I am shocked and amazed, Jack," Tory said. "But I remain convinced that this person is only one of nearly two thousand law-abiding, kind, and generous residents of this special community. We—I mean law enforcement, with the community's help—will apprehend this person and bring him to justice. We will survive this and emerge the stronger for it. Sanctuary, Maine, will continue to be a wonderful place to raise a family, retire, or invest in a one-of-a-kind home."

He smiled.

"How was that, Jack?" Tory said.

"Very good," I said.

He beamed. "Glad to help out."

I photographed Tory standing at attention by the "Sanctuary Opportunities" board out front, the one with the snapshots of new listings. In his blue Sanctuary Brokers polo, he struck a vaguely military pose, like he was about to depart for the D-Day invasion and had just kissed his sweetheart good-bye.

I left him on the pillared porch and walked across the common, past the monuments and geraniums. The store was busy but it was almost eleven, and I had enough for a follow up. Tory. Scalabrini. The Johnsons.

And a family to protect, too.

I climbed into the truck, unloaded my gear on the passenger seat. Backing out, I waited for a car to ease past, saw that it was Russell, ex-CIA or whatever the hell he was supposed to be. I considered stopping, getting a quote from him, too, then looked at my watch, decided no. He parked and I pulled out, circled the common, drove past the big houses, the bunting-draped theater and café, and headed for home.

A mile out of town, woods on my right, the river at the bottom of the little valley to my left. I had my phone out, pressing "H" for home, when I heard a motor roar. A pickup in the rearview, big and white, pulling out to pass. I eased over to let it by, glanced at the truck as it passed.

An old Dodge Ram, white with rust on the fenders, mud spatters behind the wheel wells. I recognized it from one of the fires, the two youngs guys, too, their baseball caps on backwards. They looked at me, pointed to the roadside. Ten feet ahead, they pulled right and slowed. I braked and heard another roar behind me.

Another truck in the rearview, this one familiar. The primer-black Chevy from the fire station. Ray and Paulie.

There was a turnoff at the edge of the woods. I swung in, Ray and Paulie behind me, the Dodge skidding off onto the gravel and wheeling around. The trucks pulled up beside me, parked nose to nose, blocking the view from the road.

I got out. Ray-Ray opened the passenger door of the Chevy and a beer can fell out. Bud Ice. He slid down and stood in front of me, scowling, fists clenched at his sides, swaying slightly in his unlaced work boots. Paulie came around the back of the truck, stood to my left. I could see myself in his mirrored sunglasses. The guys in the Dodge stayed put.

"Starting a little early, Ray-Ray?" I said.

"None of your fucking business," Ray-Ray said.

"Well, at least you brought a designated driver. Way to step up, Paulie."

"Shut the hell up," Ray-Ray said. His fists were clenching and unclenching and he was rocking in place, took a step forward. I stood my ground. He stopped.

"You talked to the state cop. Gave him my name."

"Yes."

"You said I blamed that freakin' Goth geek for the fires."

"Correct."

"Now that statie thinks I was the one beat the crap out of the kid."

"Did you?"

"No fucking way. I wouldn't waste my time."

"Well, good for you. You don't have anything to worry about."

"He don't believe me. Said he's gonna be watching me, talking to other people about me."

"That's his job."

"Cop said if he can prove I did it, I'll get ten years."

"Woodrow dies, whoever did it could get twenty-five," I said.

"I ain't done nothin'," Ray-Ray said.

"Then you can sleep easy, your conscience clear."

"If I'm gonna friggin' take a fall when I ain't done nothin' wrong, I might as well do something wrong anyway."

He was rocking more, the right arm bending. Even as I got ready I felt a pang of pity, a kid probably talked into this by his buddies, and now there was no way out.

"That makes no sense, but whatever, Ray-Ray."

"You're done."

"Maybe you're drunk. Maybe you're just foolish. Maybe both. But you're really only hurting yourself here."

He shuffled a foot closer, turned his left shoulder toward me. One of the guys from the Dodge shouted, "Take him, Ray-Ray," and held up the phone. A video called "Reporter Beatdown" was about to go viral.

Paulie looked nervous.

"Your dad gonna like this, Paulie?" I said.

"Shut up," Paulie said, and moved to flank me, blocking my escape. I looked at him.

"Don't worry, chump. I'm not running. What I'm doing is going home to my family. And I'll go through you guys. Over you. Whatever it takes."

"Come on, Ray-Ray," the Dodge kid said. "Shut his mouth."

"Some things you can't let somebody get away with saying," Ray-Ray said. "And payback's a bitch." He launched himself at me, the right coming over, catching my shoulder, and then I was in tight, got my arm around him, his punches hitting my back. We spun and he got a shot in, hit me in the ear, the pain electric, someone yelling "Get him, Ray" as I drove Ray-Ray into the side of my truck, bent him back over the bed.

He whipped back, lithe and strong, and I punched him in the throat before he could get his weight on his feet. He sagged and I felt Paulie coming, a punch to the back of my head, arms pulling at me. I elbowed him, caught his face, shoulder. Ray-Ray was up again, swinging wildly, both arms, and I drove into him, arms in front of my face. His punches hit my forearms, jolted them numb, and I backhanded him in the throat again but he threw me back against the truck.

Ray-Ray was coming, fist cocked, bobbing and weaving like a boxer. The guys from the Dodge were close, phones up, and Paulie grabbed me by the shoulders, pulled me away from the truck. He had me by the shoulders, tried to trip me, spin me to the ground. I stumbled, stomped his foot, hit him in the face, got loose, stepped back to the truck bed, came up with a lug wrench.

They backed away.

"That ain't a fair fight, dude," one of the Dodge boys said, and the other started for their truck.

"You ain't got the balls to use that," Ray-Ray said, and he lunged at me and I swung the wrench, hit him hard on the collarbone and he grimaced, dropped to his knees.

The Dodge boy was pulling something from behind the truck seat and I moved, rammed the door into him, heard him grunt. I ran for my truck, got the door closed, the motor started. Paulie reached through the open window, got both hands on my throat, and I jabbed him in the chest with the sharp end of the wrench, jammed the shifter down, floored the truck, and he fell away. The truck crashed through the brush on the edge of the woods, bounced over a rock, and fishtailed onto the road.

In the rearview I could see Paulie getting up from the ground, Ray-Ray on his knees, clutching his shoulder. One Dodge boy was by Ray-Ray, the other in the cab of the truck. I rounded the curve, reached for my phone.

I punched in the numbers: 9 . . . 1 . . .

I paused. If I was part of the story, I couldn't write it. And I wasn't giving this one up.

I put the phone back down. Blood dripped from my nose down my chin and onto my lap and I wiped my face with the back of my hand. I picked up the recorder. Pressed the button and talked.

"In an interview, Ray-Ray denied any involvement in the assault on Woodrow Harvey. 'I ain't done nothin', Ray-Ray said."

15

"You gotta be more careful," Sophie said. "If I'm not careful, I fall down, too."

She walked gingerly across the kitchen like she was on a tightrope.

"Like that, Daddy," she said.

"Okay, honey," I said. "I'll remember that."

She turned, kept tightrope-walking into the hallway and up the stairs.

"Well?" Roxanne said. Clair stood at the counter behind her. He was sipping coffee and eating an M&M cookie.

"Not everyone in Sanctuary appreciates my presence," I said. I moved to the table, took a cookie from the plate. A bite.

"Very good," I said.

"You remember what I told you about leading with your left," Clair said.

"Two of them. I wasn't sure who I was leading at," I said.

"Two of them?" Roxanne said. "Did you call the police?"

"That's what got them all riled up to begin with."

Roxanne gave a short sigh.

"So this is going to be one of those stories?" she said.

"Gripping and compelling?" I said.

"I was thinking more like dangerous and disruptive," Roxanne said.

"Ah, they were just kids," I said.

"The firebugs?" Clair said.

"Who the hell knows," I said.

I told them the bare-bones story. Woodrow and the assault. Scalabrini rousting Ray-Ray. Tory and his concerned citizens. Ray-Ray and friends accosting me to demonstrate his innocence.

"A flaw in that boy's logic," Clair said.

"But the best of intentions," I said.

"You don't think he attacked this other kid?"

"If he did, he's a hell of a liar, and I don't think he's smart enough for that. About as complex as a Labrador."

"Somebody did it," Clair said.

"And somebody is setting the fires," I said.

"Clear as mud," Clair said.

"That it is," I said.

Roxanne got up from her chair.

"Nothing from Foley?" I said.

She shook her head again, moved to the sink and started washing the mixing bowl, the cookie sheets. There was clanging and banging and Clair looked at me, said he'd head home, if it was okay. Roxanne paused, turned to him and said, "Thanks, Clair."

"Anytime," he said.

We stepped out onto the deck. The sun slipped behind fast-moving clouds, then back out again.

"Hope you gave as good as you got," Clair said.

"Took a lug wrench to get them off," I said.

"Good thing you had your Sears and Roebuck roadside tool kit."

"You'd be visiting me in the hospital."

"No cops?"

"I get paid to write the stories," I said. "I don't get paid if I'm in them."

We stood for a moment, watched the scudding clouds. Beyond them two jets left contrails against the blue. London to New York. Dublin to Boston.

To the passengers peering out the cabin windows, we were invisible in a sea of green.

"How was Roxanne?" I said.

"Fine, as long as she's distracting the little one. Keeps both their minds off it."

"See you got out the Glock."

"Better safe than sorry."

"Your intimidating presence would probably be enough."

"Not taking a chance," Clair said.

"Yes," I said. "But he sounds like a coward."

"Even cowards," he said, "can have a flair for the dramatic."

"And telling a real threat from melodrama?"

"Not my problem," Clair said, and he went down the steps, across the yard, and down the path into the woods. Just as it had been in Vietnam all those years ago, in seconds he was invisible.

I looked in, saw Roxanne and Sophie reading on the bed in Sophie's room. Scuffy the Tugboat, a tattered copy. Roxanne looked up and I mouthed a silent kiss. She managed half a smile, kept reading. Sophie turned the page.

I went back downstairs to the study, sat down in the chair, flipped the laptop open, picked up my notebook. There was dried blood on the cover, a smear from my hand. I touched my lip and began to work.

First thing was a call to Kerry at the *Times*. Vanessa the editorial assistant said Kerry was in a news meeting; no, she was out. I waited, heard clicks as the call was transferred.

"McMorrow," she said.

"O'Brien," I said.

"Your story's going outside," she said. "Everybody likes it. The idyllic Maine town, residents grappling with an arsonist in their midst."

"They're doing more than grappling," I said.

I recounted the day's events, sans the altercation.

"So they're policing themselves," she said.

"Trying," I said.

"Self-reliant Mainers."

"Except half of them are from away. There's a whole crew from inside the Beltway."

"Maybe when you move there you take on the characteristics of the natives," Kerry said.

I thought of Ray-Ray and Paulie, the Dodge boys.

"Could be," I said.

"Can you do it in three hundred words? I'll offer it as a sidebar. Three hundred bucks."

"You got it."

"And we need to get to this teenage boy, or at least his family. I'm picturing a photo of them outside their pretty Maine house. Did Fred Lawn call you? I'm going to send him up to shoot. I mean, did they think moving to this small town was going to save their troubled son?"

"Not yet, and I don't know," I said.

"But you'll find out."

"I will."

"Let's do that one for Wednesday, Jack. Six hundred words?"

I thought of Roxanne, Alphonse, having to enlist Clair again. The money.

"It's a deal," I said.

"You're really rocking this one, McMorrow."

I touched the scrape on my neck.

"We aim to please," I said.

"Oh, by the way—how's that thing with Roxanne going? The kid who died in custody?"

"How did you hear about that?"

"AP," Kerry said.

"There's more," I said. I told her about Alphonse escaping from the funeral.

"No shit. How'd he do that?"

"Bathroom window."

"Huh."

"Yeah. Good times."

"Jeez, Jack," Kerry said. "I thought Maine was supposed to be such a nice place."

I got to work, pausing now and then to listen to the sound of Roxanne reading, Sophie's chirpy voice chiming in. I couldn't hear the words but I could imagine them. "I like this part. . . . That horse looks like Pokey. . . . If we read Pokey a book, would he understand?"

And then it was quiet and I listened. Still nothing. I eased out of my chair, crept up the stairs, poked my head in. They both were asleep, Sophie's head on Roxanne's chest. I smiled, went back to work on the sidebar: VIOLENCE ERUPTS AS TOWN TURNS ON ITSELF.

The trick was including a description of the town, the landscape, the window boxes and gray-painted porches, but not hitting the readers over the head with it. I toyed with different leads, decided to write it straight:

SANCTUARY, MAINE—*A teenage boy rumored to be a suspect in a spate of arson fires here was savagely beaten Monday and left for dead on the edge of a logging road.*

Woodrow Harvey, 17, who recently moved with this family to this seemingly peaceful community along the Sanctuary River, was in critical condition at Central Maine Medical Center in Lewiston, where he was flown from the scene by emergency helicopter.

He was found by loggers as they arrived for work early Monday morning.

"This was not a fistfight," said Detective Arthur Scalabrini of the Maine State Police. "It appears that someone intended to do serious damage."

From there I added a general description of the town, moved into Tory saying that the citizen patrol would get under way as soon as possible.

He said many town residents have permits to carry concealed firearms, but he did not know whether they would be armed while patrolling.

Stevens said the attack on Woodrow Harvey would not affect the patrol's plans to police the town's roadways at night. "Until the authorities declare that they have a suspect in custody, then we will remain vigilant," he said. "I don't know that this young man has perpetrated any of these crimes. And if he didn't, somebody else did, and they're still out there."

There was more. Tory vouching for the community, two thousand upright citizens, etc. That's the kind of people we are.

But exactly what kind of people were they? Certainly not the kind that Tory described in his brochures; not all of them. I licked my lip. The swelling was gone, but it was still sore.

More time on the phone. Calling the hospital. Woodrow still listed as critical. Were his parents there? They could not provide that information. Could he get a message to them? No, but maybe a call to the floor. I called, the phone rang. No answer in ICU.

A message left on Scalabrini's cell phone with questions I should have asked earlier. Too concerned with being a witness. I scowled, waited for the beep. Would State Police be adding to its patrols in Sanctuary? How many detectives were on the investigation? Was it legal for citizen patrol members to carry weapons? Was he concerned that the assault on Woodrow Harvey was the beginning of vigilante activity in the town?

I rang off.

There was stirring upstairs, Roxanne's footsteps crossing the room, then on the stairs. She came into the kitchen, gave me a wave on the way by. I heard the water run, Roxanne filling the teakettle.

"You want some?" she called.

"Sure," I said.

More clattering, then the water hissing, then quiet, then Roxanne: "Oh, no."

"What?" I called.

"Beth."

"What about her?"

She came in from the kitchen, her cell phone in hand. Crossed to the desk, held the phone up in front of my face. A text.

> OMFG IF IT AINT ONE THING ITS A FUCKEN OTHER . . . SO SICK OF
> THE PETTY BULLSHIT I COULD PUKE . . . CAN WE TALK?

"Is she going to call?" I said.

"Keep going."

> GOT REPORTERS CALLING . . . SO CALLED FRIENDS REAMING ME
> OUT ON FBOOK . . . FUCKEN PHONSE STRIKES AGAIN . . . RUINS
> MY LIFE EVEN WHEN HE AINT HERE . . . DRAGGIN ME DOWN BAD
> . . . B THR N 5

"Here?" I said, but Roxanne was already headed for the front door. I followed her and we stood side by side and watched, listened.

"She thinks she can just show up for a pep talk?" I said. "Doesn't she get that you don't do that job anymore? She can't just—"

Roxanne held her hand up. We listened. A car, loud exhaust, coming from the Freedom end of the road. The noise got louder.

"She won't be sneaking up on anybody," I said.

Roxanne's jaw was clenched, her face tense, eyes narrowed. We waited and then the exhaust noise subsided, no car in sight.

"Clair," I said.

We stepped out and crossed the lawn to the road. Looked right and saw Clair's truck backed across the road, Beth's beater behind the roadblock. Clair was leaning close to the driver's window.

"Sophie," Roxanne said.

"I'll stay," I said.

She started up the dirt road, walking quickly, arms swinging, back straight. Roxanne all business was a formidable force. I waited in front of the house, watched as she approached the car. Beth got out, looked like she was crying. Roxanne put her hand on Beth's shoulder. Clair stood to the side with his arms folded. Roxanne turned to him and he nodded, stepped to the big Ford and climbed up into the cab and pulled it out of the road.

Roxanne and Beth got in the car and Beth started it, rumbled down the road toward me. She pulled up in front of the house, looked up at me. Smiled weakly, wiping her swollen eyes. Roxanne got out, came around the car. She gave me her warning look.

"Beth says she heard from Alphonse," she said. "She wanted to tell us in person."

"How thoughtful," I said.

"I told her I'd make her a cup of coffee."

"Sure thing," I said.

"We can talk on the deck."

Behind Roxanne, Beth was clambering out of the car. She reached back in and came out with a jug of coffee brandy.

"This is for you guys," she said. She held the bottle out. I took it. It was plastic. To her credit, it hadn't been opened.

"You shouldn't have," I said.

"Roxanne told me a long time ago," Beth said. "You don't show up empty-handed."

We assembled on the deck, Beth and Roxanne in chairs, me leaning against the railing. Beth was wearing white dungaree shorts, pink flip-flops, and a black peasanty-looking top. She was skinny, not in a healthy way, a yellowish pallor to her pale skin. There was a blue barbed-wire tattoo around her right ankle. They had coffee. I had tea. The brandy bottle sat on the table like a centerpiece.

"So where is he?" I said.

"Alphonse?" Beth said. "I'm not sure."

"I thought you said you heard from him," Roxanne said.

"I did. But he didn't say where he was, exactly."

"A state? A region?" I said.

Beth looked at me.

"He said he met this girl," she said. "Snoopy."

"Like from Peanuts?" I said.

"Who knows. It's her street name," Beth said.

"Know her real name?"

"Nope."

"This the one, he knew her brother in prison?"

"Yeah. They been writing. Some girls do that. Skanks and losers."

"Where is this one?" Roxanne said.

"In Massachusetts. Some place I never heard of."

That did not narrow it down.

"Was he with her when he called?" I said.

"He didn't say. He just said he finally found somebody who understands him."

"No mean feat," I said.

Beth looked at me.

"So was he going there?" Roxanne said, hope in her voice. "To see this woman?"

"I think so. I mean, he's been in jail for like, five months. He's gonna want to get—"

She paused. Looked at me. Mixed company.

"What else did he say?" Roxanne asked.

"He said he was sorry for messing up the memorial service. He said he just couldn't handle it, had to get out of there."

"Convenient time to need to be alone," I said.

"Yeah, well," Beth said. "It's always been totally about him."

"No doubt," I said.

"Where'd he get the phone?" Roxanne said.

"Bought a TracPhone at a supermarket."

"You have the number?"

"On my phone."

"We need to tell Foley," I said. "Maybe they can trace it, figure out where he is."

"What else did he say?" Roxanne said.

"He said he was feeling conflicted," Beth said. Therapy speak. She sipped her coffee. Looked at the bottle, then at us. I nodded. She reached, snagged the bottle, and unscrewed the cap. The coffee got a big glug. She sipped and her eyes brightened.

A cloud moved over the sun and then passed. Beth stretched out her legs, rubbed her thighs. There were dots on the inside of her left leg that looked like track marks.

"Conflicted about what?" Roxanne said.

"Well, about Ratchet."

Beth hesitated.

"About how he died. Whether he should be taking off with this girl. I mean, I'm sure they'll be partying and everything."

"Escape from your son's funeral to go play with your new girlfriend," I said.

"Yeah, well, like I said, it's always been about Alphonse. He only thinks about himself. There's a word for it."

"Narcissist," I said.

"No, that's not it," Beth said.

"So how do you think he was going to resolve this conflict?" Roxanne said.

Beth drank the coffee, eyed the brandy. Held off.

"He said he could go party with Snoopy or he could—"

She paused. Looked away.

"He could what?" I said.

"He could do the right thing," Beth said.

"Which is?" Roxanne said.

A longer pause. Beth was looking out at the gardens, flecks of color against the green wall of the woods. I looked, too, watched a hummingbird flit from flower to flower and away.

"He said he could stay in Maine and revenge his son's death."

"That would be the right thing?" Roxanne said.

"Yeah," Beth said.

"How often does Alphonse do the right thing?" I said.

"Like, never," Beth said.

"Then I like our odds," I said.

"Right," Beth said.

"And does he know what will happen if he comes here?" I said.

Roxanne turned to me, held up her hand, said, "Now, Jack—"

"I'll shoot him on sight," I said. "If Clair doesn't get him first."

Beth looked at me, shrugged, said, "Makes no difference to me. I hate the bastard."

And then she turned away and I followed her gaze to Sophie, standing in the doorway. She was rubbing her eyes with one hand, holding her blanket with the other.

"You were all talking," Sophie said.

"Oh, honey," Beth said, smiling. "Did we wake you?"

She turned to Roxanne and stage-whispered, "She's so freakin' adorable."

Beth stood, held out her arms. It was all I could do to not jump up and hustle her off the deck.

"Oh, honey, come sit with me," Beth said. "You can wake up slow."

16

I called Trooper Foley on his cell. He was at a car accident in the town of Washington, ten miles from Prosperity. He said he'd be over ASAP.

Beth was talking about Ratchet, the cute things he did. He did not have a long life about which to reminisce, and Beth had missed a chunk of it, but she stretched it out. How he had a mop of dark hair when he was born but then it all fell out and grew back blond. How he never sucked his thumb but he did suck his toes. How his first word was Mama, and he never said Daddy, ever, not once. She smiled at the thought. It was terribly sad.

Sophie, standing and leaning against Roxanne's legs, blanket pressed to her cheek, stared at Beth and listened.

"So every minute with your little one, it's just, like, awesome," Beth said, eyes misting. She looked at Sophie.

"Oh, if I could do it all over again," Beth said.

"Don't go there," Roxanne said. "You can't undo the past."

"I know," Beth said, and she started to cry, her lips pressed together, fist pressed to her mouth. Her fingernails were deep purple. "I just miss him so much."

"I'm sure you do," Roxanne said, as Sophie suddenly ran from the deck into the house. There was a clattering noise from the kitchen, a chair being pulled across the floor. I was starting to go to check on her when there was a flurry of footsteps and she was back. She had a cookie in her hand and she trotted to Beth and held it up.

"Don't be sad," Sophie said.

Beth smiled through her tears and took the cookie.

"Oh, sweetie, I'm sorry. It's just that I loved my little Ratchet so much."

"My mommy and daddy love me," Sophie said.

"I know they do, honey," Beth said. "And you know what? I love you, too." She sniffed. Took a bite.

"If I can't have my little boy, maybe I can have you."

Roxanne and I exchanged glances.

"Like a substitute," Beth said. "A substitute family. You know, I never had a family like yours. My daddy, he wasn't nice to me, and he was really mean to my mommy."

Sophie's eyes narrowed.

"And then I had a boyfriend and he was mean to me, too. And I made some bad decisions."

"Oh, Beth, I don't think—" Roxanne said.

"So don't ever take drugs," Beth said, leaning toward Sophie. "Drugs are a bad thing."

"What are drugs?" Sophie said.

And there was the sound of a car, a police radio. I whisked Sophie up into my arms and went to answer the door.

Foley talked to Beth on the deck while we waited inside. Sophie asked Roxanne about drugs again, and Roxanne told her they were a grown-up thing and some of them made you better and some of them made you sick. Sophie asked if drugs made Beth sick, and Roxanne said yes, but now she was feeling better.

"Is she part of our family now?" Sophie said, and Roxanne said, "Not exactly."

Foley had Beth's phone and was copying something onto his notepad. Alphonse's number. I heard bits and pieces, then Foley saying, "I'd like you to talk to some other investigators. And then maybe we should have you call him back."

They walked around the house to the road and then Foley knocked at the front door. I answered it and looked out, saw Beth in the backseat of the cruiser.

"I'm gonna take her to a couple of the people in CID," he said. "We'll try to get him on the phone, see if we can get him to reveal a location, maybe trace the call to a tower."

"Great," I said. "Can you let us know? Especially if he's far away?"

"Sure," Foley said. "It's a concern for you and your family, I know."

"He shows up here, I can't guarantee his safety," I said. "Just so you know that, too."

"We'd prefer that you let law enforcement handle it, Mr. McMorrow."

"It isn't only me that you have to worry about."

"You mean Mr. Varney?" Foley said, looking in that direction.

"He cares a lot about my wife and daughter."

"Like I said," the trooper said. "We would prefer to handle this."

"Like I said."

"I'll call you," Foley said.

Pokey was frisky, relatively speaking. In the paddock he was moving at almost a trot, Sophie bouncing in the saddle. She lifted herself up on the stirrups and got the rhythm of it, and for a minute looked like a little jockey on a small, hairy racehorse. Roxanne turned at the end of the lunge line, saying, "Good girl." Clair and I leaned against the fence. We were talking about Mozart, our topic for the Ballantine Book Club. And then Clair said, "This girl."

"Today she told Sophie not to get involved with drugs," I said.

"She know what drugs are?"

"She does now, sort of."

"Hate to be a pessimist," Clair said, "but everything she's got to deal with, odds are she'll start using again. And it won't be pretty."

Pokey and Sophie circled, like Roxanne was a millstone and they were grinding wheat.

"In the war," Clair said, "the North Vietnamese Army was straightforward. They had different uniforms from ours."

"They were the enemy."

"The Vietcong, whole different animal. Obsequious villagers during the day, toss a grenade in your hooch that night."

"So Alphonse is NVA," I said.

"And she's the VC. Smiling at you, 'Hey, Joe. Hey, Joe.' Underneath she's not mentally sound, this girl," Clair said.

"I don't know. I'm beginning to think of her as sort of screwed-up but well-meaning."

"She's a time bomb, Jack. Even if she doesn't know it. Takes all of her effort to maintain the facade. Grieving mom. Sort of your friend. Troubled woman, but a good person at heart."

"She's working at it," I said.

"One of these days she's gonna fall apart. Self-destruction. Whatever reason. These people are broken, Jack. Not their fault."

"Something tells me her life as a kid was pretty hellish."

"I'm sure it was, and I'm sorry for her. But you don't want to be too close when she blows up."

"It just seems cold to think of it that way. Her little boy dead," I said.

"You protect your own," Clair said. "Once that's done you can try to put Humpty Dumpty back together."

Pokey snorted as he passed. Shook his head.

"We're just trying to stay out of court," I said.

"I know that. But I think Roxanne is getting bad advice."

"You should tell her."

"I will," Clair said. And he did.

I was in the box stall with Pokey and Sophie. We were brushing him, making his mane beautiful. Sophie was saying maybe we could get some barrettes. I said boy horses didn't wear barrettes. Sophie asked why not. I was trying to formulate an answer when I heard Roxanne, in the tack room with Clair.

"If I thought that way, I wouldn't have spent fifteen years doing what I did."

"I know that," Clair said.

"Yes, she's got a substance abuse problem. And yes, that made her a crappy mom. But that doesn't make her a bad person."

"I'm not saying she's bad; I'm saying she's dangerous. She's dangerous to be around."

"I didn't invite her, Clair."

"I know. But I'd make sure she doesn't come back."

"I declare her the enemy, that's how she's going to act."

"Well, that's the reality."

"Clair, don't you understand?" Roxanne said, her voice raised.

I picked up Sophie, held her up to Pokey's mane, said, "You missed a spot." She began to brush and I said, "Good job." Still, Roxanne's words could be heard from beyond the wooden walls of the stall.

"I made a decision, and as a result of that her son is dead."

"Not your fault," Clair said. "You weren't there. You had nothing to do with it."

"But I did."

Her voice was breaking now.

"If I hadn't pulled him, maybe he'd be alive right now. Not perfect, but going along."

"Or he'd be dead at someone else's hand," Clair said. "Or abused. Or molested."

"I was part of it, Clair. I set off the chain of events."

"But that's not logical. Like saying, if I'd turned left at the corner instead of right, I wouldn't have hit that squirrel."

"But he wasn't a squirrel," Roxanne said, crying now. "He was a little boy. An innocent little boy with big brown eyes and a sweet smile and he didn't deserve to die."

Sophie stopped brushing. We could hear Roxanne sobbing. Sophie's eyes were filling with tears.

"Mommy's crying," she whispered.

"Yes, it's a sad thing," I said.

"I think I need to give Mommy a hug," Sophie said.

"In a minute," I said. "Let's get Pokey all set."

I did, holding Sophie, her arms wrapped tightly around my neck. I unfastened the lead from Pokey's bridle, took the bridle off, and dumped a scoop of grain in his trough. He was snuffling up the grain when we gave him a last pat on the neck, stepped out, and fastened the door closed. I hung up the brushes and the bridle and we walked down the passage and out into the yard. Roxanne and Clair were leaning over the fence. His big arm was around her shoulders, his T-shirt damp with her tears.

I walked over and Roxanne turned and took Sophie from my arms. They hugged and Roxanne kissed Sophie's cheek and Sophie kissed her back. Roxanne smiled and Sophie slid to the ground, ran off toward the house, where there were kittens on the back steps.

"I didn't mean to upset you," Clair said to Roxanne.

"I know," Roxanne said. "It isn't you. It's just all bottled up inside me."

"You're taking too much of it on," I said.

"But a little boy is dead," Roxanne said. "He was three, and he's dead."

"I know. It's terribly said. Awful. But you didn't do it. Not on your watch."

"My kids," Roxanne said. "The watch doesn't end."

She turned away, walked toward the house. I turned to Clair, gave him a pat on the shoulder and followed Roxanne. She was picking Sophie up as Sophie snuggled with the cat, a tiny orange tiger. It scrambled down, ran to its mother, one of Clair's barn cats, lying on the step. Sophie whispered to her mom and Roxanne said, "He's too little to leave his mommy. Maybe when he's a little bigger."

Sophie slid down, too, and we crossed the yard, started down the path, Sophie twenty feet in front, walking point.

"I thought you were allergic to cats," I said.

"I'll be fine," Roxanne said.

"You don't have to do that. I mean, just because . . ." I hesitated.

"Because what?" Roxanne said.

Because you're overcome with guilt, I thought. Because you want to prove to yourself that you're a good person, a good mother.

"Because the cat needs a home," I said.

Roxanne didn't answer and we walked down the path between the alders and birches and then a big clump of lilacs, at the edge of our backyard. Sophie was singing "I'm going to get a kitten," over and over. We went in the sliding door off the deck, and I stood in the kitchen and listened. The house was still but for Sophie's singing and the clank of dishes as Roxanne emptied the dishwasher. Then she herded Sophie up the stairs and I heard the water run. I went to the front windows, one side of the house, then the other. The road was empty, the woods still.

Until next time.

I climbed the stairs to the sound of splashing. The bathroom door was open and steamy, soapy air was floating from inside. I stepped in. Roxanne was sitting on the closed toilet seat, her legs crossed. Sophie was in the tub, shaping her hair with shampoo suds.

"Look at me, Daddy. I have a . . ." She looked at her mother.

"A Mohawk," Roxanne said.

"A Mohawk," Sophie said.

"Very nice," I said. "I think that should be your new hairdo."

"Mommy could get one, too," she said, "so they know she's my mommy."

"I'll pretend I don't know you," Roxanne said.

Sophie laughed. Squashed her Mohawk down. I stepped outside of the room and Roxanne followed. She took a deep breath, stood with her arms folded across her chest.

"Don't do this," I said. "Don't torment yourself."

"Easy to say."

"None of it is easy. It's awful. Horrible. But it's not your fault. And Sophie's starting to notice."

"Well, I'm sorry, Jack," Roxanne whispered. "Sorry if I can't just breeze along like nothing happened, like a little boy isn't dead, like my decision didn't put him in a place where his life ended. Sorry if I'm a little down in the dumps about it. Sorry if I can't be sexy and loving and the perfect mother and the perfect wife and smile my way through the day while we may be sued and the mom is cracking up and some nut-job druggie is on the loose and my husband is being pursued by some horny drunken artist woman and seems to like it."

"I'm not being pursued," I said.

"No, and everything is just fine in your world, Jack. Sorry if I'm such a downer."

And she turned away, stepped into the bathroom, and said, "Time to rinse, soapy monster."

That night the tension didn't ease, Roxanne simmering, me brooding, Sophie chirping and chatting. She wanted extra books at bedtime and we sat with her perched between us and a stack of books beside her. Blueberries for Sal. One Morning in Maine. The idyll that was Robert McCloskey. Sophie asked how old the girl was in the pictures. She asked why we didn't have a boat. She asked if she'd ever have a brother or sister. She asked if Beth had any other children. She said she was going to get a tattoo when she grew up. Like Beth. It was going to be a picture of Pokey.

Halfway through Make Way for Ducklings, Roxanne's phone buzzed. She sprang off the bed, was down the stairs in a flurry of steps. I heard her say, "Yes, uh-huh. Okay. Great. No, I'm so glad you called." I felt my body relax. Sophie said, "Mack, Lack, Quack."

Roxanne came back upstairs, into the room. She looked better, around the eyes. I got up, went with her to the hall. Sophie was quacking. Roxanne said, "They tracked the phone. Something about triangulation, with cell-phone towers. He's in New Bedford, or around there. Police down there are looking for him. Foley said he thinks they'll pick him up soon."

"So you can relax," I said.

"You, too," Roxanne said, and she smiled, gave my hand a conciliatory squeeze. I squeezed back. Sophie called, "You guys are missing the best part."

We went back in and sat. Roxanne started reading. The ducks were eating popcorn, tossed from a swan boat. Roxanne turned the page and looked at me and smiled.

We made love that night after Sophie was asleep. It began with a touch, Roxanne's hand on my shoulder. Then a gentle kiss. Then a quiet relentlessness, like this was going to happen, let nothing and nobody stand in the way. We didn't talk. Our sighs were barely audible. We were righting the topsy-turvy world, one kiss, caress, squeeze, thrust at a time. And then we lay together, Roxanne's back tucked into my front, my arms around her, just under her breasts. I felt the in-and-out of her breathing, the touch of her feet as she intertwined her legs with mine. She leaned down and kissed my arm. I kissed her neck. She said, "We're going to be okay, aren't we?"

I said, "Yes, we are."

And then we were quiet. A robin cackled somewhere, disturbed on its roost. A June bug banged the screen. My phone rang, a distant but insistent buzzing.

I felt Roxanne tense as she untangled her legs from mine. I rolled out of bed, picked my boxers up from the floor, and pulled them on. Went down the stairs, saw the phone blinking on the kitchen counter. I picked it up, said, "Yeah."

"Jack."

"Lasha?"

"Am I calling too late?"

She was whispering.

"No, it's fine."

"I thought you'd want to know."

"What?"

"There's another one."

"A fire?"

"A house," Lasha said.

"Right now?"

"Call just went out. Somebody saw flames."

"Anybody hurt?"

"No," she said. "Nobody was living there. It was for sale."

17

The fuel gauge in my truck had quit a few months back but the trip thing worked, and I could safely go 300 miles between fill-ups. At the stop sign at the end of Route 220 I glanced down, saw 321.8.

"Damn," I said. I drove east on Route 17 until I hit the Quik-Mart. I pulled in, checked my wallet for cash, started pumping. Watched a swarm of mayflies swirling around the lights above my head. Then there was a splash as the gas pump went past full and splashed gasoline down the side of the truck. A voice said, "Nobody light a match."

I looked around the pumps. A beat-up Jeep Cherokee, primer-black, over-size tires. The guy had his back to me, finished pumping. Army fatigue jacket over a black hooded sweatshirt. He turned to rack the hose. A hard, lean face, a couple of days' worth of beard. He looked at me. An alertness in his eyes, dark and staring with a sort of wired wariness.

"Teach me to watch the bugs," I said.

"Good for you," he said. "Nobody sees nothin' anymore."

And then he climbed up into the Jeep, slammed the door shut. The windows were blacked out and he was just a shadow behind the glass. I heard the woof of a dog, the guy saying "Backseat." And then the Jeep pulled out and away.

I watched, thinking there was something very different about him. Like he was on some sort of mission and the rest of us were just bystanders.

I stepped across the puddle, went into the store, and took a napkin from beside the hot-dog steamer, wiped my hands. I fixed a coffee and paid, went back out to the truck. The gas had mostly evaporated. I spilled coffee on my jeans, cursed, and went on my way.

The sign was by the road. CALL TORY OR RITA. There were pickups parked up the driveway, red dash lights flashing. When I got out of the truck, I could smell the smoke, primal and acrid. As I trotted up the drive through the trees, I could see the orange glow. Coming out of the trees, I could hear the crackle and pop.

It was a little after eleven. The house was a big colonial that overlooked the river. A circular drive paved with gray pebbles, carriage house connected to the house, a barn beyond that. Fire spilled out of the roof of the main house, shooting twenty feet into the dark sky. Firefighters clomped by in their big boots, shouting to each other as they unraveled hoses, hooked them up to a pumper truck. Hoses were trained on the fire from two sides, like guys pissing on a campfire.

I took a picture.

I backed out of the way as a second tanker started moving, edging closer to the blaze. I spotted Ray-Ray holding a hose, one shoulder pulled forward. Paulie and Casey strode by, Casey carrying an ax—a disturbing sight. Chief Frederick was directing the operation, waving the tanker back with two hands, like one of those guys who direct planes on the runway.

He turned, saw me and scowled. I fired off another shot, just to make him flinch. Another firefighter was trotting by and Frederick reached out, grabbed him by the shoulder, said something and pointed back at me.

The firefighter looked, trotted over. It was Peter Johnson, the trucker. Behind his plastic face shield he looked apologetic.

"Jack," he said.

"Hey," I said.

"The chief says he can't have civilians in front of the fire lines."

I could tell his heart wasn't in it.

"I'm not a civilian. I'm the press."

"I know, but he said—"

There was a whoosh and we turned as flames burst through the roof near the ridgeline. I snapped off three shots.

"When they go, they really go, don't they?"

"We'll knock it down," he said.

"Place was vacant?"

He looked toward the flames, hesitated.

"It was for sale."

"But was anyone living there?"

"I don't know. People are saying—can this be, whatever you call it?"

"Off the record? Yeah."

"People say the owner, he may have come up. To check on things. Listen, I gotta go."

"And he's in there?" I said. "Jesus. You couldn't go in there and get him?"

Johnson stared at the flames. "It was fully involved. I mean, there was no way to get in there. We tried. The heat, it was … Somebody said he was in there. If he was …" He shook his head.

I looked toward the building. The garage was part of an attached shed. The building was a mass of fire, the framing showing as a dark crisscross of lines. The silhouette of a car was barely visible.

Flames burst through the roofline, cinders rising into the dark sky like a volcano was erupting. Flashing lights and smoke and heat and people shouting—I could see how the arsonist could get off on this. The power to create this amazing thing.

Johnson turned and trotted away, his figure silhouetted against the firelight. I watched the flames, prayed there wasn't anyone—

"Oh, my God."

I turned. It was Rita, running across the yard toward me, her face wan and washed-out, hair tied back. Yoga pants and flip-flops and her company fleece. Tory behind her, jeans and the company polo untucked. His hair was askew, eyes wide and mouth open. They trotted by, Rita saying, "Oh, my God. Not another one. Oh, dear God. No. Where is Dr. Talbot?"

Tory passed me, too, his boat shoes untied and flopping. He stopped beside her, hands at his side, and stared at the blaze, the flames shooting from the roof. A portly firefighter moved to them, explaining the situation and waving them back like a farmer herding sheep out of the road. When he'd driven them to me, he stopped.

"I cannot believe this," Rita said. She gave Tory a disheartened look. "We had this couple."

"Seriously interested," Tory said. "If they liked it, they were gonna pay cash."

"He just came up to clean a few things out," Rita said, putting her hands to her mouth like she was praying. "His wife died last year. This was a summer place."

"Where is he from?" I said.

"Westport, Connecticut," Tory said. "Vascular surgeon. Retired."

"It was just too much for him," Rita said. "Without Mrs. Talbot."

"No kids," Tory said.

I watched what was apparently Dr. Talbot's funeral pyre, listened to the crackle of burning beams

"What's his first name?" I said.

"Bert. For Bertrand," Tory said.

"He'd say to me, 'Please, Rita. Call me Bert.' Oh, he was such a sweet man. A real gentleman."

"There's always a chance he isn't in there," I said. "The heat was too strong for the firefighters to make a search. We won't know for awhile." Flames spread across the roof, chimneys silhouetted against the smoke. "Maybe he got out."

The firefighters started a new hose on the roof. Water gushed. Steam rose into the sky. A window blew out of the dormer on the second floor, glass shattering, and the crowd took a step back.

Rita bit her knuckle. Tory shook his head.

"Who do you think would do this?" I said. "I mean, this isn't some old barn."

"A very sick person," Rita said.

"But not Woodrow, that high school kid," I said. "He's in the hospital."

"I never thought it was him," Tory said.

"Seems somebody did," I said.

"I think it's pretty clear," Tory said.

"Tory's been thinking about this," his wife said.

"I'm sure," I said.

"That kid couldn't move around town like this," Tory said. "Clomping around in his big boots and coat? No offense, but that big flabby goof? No way."

"So who, then?" I said. "And why?"

Tory stared at the flames, lost in his own thoughts. In the end it was Rita who stepped in.

"There's this army veteran," she said."

"Really."

"Afghanistan or one of those places. They come back with all sorts of problems, you know. It could be him."

"I suppose some of them do," I said. "Who's this guy?"

"I really shouldn't say."

"Between us. Just so I know if his name comes up later."

Rita hesitated. Tory was still staring at the flames, his eyes glittering in the firelight. I waited.

"Louis," she said. "Louis Longfellow. He's from here, too."

The wind shifted and smoke billowed over us. We moved. Two women saw Rita and came over and gave her big hugs. Condolences, apparently—but for what? The lost commission?

The two women moved away.

"So this Louis?" I said.

"Right," Rita said. "Grandparents grew up here. Mr. and Mrs. Longfellow. His parents sold the house. They live outside Philly. Ardmore, I think. I may have that wrong."

"That's okay."

"You know the big center-chimney cape on the River Road? With the big red barn?"

I shrugged. Tory still stared, said nothing.

"Well, the family, Louis's parents, sold the house and five acres to an obstetrician from Rhode Island—this was ten years ago—but the family kept the rest of the land and a camp. Two hundred eighty acres, two thousand feet on the river. Three years ago I could have gotten eight hundred thousand for it, easy."

"Huh," I said, thinking this was a cold sort of conversation to have while somebody burned.

"Used to be the out-of-state money only wanted coastline. But the coastal market is totally through the roof, so rivers are being discovered, especially if you have ocean access."

Her eyes gleamed in the firelight.

"I see."

"Ginny Longfellow died last year. Ovarian cancer."

"I'm sorry."

Rita didn't appear to be. "Dan, that's for Danforth, he's like fifteen years older than her. I think he's in assisted living."

We stood. The fire crackled. A tanker backed out, horn beeping, and was replaced by another.

"Louis," I said, directing the question at Tory. He seemed to have checked out.

"Only child," his wife said. "I make him for a bit of a black sheep. I mean, the army? With all this family money behind him? And it isn't like he went to West Point or anything. He just joined up like some, I don't know . . . dropout."

I thought of Clair. He and Rita would not hit it off.

"I actually went out and knocked on the door of this place where he lives, Tory and I—just a cabin, really. You'd have to bulldoze it."

"Did he come to the door?"

"No. I knocked a couple of times, turned around to leave. And he's standing there. With a gun. A rifle. And this gigantic dog."

"What'd he say?"

"I introduced myself. Held out my hand."

"He didn't take it?"

"No way. Said one word. 'Go.' That was it."

"So you did?"

"Hey, I know when a deal isn't forthcoming. I put my card on the porch floor and vamoosed."

"Good decision."

"He's clearly mentally ill. PTSD, or whatever you call it."

"Doesn't mean he's an arsonist."

"That's what Harold said," Rita said, leaning closer. "He said he was thinking it was the kid, Woodrow—the way he wouldn't look at anybody when he came into the store. I said, 'Harold. What about Louis Longfellow? Probably trained in explosives, who knows what else. He could burn a building down in his sleep.' "

"Harold wasn't going there?"

"No," Rita said, rekindling some indignation. "But he didn't see this guy's eyes. Like a dog has, just black and burning. Him and the dog, they're sort of the same."

The wind shifted and embers floated over our heads and away. Some people in the crowd were covering their heads, like it had started to rain.

"Having emotional problems because of combat doesn't mean you burn people in their homes," I said.

"Who knows what goes on in that spooky bastard's head," Rita said, clapping manicured fingers over her mouth. "I can't believe I said that."

"So the patrol," I said, turning to Tory. He shook himself loose, looked at me. "Uh-huh."

"You all gonna go knocking on this Longfellow guy's door?"

"Police knock, Jack," Tory said. "We just patrol."

"Can I go along sometime?" I said.

I glanced at him, saw a flicker of doubt.

"I don't know," Tory said. "I mean, there's the liability. What if something happened?"

"I'll sign a release."

There was a crackle, a billow of flame. Tory and Rita took a step away. I stayed with them.

"Ask the committee," I said.

"Sure, Jack," he said. "Sure."

At 11:35 the roof collapsed, flames billowing, sparks cascading down, the crowd saying "Ooohh," like it was fireworks, the grand finale. The firefighters stayed outside the house, pouring water on the mess. The shed was half-burned, the shell of a vintage car visible through the charred doors. They saved the barn—with Dr. Talbot's Mercedes sedan inside.

I texted Roxanne and she texted back. I called. She answered. She had news. The doors were locked, she said, and Sophie was asleep, in bed with her.

"But that's not the news," she said. "They found Alphonse's lady friend."

"They got him?"

"Foley called," she said, as I plugged an ear and bent to hear Roxanne's whisper over the fire noise. "New Bedford police broke down the door of an apartment. This woman Snoopy was hiding under the bed."

"And Alphonse?"

"She said he wasn't there. Never had been. She said he turned out to be a jerk, so she dropped him off in Portsmouth."

"So he's out there."

"The whole time they were chasing the phone."

"So she was bait," I said.

"If he's that smart," Roxanne said.

"Nobody has ever said he wasn't. They have any idea where he is?"

A pause.

"No," she said.

The implications raced through me. Portland. Or New York. Or Prosperity, Maine.

"You tell Clair?"

"I will."

"He'll need to know. That now we have two of them out there."

A crackle on the line. Roxanne's voice garbled. I made out the word "somewhere."

"Something happened down here," I said. "Can you hear me?"

There was no reply, just static. I told her not to worry, that it would work out, but she was already gone.

I put the phone away, stood for a minute.

Two fronts. Two very different crazies, one calculating and vicious, one distraught and angry and vengeful. Two different minds to try to fathom, two people with very different capabilities. Beth might drive her car through our front door. Alphonse might try to work it for money. But both of them knew our soft spot, the place they could hurt us most, gain the most leverage, make us kneel before them.

Sophie.

I swallowed. Tried calling Roxanne back, but the phone beeped, the screen saying UNABLE TO PLACE CALL. I put it away and looked around, the fire scene reappearing like I'd just come to. I took a long breath and went to work.

Working my way through the crowd, I picked out Frederick standing on the running board of a pumper, talking on the radio. I walked toward him and he saw me and turned away. I needed somebody more official than the real estate people to say something, and the chief was as official as I could find. I stood and waited, and a minute later a maroon Suburban pulled in, blue strobes flashing, and Davida Reynolds got out.

There were two fire marshal's office investigators, Reynolds and an older man—chunky, thinning gray hair, mustache—both of them wearing blue jumpsuits and black boots. They opened the side doors of the truck and took out hard hats, and they were putting them on when I approached them.

"Inspector Reynolds," I said.

"Mr. McMorrow," she said. "You are the newspaper's man on the scene." She turned to the other guy. "This is Jack McMorrow. *New York Times*."

The other investigator looked at me warily.

"Long way from home," he said.

"About twenty miles," I said. "And you are?"

He glanced at Reynolds. She nodded.

"Derosby," he said.

I put my notebook in my left hand, held out my right. He was holding a video camera and he switched it to his other hand and shook gingerly, like I might have a disease.

"Filming the scene?" I said.

"Most serial arsonists like to admire their own handiwork," Reynolds said.

I looked at the burning house, thinking there wouldn't be much left of Dr. Talbot if he was inside.

"Upped the stakes this time," I said.

"Either way," Reynolds said. Derosby panned the camera across the line of townspeople. I started to take notes.

"Hard to picture a murderer being in this crowd," I said,

"They look just like the rest of us," Derosby said. "Except they kill people."

I scribbled, catching up, flipped the page.

"Pretty cold-blooded," I said. "If they knew a man was in there."

"May not have thought the owner was home. For-sale sign and all."

"Still," I said.

"I know," she said. "Upping the ante. They can't control it. Any more than a serial killer can just stop."

Reynolds turned to the back of the Suburban and began putting on a jacket and gloves. She took a headlamp out, strapped it to her hard hat like a miner.

"Who retrieves the body?" I said. "If there is one."

"We do," Reynolds said. "This is our crime scene."

A grisly task, pulling a body from the ashes. A skeleton? A torso? I wondered if you ever got used to that, picking at a charred body that had just been a person. Dr. Talbot, the sweet old gentleman. Call me Bert.

I watched Reynolds, then realized Derosby was watching me.

"Been to a lot of these fires?" he said.

There was an edge to it, and I looked at him.

"Last two," I said. "Don Barbier's barn and this one."

"Made it quick, for someone who lives out of town," Derosby said.

"I got a call, soon as it was reported."

"Who was that?" Derosby said.

I looked at him, surprised.

"A confidential informant," I said.

"You know this person's name?" he said.

"Sure I do," I said. Our eyes locked, held. Derosby looked away, out at the crowd, nodded to me and said, "Good meeting you," like it wasn't. And he walked off, the camera held low against his calf. I watched as he sauntered to the far end of the house, turned back and started filming.

18

Once the roof was gone, the fire gave up quickly, the building collapsing on itself. The boys poured a steady stream of water on the smoking rubble.

Frank Derosby filmed the bystanders and then he filmed the fire. Then the bystanders again. I looked around to see if anyone new had arrived. I saw Russell and Don Barbier, one of the high school girls from the store. She was with her boyfriend, a big doughy fellow, and he kept his arm around her waist, like someone might steal his date.

I heard barking behind me, headlights coming up the drive. We all turned. It was a dark Crown Vic, gray, unmarked. There was a dog in the back, a black Lab that was bounding from side to side. The car parked and the driver—thirtyish, blue jumpsuit, baseball cap—got out and walked past the crowd to the far end of the house, where Reynolds and Derosby were pointing up at the burned and teetering wall. They talked.

The dog was at the side window, a metal grille where normally there was glass. The guy opened the door and the dog went still as the lead was snapped onto his collar.

"They gonna use the dog to find the bastard?"

I turned. It was Lasha. I smelled alcohol, heard a barely perceptible slur.

"I guess. Maybe he came out of the woods, lit the place, and went back that way."

She looked at me, her eyes vague. The mane of hair, a dungaree jacket, a loose-fitting white blouse, a baseball cap that said NYPD.

"Or she," Lasha said.

"Thanks for the tip on this one," I said.

"You're welcome. I've got a lot more. Your way home, stop at the house."

"Anything good?"

Lasha stepped closer. I could smell perfume, mixed with the alcohol. Lasha was drunk.

"Yeah. Something very good. It may—"

"You know somebody might be in there," I said.

Lasha froze, her mouth open. "Oh, my God," she said, and then the dog bounded out of the car, woofed a couple of times, and put his nose to the ground and began to course. He moved toward the house, the handler trotting behind. I took a picture, the strobe going off like a muzzle flash. They went to the back of the house, the walls half collapsed, and turned the corner. They were on the side that faced the woods.

We watched and waited. Then they came back, the dog first, the handler in tow. He let out more lead and the dog ran past the house, toward the crowd. He slowed and began sniffing each person he passed. Two firefighters moved past him, dragging a hose, and he gave them a sniff and bounded on. Rita and Tory and the women, Russell and Harold from the store, the teenage girl and her boyfriend, the girl leaning down to try to scratch his ears, the handler saying, "Please don't touch him, miss." The dog continued toward us. He sniffed at Lasha's feet, red-painted toenails on display in her sandals And then the dog moved to me.

Sniffed my running shoes, one, then the other.

Stopped. Looked up.

Sat down.

"He likes you," Lasha said.

"Accelerant dog," I said. "He smells gas."

The handler moved up behind the dog, leaned down and said something. He tried to pull the dog away but he wouldn't move. Just sat and looked at me and panted.

"He's got a hit," I said.

The guy looked at me. He was young with a chiseled face that showed nothing. The dog looked at me, his mouth open, tongue lolling. My new best friend.

"Good job, pup," I said. He whined.

"Is he gonna just sit there?" Lasha said.

"Until they release him," I said, looking up to see Reynolds and Derosby approaching.

I waited. They walked up to the handler, looked at him, the dog, me.

"Mr. McMorrow," Reynolds said, smiling. "What you got on your shoes?"

"Gasoline," I said.

"How'd you do that, sir?" Derosby said, like we'd never met.

"Filling up my truck on the way over here. The pump at the store didn't shut off right. Some spilled on the ground. I probably stepped in it."

Lasha moved close by my side, slipped her arm through mine. "Hey, wait a minute, officers. I was the one who called him to tell him about the fire. He was home."

"It's okay," I said. "They have to ask—"

"Well, sure, but they're making it sound like you're a suspect or something."

"Everybody's a suspect," Reynolds said, half-smile in place, "until we cross them off the list. It's like musical chairs. You eliminate people one by one, and after a while there's only one person left."

"But he told you what happened," Lasha began.

"What store was this?" Derosby said.

"The one on 17. The Quik-Mart."

"How long ago?" he said.

"I don't know. An hour, maybe."

"Do you know who he is?" Lasha said. "Jack works for the *New York Times*. He's not some—"

"Anyone see this happen?" Derosby said.

"Yeah. There was a guy there, filling up, too. He said, 'Don't light a match.' Or something like that."

"You know him?" Derosby said.

"No."

"Your truck here?"

"This is nuts," Lasha said. She pulled me closer protectively.

"It's parked on the road, just north of the driveway. Blue Toyota four-wheel-drive."

Derosby nodded at the handler. He pulled on the lead and the dog leapt to his feet, shook his head. Another yank and they were off, moving past the last of the bystanders and then down the driveway. Lasha turned and watched them go, then turned back. She hadn't let go of my arm.

Reynolds looked at us and smiled, like she'd caught us necking behind the barn.

"So," Derosby said to Lasha. "You are?"

"Lasha Cabral."

I felt her arm slide out from mine. I hoped she wouldn't take a swing at the guy.

"And you called Mr. McMorrow because—"

"To tell him there was another fire."

"And you heard about it?"

"On the scanner."

"And what did you tell Mr. McMorrow?"

"That there was another one," Lasha said.

"Another—"

"Another arson fire. Somebody torched another one. You know he's writing a story, right? I thought he'd want to know."

Derosby looked at her, eyes narrowed, like he was trying to see through her disguise.

"And what made you think this was arson, ma'am?" Reynolds said.

"This is Sanctuary, Maine," Lasha said. "What other kind of fire do we have?"

Lasha moved toward the fire, joining the crowd.

I turned away, started down the driveway. I was thinking of headlines: MAINE TOWN BANDS TOGETHER AS ARSONIST FINALLY KILLS. But what would the subhead be? With a kid beaten into a coma; a bunch of vigilantes turning their sights on the next outcast.

The woods on both sides were dark and deep, and I found myself staring into the rustling blackness. I could hear the noise of bugs and frogs, scratching of a mouse or mole in the leaves. An owl slipped across the drive and into the woods. It was a dark shape, a blur and gone. I thought of the arsonist, moving just that way through the dark woods. And then a flicker, a dot of flame.

There were a few trucks still parked in the grass along the road, four-wheel-drives rammed into the ditch. I got into the truck, put my gear on the seat beside me, started the motor. Moths and bugs swarmed the lights and I drove through them and onto the road. There was an intersection fifty yards up—right to the town center, straight along the ridge. Lasha's house.

I slowed and then caught it. Movement in the brush to my left. I pulled over and backed up. Looked into the woods and this time saw nothing. Put the truck in gear.

Saw it again.

Someone was standing there, at the edge of an opening cut into the brush. I saw a hat when the head turned. A car was coming up behind me and its headlights were reflected in the woods.

I pulled ahead, drove a hundred yards up the road, over a rise to the right. I pulled over into the brush and killed the lights. Got out and started back. Halfway down the hill, I stopped. The person was coming out of the bushes at the side of the road. I stepped to one side, stood in the grass at the edge of the trees. It was a man, coming toward me, a big dog beside him. He moved quickly, in a half-crouch, something between a walk and a trot. I watched as he turned, looked over his shoulder. Headlights came over a rise in the distance and he and the dog moved to the side of the road, against the woods, and froze. Disappeared.

The car approached, then turned right at the intersection, headed for the town center. There was a moment when we both stood in the darkness and then he and the dog moved out of the grass, onto the road. The same half-trot.

Twenty yards. Boots tapping the pavement. Quick economical movements.

Ten yards. A guy. Dark hat, some sort of dark jersey.

I stepped out.

He moved to his right, across the road. I crossed, too. Held up my hand like a crossing guard.

"Louis," I said.

It froze him. The dog, too. It didn't bark.

I stepped closer.

"I'm Jack. Can we talk?"

He unfolded from the crouch, grew a foot. The dog circled him, stopped and looked at me. The guy from the gas pumps. Tall, thin, dark beard and the black deep-set eyes. Jaw that stuck out, like it was perpetually clenched. An old-fashioned face like something from a daguerreotype, a farmer on the prairie. He took two steps to his left but I moved, too, and blocked him.

"Louis, I'm a reporter," I said. "I've heard them talking about you."

He took a step backwards.

"The patrol," I said. "The guys in town looking for the arsonist. You're the next suspect."

He looked at me. Didn't answer.

"Why are you out here?"

A moment and then, "We walk at night."

"Why here?"

"Why are you here?" he said.

"The fire."

"Me, too. We could see it from up on the ridge."

We. Him and the dog.

"You know they think someone died in this one?"

"No," he said, and he withdrew to a place somewhere behind the black eyes.

"Some people in town are thinking you might be the one."

"The one what?"

"The one setting the fires?" I said.

"Why would I do that?"

"I don't know that you would. But they think maybe 'cause you're a troubled combat veteran."

He looked away, scowled. He shook his head, like it was one more thing.

"They don't know shit about combat. They don't know shit about trouble."

Echoes of Woodrow.

"I don't want to be in the newspaper."

"You may not have a choice."

"What?"

"If other people are talking about you. I can't ignore that."

"What if I say no?"

"Then your side doesn't get told."

"My side of what? All I want is to be left the hell alone."

"Sometimes things don't work out," I said.

A flash of temper in the dark eyes.

"This is nuts," Louis said.

Headlights flashed behind him, leaving the fire scene. He looked back. Shifted uneasily, like a nocturnal animal caught in a spotlight.

"Can we talk?" I said.

"No, thanks."

I held a card out.

"You can call me," I said.

"I don't have a phone," Louis said, and he broke past me, grabbing the card on the way by, like I was passing out strip-club leaflets on 42nd Street.

"I'll come to you," I called as he trotted up the road.

A pickup was approaching and I moved into the brambles, waited. The truck passed, a firefighter at the wheel talking on a cell phone. He hit the high beams and the lights flooded the road. Louis and the dog were gone.

I sat in the truck in the dark. It was 12:35. I texted Roxanne again. Waited for a reply. Nothing. I wrote out my conversation with Louis, every word that I could remember. The quotes were underlined. *Why would I do that?*

I wrote my impressions, a physical description. And then I sat back in the seat and wondered. Should I call Davida Reynolds, tell her who I'd run into? Was I reporting the story or becoming part of it? God, I needed more on this Louis guy, the rest of them, too.

The woods were loud, a cacophony of peeps and scritches and hoots. I added the sound of my keyboard clicking. A text to Lasha: YOU UP?

The phone beeped. No service. I sat for a minute, mulling.

Started the truck. Drove.

Lasha's house was a mile farther up the ridge, the driveway climbing from the road through the woods. A fox trotted through my headlights halfway up the drive, gave me a quick backward glance, and leapt into the trees. The woods here were teeming with life: bugs, birds, animals, arsonists, skulking ex-soldiers.

There was a light on by the front door, moths swirling around it like electrons. Another light on in the ell of the house, the kitchen. More lights showing in the studio. I pictured Lasha working in a nightlong frenzy, then collapsing for a couple of days, creatively spent.

I parked beside her Jeep, walked to the side door and knocked. No answer. I peeked in the window, saw the kitchen table, an empty bottle of Geary's. I turned the knob. The door opened. I took a step in. Thought of Lasha's shotgun and called.

"Lasha. It's Jack."

No reply. I took two more steps and stopped. Called again. To my left was the main house, a kitchen showing, a big harvest table. Lonely dinners. To my right was a door that led outside, then 10 feet to the studio. That door was closed. I walked over, paused and tentatively tried the knob. It turned. I pulled the door open and it gave a haunted-house creak. I stepped over the threshold into Lasha's world.

The horses were still frozen in mid-panic, eyes bulging and teeth bared. Some sort of Viking-looking guy had his throat thrown back, a spear pressed against it by an invisible assailant. His eyes were defiant: Go ahead. Kill me. There was a half-carved eagle clamped onto the workbench, like it was bursting out of the wood. Chisels on the bench.

One on the floor.

Blood on the blade. Blood spatter around it.

I froze. Listened. Reached into my jeans pocket for my knife. Slipped it out and pared the blade back. I peered into the dimly lit corners of studio, the grimacing figures staring back silently. I turned back toward the house.

Something hit the floor behind me. I whirled, knife low and ready.

A ginger-colored cat was crouched on the floor by the bench. I looked up, saw the edge of a loft. Looked back down. The cat was licking its mistress's blood from the floor. It was a splotch the size of a quarter. Droplets sprayed next to it. Then another splotch, this one bigger. The cat moved to it, began lapping. I could hear purring. There were drops leading away from the chisel, a dozen or more. I followed them six feet. They stopped. So did I.

I listened, waited. Started for the door to the house. The cat bolted past me, slipping between my legs, trotting into the house. I followed.

Into the kitchen. Another empty beer bottle on the counter, a half-empty bottle of Irish whiskey. Bushmills Black. There was a light on over the microwave. The refrigerator whirred. The cat went to a bowl of food on the floor and sniffed. I stepped into the dark hallway, the Swiss Army knife in my right hand.

Stopped. Took two more steps.

Froze. Listened.

There was a rattle to my right. I listened.

A whimper.

I stepped toward the noise, saw a closed door. The whimper again.

I moved to the door, reached for the knob. Turned it and pushed.

"Lasha," I said.

She was sitting on the closed toilet seat in the darkness. Her left hand was wrapped in a towel and she was barefoot, her sandals under the sink. She turned and looked at me.

"Are you alone?" I said.

"Yes," she said. "I just got home. Decided to work on the big horse, his hoof."

I reached for the light switch, flicked it up. A light glowed dimly on the wall above the sink. I saw a puddle of blood on the floor. Her shirt was speckled red.

"Blood," Lasha said. "It's a bitch to get out."

She smiled at me.

"I heard something."

"Where?"

"Outside. And I got distracted or whatever. And the chisel slipped."

"And you cut yourself."

"Bad," Lasha said. "I don't think I got an artery or anything."

"You work when you've been drinking?"

"I do everything when I've been drinking," Lasha said. "And besides, I had an idea."

"Let me see the cut," I said.

I moved to her and she held out her arm. I held it with one hand, unwrapped the towel with the other. She closed her eyes when I pulled the towel aside.

It was an L-shaped slash where the chisel had gone into the palm of her hand, then sliced a furrow past her thumb. The skin and muscle flapped loose. Blood oozed from the wound, then started to flow, then drip.

"You need stitches," I said. "You okay to move?"

She reached out and clutched my arm with her good hand.

"Can I tell you something, Jack?" Lasha said softly.

I looked at her. There were freckles on her nose and crow's-feet beside her eyes, brown and steeped in sadness. A drop of blood fell from her hand and landed on her foot. She had one foot on top of the other in a way that reminded me of Sophie. There were gold rings on two of the toes on her right foot and her toenails were painted blood-red.

She began to cry. Silently, tears spilling one by one.

"It's all right," I said. "They'll fix you up."

"Jack," Lasha said.

"Yes," I said.

"I was sitting here. I was thinking I really like this shirt. It'll never come out."

"We'll soak it," I said. "Cold water."

"And then I had this thought. I thought, I just missed the artery. And I thought . . . I thought maybe I'll cut it again. Maybe I'll just let it bleed. Maybe it would be better . . . better to die."

"Lasha, stop it."

"Because I'm lonely, Jack. I'm so lonely. And that man died and this town is freaking me out."

"It'll be okay," I said. "You're just upset."

"But what if this is it? What if I'm alone the rest of my life? What if I end up just a lonely old drunk?"

"Don't worry about that now," I said. "Let's just get you stitched up, back to work. I saw the hawk. It's beautiful."

"It's a falcon," Lasha said. "You can tell by the wings."

"I'm a birder. I should know that."

"I'm terribly unhappy, Jack," Lasha said.

"It's just the whiskey," I said.

"Oh, the fucking Irish whiskey. Brings you up and then crashes you down."

"Right. So you'll be fine. Let's get this hand wrapped back up."

"Jack."

"Yes."

"Do you know what I want?"

"No," I said.

She looked up at me, her cheeks glistening, eyes dark and shining, mane of hair askew. She looked like the queen of some defeated desert tribe.

"I want you to hold me. No one ever holds me anymore."

I smiled, wrapped the towel back around her hand.

"I'm sure someone will. You're a very attractive woman—an interesting person, too."

"Kip, for the last six months, he didn't hold me. A peck on the cheek, the rest of him holding back like I was radioactive. And then I figured out about his little honey. Little gold digger. You know they were texting picture of themselves to each other? I mean, you know. Pictures."

"I'm sorry."

"After that I didn't want him to touch me. Ever."

"I'm sure," I said.

"I get so tired, Jack."

"Right."

I finished wrapping the towel. Blood was already beginning to seep through. Lasha held tight to my arm and pulled herself up from the toilet.

"Please," Lasha said. "Just for a minute."

"I really don't think—"

She half fell against me, her arms around my neck, her cheek against my shoulder. I had my arms at my sides and she said, "Hold me, Jack. Really hold me. Just for a minute."

I put a hand lightly on her shoulder and she reached up and drew my arm around her. Then the other. Then hugged me tightly. I felt her breasts pressed against my chest, her thighs against mine. She was bigger than Roxanne, wider and thicker, and her weight rested against me. She gave me a long squeeze and turned her head and kissed my neck. Just once, then let her head rest on my shoulder again.

"Thank you," Lasha said. "That helps."

"No problem," I said.

I tried to pry myself away but she held me tightly.

"You know what, Jack?" she said.

"I know you need some stitches," I said.

"I'm glad I didn't kill myself."

"You and me both," I said.

"You know what else?" Lasha said.

"No," I said. "What else?"

"I think there really was somebody outside."

19

"No ambulance," Lasha said. "I don't want these nosy bastards knowing my business."

We were out in the dooryard, standing by my truck, Lasha saying she needed fresh air. She'd put on clean jeans, a black T-shirt, and gold flip-flops. She was holding her bandaged hand in front of her. Towel number two was splotched with blood.

I thought about it. A half-hour to the hospital in Augusta, the nearest ER. Time to get her booked in. Forty-five minutes home. Two o'clock.

"I'll drive myself," Lasha said.

"You can't. You might pass out or something."

"I'm fine."

"I'll drive you," I said.

"You don't have to."

"I know. Let's go."

She sat beside me with her hand cradled on her lap like a kitten. I drove fast through Sanctuary, west to Route 17, and headed southwest. There was little traffic, a few trucks, no cars. We were passing the Quik-Mart when she finally spoke.

"You must think I'm such a mess," Lasha said.

"No," I said.

"I'm sorry. Blubbering on like that."

"It's okay. You were upset."

"I'm just really comfortable with you. Like I've known you a really long time."

I didn't answer.

"Thanks for doing this," Lasha said.

"It's nothing."

Another long pause.

"Your wife is going to think you're fooling around."

"No, she won't," I said.

"Why not?" Lasha said.

"Because I wouldn't."

She gave a little snort.

"Must be nice," Lasha said. "What's her name?"

"Roxanne."

"Like the song?"

She sang it, Sting's falsetto. Put on your red light. She had a nice voice.

Another pause.

"I hope your Roxanne knows she's very lucky," Lasha said.

"I'm the lucky one," I said. "She saved me."

"From what?"

"From myself," I said.

She looked at me, then straight ahead. We rode in silence for a mile or two, the headlights tunneling through the darkness, the truck tires thrumming on the pavement. A beetle smashed the windshield, left a viscous smear.

Lasha touched her hand, winced.

"Starting to hurt?" I said.

"Throbbing," she said.

"Shock's wearing off. They'll give you something."

Another mile and I said, "So what is it? What did you find out?"

Lasha turned, looked at me closely.

"That's why you're taking me, isn't it?" Lasha said.

"No, I'm taking you so you don't bleed to death. But we might as well do something constructive."

"It's probably nothing."

"What's probably nothing?"

"Harold at the store," Lasha said.

"What about him?"

"Like I said, it's probably nothing."

"What?"

"He torched his house. For the insurance."

"You're kidding me. When?"

"Fourteen years ago," she said. "I searched the *Bangor Daily News* archive. It's all online now."

"Searched for what? Harold?"

"Arson and Sanctuary, Maine."

"Is that the only thing that came up?"

"Yeah."

"He was convicted?"

"Went to jail for three years and had to pay, like, ninety thousand in restitution. To the insurance company."

"Huh. Folksy Harold. Knows everybody."

"And everybody must know this," Lasha said.

"Nobody told me," I said.

"That's because you're like me. We're outsiders."

I drove, mulling it. We passed a boarded-up ice-cream stand, a farmhouse with an overgrown lawn, for-sale sign staked out front. All of it so much tinder.

"A fraud arsonist is very different from a thrill arsonist," I said. "One's dishonest and the other's nuts."

She went quiet again, stared at her hand.

"I guess it wasn't that interesting," she said.

I shrugged.

"Maybe I oversold it," Lasha said, "hoping you'd come up to the house."

"So I could drive you to the hospital after you chiseled your hand open. You are devious."

It was a joke. I smiled, glanced at her, but she wasn't smiling, and then she turned and looked away. For the rest of the trip, Lasha rode in silence, staring out the window at the darkness. I considered her tip about Harold—jokey, small-town Harold—and wondered who else in town was not what they seemed.

There had been a car accident, high school kids in Chelsea hit a tree, nobody wearing seat belts. The ER was packed with parents, brothers, and sisters. Some were in pajamas. Many of them were crying.

The woman behind the glass said it would be a while before Lasha could be seen. We stepped away from the counter and I turned to her.

"You go," she said. "I'll wait. I'll be fine. I'll get a taxi home."

I hesitated.

"Go home to your honey, Jack McMorrow," Lasha said.

So I did.

In the parking lot I texted Roxanne again. I said I was on my way home, would see her in an hour. She didn't reply, which meant she was asleep.

I headed out of the parking lot, crossed the bridge over the black ribbon of the Kennebec River. Prosperity was thirty miles northeast of Augusta, in the wooded hills west of Belfast. Sanctuary was twenty-five miles east. I took the long way home.

It was a little after one when I came through Sanctuary again. At the fire station, the bay doors were open, lights on, trucks backed in. There were a few pickups in the lot, Chief Frederick's Ford, Ray-Ray's Chevy among them. I kept going.

I drove down to the river, crossed the bridge, and climbed to the ridge on the other side. With the exception of the fire station, the town was dark and quiet, still under the pale blue moonlight. At the top of the ridge, I turned right and drove. On the side of the road, a deer turned and stared. I glanced in the mirror, saw it vault into the woods. I looked back to the road, saw the mailbox, braked, and turned off the road, up Lasha's driveway through the woods.

The dooryard was dark; outside lights on a timer? There was a light on in the kitchen, glowing dimly. I killed the truck lights and rolled to a stop. Shut off the motor and sat.

It was still. I thought of Lasha asleep out here in the dark, the house surrounded by miles of woods. Lasha alone.

I got out of the truck, reached behind the seat, and took out a spotlight. I pulled the trigger and the ground went white, the million-candlepower beam illuminating the grass and weeds and bugs. I turned it off, and walked slowly along the side of the studio shed. The workbench was on this side of the building, toward the rear. If Lasha had heard someone, where would he have been?

I walked slowly to the end of the building and stopped. Stood. Listened. Sniffed. Stepped around the corner of the building, flicked the light on.

And there it was.

It was on the ground by the wall. I took a step closer. Sticks and bark and grass had been piled against the wall's cedar shingles like a squirrel's nest. On the grass beside the pile was a long, white, plastic lighter, the kind used with a barbecue grill. I leaned down close to the pile and sniffed and smelled the gasoline, saw the shingles darkened where it had been splashed.

Had Lasha scared the arsonist away, screaming when she cut her hand? Why hadn't he just lit it and run? Would he be back to pick up his stuff? And if he was a thrill arsonist, like Reynolds believed, wouldn't he still be letting the Talbot fire soak in? Would he walk through the woods and start another one? Or could it be two people, two arsonists, each hiding in the other's shadow?

I stood and turned, played the light across the back field. Two pairs of eyes glowed and I flinched, but then they disappeared, and I heard the sound of crunching and crashing as the deer leapt through the brush.

I left a message for Davida Reynolds on her cell phone. When she called back, I had crossed Route 17, was two miles north on 220, in the town of Washington. I turned around.

She met me at the Quik-Mart, the Suburban backed into the far corner of the lot, the motor idling. Reynolds was sitting in the truck, sipping a coffee. I parked next to her and she cleared stuff off the passenger seat. I got in, my feet propped up on a stack of folders and notebooks.

"When do you sleep, Mr. McMorrow?" Reynolds said.

"When you do," I said.

"Hey, just another all-nighter. Like college. I think of it as Organic Chemistry. What do you think of it as?"

"Cash money," I said.

She sipped. I smelled vanilla roast.

"Was he in there? Dr. Talbot?"

"This for the record?"

"Yes."

"We found the remains of one person. We believe it to be Dr. Bertrand Talbot, the homeowner. Identification will come after examination of the remains by the state medical examiner."

"Shit," I said.

"You got that right," Reynolds said.

"I suppose it was just a matter of time."

"Every arson is a potential homicide," she said. "Fire is a lethal agent."

"Think they knew he was in there?"

"I tend to doubt it. Place is dark, has been empty. May have scouted it and thought it was clear."

"Poor man."

"Yes."

"Where was he?"

"Front hallway. Downstairs. He almost made it."

"Smoke?"

"Everyone asks that," Reynolds said. "Nobody wants to think of someone being conscious as they're burned alive."

"So?"

"Smoke in the lungs and then burned."

"Doesn't answer the question."

"Most likely unconscious before the fire got there," Reynolds said.

"Glass half full?"

"He's got family, Mr. McMorrow."

I looked at her. Paused.

"I have something else for you," I said.

She drank coffee, swallowed, said, "What's that?"

I told her about Louis Longfellow lurking in the woods. After I recounted our conversation, she said, "Would have been nice to know this sooner."

"Sorry. I got caught up with Lasha."

"I sent Frank Derosby over to the artist's place, by the way."

I told her where Lasha was and why.

"Maybe Lasha should stay somewhere else until they catch him," I said.

"Or her," Reynolds said.

It took me a second.

"You mean Lasha herself?" I said.

A sip and shrug.

"She got your attention, didn't she? Cuts her hand and gets you to play doctor."

"Hey," I said. "She's not like that."

"Maybe not. But bottom line, Mr. McMorrow, nobody's ruled out until—"

"I know. You told me."

"A little grumpy, Mr. McMorrow?"

"No, just tired."

"Well, you've been busy. When do you have time to write?"

"Good question," I said. "For the record now: You don't think the person was scared away at Lasha's place?"

"Could have been. Or could just enjoy messing with us."

"What was your degree in from Bowdoin?"

"Psychology."

"Good thing."

"Very good. This is all about human behavior."

"Speaking of which," I said. "Very different kind of thrill, jerking people around. Lasha's place. No flames, no fire trucks, no crowds. If he didn't want to light it up, haven't we just diverged into a very different sort of arsonist. More subtle? Clever?"

She looked at me.

"Interesting theory."

"And another thing," I said, and I told her about Harold and his arson conviction.

She said she knew about Harold's record. "But fraud arson and thrill arson are—"

"I know. Again, completely different motivation. But you know they're gonna go after Longfellow for this."

"People are afraid," Reynolds said. "Understandably. An arsonist is a killer who's been lucky. And this one's luck just ran out."

"What if Louis has nothing to do with any of it?"

"Life's unfair. An accomplished physician and good man was just burned to death in his own home. It's my job to bring the score a little closer to even."

She took a long pull on her coffee. A pickup pulled in, parked at the gas pumps.

"You want to see where I stepped in the gas?" I said.

"No, that's okay."

"Because you believe me?"

"Because I already looked. They spread that kitty-litter stuff on it."

"Ours is a relationship built on trust," I said.

Reynolds grinned. We sat. I held my notebook on my lap. The guy pumping gas into the pickup looked over at us curiously, like he'd made us as cops or lovers.

"Is it me, or does Sanctuary have an awful lot of undercurrents," I said.

"Oh, all small towns do," Reynolds said. "We just don't look closely enough. Or we choose to ignore them."

"Don't let the facts get in the way of the idyllic myth."

"You got it, Mr. McMorrow. Hey, one more thing and I'll let you go."

"What's that?" I said.

"My colleague," she said. "Derosby, he's—"

"You don't have to apologize," I said.

"Oh, but I'm not, Mr. McMorrow," Reynolds said. "Like I told you, solving an arson is—"

"Like musical chairs. And I'm still walking 'round and 'round?"

"You and some other people."

"Torching buildings so I can write about it? Seems like a reach."

"Cash money," she said.

I didn't answer.

"Hey, don't get all huffy," Reynolds said, turning to me. "He didn't put you at the top of the list."

"But not at the bottom, either?"

She didn't answer.

20

I walked through the silent house, checked Sophie in her bed. She was asleep with her arms thrown up over her head, her head back and mouth open. I took a book from the bed and put it on the shelf, pulled the sheet up to her waist. She stirred and turned on her side, kicked the sheet back off. Warm-blooded.

I walked out of the room, down the hall, and into our room. Standing by the bed, I took off my jeans and T-shirt, slipped in beside Roxanne. She murmured, "I'm glad you're home," and then went back to sleep. I lay on my back. Looked at my watch in the dark, the green luminescent hands showing 2:40.

Then 2:55.

And 3:12.

At 3:20 I eased out of bed, picked up my clothes, and padded out of the room, down the stairs. In my jeans and T-shirt, I went to the kitchen, took a Ballantine from the refrigerator. I took the beer out on the deck and sat. The stars were glistening in the western sky, already fading to the east. A robin clucked in the woods, then was quiet, still too early to start in for the day. I sipped the beer and studied the stars, picking out the few constellations I knew. The Big Dipper. The Swan. The Archer. My father showed them to me and I had shown Sophie. She'd said, "Was your daddy an astronaut?"

I heard coyotes yipping on the ridge a half-mile back. The flutter of a bat passing close. The croak of frogs in the woods. The rustle of a mole or mouse in the garden along the steps. The hoot of a barn owl from beyond the house, across the road.

And a footstep.

It was 4:05. He was standing at the edge of the deck, fifteen feet away. I'd heard the mice but I hadn't heard him coming. He moved closer.

"Just getting up?" I said.

"Been up a while. You?"

"Couldn't sleep."

"Guilty conscience."

"That would be me," I said.

"No doubt," Clair said.

I got up and we walked around the house to the road, so we wouldn't wake Sophie and Roxanne. At the road we went right, talked as we walked. I told Clair about Dr. Talbot, and he shook his head, was quiet and somber. I went on to Louis and Lasha, Derosby and Davida Reynolds. Gas on my shoes. Louis some more.

"People react differently," Clair said.

"To the violence?" I said.

"To war in general," he said. "It's not something you can understand until you've seen it."

"This guy is definitely troubled."

"Could have been troubled long before he enlisted," Clair said.

"And then Iraq?" I said.

"Where was he?"

"I don't know. Someone said they thought he was a machine gunner. You know, on top of the Humvee."

"You're out there when all hell breaks loose."

"And your buddies are getting their legs blown off," I said.

"And you're taking fire from three directions," Clair said. "Some complex ambushes in Iraq. IED detonates first, then they pin you down with small arms and rockets. RPG is a serious weapon."

We turned, started back. Dawn was easing in from the east, the sky lightening. "Well, whatever it was, Louis is messed up."

"Living all alone. Worst thing for a guy like that. You have to talk it out, purge the demons. Otherwise, they can eat you up from the inside, like cancer."

We were in front of the house, the window of Sophie's room glowing faintly. Her nightlight.

"Speaking of which," Clair said.

"Which what?"

"Demons. Roxanne."

"What about her?"

"This is really bothering her, Jack. This little boy."

"I know," I said.

"I came by. Midnight, a little after. She was out back, standing on the lawn. Crying. She said she didn't want Sophie to hear."

Midnight, a little after. I was holding another crying woman.

"The mother–"

"Beth."

"She called her, drunk and hysterical. Said she had nothing to live for without the kid."

"Could be true. What did Roxanne say?"

"I don't know. Tried to calm her down, but all she kept saying was that the boy was her responsibility. Said, bottom line is, he died on her watch."

I swallowed.

"I'll talk to her," I said.

"You just don't want it to fester, Jack," Clair said. "With her being with the little one all the time, she can't let it out."

"But I can't do stories staying here. And we need to make money."

"Hey," Clair said. "Don't you go guilt-tripping, too. Your job is to keep her together."

"And write this story," I said.

"And stay out of jail," Clair said.

"Yes," I said. "There's always that."

I fell asleep at 5:00, listening to the sound of Roxanne's breathing, in and out, like gentle waves washing up on a shore. At 7:40 I woke to the sound of clattering pans and chattering Sophie.

They were downstairs and I could smell pancakes, coffee. Then I heard Sophie's footsteps on the stairs, Roxanne saying, "Quiet, honey. Don't wake Daddy."

The refrigerator door closed. The microwave beeped. The door to the bedroom clicked. I looked over from the bed. Saw Sophie peering from behind the door like a nosy jailer.

"Daddy's awake," she called, and barged in, took four running steps and leapt onto the bed.

"We're having pancakes," she said. "Mom made extra for you."

"Great, honey," I said.

"Let's eat," she said, taking my hand and tugging. I threw the covers back, let her drag me out of the bed. I pulled my jeans on, a T-shirt, and picked her up and carried her downstairs.

"Daddy's very hungry," Sophie announced.

"Well," Roxanne said. "Then Daddy came to the right restaurant, didn't he?"

"Right," Sophie said, and she slid down and climbed up into her chair. I walked to Roxanne, who was pouring orange juice, put my hand on her hip and kissed her cheek.

"Hands off the help," she said.

I sat and Roxanne served the pancakes. Sophie and I helped ourselves to melon and grapes. Roxanne sat and we passed the syrup and then raised our juice glasses for a toast. "To the chef," I said, and Sophie said, "That's our mom," and we clinked our glasses. Roxanne was smiling, her pretty brown eyes and her pretty mouth, and I wondered if Clair had just caught her at a low moment.

We ate, sipped coffee and tea. Sophie was saying that she wanted to get Pokey a wagon so he could pull the whole family in it and we could take it to the store. I said maybe we could, and then Clair was on the deck and Sophie was running for the door, dashing back in to get her cowgirl hat and back out the door, where Clair was waiting.

He waved to us. We waved back. He and Sophie went down the steps and headed for the path through the woods to the barn.

"So," I said.

"So," Roxanne said.

"Someone died in the fire in Sanctuary last night," I said.

I told her who, and how. Roxanne closed her eyes and sighed, like more weight had been lowered down on her.

"You okay?" I said.

"Yeah. The poor man. I mean, it's just all too much. It's like the whole world is spinning out of control."

"Just a small piece of it," I said.

"With you and me right at the center," Roxanne said.

I squeezed her shoulder. And then I told her the story of the rest of the night. When I was done, the coffee was gone.

"This woman's got emotional problems," Roxanne said. "And she's infatuated with you."

"She's just lonely," I said. "And sad."

"Why would someone try to burn down her house?"

"I don't know. I don't know that they really did."

"Is this Louis guy dangerous?"

"Probably not," I said. "It's the rest of the place I wonder about."

"You don't think this investigator really thinks you're the arsonist?"

"No. I think she likes playing with people's heads. Throw something out there, see how people react."

"Nice," Roxanne said.

"She's very smart."

"Good for her. Tell her to leave you out of it."

"I think she likes me, actually."

"Well, aren't you Mr. Congeniality."

Roxanne got up from the table, took her plate and glass and cup to the counter. I got up and did the same, then stood beside her. I put my hand on her hip again. She stood still, staring out the window at the yard, the trees, nothing at all.

"Clair told me you were upset."

"Yeah, well, that's the reality of it."

"You know you didn't hurt Ratchet," I said.

"Didn't help him," Roxanne said.

"You want to talk to somebody?"

I felt her tense.

"I'm fine."

"Great, if you really are. But if you're just holding it in—"

"I'm really okay."

"You sure?"

"As okay as I can be. I mean really, Jack. Sometimes I'm not sure you understand how this feels. It's not just that some little boy died. It's that I was the one—"

A noise at the shed door. More a thump than knock, like someone had delivered a bag of flour, tossed it onto the step. I crossed the kitchen, listened. There was another thud, fainter than the first. Roxanne stood behind me as I lifted the latch and pulled.

And Beth toppled headfirst into the room.

21

⎯⎯ᴍ⎯⎯

"Oh, my God," Roxanne was saying. "Beth. What happened? What happened to you?"

I turned her over. She looked up at us, woozy, her eyes unfocused. Both hands were bloody and there was more blood on her cheek, her chin. Roxanne rose, went to the sink, and ran water. I pulled Beth's sweatshirt sleeves up, saw that the blood was thick, starting to dry. Roxanne came back with a bowl of water and towels and knelt and dabbed at Beth's hands and wrists.

I felt a tidal wave of déjà vu.

"Call 911," she said.

I peered at the cuts on Beth's wrists, said, "Wait."

Roxanne rinsed the towel and the water in the bowl turned pale pink. She dabbed some more and said, "Beth, what the hell did you do this for? What were you thinking?"

"I wanted to die," Beth said weakly, with sour alcohol breath. "I just wanted to die."

Beth cried softly. Roxanne dabbed and rinsed. I looked at the hand that was less bloody, saw the cut on the upper wrist toward the hand. It was a quarter-inch long and ran parallel to the tendon, well above the veins. If Beth had intended to kill herself, she hadn't come close.

"So what are you doing?" I said to her. "Trying to spread the guilt around?"

"Jack, no," Roxanne said.

I looked at her. "She didn't want to kill herself. She wanted to make you suffer."

"Jack, please."

Beth looked at me, then at Roxanne, and the crying turned to sobs. Then coughing, and sobbing again, back to crying. When the crying subsided, Beth said, "You don't know what I'm going through. You can't know how I feel."

I reached over and took the towel and bowl from Roxanne and started on the right wrist. "No, I can't," I said. "And I don't intend to ever find out."

Over coffee at the kitchen table, Beth's bandaged wrist raising and lowering with the cup, the truth slowly leaked out.

She'd selected a steak knife with a sharp tip and sterilized it with rubbing alcohol. If you're going to kill yourself, the last thing you need is an infection. She'd put the knife in a plastic grocery bag and headed for Prosperity, pulling over to buy a couple of big cans of hard cider, "a good morning drink, 'cause it's kinda like juice."

Beth finished one can of cider on the drive up from her apartment in Gardiner, pulling over when the car conked out just past the intersection of 137 and the Dump Road, two miles from our house. "Ran out of gas," she said. "The thing said an eighth of a tank, too."

Sitting in the car, she'd jabbed her right wrist (she was left-handed) and watched as the blood flowed. Dripped, not gushed.

"Everyone thinks I practically did it, like I killed Ratchet. Like, if I'd been a good mom, none of this would have happened."

Exactly right, I thought, leaning against the counter.

"Beth," Roxanne said. "You made mistakes. But you had no way of predicting this. Nobody could."

"I was doing better," Beth said. "I was off the junk. Was gonna get some training, remember? Get a job."

Talk, I thought. All talk.

"You can still do all that," Roxanne said. "You should. There's no reason to settle for this."

This being faking a suicide attempt to manipulate the person who'd tried to help you.

Beth stared into her coffee cup.

"I don't want to sue anybody," she said. "But the lawyer says—"

"I can't talk about that," Roxanne said. "Not at all."

"Well, I don't. I just want to get on with my life, make something of myself, you know?"

"You should," Roxanne said. "You have a lot to offer, Beth. I can see you working in a nursing home. Remember we talked about you getting a CNA certificate?"

"I really like old people," Beth said. "They're so, like, sweet."

Hide the meds, I thought.

"See? You're already up for it. Who were you working with, at the end?"

"Sylvia and a new guy named Marco. He was wicked chill."

"Well, you should talk to them. See if they can set up some vocational rehab."

"Okay."

"Because it would be so much better for you to look forward. Do it for Ratchet."

A little close to the edge, honey, I thought. Counseling her not to dwell on the past, when her kid died in your agency's custody.

"I will, Roxanne," Beth said, smiling. "I'll do it. I'll show these assholes—sorry. I'll show them that I'm a good person. You know what they call me on Facebook? JSM. For junkie-slut-mom."

"It doesn't matter what they say," Roxanne said, looking at me. "This is your life. You have to take control of it."

"And make Ratchet proud of his mom," Beth said. "And then I can see him in Heaven, right?"

Now she was calling on Roxanne to offer a guarantee of an afterlife.

"I hope so, honey," Roxanne said. "I truly hope so."

Roxanne was thumbing her iPhone, looking up phone numbers of people in vocational rehab. Beth was having a second cup of coffee. I was in the study next to the kitchen, checking e-mail.

I scrolled down, saw the note from Kerry at the *Times*. The subject line: GOOD NEWS.

McMorrow:
Was talking up the arson story at the news meeting. Bad news is that it got bumped from the cover. Good news is that with the death now, they want it for the Magazine. Like the idea of the demon within. They even have a head: AN IDYLLIC TOWN BURNS, FROM THE INSIDE OUT . . . ARSONIST CAUSES 'PERFECT' MAINE COMMUNITY TO LOOK HARD AT ITSELF.
Good luck. Call Ryan Hockaday (202-555-9997) about specifics. Congrats, McMorrow!

The *Times* Magazine. A bigger story. A bigger paycheck. More time. More work.

I leaned back from the laptop, scanned the notebooks on the desk. Picked them up and flipped through them, put them down. I grabbed the phone, dialed the number. It went to voice mail. I left a message, my name and number. Put the phone down and reached for a legal pad and started a list:

Woodrow
Woodrow's family
Louis Longfellow (bring Clair, see if he'll open up)
Lasha, her fear of living alone
Harold, his past dredged up
Citizen patrol: What will they do if they find arsonist is one of their own? Armed? Will they shoot?
Davida Reynolds: How is arson different from other crimes? How is this different from working a straight homicide?
Don Barbier: Did he pick the wrong town for his house flip? Why Sanctuary?
Tory, real estate boom and bust? From "Hidden Treasure" to

arson town—a broker's nightmare

The Johnson family: How can you leave your wife and children home alone in a town where an arsonist is roaming (your kids have to eat)

Chief Frederick: He thought he had the town under control; now he has a tiger by the tail

Paulie and the boys, from firefighters to vigilantes.

I stared at the list. What would I get for a word count? Three thousand? More for online? Online slide show? Video? What had I left out? Russell, rumored to be ex-CIA, from the Think Tank. I added him, looked it all over. It was enough for a start. Some would talk, some wouldn't. One interview would lead to another.

I turned from the desk, looked into the kitchen. Beth had gotten up from her seat, was taking a piece of paper from Roxanne. Names and phone numbers. Roxanne saying, "Promise me you'll get right on this."

"Oh, I promise," Beth said.

Her word was her bond, no doubt.

And then Roxanne again, "You sure you're okay to drive?"

"I'm fine. I only had one drink. After I . . . after I cut myself, I didn't feel like drinking anymore."

"Where's your car?"

"Down the road. I walked the last part."

"I'll drive you to your car," Roxanne said.

I walked into the room.

"I'll do it," I said. "I have to go anyway."

Beth looked at me warily. "Oh, that's okay," she said. "I can—"

"I don't mind. I'm driving right by it."

Beth got up slowly. I went to the door and held it open for her. Here's your hat . . .

She went out first, Roxanne and I hanging back.

"The *Times* Magazine wants the story," I said.

"Wow," she said. "That means—"

"Twenty-five hundred, at least."

"Great," Roxanne said.

"But a much longer story. More time away."

I looked out the door. Beth was standing there, listening.

"I'll be right there," I said.

"Just a minute," Roxanne said.

Beth turned, walked slowly to the car.

"This thing with Beth," I said.

"It was a cry for help," Roxanne said.

I looked at her.

"I know you don't like her," Roxanne said.

"It's not that. I feel bad for her. I mean, God, I can't imagine what she's going through. But I just want her out of our life."

"And the best way to do that is to encourage her to make a better life for herself."

I looked away, shook my head.

"Jack," Roxanne said, and we were out the door.

Beth was standing in the driveway by my truck. We were walking toward her when she turned and looked up the road.

"Oh, look," she said. It was Sophie on Pokey, Clair leading the pony down the dirt road. Sophie had the reins in both hands and was rocking in the saddle. The three of us stood at the end of the driveway and waited. When she was thirty feet away, Sophie risked a brief wave, then took the reins with both hands again.

"Oh, my God, how cute is she?" Beth said, smiling, eyes narrowing. There was something faintly predatory about it.

"Very," Roxanne said.

"What a lucky little girl, to never have any problems," Beth said, in an odd, suddenly singsong voice. "To never have anything go wrong. Living the dream, you know? You just wonder how long that can keep up before—"

"Let's go," I said.

She looked at me. Gave me the same creepy smile. I started for the truck, waited for her to catch up. I kept her in front of me the rest of the way, held the door open for her. She climbed into the passenger seat and I closed the door. Beth sat facing straight ahead, the smile in place.

I walked to the group, and said, "Good job, honey."

"Pokey got tired of going in circles," Sophie said.

"I'm sure, doll," I said. "Don't want him getting dizzy."

Pokey looked at me with his big dark eyes, snorted and nuzzled, looking for a carrot or an apple.

"I'll be back late," I said to Roxanne and Clair. "I'll call."

Clair looked up at the truck, Beth turned to watch us, and Clair said, "Sorry I missed her."

"She walked in from the Dump Road end."

"Has some issues," Clair said.

"I guess," I said. "Roxanne can fill you in."

"But we're working through them," Roxanne said.

"What's issues?" Sophie said.

I took a five-gallon gas can from the shed. It was two-thirds full. Three gallons, sixty miles. Enough to get Beth on her way. Burn a house or two. I put it in the back of the truck, climbed in, and looked at her. She looked straight ahead.

I backed out of the driveway, started down the road, gravel rattling under the big tires. Beth reached over with her left hand and pulled her seat belt on. She couldn't get it to click in and I reached down and helped her.

"Thanks," she said.

I didn't answer.

"I know you don't like me," Beth said.

Again, I didn't answer.

"You don't want me around your perfect little family. Well, I'm sorry if my life hasn't been like a fuckin' fairy tale. I never had no golden spoon in my mouth."

We crested the rise, drove into the shadows between a long line of oaks, birches between them. Doves flushed from the sand along the roadside.

"Silver," I said.

"What?"

"It's silver. The expression. Born with a silver spoon."

"Whatever. I'm just sayin' I never caught a freakin' break. You got your cute little family. My father, he was in jail, out just long enough to knock up my mother with me. Ma, she brings home one loser after another. Finally, one decides he's gonna have me, too. I'm like, 'In your dreams, you disgusting freak.' I'm out the door."

I waited. We were almost to the Dump Road. I slowed.

"How old were you?"

"When?"

"When you left home."

"It wasn't a home. It was a freakin' dirty apartment with a drunk guy farting on the couch."

"And you were?"

"Fifteen."

"Where'd you go?"

"I knew this kid, Sammy. We used to get kicked out of school at the same time. I called him up, went over there. Nobody cared if I stayed. One more kid in front of the TV, you know? But he had an older brother."

"Alphonse?"

"Right."

"And the rest is history," I said.

"Yeah, well. You do what you gotta do."

"Which is?"

"I learned to party. Never even been drunk before, fifteen years old."

"Hard to believe," I said. "And then you got pregnant?"

"Yeah, but not by Alphonse. Not the first time."

"Where's that baby?"

"I lost him," Beth said."

"I'm sorry."

"Yeah, well, I was too young anyway."

I turned onto the Dump Road. An oncoming pickup passed us and the driver lifted his fingers off the steering wheel in a country wave. I lifted back.

"And then Alphonse was back?" I said.

"He was always around. We just never hooked up before that."

"Still partying?"

"Yeah, well, Alphonse and his friends, they were hard partyers. And then Oxy."

"And you learned that, too."

She shrugged.

"Hey, it feels pretty good. People make it sound like drugs is this evil thing. And yeah, maybe it is, but for a while there, you're just floating, baby, feeling better than you ever felt in your whole freakin' life. You're just chillin', so freakin' zonked that nothin's gonna bother you. All your troubles. Poof. Gone."

"Until they come piling back on."

"Yeah, well, getting pregnant again. This time Ratchet comes along and Alphonse gets busted and they put his ass in Windham—the correctional center? And then it's just me and the baby and, dude, it's stressful having a kid."

"Sometimes," I said.

"Well, I was all by myself."

"So are lots of parents."

"I had a hard time staying off the stuff. I mean, with Alphonse around, it was like, party central. Without him, it was all his friends. Same shit, different day."

I didn't answer.

"And that's when I first met your wife."

We were approaching the two-lane road. I looked right, then left, saw Beth's car on the shoulder a hundred yards up. I drove past it, did a U-turn, pulled up behind it and parked.

"Yeah, well, I'm glad we had this chance to talk," Beth said, looking at me, giving me an earnest smile. "So you know where I'm, like, coming from."

"I know where you're coming from," I said. "But I want you to go back there."

"What?" Beth said. "I thought you and me, we could reach an understanding."

"I'm very sorry about your son. And I'm very sorry for your troubles. Sounds like you got dealt a crappy hand all around."

"I did. I never had—"

"I want you to do better. Find some peace for yourself. But I don't want you around my family. I don't want you around my daughter."

She looked at me, her eyes hardening, narrowing, a cat about to snarl.

"What, you think I'm gonna hurt your precious little girl?" she said.

"I don't know what you're going to do, Beth," I said. "That's the problem. To be honest, you scare me."

I opened the truck door, took the keys from the ignition. Beth caught it and her eyes narrowed.

"I'm not gonna steal your fucking truck," she said.

I walked to the back of the truck, took out the gas can. She slid out as I flipped the filler door open, unscrewed the cap, tipped the can up. The gas sloshed back, onto the ground and my shoes. The dog would still like me, I thought. I rattled the spout, got it in deeper, let the gas run. Beth came and stood behind me. I shook the last drops out, pulled the can back, and screwed the filler cap back on.

"There you go. Three gallons. I'd fill it after forty."

A car passed, swerved way wide, and drove on. Beth turned and watched it round the curve and disappear. She turned back, got in my face.

"Your wife's being nice to me," she said. "Why are you being such a dick?"

I didn't answer.

"You should be nice to me, too," she said. "Maybe instead of writing about some stupid shit-ass fires, you should be writing about girls who get their babies stolen away by the State. The State killed my baby, Ratchet. I could own you."

"Yeah, but only if you can convince a jury that the foster mom was negligent. If you can convince a jury that Roxanne was negligent."

I walked to the truck, put the empty gas can in the back, and walked toward her, still standing by the side of my car. A log truck approached, roared by. A burst of dusty wind blasted the roadside. Beth smoothed her hair, then gave it a defiant shake.

"Yeah, well, you just better hope I decide to sue, Jack," she said.

"Oh, yeah? Why's that?"

"Because suing somebody, that's me being nice."

She got into her car, cranked the starter, reaching across with her left hand. After a minute the motor started. She put the car in gear and floored it. The tires spun in the gravel, caught on the pavement, and in a few seconds, she was gone.

If only.

22

Central Maine Medical Center was in Lewiston, perched on the side of
a hill, overlooking a spotty downtown and big brick mills, where, in better
times, they used to make things like bath towels. There was a clock in the
tower of the biggest mill, but it was stopped. The last worker out of the gate?

I approached from the east, navigated a long loop of one-way streets.
One skirted a mill canal, water somewhere down there beyond the railings.
Another passed a park where burka-wrapped Somali mothers watched their
kids playing on swings. I rolled down the main drag, saw people walking in
ones and twos, some of them carrying the same brown sandwich bags, takeout
from a soup kitchen.

It was a poor-looking crowd but law-abiding, or at least on probation,
the harder criminals still sleeping in the surrounding tenements. In places like
this, like jungles and forests, predators were nocturnal.

I turned right and left, pulled into the hospital's main entrance, found
the visitors' lot and parked. Walking back, I strode through the electric doors
and a gray-haired man in a light-blue coat greeted me like I'd just walked into
Walmart. His name tag said HERB, and he asked me if I needed help. You bet,
I thought. With a grieving and unbalanced young woman, a serial arsonist, a
news story that just keeps growing.

"I'm here to see a patient," I said. "His name is Woodrow Harvey."

Herb stepped behind a wooden counter, whispered to a gray-haired woman in the same blue coat. She tapped at a keyboard, peered at a monitor, whispered back to Herb. He frowned and stepped out from the counter.

"That patient is in critical care, fourth floor east."

"Thanks," I said.

"Are you family?" he said.

"No," I said. "A friend."

"Because they're pretty strict about visitors in CCU. And that patient, he has an R beside his name. For restricted visitation."

"I would hope so," I said. "All he's been through."

The elevator took me to fourth floor west. I walked past the nurses' station, followed the signs to the east wing. The corridor led into an open waiting area, people sitting as far apart as the plaid couches and chairs would allow. The television was set to a game show, on mute, the contestants jumping up and down in excitement, captions running across the screen.

The nurses' station was at the far end of the room. I walked over, waited until a young guy hung up the phone. He was in green hospital scrubs, a stethoscope slung around his neck.

He looked up.

"Hello," I said. "I'm hoping to see Woodrow Harvey. Or his family."

I smiled. He looked me up and down.

"You family?"

"Friend."

"I'm afraid visitors are restricted to immediate family," he said.

"Are they here?" I said.

"His mom is in the room," the guy said. "I mean, they come and go. As you probably know—"

"I know he's in a—"

"Right, so they just sit."

The phone buzzed and he peered at it, reading the number, then reached for the receiver.

"Listen, Woodrow's sister's here. She can probably tell you when Mom's coming out."

He started talking into the phone.

I walked back to the visitors' area, scanned the people for sister material. A girl and a boy, maybe ten and twelve, peering at the TV. A woman in her twenties, heavyset and mannish, texting furiously. A girl, thirteen or fourteen, in shorts and flip-flops, dark-rimmed glasses and hair tied back, staring into a laptop.

I walked over, sat down next to her. She had earphones in, was chewing her nails.

"Hi," I said.

I put my hand out, waved it in front of the screen. Her head jerked back and she yanked the earphones out, looked at me.

"Hello," I said. "Are you Woodrow's sister?" I smiled.

"Who wants to know?" she said.

"Jack McMorrow," I said. "I'm a reporter."

"Oh, you want the deputy. He sits at the door of Woodrow's room. I'll get him. I have family clearance."

She started to get up.

"Wait," I said.

"You want my mom?" she said.

"Sure, but first could I talk to you?"

She looked at me, then around the room.

"What newspaper?" she said.

"*New York Times*," I said, handing her my card.

"Really," she said. "You're the one."

"Who's writing about the fires," I said. "I'm Jack."

I smiled and put out my hand. She took it and squeezed, her fingers moist from her mouth.

"I'm Willa," she said.

"Nice to meet you," I said. "Well, sort of. Under the circumstances."

While she shut something down on the screen, I looked at her. Her hair was wavy and dark, corralled into a ponytail. The glasses were rectangular and possibly stylish. Her skin was fair and flawless with a barely discernible pinkish glow. She wasn't pretty, but her coloring was striking. She closed the laptop and looked over at me with an intense, assessing stare.

"So why do you care about my brother?"

"Because I'm writing about the fires—"

"I heard about how they killed that old doctor."

"Yeah. Very sad."

"Totally sucks," Willa said.

Another pause as she chewed her lip, took out a tube and smeared her lips. Strawberry.

"My brother never set anything on fire," Willa said. "Woodrow never did any of that."

I slipped my notebook out, a pen from the other side of my jeans.

"Apparently not," I said. "But he's still part of the story."

"Because kids trash him on Facebook?"

"Yup."

She thought for a second, her nails drumming the top of the laptop.

"You never do anything wrong and somebody says you did a crime, so all of a sudden you have to be in the story? That's not fair."

"Life's not fair," I said. "When it is, it's by accident."

"And now he can't even defend himself."

Her eyes filled, wet beneath the lavender eye shadow.

"I'm sorry, Willa. How is he . . ."

"Doing? He's not doing anything. He's in a coma. They induced it. He's got a drain in to keep the swelling down. On his brain."

"Is it going to be okay? Have they said?"

"Okay for somebody who got his head kicked in," she said. "As in, no."

"Why would anybody do this to Woodrow?"

"They don't need a reason, except they're hateful, horrible people."

"Not all of them. He must have some friends."

"Sure. There's lotsa good kids, but there's some really bad ones, too. It's like the rules don't apply to them. And they decided to make my brother's life hell."

I wrote that down, looked up to see her reaction. Her jaw was set, defiant. She was going to defend her brother.

"Why did they pick Woodrow?" I said.

"Because he's different. He's not a redneck like them. And he's not gonna kiss their butts."

"You came from the city, right?"

"Portland. It's barely a city."

"But way more of a city than Sanctuary."

"Sanctuary's barely a town. Hicksville in the middle of nowhere," Willa said.

"You didn't want to move there?"

"You kidding?"

"So why did you?"

Willa hesitated, looked toward the closed door to the unit.

"My parents thought Woodrow needed a change."

"He didn't like Portland?"

"These jock guys down there were bothering him. They'd say things, get him to fight and stuff, and he'd get in trouble."

"But when he got up here it wasn't much better?"

"Instead of jocks it was rednecks."

"That's too bad," I said.

"Yeah, it sucks," Willa said. "Because he's a really good kid. He just has sort of a temper. He's on the spectrum, you know."

"I heard," I said.

"Asperger's. It's like autism. But not really that bad. It's a condition, like asthma or something."

I wrote that down.

"Autism is a medical condition, like asthma or something. They have no right to discriminate against him."

"No."

"Once they figured out that he had a temper, they just kept going at him."

"Baiting him?" I said.

"Right."

"They put a video on YouTube of somebody biting the head off a bat and they said it was Woodrow, but it wasn't. They got blood from some meat and smeared it on his locker, said he'd been sacrificing animals. They held him down and put a dead squirrel down the front of his pants."

"That's sick," I said.

"When he got in fights with them, like, after school, they put that on YouTube, too. Woodrow all beat-up and dirty and crying."

"Did he lose the fights?"

"Some of these guys are bigger than him. And stronger. Woodrow's tall but he's not a fighter. He's really pretty gentle."

"With you," I said.

"Yeah. He's a wicked good big brother. They figured that out, so they'd say things about me and he'd go freakin' crazy."

We paused. I caught up with her in my notes. I saw her glancing toward the door.

"So your parents, they must be devastated."

"Yeah. And they feel even worse because it was their idea to come here."

"You going to move?"

"They say they bought the house at the peak of the market," Willa said. "If they sell now they'll lose a lot of money."

"So you're staying?"

"Me and my mom are. My dad, he's got this girlfriend. Jessie. So he's here but he's not here, you know? But yeah, I guess you could say right now we're just thinking about Woodrow, how he's gonna be."

She suddenly seemed smaller, more beaten down.

"We don't know. Until they let him wake up. He could be—"

The heavy woman looked over at us, scowled at me.

"These bullies," I said. "Do you think they beat Woodrow up? This time, I mean."

Willa looked down, flipped the laptop open and closed. Left it closed. Glanced toward the door.

"I don't know," she said. "I kinda doubt it."

"Why?"

"Because there was nobody else there to watch."

"Nothing on YouTube," I said.

"Nobody to show off for."

"In the middle of the night, out in the woods," I said.

"Right."

Willa hesitated, pushed her glasses up.

"And besides," she said. "If they killed Woodrow, who would they have left to pick on?"

"I see," I said. "But if it wasn't these bullies, then who?"

"I don't know," Willa said. She ran a hand through her hair, took it out of the elastic thing, put it back in. I put my pen down on the notebook, the interview coming to an end. Willa saw that, leaned closer.

"I have a theory," she said.

"What's that?"

"What if the fire-starter freak, he didn't like it that people were saying it was Woodrow."

"Stealing his limelight?" I said.

"Right. So he has to show it isn't Woodrow."

"And to do that—"

"He has to hurt Woodrow. Put him in the hospital," Willa said. "And then burn another place."

From the mouths of babes.

It was so smart, a piece of the puzzle that I'd been turning around and around, and this kid had just dropped it in place. I was still considering how it fit when Willa raised her eyebrows, nodded, then looked over my shoulder.

There was a clacking, the door to CCU opening. I turned as a woman walked out, a straw bag clutched in front of her. She saw us and we both stood. I waited for her to approach, then said, "Mrs. Harvey."

She looked like her daughter—tall and pale, dark hair pulled back, angular frame, awkward walk. Her eyes were glazed with worry and exhaustion and fear.

"Yes," she said, and I gathered myself up for the part of the job I hated most.

"I'm Jack McMorrow. I'm a reporter. I'm really sorry to bother you, but I couldn't reach you at home. I'm writing a story about the fires in Sanctuary. I'm very sorry about what's happened. Actually, I've met your son. He was—"

Her face tightened into a scowl, then a sneer of disgust. "I have no comment for the press," Mrs. Harvey said.

She reached past me, yanked her daughter by the wrist, wheeled around. As they strode away, Willa turned and our eyes met. "Sorry," she mouthed, and they were into the corridor and gone. The heavy woman in the waiting room glared, her eyes filled with loathing for me and my kind.

"Bothering people in a hospital," she said. "You should be ashamed of yourself."

"Sometimes I am," I said.

I slipped my notebook into my back pocket, the pen, too, then walked to the wooden door to the unit, peered in the window. There was an intercom button on the wall, and when a young man and woman came up behind me, I stepped aside. The guy reached for the button, pushed it, and said, "Steve Gaylord to see Butch Gaylord." Someone buzzed the door and he pulled it open, held it for the woman. The woman held the door for me.

I followed them past the nurses' station, down the corridor. The walls were glass, and so were the doors to each room. I walked along, looking left and right. The rooms were filled with electronics and pumps and tubes, blinking lights. The patients were plugged in, connected to IVs. There was a middle-aged woman, her belly bloated. A guy in his twenties, his arms and one leg in casts, a Red Sox banner stuck on the wall.

And then in the next room, an empty chair outside the door, a book on the floor. Doctor Sleep. Stephen King.

I stopped, said, "Oh, Woodrow. I'm sorry."

He was on his back in the bed, the whole thing behind the glass like a body lying in state. His eyes were purple and yellow and swollen shut, and the top of his head was bandaged. There was a tube running from underneath the bandages at the side of his head, tubes coming from his nose, an IV connected to his arm, a catheter tube from underneath his hospital gown at his waist. The machine beside him blinked red and green. There were flowers on a table, get-well cards set up in a row on the radiator. I could see one had been signed by a bunch of people, like it had been passed around a classroom. I looked back at him, the angry, confused kid in the long black coat, now pale and broken.

He didn't deserve this. He didn't deserve any of it.

"I'm gonna find out who did this, buddy," I said. "I'm gonna make sure they—"

And then I heard voices coming from the other end of the hall, the squawk of a police radio. A sheriff's deputy, an older woman in brown and tan, turned the corner. She was chatting with a guy in scrubs, pushing a cart. I turned and headed for the exit. When I got to the door, I pushed. It was locked. I turned to the station, smiled at the woman standing there.

"Could you buzz me out, please?" I said.

She looked down at the counter, picked up a pen. "And who were you visiting?" she said.

"Mr. Gaylord," I said.

"And your name is?"

"Jack," I said.

She peered down at the sheet, but she buzzed the door as she spoke and it swung open and I walked through, heard it click shut.

23

We were in the parking lot of the Quik-Mart again, standing beside Davida Reynolds's idling Suburban. She was waiting for Frank Derosby, who had been interviewing people about the Talbot house, tracking down those who lived on the back side of the land that abutted Lasha's property. The usual questions: Did you see anything unusual? A car or truck parked by the side of the road? Someone walking in the woods? Someone driving away fast when everyone else was hurrying to the scene?

"So a serial arsonist assaults someone to keep them from taking credit for the fires?" Davida Reynolds said.

"That's the theory," I said. "Take them out of the running. Woodrow's sister came up with it. She said she wondered if the real arsonist was mad that other suspects, like Woodrow, were stealing all the glory."

"Adds a whole other layer of craziness to the perpetrator."

"Can't they be nuts in more than one way?" I said.

"Sure," Reynolds said. "But what about this: What about the firebug trying to kill Woodrow because Woodrow knows who he is."

"And now he's praying to hell that Woodrow doesn't wake up," I said.

She looked at me, flashed a weary smile.

"You know, I liked it better when we had the case locked. It was just you lighting fires to fill the news pages."

"If only life were so simple," I said.

I pulled out as Derosby, in his own Suburban, this one dark gray, pulled in. I saluted as we passed and he glared back.

I headed east, then turned off and followed the back roads to Sanctuary. It was a route that made me think of the watershed here, streams running through the hollows, flowing into bigger streams, and then the Sanctuary River. There was an inevitability to it, like the questions that drew me to the troubled town, and would until they were answered.

I slowed as I called home, waited. Roxanne answered, Sophie's clatter and chatter in the background.

"Hey," I said.

"Hi, honey," she said.

"Hi, honey," Sophie called, laughing.

I asked what they were up to.

"We're going to look at the school," Roxanne said. "Get the lay of the land before the big day of—"

"Kindergarten," Sophie shouted.

"We're going to check out the playground," Roxanne said. "See if we can see the kindergarten classrooms. Eleven more days, right, honey?"

"Nine, ten, eleven," Sophie said.

"Nothing from Beth?"

"Not a word."

"Good," I said.

"How was she with you?" Roxanne said.

I hesitated.

"Fine," I said. "She definitely had gotten herself together. Talking about her plans."

"Great. Maybe that was just a bump in the road."

"Right. And the next bump, she'll be somewhere else."

A pause and I said, "How are you doing?"

"I'm good."

"Better?"

"Yes. Something about the light of day and Sophie."

"Yes," I said. "There is."

I asked how long they'd be gone and she said a couple of hours. Unless they decided to go to Bangor to go school shopping. If they did that, they'd get supper there.

"Girls' night out," I said.

"We'll see."

"Call me," I said.

"You'll be—"

"Talking to people. For the story."

I told her about Woodrow, the hospital, Willa and her theory.

"And I caught the investigator. Now I'm headed into town. Check in with Lasha. Some other people."

"The artist who cut herself."

"Yeah."

"A lot of that going around," Roxanne said.

"Yes," I said. "I guess there is."

There was a pause, Roxanne telling Sophie to go find her other sandal. Sophie running off, Roxanne saying, "Sorry." Another pause and then Roxanne said, "This artist woman."

"Yeah?"

"Tell her to keep her hands off my man."

I chuckled. Roxanne didn't.

I called but Lasha didn't answer. I texted and she didn't reply, so I drove through town, past the common, and up the ridge, rattling up the drive. Lasha's Jeep was parked in the dooryard. I parked beside it, walked to the side door. There was music coming from the studio. Alison Krauss playing loud, over the buzz of a power tool.

I knocked and opened the door, crossed the kitchen, and opened the door to the studio. Alison was playing the fiddle. Lasha, her back to me, was running a palm sander over the falcon's wings. I waited for the fiddle solo to end and knocked on the doorjamb.

Lasha whirled around, startled. Saw me and put a hand to her chest.

"Oh, you scared me," she said.

"Sorry," I said.

She turned off the sander. Walked to the shelf and the stereo and turned the music down. I crossed toward her.

"I called and texted. You should keep the door locked."

"I was going in and out. It was a pain."

"When did you get home?"

"Around four. Slept for a few hours and woke up all recharged."

I looked at the falcon, the graceful curves and deadly talons.

"It looks beautiful."

"I'm not sure beautiful is what I envisioned."

"Powerful, then," I said.

"Closer," Lasha said. She touched the bird's wing, running her fingers over the contours, then frowned, like it wasn't quite right. She was wearing jeans and a red union shirt, her hair pulled back with a blue bandanna. Her hand was bandaged, but there was a glow to her. If Lasha was given to deep mood swings, this was her peak, when she was working.

Sober. Happy.

"How's the hand?" I said.

"All right. Sore."

"How many stitches?"

"Eight."

"Decent cut."

"Well, I keep my tools sharp."

"Hear from the cops? The fire marshal's people?"

"Yes. A young woman came to talk to me."

"Reynolds."

"Yeah. She was nice, but I think she was trying to figure out if I was crazy. Like maybe I faked the whole thing."

"Don't take it personally," I said.

"Oh, I didn't. Actually, it was kind of interesting. The way her mind works, the questions she asked."

"Like what?"

"At first she was sort of focused on me, asking me stuff and then just watching. It was like it wasn't what I was saying—it was how I was saying it."

"That's about right," I said.

"But then there was this shift and she started asking me about everybody else."

"You tell her about Harold and his record?"

"Yeah, but she already knew."

"Woodrow and the army guy?"

"Them, too, but it's like I told her; those are the obvious ones. The outsiders."

"The outcasts," I said.

"Which I'm sort of one of. I mean, I'm not living out in the woods or wearing black overcoats in the summer."

"But you make giant wooden monsters," I said.

"Mythological creatures. But yeah, I'm sure they think I'm way out there."

Lasha smiled again, gave a little laugh, and it was charming. If she was like this all the time . . .

"So what did you tell her?" I said.

Lasha walked to the falcon, picked up a cloth from the table, and started wiping the wings.

"I told her, if it's not obvious that it's the obvious ones, then it's got to be somebody right in the middle of it all. Somebody you think you know, but you really don't."

"Like who?" I said.

Lasha wiped.

"Like me," she said. "Or any of us. When you think about it, you only know the outside shell."

"I feel like I know you a little more than that," I said.

Lasha glanced at me and smiled knowingly.

"Jack, last night."

"Yeah."

"Thank you. You were truly a friend in need."

"No problem."

"And the other thing?"

"What's that?"

"You know. When we kissed?"

I recalled her kissing me, that peck on the neck.

"Well, I'm not sure we—"

"I didn't mean anything by it. I know you're happily married, with a little girl. You're a nice guy, that's all. I mean, I think we could be friends. I'd love to meet Roxanne."

She turned and wiped the falcon with her bare hand. Found a rough spot and touched it with her fingers.

"Yeah, well, maybe sometime. When the story's done."

"Oh, yeah. Because now I'm—what do you call it? A source?"

"Right. And speaking of which, can we talk for a minute? For the story?"

Lasha turned to me, leaned back on the table. The falcon eyed me from over her shoulder.

"Sure."

I took out my notebook and pen.

"After what happened, are you afraid to live out here alone?"

"Yes, but I'm not running away," Lasha said.

She waited for me to write it down.

"Because this is your home?"

"It's my home. It's my studio. It's where I create."

"But at night? Will you be able to sleep?"

"Sometimes I sleep at night. Sometimes I sleep during the day," Lasha said. "Nobody should come here assuming I'm asleep."

I scrawled.

"But if they do?"

Lasha looked behind me. I turned, too, saw a shotgun leaning against the wall.

"That loaded?"

"Double-aught buckshot," she said. "The guy at the gun shop said it'll cut you in half."

"You'd shoot?" I said.

"After fair warning," she said. "Come on, I'll show you."

She walked to the gun, picked it up, and stepped out the door, through the kitchen and outside. We crossed the grass and walked out into the back field, Lasha carrying the shotgun in the crook of her arm. There was a path where the grass was beaten down and we followed it. I walked just behind her, on her right side, away from the barrel, notebook in hand.

Ahead of her, fifty feet from the edge of the woods, was a sign, a piece of plywood nailed to a post. She pointed left and right, and I could see that she'd put up a half-dozen of the signs, fifty yards apart. We reached the first one and stepped past it and turned. The words were neatly painted.

TRESPASSERS AND ARSONISTS

WILL BE SHOT

I slipped the phone from my pocket, took a picture. The sign, Lasha, the shotgun. Send this to Hockaday, give him a taste.

"First it was Kip, that lying piece of crap. Now it's this guy, the goddamn coward," Lasha said. "I'm tired of being pushed around, Jack."

"Well, that's pretty clear," I said.

"I decided this morning, came to me as soon as I woke up. It was a total epiphany."

"Yeah?"

"I decided right then: I'm not gonna run from these men. I'm gonna stand and fight."

We stood and looked at the sign, poking out of the grass like a gravestone, the words a defiant epitaph.

"Then you probably ought to do a couple more things, Lasha," I said.

"What's that?" she said.

"Cut way back on the drinking," I said. "Turn down the music. And lock the freakin' doors."

Heads turned when I walked into the general store. Harold glanced up from behind the counter, then busied himself bagging groceries. The girl working with him saw me and stage-whispered, "That's the guy I was telling you about." Harold nodded and kept bagging.

I walked through the store to the sandwich counter, looked up at the menu board. A teenage boy wearing a baseball cap backwards walked up to the counter with a pad in hand. I asked for a tuna sandwich on whole wheat, with lettuce, tomato, and horseradish. He scribbled it down.

"The name is—" I said.

"I know who you are," the kid said, tearing the page from the pad. "You're the reporter."

His tone said that this was not a good thing.

He turned away, showing the front of the hat. It said SKI-DOO. I went to the cooler and took out a bottle of orange juice. I was standing back from the counter when Eve Johnson came down the aisle, alone.

She saw me. I smiled, said hello.

"Where are the kids?" I said.

"In the truck with their dad," she said. "Mom's night off from cooking. We're getting sandwiches."

"A picnic?"

She hesitated, a troubled look crossing her face, just a flicker.

"No, we'll stay home, I guess."

"Peter not going on the road?"

"No, he's taking a little break."

The baseball cap kid came up and took Eve's order. Five foot-long ham and cheese, two with peppers, three without. He scribbled, turned away. She turned to me. I moved closer.

"How's everybody doing?" I said.

"Oh, they're . . ."

She paused.

"I don't know if I want to be in the paper, even if it is the *New York Times* or whatever."

"I'm just interested in how the fires are affecting people's lives. Regular people. People like you, with families."

She moved toward me, away from the counter.

"Well, here we are. Usually once a week, if Peter's home, we go to Rockland or whatever. Go to Subway, eat on the waterfront there, in the park. Fridays, me and Pete, if he's home, we get a babysitter, go to a movie, have a drink, sit and talk. With him driving so much, we need to reconnect, you know?"

"I'm sure," I said, slipping the notebook out.

Eve looked at it, uneasy.

"So now you stay home. Because of the fires," I said.

She hesitated, then looked up and nodded.

"Pete says we can't leave the house empty after dark. He says it's inviting trouble."

"You leave lights on?"

She smiled. "Hate to see our electric bill next month."

"How does all this make you feel?" I said.

"Like a prisoner," Eve said. "A prisoner in my own home."

I wrote that down. Looked up at her.

"This is really a nice town," she said. "It's not like this. It's like the whole place just went off course, you know? And once it starts, it keeps feeding on itself. People looking at each other differently, not trusting."

I scribbled, underlined. That was the story. A small town upended, the foundation of trust shaken.

"How long are you prepared to keep this up?" I said.

"Pete says until they catch him."

" 'They' being—"

"The police. The fire investigator people. The patrol."

"The citizens," I said.

"Right."

"Is Pete on the patrol?"

"He hates leaving us alone," she said. "Most of the men on it don't have families. It makes him feel like a wimp or something, which he hates."

"I'm sure he would."

"Because this is his town, really. He grew up here, his parents grew up here, his grandparents. I'm from Bangor. I like it here, but he feels it's his duty."

"Uh-huh."

"But after what happened to the doctor, he can't take any chances. With the kids and me."

"The house," I said.

"He went into the garage, took out all the gas, stuff that's flammable. The gas for the mower, he keeps that in his truck. Even put the gas grill away, down in the cellar."

"Must be hard to sleep at night, thinking that this person's out there."

"Oh, Pete, he sleeps during the day now, when he can. Nights he's up watching."

"With a deer rifle across his lap?"

"Oh, I told you he's a trucker," she said. "Rifle isn't much use in a truck."

"So, what? A nine-millimeter?"

"Three fifty-seven," the young mom said. "Pete, he says it's got stopping power."

The baseball-cap guy came back, said my sandwich was ready. I took it from the counter, thanked Eve for her time, and headed for the front of the store.

Harold was at the register, and the teenage girl was loading frozen vegetables into the cooler off to the right.

Harold smiled, said, "How's Mr. McMorrow today?"

"Jack," I said.

"Yessir," he said.

He rang up my sandwich and drink. I handed him a ten-dollar bill and he slid the drawer out, counted my change and handed it to me.

"We thank you kindly," Harold said.

I stood there for a moment, then said, "May I ask you a question, Harold?"

I nodded toward the door. He blanched, the smile long gone. I walked toward the door and he followed. We stepped outside, stood by the bench and the petunias. A truck drove by and the driver beeped. Harold waved.

"Harold," I said. "I've been talking to people in town."

He knew.

"That," he said, "was a long, long time ago. I paid my debt to society, whatever you want to call it. It ain't got nothin' to do with what's going on here now."

"Well—"

"Nothin' to do with it. I've worked long and hard to get back to where I am. You go dredging all that up again, mister, I'll be ruined. Work in this store eighty hours a week, here at four forty-five every morning, middle of the goddamn winter, twenty below, down here every time the power goes out, feeding that generator every—"

"Harold," I said. "Easy."

"Nothin' easy about it, all of that brought back up in the goddamn New York—"

"I want to ride with the patrol, Harold," I said. "Think you can make that happen?"

He looked at me, edged closer.

"And forget the rest of it?"

"If I get enough of what's going on now, I won't need to go digging up the past."

He looked at me. I could hear his breathing. Inhale. Exhale.

"You aren't as easygoing as you pretend to be," he said.

"Likewise, I'm sure," I said.

"Eight o'clock. Quik-Mart."

"Who's gonna be with you?"

"Russell. Barbier."

"Will they object to having a reporter along?"

"No," Harold said. "I won't let 'em."

It was a little after four. I walked to the truck, got in, and quickly went over my notes, fleshing out the stuff I'd gotten from Eve.

I'd use the idea that the men in town had to join the posse, protect the women and children. Pete sitting up at night with a .357 on his lap, removing the gasoline from the garage. I thought of my own house, with gas in the shed for the chain saws, the mower. Enough extra gas on hand to send Beth on her way.

Should I move it? Wait a minute, I didn't live in Sanctuary. This wasn't my battle to fight. I thought again. Sure it was.

A white-haired lady walked past my truck and into the store, canvas bags in hand.

I picked up the phone, called Roxanne. Waited.

"Hi, Daddy," Sophie said. "I answered."

"Yes, you did, honey. How are you doing?"

"Good. We're in a store that's all kids' stuff."

"Have you found anything good?"

"I got new sandals and shorts and a dress that's orange and pink and yellow."

"Wow."

"It's very colorful," Sophie said. "Mom says it's—"

She put her hand over the phone and came back on.

"The latest."

"Well, you are going to be so ready for kindergarten. Are you coming home soon?"

Sophie covered the phone again. This time it was Roxanne who came back on.

"Hey," she said.

"Hey, yourself. Having fun?"

"Yeah. We're outfitting our fashion plate."

"I'm sure she'll be the best-dressed kindergartner in town."

"You only do kindergarten once," Roxanne said.

"What's your plan?"

"*Frozen* is at the movies here. She wants chicken nuggets for dinner. She got your gourmand gene."

"So you'll be home when?"

"Nine-ish. She'll sleep the whole way home."

"I'll be late," I said. "I'm riding with the citizen patrol."

The white-haired lady came back out. Harold followed her to her car, carrying one of her canvas shopping bags.

"When?"

"We start at eight."

"I won't wait up," Roxanne said.

"Clair will be around."

"We'll be fine." Her new face. "What are you going to do until eight?"

"Another interview or two," I said. "I'm checking them off, one by one."

The phrase prompted something, a significance I couldn't quite grasp.

I was searching for it when Roxanne told me to be careful. I said I would. I said I loved her. She said she loved me, too. Sophie kissed the phone and they were gone. Harold put the bag in the backseat of the woman's car, closed the driver's door for her. He didn't look at me as he walked back to the store.

I rang off, called Clair. He answered, the clank of a tool, music in the background.

"Mozart's Marriage of Figaro," I said.

"You're getting better," he said. "But it's Vivaldi."

"Same tights and wig," I said. "What are you doing?"

"Nothing much," he said. "What are you doing?"

"Chatting," I said.

"Knock yourself out."

"Next up, the Iraq War vet."

"Want some help? I'm thinking you might need some street cred."

"Sure. You guys can trade war stories."

"While you knit or whatever," Clair said.

"There you go," I said.

"Forty minutes."

"The town common."

"I'll look for the guy doing nothing," he said.

"If I'm napping, just knock," I said.

Louis Longfellow lived a couple of miles past Lasha's off the Ridge Road, on the valley side. His driveway was a narrow cut into the woods, the opening marked by signs nailed to trees. They said PRIVATE and NO TRESPASSING.

There was a steel cable on one of the tree trunks, an eye bolt screwed into the trunk of another, a big padlock hanging from the eye. The cable was used to bar the entrance, but when we rolled up in Clair's truck, the cable was down. We drove in.

The driveway was more of a path, two wheel ruts that deepened on the S curves where the road snaked its way downhill toward the river. The big Ford jounced along, turning left and right, stuff rattling in the toolbox in the truck bed.

"Can see why he doesn't get out much," I said.

"And nobody gets in," Clair said.

"Keeping the world at bay."

Clair was quiet. The truck bounced and heaved.

"When I got back from my first tour, we were living on a farm in North Carolina. Kids were in school, Mary at home. I spent the first week sleeping in a cow shed a half-mile from the house."

I looked at him.

"You go from lying on your belly in the jungle, holding your breath, not making a sound for hours. Not a cough or a sneeze, not scratching that itch because the enemy is walking by six feet away, and there's five of you and a hundred of them, and one sniffle and you're all dead. And then you're in a bed with white sheets and a shower every morning and your wife tippytoeing around you, being so nice and patient and just waiting for you to open up to her."

I waited.

"And you can't explain it, what you've seen. And when it comes down to it, nobody really wants you to."

"So you shut it all in," I said.

"Until you make it over that hump," Clair said. "Or you end up shutting the world out."

"Retreating to a place like this."

We had emerged from the woods into a small clearing. There was a log cabin to our left, an open porch on the front. There was a line of orange marigolds and red geraniums on the porch, planted in white five-gallon pails. The black Jeep was parked beside it, sitting high on its oversize tires. A four-wheeler and a snowmobile, an older one. Unidentifiable stuff under dark-green tarps.

Clair turned the truck toward the house, parked beside a vegetable garden, aluminum pie plates hanging from strings to keep away birds. A scarecrow wearing a ragged red T-shirt that said CAMDEN, MAINE.

Clair shut off the motor. I eyed the house and waited. Five minutes, ten. Clair calm and still. A half-hour went by. Clair still didn't speak, the Zen of the Recon Marine.

"Let's just go," I said finally.

"He's here," Clair said. "He's watching. Just wait."

We did, another ten long minutes. I listened to the birds: crows, then a pair of ravens. Cronk, cronk, Sophie would say. Clair was listening, too. He said, "He's coming."

"I don't see—"

"Behind us."

There was a galloping sound and I turned toward it, flinched. The dog, the same one from the road, skidded to a stop beside the truck. In the daylight he was black and even bigger, some kind of giant Baskervillian hound. He didn't bark and he didn't take his eyes off of me.

I turned and looked left and there was Louis, standing ten feet from the truck, driver's side. There was a rifle slung over his shoulder by a tan canvas strap. A handgun in a brown leather holster set low on his hip.

"Hey, Marine," Clair said.

Louis didn't answer, just stared. Clair added, "Mind if we get out and talk?"

"I'm gonna take that as a yes," Clair said, and he smiled. He opened the door and got out. I popped the door, eased down and out of the truck, came around and stood beside him.

"Hey, Louis," I said.

"Didn't teach you to read at the newspaper?" Louis said.

"The signs?" I said. "The cable was down, and it's important that we talk to you. This is Clair; he's a friend of mine, and sometimes he works with me."

Louis, his expression dark and brooding, looked at Clair. The dog stared, too.

"Marine Corps, huh."

"Force Recon," Clair said.

"Vietnam?"

"From '66 to '70."

"Where?"

"Mostly along the Laos border. Based out of Phu Bai, Gia Vuc, Kham Duc."

"We lost Kham Duc," Louis said. "I read about it."

"Yes," Clair said. "That was a very bad week."

A long pause. The dog sat down and swallowed, then panted, showing his salmon tongue and Tyrannosaurus teeth. He looked at Clair, then at me.

"Iraq?" Clair said.

"Yeah."

Louis hesitated, then choked it out.

"In '06, '07," he said. "Kilo Company, three-eight."

"Ramadi," Clair said. "What was it the Marines used to say there? 'Another day in paradise'?"

Louis said, " 'Another day in hell.' "

"IEDs?" I said.

He looked at me, the non-Marine, then decided to answer.

"IEDs, firefights," he said, taking on a lecturing tone. "Didn't mind the firefights. They were trying to kill you and you were trying to kill them. And then an hour later you were handing out soccer balls, pretending the locals didn't hate your guts, wouldn't just love to disembowel you and feed your bleeding intestines to their dogs."

There was a pause as we took it in.

"But you survived it?" I said. "I mean, not wounded?"

Louis looked at me like I was the dumb kid in the class.

"Everybody's wounded," he said. "Some on the outside, some on the inside, some both." He glanced at Clair. "He understands. You can't."

Louis looked back at the house and said, "I guess you might as well come and sit down."

He looked at the dog, nodded. The dog got up and bounded to the house and up onto the porch. There was a blanket on the floor and he circled once and lay down.

We followed him, climbed the steps. There was a makeshift table, a piece of plywood on sawhorses. A brown pint beer bottle on the table, a pack of Camel cigarettes, a tuna can for an ashtray. A stack of books, hardcovers. The one on top was something about North Africa, World War II. I could see another one about Vietnam. Michael Herr. A Louis L'Amour Western, for a guy who had seen his own Wild West.

Louis unslung the rifle and leaned it against the wall of the cabin. There was only one chair. Louis went to the end of the porch, picked up two wooden crates. He turned them over and shook and kindling and sawdust fell out. He put the crates down by the chair and table upside down. We sat.

"Cigarette?" he said.

We shook our heads. He slipped a lighter out of the pocket of his cargo pants, a silver Zippo with a red Marine Corps emblem. He flipped it open, lit the cigarette, snapped the lighter shut, and put it on the table.

"Force Recon," Louis said, his voice soft and low. "Officer?"

"No. Master sergeant."

Louis considered it. Clair continued.

"Very different game, fighting in a jungle, compared to those towns you were in," he said.

"Hot as hell," Louis said. "I got used to that, the heat. But everything's this reddish brick color. Had a hard time with that. The sameness."

The flowers, explained.

Louis was quiet, lost in the past. Then he faded back in. He drew on the cigarette. There was a tattoo on his forearm, a rifle and helmet, an empty boot. Under it was written NEVER FORGET.

"You lose a lot of friends over there?" I said.

I got the look again.

"Yeah," he said.

A long pause and then he said, "They give you what you never had and then they take it away."

"In an instant," Clair said. "One minute you're talking to a guy, knows you better than your wife, you'd die for him. And then the next minute he's gone."

Louis looked at him. "And the next day it happens again," he said.

"And the day after that," Clair said. "And you just have to keep going. So it's this grieving that never gets done."

The dog shifted and grunted. His head was on his big paws but he was still doing the guard thing, looking from me to Clair and back again, his mahogany eyes flickering.

Louis suddenly dropped the cigarette in the can, got up.

"You want a beer?" he said to Clair. "Can't not offer a beer to a Marine." Then to me. "You, too."

"Sure," Clair said.

"Thanks," I said.

Louis got up, the handgun still on his hip. It was a revolver, not a big one, maybe just a .22. He saw me staring and said, "Gun like this way out here—it's like you have a silencer."

He pushed the door open, a windowless massive thing made of two-inch planks, like something from a medieval fortress. We heard his boots cross the room inside, then come back. He emerged with three of the brown bottles, a pint glass, two canning jars, and a soup bowl. He gave the glass to Clair, and he and I had jars. The dog got the bowl.

"Excuse the glassware," he said. "Don't usually have company."

"You make the beer yourself?" I said.

"That I do," he said. "This one's brown ale. Yeast on the bottom, so pour it slow."

We did. Louis raised his jar to Clair. "Semper fidelis," he said. They clinked and then he turned to me and we tapped jars. "Sláinte," I said.

We drank. The ale was pretty good. Louis leaned down and poured some from his jar into the dog's bowl. The dog got up and lapped. His back came up almost to the top of the table.

"What's his name?" I said.

"Friend," Louis said. The dog whumped his big tail back and forth.

"What kind of a dog is he?" I said.

"Big," Louis said.

We sat and sipped and looked out. A hermit thrush was calling from the woods, like Pan on his flute. The river flickered through the trees below the house. The air had thickened in the past couple of hours, and the sky was darkening to the southwest. More Vietnam than Iraq. Maybe why Louis hadn't moved to Arizona.

"Gonna rain," Clair said.

"In Anbar that would be a sandstorm coming," Louis said.

We looked at the slate-gray sky.

"What was that like?" I said.

"Horrible. Gets in everywhere. Your food, your mouth, your eyes."

We drank.

"Vietnam," Clair said. "Thickest, heaviest rain you've ever seen. For days. Boots, clothes, blankets. Nothing ever got dry. Everything rotted, even your feet."

Louis drank, seemed to be considering that.

"Well," he said, "the world is rotting, when you think about it."

I hadn't.

"Why'd you come back here?" I said.

He didn›t answer.

"You know people? From coming here with your parents?"

"What?" he said. "You've been inquiring about me?"

"Your name came up," I said.

"Came up here to be left alone," Louis said.

"Didn't want to stay in the Marine Corps?" Clair said.

"Wasn't an option," he said.

He put his jar down on the table and looked at me.

"What is it?" he said. "What's so important you show up with a military escort?"

I put the jar down, took out my pad and pen, and laid them in front of me on the table.

"I'd like you to be in the story," I said.

"Why's that?"

"Because you're one of the outsiders. Like I said, you're one of the people they're eyeing as possibly being the arsonist."

"Like I would kill that doctor?"

"I guess."

"And the other 'suspect' is that kid?"

"Yeah."

"They know who beat him up?"

"I don't know. I don't think so."

Louis reached for the cigarette pack and shook another one out. He lit it and drew deeply, raised his head and exhaled.

"So I'm supposed to defend myself against these anonymous accusations?"

"You can say whatever you want."

He smoked. Took a swallow of ale from the jar. Leaned over and sloshed a little more into the dog's bowl. The dog lapped.

"Okay," he said. "Here's my statement to the press."

He drew on the cigarette, exhaled slowly so the smoke clung to his face.

"It's funny how some people get classified as outsiders," he said. "I've been coming here since I was a baby. My parents had a house in Sanctuary, their parents before them. I come here now, I see all these new people. Retired folks from New York and New Jersey, people moved over from the coast, the businesspeople. But I'm the outsider. That kid, just 'cause he looked different, walking around in the middle of the night."

"You saw him?" I said.

"Yeah," Louis said.

"He see you?"

"No," he said.

He smoked. "Why do you walk at night?" I said.

Louis exhaled.

"Like to know what's around me. Only way to know that is to do patrol."

"So you watch people in town?"

"Sometimes. Sometimes I watch people watching people. You'd be surprised what you see."

"I suppose so," I said.

"Not surprised they beat the crap out of the kid in the coat. Didn't do anybody any harm, did he? What is it he has?"

"Asperger's."

"Jesus. And that gets him nearly killed. People are sick, you know. Problem is, some of 'em see outsiders as a threat, even this poor kid. Rejection of the pathetic social order they live under. That kid's saying, 'Screw all of you. I don't need you. You're nothing.' "

"And that causes them to question their own value," Clair said. "Which is uncomfortable."

"Yes, it is," Louis said, flicking an ash. "I've always been an outsider. When I was a summer kid here, local kids thought I was weird. When I was at boarding school, I didn't fit there, either. Maybe 'cause I was up here in Maine every summer, running around the woods by myself. I was on my own, building cabins, tree forts, even a tunnel once."

He looked to Clair.

"Read about the Vietcong. I read all the time, every military book I can find. The VC and their underground hideouts. Amazing ingenuity. Mine had a trapdoor kind of thing, vent holes with pipes sticking out."

He smoked, tapped the cigarette on the edge of the can.

"Fuckin' A, man. Talking more today than I have in the last six months."

He raised the jar. "Must be the truth serum. Anyway, when I joined the military, my family, they thought I'd lost my mind. Turned out the only place I felt like I belonged was in the Marine Corps. Only time I felt I could really trust people. Shit we went through, people were laid bare, you know? We knew each other to the fucking core."

He looked at Clair.

"You know what I'm saying. You can trust a fellow Marine," Louis said.

"Trust him with your life," Clair said.

"So why didn't you stay?" I said.

Louis shrugged. The dog perked up at the slight movement.

"Shit happens. I had some things to deal with when I got back from Anbar. First I was in San Antonio, the VA there. Then I went to Bethesda, the naval hospital. That was for mental health stuff. Depression. I mean, I was a little sick with it before I went, now that I look back on it. Then you come back all the way from hell and nobody cares. About any of it. Not one iota. You're over there fighting for your life, your buddies getting blown to shit, and you get back here and it's like it ain't even happening. Nobody here gives a rat's fucking ass."

He looked at me.

"They gave Fallujah back to the friggin' Taliban."

He said it like it was somehow my fault.

"Yeah," I said. "I read the stories."

"Guys died to take that place. Guys way braver than me. And then we just let the insurgents walk in and raise their freakin' black flag. I saw it on the front page of the paper at the store. I'm standing there and I look around.

Nobody even notices. Guys got killed there. Guys got their legs blown off. Guys got burned alive."

Now he looked at Clair.

"So it's all a big joke, and the joke's on us. Never mind. Forget it ever happened. I mean, Jesus. Some of us were just kids, you know? We threw those kids away. For nothing."

"Vietnam," Clair said. "You can go there on vacation now. Scuba diving. Lie on the beach."

"So what the hell is it all about, then?" Louis said, looking up at him, the anger fading, the question real.

Clair hesitated, took a long swallow of Louis's beer.

"Every society has a warrior class. Without that we have anarchy. You'd see way more suffering, way more carnage. We fight to keep humanity from going totally crazy. Somebody has to step up."

Louis considered it. Turned his jar in his hand.

"Pretty fucking abstract," he said.

"All I got," Clair said.

We were quiet, the three of us and the dog. A pileated woodpecker called from somewhere in the treetops, a primeval sound. Bees bounced around in the flowers.

"Well, you Vietnam guys—at least nobody was spitting on me," Louis said. "Somebody spits on me, they may not be alive when they hit the ground. Anyway, the docs—the shrinks, I mean—they decided what with everything going on with me, my 'adjustment issues,' maybe it was better I took my disability."

I glanced at Clair. He was listening closely. Waiting.

Louis had darkened like the sky. Scowling, he tipped the jar and finished his beer.

"San Antonio VA," Clair said. "WIA?"

Louis stubbed out his cigarette in the can.

"The Humvees, the early ones—they were like tin cans. You know a lot of guys lost legs, feet. But the thing is, even if you don't get your legs blown off, you're stuck in the goddamn thing. And it's full of fuel and ammo and the enemy, they're following up with RPGs, small arms. So the vehicles, sometimes they—"

He stopped.

"Catch fire," I said.

Louis stood up, leaned down, and pulled the left leg of his pants up above his knee. His calf was a mass of pink and red and purple scars, the muscles misshapen. He reached to his right leg and pulled that pant leg up, too. It was the same—hairless, disfigured, scars from skin grafts and surgeries.

"Battle of Ramadi," Louis said. "Some guys got tattoos."

He dropped the trouser legs, sat back down. Pointed at my notebook.

"So am I a troubled veteran? Yeah, maybe I am. Do I have a thing about fire? Yessir. Wake up at night with my legs on fire all over again. So would I go around town burning down buildings?"

He leaned back in his chair, watched me scrawling in the notebook. The dog sighed.

"You all are the experts," Louis said. "You tell me."

24

The sky darkened overhead and the rain did come; wind, too. It blew in gusts and the rain drummed on the roof of the truck, skittered across the parking lot of the Sanctuary General Store. Clair had been quiet on the ride back down the ridge and into town, and now we sat as I went over my notes, rewriting phrases, picking out the best quotes. Some guys got tattoos.

I waited and finally Clair spoke.

"It's eating him up," he said. "Some vets are like that. They chew on it, ruminate on it, steep themselves in it."

"Bitterness."

"More that they can't reconcile what they've gone through," Clair said. "You try to find a way to make it make sense. The death. The destruction. The horror. You need a reason."

"But you came through it. Why not Louis?"

"Troubled to begin with, maybe? Less to fall back on when the Marine Corps was taken away. I had Mary."

"Think he's the fire starter?" I said.

"Would be a certain symmetry to it."

"Society burned him, so now he's burning it back."

"And he didn't deny it," Clair said.

"He could have just lied," I said.

"Marines don't usually lie to other Marines."

"Semper Fi."

"Yes," Clair said. "Speaking of which—"

"You've got to get back to Mary."

"And I'll check in on Roxanne. And my little girl."

"Thanks," I said. "I'll be home after the patrol."

"Watch yourself."

"Oh, I think it's going to be just riding around, talking."

"Well, you ought to be fine then," Clair said, "Mr. Chatterbox."

He smiled. I climbed down out of his truck and walked to mine. The big Ford rumbled off. I followed him as far as Route 17, where he went right and I went left, as far as the Quik-Mart. I pulled into the back of the lot and parked.

It was 6:20 and I was hungry and thirsty, so I went into the store and bought a ham-and-cheese sandwich, a bottle of water, and a coffee. I took it out to the truck and laid it all out on the passenger seat: my dinner, my notebooks. I ate and drank and listened to jazz on public radio. A show about Chet Baker. I took a blank legal pad and put it across the steering wheel.

Made a list, starting with the three most recent structures that had burned. Then a rough map of Sanctuary, with X's for their locations. Barbier's barn and the Talbot house on the east side of the river, the poultry barn on the west. Woodrow was attacked on the west side, south of the town center just a couple of miles from the shed. Would the arsonist start close to his home and then go farther afield? Would he start farther away and grow less cautious as the need for fires increased?

Maybe Woodrow was beaten by Ray-Ray and Paulie, payback for starting all this trouble. Or what if Woodrow had been attacked by the arsonist himself? Were arsonists violent in other ways? Burning the house with Dr. Talbot in it—that was very different from beating somebody with a club. This would be a good question for Investigator Reynolds.

What were they focusing on? A question for Trooper Foley.

I finished the sandwich. Took the lid off the coffee. Sipped. It was strong, a little burned, but it was hot, and it was raw in the rain, even though it was August. I sipped again, the cup in front of my face as Don Barbier's truck—a big black Dodge with ladder racks and toolboxes—pulled in and up to the gas pumps. He got out, reached for the hose. Tory got out of the passenger side, said something to Barbier. They both were wearing black—jeans and T-shirts.

He didn't look over as he walked into the store. Barbier stood at the pumps. Gassing up for the patrol? Tory going in to get supplies? Coffee and doughnuts? Some rope for the lynching?

I put the pad down and, taking my coffee with me, got out of the truck and walked over.

"Don," I said. "How's it going?"

He looked up, startled, but only for a moment.

"Jack," he said. "Hear you're going to be joining us."

"That's right, if you don't mind."

"Hey, the more the merrier. And maybe we can pick your brain a little on this thing."

He eased the nozzle out of the truck and hung it back on the pump, looked over my shoulder.

"Tory," he said. "Jack's ready to roll."

I turned. Tory had a cardboard tray with two coffees and several hot dogs.

"Shit," he said. "I forgot the napkins."

"I'll go, bro," Don said. He turned to me.

"Coffee?"

"Sure. Black." I'd almost finished my other cup, and knew I'd need the caffeine.

"You got it."

Don jogged to the store, swung the door open, and went inside. Tory leaned into the truck and arranged the food on the console between the front seats. I stood by the open back door and waited.

"Ever expect you'd be doing this sort of thing in Sanctuary, Maine?" I said, slipping the notebook out.

"Heck, no," Tory said. "Gorgeous setting, pretty little town that's gotten some national press. Who would've thought somebody would want to burn it down?"

"Where did you and Rita come from?"

"Chesapeake Bay area. South of Annapolis. Opportunities there had flattened out. You need a place on the upswing, ride the crest of that wave."

"To make money, you mean," I said.

"To be successful."

"What's all this doing to the wave?"

Tory looked at the notebook.

"Just a blip, Jack," he said. "This area is coming on like gangbusters. The wave is sweeping in from the coast. Camden. Belfast. Rockland. Those have peaked out. People are realizing that this is just a wonderful area."

"So, catch this person, get back to business?"

"You got it, Jack," Tory said. "Rita and I, really, it's our calling, to bring people to Sanctuary and enhance their lifestyle. A couple of months, this will all be forgotten. Ancient history. Like the Romans or whatever."

The Romans. I wrote that one down, was still scribbling when Don came back with my coffee. "One for you, Jack," he said, and then, to Tory: "Gonna have to watch what we say, with a reporter in the truck. Jack, you keep writing about this fire stuff, and nobody will ever want to move here."

"Well, that's why we have to nail this frigging clown," Tory said. "Nail his ass."

An urgency in his tone, beyond the guy talk. I guess if I was losing money by the minute . . .

"Let's roll," Don said. I walked back to my truck, collected my stuff, and came back. I got in the back, driver's side. I looked up, saw two rifles on the gun rack.

"What season is it?" I said.

"Varmint," Don said.

We roared off, turning on the Sanctuary Road. Sitting in the back, in the dark, I reached for my notebook and wrote that down, too. Tory had turned and he saw me writing and seemed to wince, probably feeling property values plummet with each good quote. I decided not to mention the *Times* Magazine.

Russell and Harold were waiting in the parking lot by the common in Sanctuary, dressed in black, too. I felt like I was headed for a poetry slam.

I moved to the middle and Harold got in beside me, gave me a knowing look. He'd fulfilled his side of the bargain. Russell got into the truck on the other side, putting a black canvas duffel bag on the seat beside us. He nodded at me, said, "Mr. McMorrow." I nodded back, said, "Russell. So what's in the bag?"

He looked at me, seemed a little irritated. I wondered how Harold had twisted their arms into letting me come along.

"Spotlight," he said. "Some other equipment."

"Like what?" I said. "Just curious. What do you bring on a citizen patrol?"

A little sigh, an eye roll. But he unzipped the bag, took out a spotlight, one of those million-candlepower lights that plugs into the cigarette lighter. A plastic bag that had 89977-RESTRAINTS USGOV stamped on the outside. Inside were plastic handcuffs, the kind you saw used on insurgents in Afghanistan and Iraq. He reached into the bag and took out another item: a pair of bulging goggles. Night-vision.

"Wow," I said. "Serious business."

"This is no game," Russell said. "Ask Dr. Talbot. Oh, sorry; too late. Remember, Mr. McMorrow: The only difference between arson and murder is luck."

I held up my notebook.

"May I quote you?"

"Do I get to vet the story?" Russell said.

"No," I said.

"Do you have to use my name?"

"Yes," I said.

"I'd rather just be described as a former government operative."

"What did you actually do, Russell?" Tory said.

"I'd rather just be described as a former government operative."

"Tell him what you really did, Russell," Tory said.

"Classified," Russell said, his lips clenched tightly.

"You heard of black ops, Jack?" Don said.

"Easy," Russell said.

Don smiled, said, "This piece of shit isn't gonna know what hit him."

We rumbled out of the town center, headed southwest. It was dusk, misty and overcast, and soon we were on a country road with only a few houses. Tory got out a map and unfolded it. He reached up and hit the overhead light and said he'd marked the houses he and Rita had on the market.

We drove down and along the river, pulling in where Tory pointed out vacant houses for sale. Don and Harold stood by the truck, the motor idling and lights on, a rifle in hand, while Russell, Tory, and I walked around the houses, looking for signs of any sort of intrusion. Russell shone the spotlight on surrounding yards and fields, illuminating deer, foxes, raccoons, and a skunk.

After two hours, we'd finished Tory's list and had made a complete circle of the town. It was after ten and Russell said, "Now we sweep for suspicious persons. Parked cars."

Away we went again, Russell grim, Tory seemingly buoyed by the idea of actually rousting someone. In fifteen minutes we found our first car, a gray Honda parked on a back road, half in the ditch. We all got out and Russell shone the light in, saw empty beer bottles on the floor. I held my recorder under my notebook, hit the button. Tory wrote the plate number down in a black notebook. Don felt the hood. "Still warm," he said. We turned to the dark woods and Russell played the light.

A pair of eyes.

Watching us from the first line of brush.

Don trained the rifle on the figure.

Russell said, "Citizen patrol. Come out slowly and show your hands."

There was a crunching, crashing sound as the person pushed through the brush. A teenage boy, his hands on his head. His white face was pale, his eyes squinting in the glare of the spotlight. He lurched toward us, stopped six feet away. He was wearing a baseball cap, red basketball shorts, a T-shirt that said FENWAY PARK.

"What is this?" he said. "Who are you guys?" He saw Harold, standing in the back.

"Harold," he said. "What's going on?"

Harold didn't answer. Russell stepped up to the kid, shone the light in his face.

"What were you doing in there?" Russell said.

"Taking a leak," the kid said.

Russell stepped around behind him. He patted the kid down, said, "Clear."

"You sure you're allowed to do this?" the kid said.

Russell came around to face the kid, said, "Sanctuary Citizens' Arson Prevention Patrol."

"Arson?" the kid said. "I was just taking a piss."

"So you are aware of the arson fires," Russell said.

"Sure, but—"

Tory stepped closer.

"Hold out your hands," he barked.

The kid took his hands off his head, held them out. "I know you," he said. "You're the real estate guy."

Tory took the kid's left wrist, held the hand up to his nose, and sniffed. Then he did the other one.

"No gas," he said.

"Please open the trunk," Russell said.

"What are you guys doing? I ain't gonna . . ." He looked at Don, the rifle by his side.

"If you don't cooperate, we have the legal right to restrain you as an imminent threat to the community," Russell said. "We have the legal right to exercise a citizen's arrest."

He reached into his back pocket and took out the plastic restraints.

"All right, all right, but there's nothing in there. The spare, some shit."

The kid walked to the car, opened the driver's door, leaned down, and pulled a lever. The trunk popped open. He walked to the rear of the car and pulled the trunk open. Russell shone the light in. There was a spare tire. A jack. A two-gallon gasoline can. Plastic.

"What's that for?" Russell said.

"In case I run out."

"Please take it out," Russell ordered.

The kid did as he was told. Russell took the can and shook it. "Empty," he said.

Russell put the can down, walked to the side of the car, and flashed the light inside. "Why do you have a lighter in there?"

"I smoke sometimes," the kid said.

"I don't see any cigarettes," Tory said.

"I'm out," the kid said.

"What were you hiding in the woods for?" Russell said.

"I wasn't hiding. I told you, I was taking a leak."

"ID," Russell said, holding out his hand.

The kid fished in the pocket of his shorts and took out a leather wallet. He slipped a license from a pocket and handed it to Russell. Russell read it aloud as Tory scribbled in the black notebook. "At 2235 hours . . ."

The kid's name was Curtis Quinn. He was sixteen, and lived on the River Road, four miles away. Russell took out his phone and took the kid's picture.

"We'll be turning your name over to the office of the State Fire Marshal," Russell said.

"For taking a piss?" Curtis Quinn said.

Russell was partway through an explanation of emergency measures in extraordinary and life-threatening circumstances when my phone rang. I turned away, put a hand over my ear, said "Hello."

Nothing, then a rustling. Lasha, I thought. Drunk again.

"Hello," I said again. "Is this—"

"Mr. McMorrow."

A girl's voice. Willa.

"We met at the hospital."

I walked away from the group, past the idling truck and onto the dark road.

"Yes, Willa," I said. "How are you?"

"Not very good," she said. "My brother."

A pause. A sniff. The scritch of a hand over the receiver.

"Woodrow?" I said. "What about him, Willa?"

"Woodrow . . . he's dead. And, well, I think you should put that in the paper. Say how this town, these awful people—"

Willa sobbed, the words sputtering out one by one.

"—they . . . killed . . . my . . . brother."

25

She was gone. I felt sick to my stomach, couldn't get a breath. I closed my eyes, said, "Son of a bitch." Turned back to the guys, playing policemen. "Son of a fucking bitch."

The kid was getting in his car. Don was putting the rifle back on the rack. Russell was taking pictures of the back of the Taurus with his phone. Harold got into the truck, followed by the rest of them. Russell got into the front seat and said, "I think he goes on the A list."

Don was nodding, reaching for the key when I said, "I have something to tell you."

They turned to me, waited. The recorder was on.

"Woodrow, the kid who was beaten. He died."

"No shit," Don said.

There was a moment of silence.

"So now it's two murders," Russell said.

"Just what we need," Tory said.

"You going to write about this?" Harold said. "For the paper?"

"A teenage boy was beaten to death. What do you think?"

Tory said. "Of course it's a terrible tragedy. It's just that—"

"This shouldn't affect this patrol," Russell said, like a boy dying shouldn't spoil the fun.

"But you know he may have been killed because somebody in town thought he was the arsonist," I said. "And he wasn't."

"We're not vigilantes," Russell said.

"When did he die?" Harold said.

"Tonight," I said. "His sister just called me. She said the town killed her brother."

"I thought he was just in a coma," Don said.

"I guess he didn't come out of it," I said.

We were quiet for a moment, even chatty Tory. The Taurus pulled away, spraying gravel.

"He came into the store once in a while," Harold said. "Never said much. Always had on that big black coat. Real quiet kid."

"He was autistic, on the spectrum," I said. "I heard the kids in school teased him, picked fights, tried to get him to lose his temper."

"Kids can be pretty damn rough," Don said.

"Could have been a drug deal gone bad," Russell said. "Might not have had anything to do with the fires."

"Now we've got drugs, too?" Tory said.

"What was he doing out there anyway?" Harold said. "In the middle of the night? You know he was always out walking the roads, in that black coat. Surprised he wasn't killed long before this just by getting run over."

"Could have been intending to steal stuff," Don said. "If it was drugs, this opiate stuff, they'll steal anything that isn't nailed down."

"Tragic," Russell said. "My heart goes out to the family. That's why we're out here—to protect the public. But keep in mind, there's always going to be a risk of collateral damage where there are civilians in the AO."

"AO?" I said.

"Area of operations," Russell said. "We can't let this distract us from our mission."

I shook my head, took my notebook out, and started writing. It was a scribble in my barely legible handwriting. I wrote down most of what they'd just said. And then I penned: A sixteen-year-old boy is beaten to death. So why does this feel like a game?

26

I asked them to take me back to my truck, my heart no longer in it.

They did, and then drove off to continue the patrol. I sat for a few minutes and gathered my thoughts, scribbled some more notes. Lifting the recorder to the light, I opened the last file, played a little just to make sure it was there. It was; their voices, the truck idling in the background. Collateral damage.

I wondered what Woodrow's family was doing. Still at the hospital? Following Woodrow's body to the funeral home? Writing his obituary, summing up his sixteen years of life? Would they collapse tonight and wake up in the morning and for a millisecond forget that their son and brother was dead?

I sighed, picked up the phone, and looked up the phone number for the State Police dispatcher in Augusta. Nonemergency. I dialed it, waited. A woman answered, her tone all-business, her words clipped. I asked for Trooper Foley. She said he wasn't on duty. I asked for whoever it was who was assigned to the Woodrow Harvey homicide. She said, "Who is this again?"

The dispatcher took my name and number, said she'd have someone call me.

I scrolled down my list of contacts, tapped in a number, and waited.

"Mr. McMorrow," Davida Reynolds said.

"Did I wake you?" I said.

"Hope not," she said. "I'm driving the back roads of Sanctuary, Maine."

"You too? I was with the citizens for a while."

"Met them twice now," she said.

"What do you think?" I said.

"Where are you?" she said.

I told her.

"Be there in fifteen," Reynolds said.

The Suburban pulled into the Quik-Mart parking lot just before midnight. I was sipping yet another coffee, eating a granola bar, had just texted Roxanne.

Davida Reynolds eased the Suburban up next to my truck. We both got out. She said, "Can't stay away, huh?"

"Nor can you," I said. "Where's your partner?"

"Oh, he's out there, too."

"Give him my best," I said.

Reynolds smiled, but only for a second. And then she said, "The kid who got beaten—"

"I heard. He didn't make it."

"Good sources," Reynolds said.

I shrugged. "I have a call in."

"CID now."

"You know who?"

"No. Just became a homicide an hour and a half ago."

"Sad to think he died because somebody thought he was the arsonist and he wasn't."

"Would be sad even if he was," Reynolds said.

We paused. An old pickup pulled up to the pumps and a guy got out. Beard, ponytail, leather biker vest. He took a gas tank from the bed of the truck and set it on the pavement and started filling it, the gushing sound carrying across the lot.

Reynolds watched him for a moment, then turned back to me. I had my notebook out.

"So can you confirm his death for me?" I said.

"I'd rather leave that to CID."

"But I won't get them tonight."

She hesitated, weighing the politics of it.

"Okay, but make sure you get CID in there someplace."

"Deal."

"When did he die?"

"I got the call at 9:03. Shortly before that."

"Do you think it's related to the fires?"

"There was evidence someone had tried to burn the logging equipment at the assault scene. So yes, we believe the death is related to the arson fires."

"In what way?"

"I don't want to speculate at this stage of the investigation."

"Okay," I said. "I will. He was either the arsonist and was killed by some-body who interrupted him, and then they couldn't call the cops, or he wasn't the arsonist, and he was killed when he interrupted the person who is."

"Or he was killed for some other reason, and the skidder was torched to throw us off," Reynolds said.

"So what is the status of the arson investigation?" I said.

"Ongoing. It's very active, as you might imagine. We've had one death. We'd like to stop this before there's another."

"You have people patrolling at night now?"

Yeah, well, sometimes you need to be a little proactive," Reynolds said. "Can't always just show up for the aftermath."

"What's your view of the citizen patrol?"

"For the record?"

"Yes."

"We welcome the assistance of the general public, but we prefer that people go about their business, be alert, and leave the investigation to us."

"They're a little scary," I said.

"Off the record? I know."

"This Russell fellow says they have a right to stop and interrogate people. Some emergency thing."

"May just scare the perp into hiding for a while," Reynolds said.

"That good or bad?"

"Kinda like to catch him now, as long as we're around."

We watched as the guy from the pickup finished pumping and screwed the cap back on the plastic jug, hefting it into the back of his truck.

"You ever read the *New York Times* Magazine?" I said.

"Sure," Reynolds said. "Bad habit. Sunday paper is a time suck."

"This story is going to be in the magazine, not the regular paper."

"Whoa. Big publicity."

"Is publicity good or bad?"

"He may back off," she said. "Or he may get off on it—want to put on more of a show."

The truck pulled away and rattled out onto the road. I watched the bugs, bats slicing through the swarm like sharks.

"Son of Sam got all upset when some nut job started calling the TV stations and horning in on his kills," I said.

"That right?" Reynolds said. "Well, you go to all that work to kill somebody and then somebody steals your limelight."

The bats kept circling and swooping. We watched and then I said, "Of course, if he'd lived to ID the person, the plan would have backfired."

Reynolds turned back to the bugs and bats, lost in thought.

"What if Woodrow was an accomplice to the fires," she said. "Maybe wanted out. Maybe Woodrow threatened to rat out his partner, so that person pounded his head in."

"And now the fires are a solo job," I said.

"Or maybe it's your artist friend," Reynolds said.

"I thought arsonists were almost always male?"

"Almost."

"Why would she do that?"

"Way to strike back at the world, after the husband dumped her," said Reynolds. "Maybe get back at the town, which she sees as representative of her ex, the bait he used to capture her. And now it's her gilded cage."

Gilded cage, filled with screaming sculptures.

"She's too open," I said. "Not nearly devious enough."

"I don't know. The thing at her house, scaring the guy away?" Reynolds looked skeptical. Or was she just watching my reaction?

"Nah," I said.

"Or maybe she just enjoys your company, Mr. McMorrow," she said. "Wants you to want to protect her."

"Doesn't need me for that," I said. "She carries a loaded shotgun."

"I don't know," Reynolds said. "I've seen her. At the Talbot house fire? This may be too forward to say, but I think she has a mad crush on you."

"Nah, she's just a little lonely," I said.

Reynolds' eyebrows twitched, and she said, "One does not preclude the other."

The interview was well over. We stood there, the bug storm swirling like a blizzard against the black sky. Looking more closely, I could see that the white plastic canopy was covered with spiders, bustling along their webs, catching moths and mayflies as fast as they could reel them in. Only from a distance was the Quik-Mart sign bright and clean.

Just like Sanctuary.

Roxanne was in bed, Sophie beside her. There was a stuffed dog beside Sophie, a kitty beside the dog. The whole crew was sound asleep. I kissed Roxanne lightly on the cheek and she opened her eyes.

"Sophie okay?"

"She wants to give you a fashion show," Roxanne said.

I smiled and Roxanne closed her eyes and fell back asleep. I circled the bed, slid my arms under Sophie, and lifted her up. She opened her eyes and saw me and then pointed back at the bed. I leaned and scooped up the kitty and the dog and carried them all out of the room and down the hall to Sophie's room. I pulled the sheet and blanket back and laid her down, put the cat on one side, the dog on the other, and covered them all up.

"Good night, honey," I said, but she was already asleep.

I slipped out of her room and walked quietly down the stairs. In the kitchen I went to the refrigerator and took out a can of Ballantine, grabbed a glass. I took it to the study, sat at my desk, and started typing, wrote a 250-word brief on Woodrow's death. I used Reynolds's confirmation, her brief comment. I added Willa's comment: "They killed my brother." And then I looked at the words again. Thought about it for a moment. Deleted the line.

She was just a kid.

I thought some more and put the line back.

I e-mailed the story and my own photos from the scene. Good enough for this story, until the real photographer showed up. Then I texted Kerry, told her they were there. They could put it up online in the morning, and everyone else could pick it up. The *New York Times* has reported . . .

I opened the beer. Drank a third of it in a long gulp. Raised the glass.

"Sorry, Woodrow," I said. "I'm very, very sorry."

And then I wrote out my notes from the night. Officious Russell and doofy Tory, the kid with the Taurus and Willa's shattered voice. Harold saying Woodrow may have been into drugs, and this becoming fact before the conversation ended. Don ready to rock and roll. This bastard isn't gonna know what hit him.

I noted my conversation with Reynolds, too, her saying it was time to be out there, not just covering the aftermath.

And then I listened. I heard frogs in the woods, something moving in the brush behind the house. I stood and went to the screened sliding door. Reached for the switch and hit the floodlights and saw a raccoon waddle away from the compost toward the woods. I watched until he disappeared, then turned the light off and went back to my desk. I drank some beer. Turned the recorder on and transcribed the conversation after I'd told them of Woodrow's death.

Tory: Just what we need.

First the doc burned, now a troubled teenage boy beaten to death. Will the bad publicity ever end?

I shook my head, went online, and Googled him. Tory, Sanctuary Brokers Real Estate.

LIVE THE LIFESTYLE.

LET TORY AND RITA BE YOUR GUIDES TO THE CHESAPEAKE BAY REGION. LOOK BEFORE YOU LEAP INTO THE CHESAPEAKE BAY AREA. TORY AND RITA WILL MAKE SURE THE INVESTMENT OF YOUR LIFETIME IS JUST THAT.

Their story lined up. The two of them had worked in Maryland for a few years, then made the move to Maine. I kept scanning, found that a real estate handout had featured them as the brokers of the month shortly after their arrival in Maryland from the San Diego area. Rita had the same smile, bigger hair. Tory was heavier, looked bulked up. The story said his hobbies were cooking, weightlifting, and "spending quality time with my awesome wife, on the job and at home." Asked about his name, Tory had said he'd gotten the nickname when he was a toddler, because his older brother couldn't say Tommy.

Huh. I'd figured it was his professional name, like radio DJs and news anchors take on. I Googled Tommy Stevens. Got a motocross racer in Indiana. A locksmith in Alberta. A guy who wrote a book about beekeeping. A wedding notice, Tommy and Sally-Jo, Oxnard, California. It would make sense if Tory had been Tory since he was three. But was that his legal name? And if so, when did he change it?

I Googled Thomas Stevens. The same locksmith popped up. Some guy who died in 1887, a genealogy thing. A computer science professor at a state college in Georgia. A police helicopter pilot in Los Angeles who got an award for rescuing people from a mudslide: "In driving rain, Sergeant Stevens piloted his Bell 206 Jet Ranger . . ."

I scrolled down, the Thomas Stevenses rolling by. Stopped.

A Thomas Stevens on a list of people described as lost. The organizers of the Class of 1988 Bangor High School twentieth reunion. "Seen these classmates? If so, tell them we'd LOVE TO SEE 'EM! Matthew Geberth, Tommy Stevens, Lasandra Lane . . ."

I clicked on the link. It went to the web page for the reunion. There were pictures of fortyish people holding drinks. Another link to the yearbook, a page for the photos. Girls leaning on birch trees. Guys in their football jerseys, standing by their pickups. And there he was. Tory—except he was Tommy then. A skinnier version, but with the same salesman's smile. He had done the business track, noted "all the laughs in accounting." His dream job: millionaire. His motto: Get rich or die trying.

Tommy Stevens was still working on it.

So what had he done? Made his way into real estate, given himself a preppy name? Still chasing that first million?

I bookmarked the page. Looked at my watch. It was 1:58 a.m. My last inch of beer was flat and warm. I looked upward and listened. No sound from my sleeping family.

Just one more.

Russell B. Witkin was a little easier. I searched for his name alongside US Department of State. Nothing. I searched for his name and Iraq War. Nothing. I tried Afghanistan. Still nothing. Then I tried US Army. And there he was.

But he wasn't in Iraq.

It was 1999. Russell was stationed in South Korea, a staff sergeant assigned to something called the US Army Materiel Support Center, Busan Storage Facility. A photo showed walls of stuff in a big warehouse, like a camo version of Home Depot. Russell was in a base news story in 2003 about personnel changes. He said he was retiring after twenty years at Busan, and would miss the important work. The story said the depot "received, stored, and issued water, fuel and clothing (packaged), building materials, and personal demand items in support of US Forces, Korea."

Night-vision goggles among them?

I smiled. No special ops. No Iraq or Afghanistan. Just keeping track of a warehouse full of boots and uniforms, bottled water, and army underwear. Clair had him pegged. Tory wasn't the only one reinventing himself in Sanctuary, Maine.

So what about Don Barbier, affable and capable, rolling into town like one of the real men in a pickup truck commercial? He said he'd been down south, out west, flipping houses, making money, being his own boss. Like Tory, he followed the real estate markets like surfers follow the waves.

I started to search for him but then looked at my watch again. It was 2:20 a.m. Sophie might sleep in until 6:30, but then would be raring to show me her new outfits. I closed the laptop and turned off the light. For a minute I stood at the open screen door and watched and listened. Let my senses come alive.

Night sounds, none of them human. A moonless night and full darkness, nothing moving that I could see. The damp smell of the woods and the grass. A lone firefly glowing in the garden, signaling to no one.

It hit me as I stood and listened. I'd been too distracted by Sanctuary, had dropped my guard. I castigated myself as I walked out onto the deck, down the steps, and across the lawn to the woods. He could still be out there, and Clair or no Clair I had to be ready. I stood in the shadows, motionless.

Listened.

Watched.

Wondered if he had the patience to outwait me, the attention span to avenge his son's death.

I stood for twenty minutes and listened to the night, and then I crossed the yard and checked the mudroom door. I went back inside, shutting the sliding door behind me and locking it. I checked the front door, made sure the window locks were on. Walked upstairs and pulled off my clothes and slipped into the bed beside Roxanne.

It was warm, she was wearing only a T-shirt, and she'd kicked the covers off. I moved close to her, felt myself stirring. Turned away and filed that one away for another night. I fell asleep with my back to hers and dreamed of a smoke alarm beeping and beeping, but I couldn't move. I tried to shout to Roxanne and Sophie to run, but no sound came out.

And then it was Roxanne talking, saying, "Who is this? Do you know what time it is?"

I opened my eyes. Roxanne was up on one elbow, talking on my cell phone, saying, "It's five o'clock in the morning, for God's sake."

I put my hand on her back and she turned, angry eyes and a scowl. "It's your lady friend," she said, tossing the phone onto the bed beside me. "Tell her to learn some manners."

I picked the phone up, said, "Who is this?"

"Jack," Lasha said. "It's me. I think I woke your wife."

"Yeah, well, what is it?"

"I couldn't sleep."

"Lasha. It's—"

"But that was a good thing, because I turned the scanner on."

"And?"

"And I made a cup of tea. And I was just sitting here and I heard the call go out."

"What?"

"Another one, Jack. A fire."

"Right now?"

"This one's right in the village," she said. "The real estate office."

"Tory?"

"And Rita."

"Was it set?"

"I don't know, Jack. But wouldn't you think?"

It was seven-fifteen by the time I walked to the end of the block and around the corner, crossed the back lots of Merrill's Antiques, the Card and Paper Shoppe, and A Stitch in Time dressmaker shop, to the back lot of Sanctuary Brokers.

Chief Frederick was there with Reynolds and Derosby, Trooper Foley, a sheriff's deputy, this one a young woman. Tory and Rita were standing to one side. Tory had his arm around her waist, like she might faint, and if she did, he'd be ready to catch her.

I walked up behind them and Chief Frederick saw me, turned and held up two hands, palms out. Reynolds turned, said, "That's okay, Chief."

I joined them. Frederick scowled. Derosby looked suspicious. The cops were neutral; not their investigation. Tory looked stricken, staring at the ground when he said "Hi." Rita looked at me and shook her head. Without makeup she looked translucent, a ghost of her made-up self.

"Check this out, Mr. McMorrow," Reynolds said, pointing at something on the ground. "This is pretty neat."

I stood beside her and peered down. There was an empty candlestick on the ground, pewter, with wax dried in rivulets down its sides. Beside it was a tuna-fish can, also filled with dried wax. Six inches from the can, a stick was poked into the ground, a piece of white string tied to it. The end of the string was burned at the tuna can. The grass was singed in a line from the can toward the door, where the grass was shriveled and brown, then burned close to the building.

Reynolds scooched over and pointed the pencil. "See, Mr. McMorrow? The ash?" There was a pale-gray ridge on the grass blades. "That was the fuse. I mean, this is very interesting." She was smiling as she pointed.

"That's candlewick. I figure he—or she—had it tacked to the door on one end, tied onto the stick at the other. A tall candle, the kind you have on the dinner table? That was in the candlestick, and I think the wick was sort of looped around it, under a little bit of tension. So you light both candles and when the tall candle burns down, the wick is freed. Maybe it's lit already, but just to make sure, it swings over so it's directly above the flame in the can. That definitely lights the wick, which starts to burn, and after a while, gets to the bottom of the door. Which just happens to be splashed with gasoline."

"And up it goes," I said.

"But by then, our perp is long gone from the scene. The timer device, crude as it is, has done its job."

"Somebody put some thought into this," Derosby said. "Somebody pretty smart."

I looked at the door, the smoke-stained bricks above it.

"Not much of a fire, though," I said.

"Oh, this wasn't supposed to burn the building down," Reynolds said. "This is somebody playing with our heads. It's like, 'You're looking for me out in the willy-wags? Well, I'm right in town. And I can burn stuff here, too.' "

"Peekaboo," I said.

"Right. Ever play that game, Marco Polo? You're swimming and one person is blindfolded and they say 'Marco,' and you have to say 'Polo.' And they listen for your voice and try to catch you. It's like, 'Here I am. Over here.' "

"But he's not," I said.

"But he was," Reynolds said.

"When?"

"Call came in—" She looked at the deputy.

"Five-sixteen a.m," she said. "Lady who lives above the stationery store saw a glow."

"So, let's do the timeline," Reynolds said, excited, like we were campers and she was the counselor. "Start with the wick. In fire investigation school they call this a micro evaluation. The candles were approximately four feet from the door. Wick burns at different rates, depending on what it's made of. Way faster without a candle wrapped around it. We'll test this one. But say the candle took two hours to burn down to the other wick, if it's a typical table candle. The wick takes ten minutes to burn to the door. We'll do a more precise timeline, but I'd say this means the person was here around three a.m."

"And back home in bed by the time the fire started," I said.

"Listening for the sirens," Derosby said.

"Or to the scanner," Chief Frederick said.

"Or watching out the window," Reynolds said.

"Or riding to the fire with the rest of the firefighters," I said.

"Hey, what is your problem?" the chief said, pointing a thick finger my way.

"Easy, Chief," Reynolds said. "We're just brainstorming."

Don had dropped the patrol members off at the store at 2:40 a.m., while the other patrol truck, the one with Paulie and the guys from the firehouse, was supposed to go until dawn. The next night, they'd switch.

He was saying this to a reporter from the TV station in Bangor. She'd arrived around seven-thirty, a video camera in one hand, notebook in the other. Blonde and pretty, in a hair-sprayed sort of way, she looked like she was playing the part of the TV reporter in a high school play.

She interviewed Tory and Rita Stevens on the front porch of the office, the sign in the background. Rita did most of the talking. When the camera came up, Tory held up his hands, said, "You don't want me. Get my beautiful wife." The reporter swung the camera toward Rita, who switched her smile on high beam.

"I'm just so proud of this town and the way it's come together," Rita said. "This will pass, and the community will be all the stronger for it. You know, there's a good reason why Sanctuary was selected as one of the nation's twenty hidden treasures by *American Living* magazine. When people move to Sanctuary, Maine, they immediately know they're in a very special place."

She held her smile for the camera. One, two, three, and cut. That's a wrap.

As spin went, not bad.

The TV reporter thanked Rita and turned and marched across the street, past the Civil War monument, across the lawn, and toward the store. I watched as Harold noticed her, said something to Don. Don said something back, then hurried across the parking lot to his truck. He climbed in, wheeled out of the lot as the reporter passed in front of him. Harold turned and went into the store. The reporter pushed the door open and followed. Corner him by the meat counter.

He'd talked to me like it was no big deal. Maybe the deal was getting bigger.

I walked to the real estate office, where the sign on the door said hours were 8 a.m. to 5 p.m. or by appointment. It was 7:55. I pushed the door open anyway. A bell jangled and I walked in. There was nobody at the desks, angry voices from out back. An argument, Tory saying, "How the hell should I know? Ask the cops. Ask the fire people. Jesus Christ, get off my back."

I stood. Waited. Walked back to the front door and reached up and gave the bell a push. It jingled again. Tory came out, saw me, and pursed his lips, impatient.

"Sorry to bother you, Tory," I said. "Have a minute?"

He turned to the back office, then back to me. "Kinda busy, Jack. I mean, it's been a hell of day."

"Just take a minute," I said. "Just a couple of quick questions about—"

"Jesus Christ," Tory barked. "Don't you know when no means no? Find somebody else to put in your fucking newspaper. I'm outta here."

He turned and walked out of the room, into the back office.

Rita came out and took his place, fluffing her hair and dabbing at her lips. She took a deep breath that seemed to inflate her smile. "Hi, there, Jack," she said. "Don't mind Tory. He's a little upset."

"Understandably," I said, taking my notebook out. "But that's what I was wondering. Why you guys? Why a fire here and not somewhere else in town?"

"I have no idea," Rita said. "It's just crazy."

"Because it looks like he had to pass by a whole line of shops before he got to yours. Why not do the first one? Then he could get away easier. This way he has to come all the way in and then walk all the way out."

"We don't know," Rita said.

"Setting that whole thing up back there, that took time," I said. "And then he didn't even get a real fire out of it. A door, that isn't much. Not compared to a few barns and a house."

Rita looked pained. "It makes no sense. No sense at all."

"It's almost like this is aimed at you personally, Rita. Doc Talbot—that's your listing. Now your office. Do you have any idea—"

Suddenly Tory was back, storming across the room.

"No, no, and no," he shouted. "I told that fire investigator woman and I'm telling you: We don't have enemies. We aren't the target of lawsuits. We haven't kept anyone's deposit. We haven't even had an argument, with each other or with anybody else. We're just living our lives, going about our business, trying to be good citizens, trying to make a living."

Rita stared at him, openmouthed.

"I have no fucking idea why somebody would light our office on fire. Or the Talbot place. Or Don's barn or that old man's shed or that skidder or any other fucking thing."

"Tory," Rita said, touching his arm. "Calm down. Jack was just asking—"

"I know what he was asking, Rita. I'm not an imbecile. And I gave him my answer. How many times do I have to say it?"

"Okay, Tory," I said.

"It's not okay, Jack," Tory said. "That's just the point. It's not okay at all."

He took a deep breath, his eyes closed. Opened them and sighed and said, "Okay. Between us, we've had one seller say she can't risk something happening to her property. One of our appointments today was to sign a contract on a six hundred thousand–dollar waterfront parcel, and they canceled."

"I see," I said.

"And we've got an investment here now, you know? Not just the listings. We own three properties. I thought with that story we were positioned just perfect. Now it's turning to shit. You know what the payments are on those? My God, we've got to turn those over. I was telling Don, let's get at least one done and moved before this goddamn market falls apart."

"Tory, you don't want all that swearing in the newspaper," Rita said.

"Oh, Jack won't put that in. Clean it all up, will you, Jack? Don't make me sound like a nut job. I'm just totally at the end of my rope. Out last night and this thing this morning—I had about two hours' sleep."

He gathered himself. Another deep breath, a half-smile, a shake of the head. But it had been a look through the facade. It was like something had been simmering for a long time.

Rita rubbed his arm to try to calm him. It was the first time I'd seen her anything but brittle.

"So you like working with Don?" I said.

Tory looked at me, startled.

"Don? Oh, yeah. Good guy. I mean, he's done this for years."

"Must have it down to a science," I said.

"Oh, yeah. He looked at the properties. Said they had good bones. Mostly cosmetics. Update the kitchens, get some granite in there. I mean, it was a slam dunk."

Rita looked at him with her big made-up eyes. "It still will be, Tor."

"I mean, this is so crazy. First Dr. Talbot, and then this kid dying—you know the last murder in Sanctuary was in 1947? Harold was telling me. Some woman hit her husband with a frying pan or something and he fell down and hit his head. I mean, this is small-town Maine, for God's sake."

"Even in the cities here," I said. "In Bangor, when you were growing up, there weren't murders all the time. It just isn't that kind of place."

He froze, like he thought he hadn't heard me right. And then he relaxed.

"Oh, I know, Jack. Our problem is, we're not used to this kind of thing. When we were in Maryland, parts of the state were just murder central. That's one of the reasons we came to Sanctuary."

"The quality of life," Rita said. "And now this."

"So why us?" Tory said, his armor back on. "The short answer, Jack? I just don't know."

He gave his wife a quick hug, looking at me the whole time.

"We'll get through this, won't we, babe," Tory said.

"Sure we will," Rita said. She looked at him, seemed relieved that she had her Tory back.

He said, "Hey, I gotta run. A shower would be nice, maybe even a shave. Can't go around looking like a homeless person." And he strode for the door, giving me his salesman's smile on the way by.

"Don't make me look stupid, Jack," he said, and the bell jangled, the door shut, and he was gone.

I turned back to Rita.

"Sorry. I didn't mean to upset him."

"Oh, it's okay. He's just been so on edge since this fire thing started. I told him that they'll figure it out. They always do."

"It is upsetting. An arsonist at work all around you."

"I mean, he's up and down all night, looking out the windows. And now this darn patrol thing. It's just eating him up."

She shook her head, her makeup perfect, her hair in place. No arsonist could keep Rita from being put together. She turned toward the back offices, then back to me, saying, "I don't know about you, but I need coffee. Want a cup?"

"Sure," I said. "Black."

"Come with me," she said.

I followed her in a slipstream of perfume and scented shampoo.

The coffeemaker was on a desk, and it looked like she'd just made a fresh pot. Rita poured, held out a cup to me. She took a small bottle of milk from the refrigerator and poured it in her cup. She sipped and sighed. I just sipped.

"I keep saying, 'Tor, worrying like this isn't going to fix it.' It just isn't like him."

"Tor," I said. "That's what you call him?"

She nodded. "And when we're alone sometimes he calls me 'Ta,' as in Ri-Ta. Silly, but that's the way we are. Just kids, really."

"Never call him Tom, or Tommy?"

She looked at me.

"Oh, nobody's called him that since he was a little boy. How did you know—"

"I read a story about you. A profile of the two of you, something in Maryland."

"Oh, that," Rita said. "I forgot about that. They had that in there, how his older brother couldn't say Tommy."

"This was in Bangor?" I said.

"Oh, I suppose. The family started there, I guess. But they lived all over the place, with his father in the military. Air Force. Tory went to, like, three different high schools."

She leaned on the edge of the table, arranged her dungaree skirt. She was fit and compact, like a piece of high-end office equipment—handsome and functional.

"My parents, they've owned one house their whole married life. Occo-quan, Virginia. Blink and you'll miss it. That's why when Tory said we should try this town in Maine, I was kind of shocked at first. But then I said it was fine with me. I grew up in a small town."

"But you didn't expect this."

"No," Rita said. "I didn't expect anything like this."

I considered it, asked one more question.

"Tory," I said. "Does he ever stop moving? It's like he's always running to the next thing."

"That's just him," Rita said, a hint of resignation in her voice. "I said that to him, when we first started dating. 'Don't you ever slow down?' He said, 'If you slow down, they catch you.' "

"Who?" I said.

"Life, I guess," she said. "For Tory, something is always nipping at his heels. He says if you're not moving forward, you're sliding back."

The phone rang in the office and Rita slid down and scurried to answer it, as if, in the midst of mayhem, a cash-buyer might still be out there. I stepped out of the office, walked a couple of doors down, and called home.

Roxanne didn't pick up, odd for 8:30 in the morning. I called her cell and got voice mail there, too. Texted her, asked her to call me. Called Clair's cell and he answered with a "Yessir."

"Hey," I said. "Pokey there?"

"Running in circles."

"I know the feeling. Pretty little girl in the saddle?"

"And another one leaning on the rail," Clair said. "How was the fire?"

"Not much of one. Whoever set it did it more to send a message."

"Saying what?"

"I don't know," I said.

"To whom?" Clair said.

"I don't know that, either."

"Good thing they assigned the crack investigative reporter."

"Very good thing," I said.

I heard Sophie in the background, a tiny cackle of laughter.

"How's things on the home front?" I said.

"Quiet. Doing a little ridin' and ropin'."

"Roping?"

"Well, we're working our way up to that. After we break some broncs."

"Great. Would you put Roxanne on?"

"Sure. And Jack."

"Yeah?"

"Watch yourself, blundering around down there. Sounds like somebody is building toward something, getting bolder. You don't want to step right in the middle of it."

"Yessir," I said.

A rattle and fuzzy hiss. Then Roxanne, her voice just this side of chilly.

"Hi," she said.

"Everything okay?"

"Fine."

"Sorry I had to leave in such a rush. Tell Sophie I'll be home for lunch for the fashion show."

"She's over it," Roxanne said. "Back in cowgirl mode."

A pause.

"It wasn't much of a fire," I said.

"Good."

"Lasha called because it was another case of arson."

"Uh-huh," Roxanne said.

Sophie in the background, "Pokey, giddyap."

"Something's wrong down here," I said. "Some things aren't what they seem."

"And some things are."

"What do you mean?"

"This woman, Jack," Roxanne said.

"Lasha," "I said.

I heard her moving, pictured her walking away from Clair.

"I know how it goes." Her voice was muffled, the hand over the phone. "You charm them, give them the soft smile, the blue eyes, your full attention. And they give you information. I understand that."

"I don't know about the charm part," I said.

"I do. And you've got her. Hook, line, and sinker."

"I don't know—"

"I do. I could tell by her voice this morning."

"Honey, she's just a source," I said.

"She doesn't know that, Jack. I promise you."

Sophie calling something, Roxanne covering the phone, saying, "Great, honey."

Then she was back.

"I'll be glad when this is over," Roxanne said. "This woman and Beth."

"What's with Beth?"

"She's been texting."

"Saying what?"

Then Clair in the background, saying, "Easy there. Say whoa, honey. It's okay."

"I gotta go," Roxanne said.

And she was gone.

I stood by the truck. Hit redial. Got Clair's voice mail. Said, "Call me as soon as you can."

I looked across the common, the red and white geraniums by the monument, the flag furling and unfurling in the breeze, people coming and going at the quaint general store. The news satellite trucks, booms telescoping into the sky.

Two more had arrived from Portland and Bangor while I was inside talking to Tory and Rita, setting up on the common with the monument and store in the background. The first reporter, with backup now, was speaking into a camera. Another woman, dark-haired in khaki slacks and a sleeveless red top, was fixing her makeup. A young guy in a Dan Rather safari vest was flipping through a notebook, the cameraman waiting.

I walked over.

The dark-haired woman was brushing something from the front of her top.

The guy, tall and blond and Ken-doll handsome, stood away from the camera and warmed up. The camera guy, stocky and shaggy-haired, in shorts and running shoes, waited.

"Yes, Sarah," the blond guy began. "I'm in Sanctuary, where, as you can imagine, it's a somber scene. First this small town was ravaged by an arsonist, who has killed one man and has authorities working feverishly to apprehend him. And now the news that Wilson Harvey—I mean, Woodrow—"

He looked down at his notes.

"And now the news that Woodrow Wilson—shit."

The cameraman laughed. "Try Teddy Roosevelt, why don't you."

"It's not funny," I said.

They turned to me.

"A kid's dead. It's not funny at all."

"Chill out, dude," the camera guy said. "We're working here."

"Is this the way you work? Thinking it's all a big joke?"

"Hey, go easy," the blond guy said.

"It's Woodrow Harvey. And he was seventeen. And somebody kicked his head in. Ever seen what that looks like? Know what it feels like?"

"Listen, bud," the camera guy said, moving toward me. "I don't know what your problem is, but I'm gonna have to ask you to move along."

He stopped in front of me, hands on his hips, chest puffed up.

"Go ahead," I said. "Make my day."

He stared at me and I stared back. Then he flinched, turned, and backed away. The blond guy scribbled in his notebook. Looked up at the camera and said, "Tensions are running high here in the town of Sanctuary, where local residents have been shaken by news that assault victim sixteen-year-old Woodrow Harvey has died."

He paused and looked at me.

"Once more," I said. "With feeling."

I walked to my truck, climbed in, set my notebook, recorder, and phone on the passenger seat. I sat and looked the place over: the general store, the red geraniums in the window boxes, the flags on the common. A Norman Rockwell scene, if you didn't mind the phonies and drunks, the murderer and the arsonist—although in fairness to Sanctuary, they could be one and the same.

As I watched, the blond TV guy was doing it for real, his expression somber and serious. An actor playing a part: the concerned journalist. As he talked into the camera, I considered my next step. Did I have enough for the magazine story? No. What was I missing? I wasn't sure.

And then Don Barbier's truck rolled out of the parking lot. How was Don feeling? Was he freaking out like his partner? I started the motor, put the truck in gear, and followed.

Don drove slowly, past the common, through the village and heading south, the direction of his house. I hung way back, catching glimpses of the black truck, the silver toolboxes. The road followed the river's course, swinging left and right, probably stamped out on the top of the ridge by horses and early settlers. A new wave of settlers here now, one of them bent on—

And then the truck wasn't popping back out. I sped up, slinging the Toyota through the S-curves, and then, when it was clear he wasn't in front of me, slowed down. There had been an occasional house near the road, a driveway or two. Had he turned off and into the woods? I was approaching Don's driveway so I slowed, stopped across the road, and looked up through the trees. No sign of him.

And then there he was, the Dodge approaching from the rear.

It slowed. I waited and caught a glimpse of Don at the wheel as he turned in. He looked like he was whistling.

I backed up, crossed the road, and drove up the tree-lined path. Popped out in the clearing. Don had parked on the side by the remains of the barn. The crime-scene tape was still there, like something left over from a party. The barn looked the same, a blackened hulk. I pulled in next to Don's truck as he got out of the cab, unfolding his long frame, pulling his baseball cap into place.

He smiled as I got out, came around the front of the truck. Gave me a manly handshake.

"Thought that was some lost tourist or something, parked down there. Then I saw it was you, Jack the reporter, digging up some dirt."

He held out his hand and we shook.

"What do you say, Jack," Don said. "How 'bout a cup of coffee? Maybe a doughnut. I got some from Harold's store. Hundred percent locally grown organic cholesterol."

He reached back into the truck, took out a box. *"Mi casa,"* Don said.

I followed him across the yard. There were rubber boots by the back door, a hose on the ground.

"Dog crap," he said. "Out behind the barn. Stuck my foot in the shit, as they say. I said, 'What the hell is a dog doing back here?' "

I thought of Louis and his hound.

"Somebody snooping around out there?" I said.

"Woulda been last night," Don said. "Wasn't warm; wasn't all dried up, either."

"Come back to the scene of the crime?"

"Don't know. But next time, I think I'll keep an eye on my own property 'stead of driving all over the willy-wags."

He opened the door and I followed him in. The door led to the kitchen, which was clean but nearly empty. Nothing on the counters. One plate in the rack by the sink. There was a coffeemaker on the table, a bag of ground coffee beside it, a box of filters. Don went to the cupboard and opened a door and the cupboard was empty, too, save for two mugs.

He took them out, went to the table and got the carafe out, filled it at the sink. Spooned coffee, poured the water in. The machine gurgled and hissed.

"Doughnuts and milk—left 'em in the truck," Don said.

He banged out the door. I heard him go down the steps, and hurriedly looked around the kitchen, poked my head into the next room. There was a folding chair, a stack of books, a TV on a box. Nothing else. It was like he was camping. I retreated to the kitchen, heard him talking. Went to the door and looked out, saw him by the truck, on the phone. I heard him say, "That the best you can do on price?"

I moved from the door, crossed the kitchen to the counter. There was a stack of mail and I flipped through it. A flyer for cable TV, addressed to Occupant. An electric bill, forwarded from Georgia Power. Fifty-eight dollars and change, billed to 587 US 41, Milner, Georgia. Another house he'd flipped?

I leaned toward the door, could hear him talking.

"Yeah, but you know I can do this myself for the cost of the shingles."

I stepped to the door, looked out. Don was between the barn door and his truck. He was carrying the rubber boots. I went back to the mail. A bill from a hospital. The Medical Center of Central Georgia. I peeked. Overdue bill from the ER for $245.55. Third notice.

And then Don was on the steps. At the door. I dropped the mail, no time to neaten the stack. Had it been neat? I hadn't noticed.

Don came in carrying a box of doughnuts and a half-gallon of milk. He put them on the table, said, "Roofers. Think just because I'm from Sanctuary, I'm made of money. Got him talking sense by the end."

He went to the sink, squirted dish soap on his hands, washed them under the faucet.

"All that talk about dog turds," he said.

He dried his hands, walked to the table, opened the doughnut box, and held it out to me. "Harold's finest," he said. They were plain doughnuts. I took one and he did, too. We both took bites and chewed and swallowed. And Don said, "So—Louis. That what you're thinking, too?"

"Crossed my mind," I said.

"It was one big turd," Don said.

"One big dog."

"I'm thinking maybe he came back to check his work."

"Or just to check it out," I said.

"Could just come by during the day to do that."

"Told the cops yet?"

"No," he said. "Hate to point fingers. I mean, he isn't the only one in town with a dog."

"I'd tell them. Don't have to accuse him."

"No, I can let them do that, I suppose," Don said.

He took another bite of doughnut. The coffee was dripping.

"Milk?"

"No thanks," I said.

Don poured coffee in the mugs, then milk in his. He handed me a clay-colored mug, painted with yellow and black stripes. A Southwest motif.

I looked at it.

"You've lived in New Mexico? Arizona?"

"Hell, yes. You reporters don't miss much, do you. Yeah, did a year in a little town called Jerome, northern Arizona. Bought a place dirt cheap, fixed it up, sold it to a lady from San Diego, just got divorced from some big shot, looking to open a B&B with her settlement. I made a serious chunk of change on that one."

"And then you moved on?"

"My job there was done," Don said.

"Where to after that?"

"Oh, jeez. Northern California, Washington State. Back to the Southwest. Flipped a place outside Taos. Nice payout on that one. Serious money in some parts of New Mexico. Taos, Santa Fe, but that got way too pricey to get in. Okay, then North Carolina, Georgia, up to Maine. May have missed a couple in there."

He finished his doughnut. Washed it down with coffee. Licked his fingers. Reached for the box and broke off a half, offered me the other one. I shook my head.

"Don't ever want to stay put?" I said.

"Nah. Hey, life's too short. Things to do, man. Places to see."

He leaned against the counter. One long, tall guy. All muscle.

"What kind of name is Barbier?" I said. "Kind of unusual."

"Well, that's because it's made up," Don said. "Story I was told was my great-grandfather, he came down from Canada. Somebody at Ellis Island there saw his name, long and French. Barbiereaux. Too many letters, I guess. Maybe a long line of folks waiting to get their papers filled out. So he writes Barbier. 'Next!' And here I am."

I smiled.

"Funny how one thing leads to another," I said.

"Yes," Don said. "It is. And then you live with the consequences the rest of your life."

"You can tell that story to your kids someday."

"Right."

"Hey, speaking of not having kids—the artist woman," I said.

"Lasha," he said.

"Yeah. You know her?"

"Sure."

"She with anybody?"

"No," he said. "Recently divorced, some guy from New York. We sort of dated a time or two."

"Really. Seems like she might be somebody fun to spend some time with."

"Nice lady," he said. "A little nuts, maybe, when she gets drinking. But I don't know. Coming off a bad divorce, I got the rebound vibe, you know? Look out or you end up with a ring in your nose."

He poured himself more coffee, held the pot up to me. I shook my head.

"So, what do you have to do to this place?" I said. "To flip it?"

Don looked around.

"Oh, paint mostly. Sand the floors. Nice pumpkin pine under the lino-leum. Needs a new roof, upgrade the electrical. But paint. Paint's big, in terms of return on investment."

"Tory your partner on this one?"

"Oh, no. I bought this from him and Rita when I first got here. Me and Tory decided to team up like a week after that. He's got three places he's look-ing to turn over, big nut to pay every month."

"This fire thing isn't helping?"

"Not hardly," Don said. "I kinda roll with whatever comes down the pike, got plenty of cushion. But old Tor, I worry about him. He smiles a lot, but underneath he's wrapped tighter than a baseball. Hard work, going around being upbeat all the time. And he's got a lot of money riding on this town."

"I'm sure he thought this was a pretty safe investment," I said. "That 'Hid-den Treasure' article."

"And instead you get some whack job burning down houses," he said. "Who would've thought?"

Don was looking away as he spoke.

"This story," he said.

"That I'm writing?"

"Yeah. Any way you could hold off on that for two or three months?"

I eyed him, shook my head. "No," I said.

"What do you make on something like this, a couple grand?"

"Something like that."

"What if we fronted you some cash, tide you over?"

I shook my head again, his intent sinking in.

"How 'bout ten grand," Don said.

"You're thinking my story's going to kill the market for your houses."

He smiled.

"Not gonna help," he said.

I didn't answer.

"You can still write the story, of course. Just give us a little time to move some of this property. Summer is prime time for this real estate stuff. You could have it come out in the fall, say October."

"I don't think so," I said.

"The amount too low? Me and Tory could throw in a little more, for the inconvenience. Say, fifteen grand. Cash. Like making twenty-five, pre-tax."

"Wasting your breath," I said.

"Think about it," Don said.

"I did," I said. "Not interested."

Don shrugged his big shoulders.

"Straight shooter, huh? Travel the high road."

"Sometimes," I said.

"Making a mistake," he said.

I paused. "Not taking the money, or writing the story?"

He waited, gave me a long look, the smile gone. "Maybe a little of both."

"Jeez, Don. That sounds like a threat."

Another long look, our eyes locked in. And then he smiled.

"Nah. I don't blame you. I told Tory you didn't get to the *New York Times* taking payoffs. But people like him, it's all about the money. And man, is he on edge."

"Why didn't he ask me?"

"He said he had more to lose. If you put it in the paper that he offered you money, I mean. More damage to do in the court of public opinion. Me, I'm nobody. I just move on. The money's sort of incidental. I'm doing what I want to do."

"Which is?"

A pause, just a beat, and then Don said, "Sticking to the plan."

"Always on the move?" I said.

"Yeah," he said. "You know the Travelers? In Ireland, England? Places like that?"

"Sure. Like Gypsies."

"Right. They keep moving, don't put down roots. Call the non-Travelers 'settled people.' "

"And you're not one of the settled people?"

"Can't do it," Don said. "Couldn't if I tried."

He looked away again. I closed my notebook, tucked the pen in the coiled binding, stuck it in the back of my jeans.

"Most people I've known who roamed like that were running from something."

Don turned toward me, gave me a defiant sort of stare. "Not me," he said. "I never run away. When I'm moving, it's because I'm looking for something."

"Find it yet?" I said.

"Coming close," he said, raising his mug. "Closer and closer."

I mulled him over as I got back in the car, headed out the drive through the woods.

Don was an odd one, hard to place. He had skills. Why would he choose this itinerant-contractor life? Who would want to be so unattached, to people or place? What straight single guy would turn Lasha down? I could see marriage, maybe, but not sex. So maybe he wasn't straight. But what the hell was he looking for?

I was a mile down the River Road when a gray Impala pulled up behind, flashed its headlights. I pulled over and the car passed me, pulled in and backed up. There were blue lights on the backseat deck. A police aerial.

Scalabrini, the State Police detective from the Woodrow scene, was getting out of the driver's side, coffee in hand, circling the front of the car and approaching my truck on the ditch side. As he reached for the passenger door, I popped the lock. Moved my stuff. He got in, reached down to his right hip, and adjusted his gun.

"Got a minute?" he said.

"Sure," I said—like I could say no.

He sniffed. Reached in his top shirt pocket for a tissue and blew his nose.

"Allergies," he said. "Tree pollen's ungodly."

"Bummer," I said.

He balled the tissue up, looked around for a place to put it. I pointed to a plastic grocery bag on the floor at his feet. He opened it and dropped the tissue in.

"Here's the deal, Mr. McMorrow," Scalabrini said, looking straight ahead. "Every time I go to talk to somebody, you've already been there. I'm talking to Woodrow's little sister."

"Willa."

"Right. She says, 'Like I told the reporter guy from the *New York Times*.' This morning I go out to talk to this army vet, guy lives in the woods with the humongous dog."

"Louis. And he's a Marine."

"Yeah. So Louis goes, 'Like I told the reporter and his friend, the Marine.' Who's that, by the way?"

"His name is Clair Varney. He lives in Prosperity."

"Louis was very impressed by him," Scalabrini said.

"The feeling was mutual," I said.

"Yeah, well. Let me see. The artist with the crazy statues. She tells me she calls you whenever she hears something relevant. Her word. You knew about this latest fire before I did. Anyway, I'm talking to the guy who owns the store. Harold. I bring up his felony record. He says, 'I explained all that to Jack McMorrow.' I'm talking to the guys from the fire department. The young kids you told me about. One of 'em is listing to the left. I say, 'What's wrong with you?' He says, 'Nothing.' We go back and forth and finally it comes out. Says you hit him with a lug wrench, cracked his collarbone."

I shrugged. "It was three on one."

"I'll take your word for that, and besides, he said he didn't want to file a complaint. So the fire chief here, just so you know—he doesn't like you."

"Sure he does. Just has an odd way of showing it."

"But again, I say, 'How well do you know these kids, Chief?' He says, 'Like I told that A-hole reporter.' "

Scalabrini turned and looked at me for the first time since the conversation began.

"So I figure, instead of chasing around after you, I'll just go to the source."

I smiled. He didn't, just kept his gaze fixed on me.

"So, Mr. McMorrow. What do you know that I don't?"

"What's wrong with reading it in the paper?" I said.

"When's that gonna be?"

"Story's for the Sunday *Times* Magazine. I don't know which Sunday."

"And I'm trying to catch a stone-cold killer, torched a house with a man in it. Beat a kid to death. I don't know why he did it, so I don't know if he's about to do it again. And as you're aware, this is in a town targeted by a serial arsonist, which by definition is a murder waiting to happen."

I took a deep breath. "I don't know," I said. "I don't usually—"

"How long you been a journalist," Scalabrini said.

"Almost twenty years."

"Why do you do it? In ten words or less."

"To get to the truth."

"Me, too. And once I get to the truth, I throw somebody's ass in jail. Punish the guilty, protect the innocent. You got a family?"

I could see where he was going, but I answered anyway.

"Yeah. A five-year-old daughter and a wife."

"How would you like it if they got hurt because a journalist refused to share information with a homicide investigator, information that will be taken in confidence, by the way."

"I guess I wouldn't like that much."

"And if I'm reading you right, you'd probably go after the person who hurt your kid," he said.

"Or Clair would," I said.

"Well, let me save you or some other dad all that trouble. Whatcha got?"

He turned away and took a swallow of coffee. Sniffed again. Sipped again. Turned back, his black eyes a little weepy.

"Well?"

"Tory Stevens's real first name is Tommy. Thomas. He graduated from Bangor High School."

"How do you know that?"

"Wasn't hard once I started looking. Found his high school picture online. Under Tommy."

"Okay. So he wanted a fancy name, better to sell houses to rich people."

"He looked sort of shocked when I brought it up. He's got some story he made up about getting the nickname when he was three."

"Not the first person who's embellished their past."

"I didn't say everything I had was blockbuster news."

"Okay. What else?"

"This guy, Don Barbier.

"The contractor guy?"

"Right. I can't find many Barbiers online. Just him, and a lawyer. And some dancer or something who clearly made up the name."

"People change their names all the time."

"Bought the house with cash."

"Maybe he's hiding from an ex-wife."

"I don't mean a check. Cash-cash. As in a stack of hundreds."

"Perfectly legal."

"Why Don Barbier? Why not David Jones? Or Darrell Smith?"

"I don't know," Scalabrini said. "Why don't you ask him?"

"I did," I said. "Sort of. About the name, I mean—how unusual it was."

"And he said?"

"Somebody monkeyed with it when his grandparents came through Ellis Island."

"Makes sense. That happened all the time," Scalabrini said. "I have a great-uncle, Guido Scala. Immigration guy filling out Guido's papers didn't have time for all those Eyetalian letters."

"Except most French-Canadians just came over the border. They didn't come in through Ellis Island. French people from France came to Ellis Island, not French-Canadians."

"How do you know that?"

"I did a paper on Ellis Island in college," I said.

"I did a paper on Beowulf," Scalabrini said. "Waiting for that to come in handy."

We sat. The motor idled behind us. The woods rustled. As always.

"Maybe the story got mixed up as it got passed down," Scalabrini said.

"Maybe," I said.

Another long sit, the detective thinking. Finally I said, "Sorry I don't have more for you."

"Oh, no, that's okay," he said. "I'm just trying to figure this thing out, maybe get somewhere before somebody else gets killed."

"I understand."

"And you seem to know these people, so I figured I'd kinda pick your brain."

"But I don't really," I said. "I feel like I don't really know anybody. I mean, I know them on the surface, but that's all."

He didn't reply, so I said, "It's kind of the way I know you. Sort of, but not really."

That got him to turn his head.

"What do you want to know?" he said.

"What do you do for fun when you're not doing this?"

He thought for a few seconds, scrunching up his face like I'd asked him to do trigonometry.

"Jeez. Well, I read books about World War Two. Just finished one on the Battle of Midway. You know we could've lost that one? Two fleets in the Pacific, Japanese trying to sneak through. Our guy happened to guess right."

"What else?"

"I fish. Bass. And I'm trying to learn how to play the guitar. Probably a midlife thing. Always wanted to be a rock star."

"Married?"

"Divorced. Cop thing."

"Kids?"

"No."

"So is this case frustrating for you?"

"Yeah. Because I feel the perpetrator is right in front of me. Has to be. I mean, who else is here? The one this morning. Weird, right? Breaks the pattern of rural and isolated locations."

"It did use the fuse thing, like the barn."

"That's true."

"And it's a good fire if you want to make sure you're not a suspect," I said. "No real damage. Lots of attention."

"Very good, Mr. McMorrow. You ever need a job . . ."

A pause. He rubbed his eyes and it made a squishing sound.

"So you don't think it's somebody from somewhere else?" I said.

"Nah. I think it's somebody local, maybe getting their jollies from torching stuff, or just benefiting from turning this town upside down. I always go back to the cardinal rule of thumb: Who stands to benefit?"

I felt a wave of uneasiness pass through me.

"Maybe," I said, "somebody who wanted the treasure to stay hidden."

Another pause, and then a car came into view, a cruiser, an unmarked brown Crown Vic. It slowed as it approached. As it passed I saw the dog mesh on the back window, the sign that said K-9 KEEP BACK.

The cop at the wheel glanced at us and did a U-turn, pulled up behind my truck. As we sat, a Suburban came up the road, from the same direction.

It approached and there was Derosby at the wheel. He did the U-turn and parked behind the cruiser.

"A regular party," I said.

I watched in the mirror as the jumpsuited trooper got out and went to the back door of the cruiser and let the dog out. He woofed a couple of times, sniffed the ground, then bounded toward my truck.

I looked at Scalabrini.

"You mind?" he said. "Process of elimination."

"No. Go for it."

The dog was sniffing the side of the truck, then circling behind and doing the passenger side. As Derosby watched, the handler unlatched the tailgate and lowered it. He said something to the dog and the dog jumped up. He sniffed around the truck bed. I watched in the mirror as he sat. The handler gave him a treat. The dog jumped down.

"Got the truck," Scalabrini said. He glanced at my feet. "You wearing those shoes last night, riding with the militia there?"

I looked down, too. I was wearing hiking boots from L.L. Bean.

"Yup."

"Wearing those when you stepped in the gas at the store, or whatever it was?"

I thought. That had been my New Balance running shoes.

"No."

"Could the dog have a sniff?"

"Sure," I said. "But do you really think I may have burned Tory and Rita's doorway?"

"I don't think anything. I just eliminate. Where'd you go after you got done with those guys?"

He didn't bother to make it sound like small talk.

"Had a chat with Investigator Reynolds up at the store. I thought this was her case."

"We're teaming up," Scalabrini said. "I knew the dog was in town, figured they'd want to cross you off the list. As long as you were here. Would you mind getting out?"

"Not at all," I said.

I opened the door and the dog was there, panting and straining on his leash. I got out and stood. The handler, the same rangy kid with the chiseled face, let him in. The dog sniffed my shoes and jeans, then moved past me. The guy pulled him back and he gave me another sniff.

No wag. No sit.

I'd passed.

I looked at Scalabrini. He looked at the dog guy. They all walked back to the car and the dog jumped back in his seat. Derosby was out of the Suburban and they talked, their backs to me. Then Scalabrini and Derosby walked back to my truck and looked in the bed. The handler came and joined them and pointed down into the truck.

Derosby beckoned me over with his forefinger. He looked down into the bed of the truck. There were empty oil cans, a plastic jug of bar oil, a couple of rusty wrenches. The bottom of the bed was coated with a paste of wood chips and oil and dirt.

"Spill gas in here recently, sir?"

Sir. I looked down, leaned closer, and sniffed. I smelled it.

"Not that I know of," I said. "But I carry chain saws back here. I suppose one of them could have leaked."

"You carry saws yesterday?" Derosby said.

"No," I said. "Last time I worked in the woods was last week."

He leaned and sniffed, too. The gasoline odor was unmistakable.

"That's not last week," Derosby said.

"No," I said. "Don't need a dog to smell that."

"Where was your truck all night?"

"Parked at the Quik-Mart on Route 17. They picked me up and dropped me off."

"You didn't notice the smell?"

"No. But I haven't been back here. I usually ride in the front."

They looked at each other.

"You got a minute more?" he said.

He gave the trooper a look. The trooper went back to the car and got the dog out again. The dog bounded around, straining on his leash. Derosby asked me to step away from the truck and put my hands out.

I did. The dog dug his way toward me, his toenails scratching at the pavement. He sniffed my hands, my feet again, swerved toward the truck. The handler tried again, but the dog wanted the truck, the treat.

"Wash your hands this morning?" Derosby said.

"Yeah. Brushed my teeth, too," I said.

And then they looked up and past me. A car was approaching and I turned, saw a silver SUV, a Mercedes. It was Tory, Rita beside him. They stared, first at the cops, then at me, our eyes locking as the car slowly passed.

27

It had turned colder, a front sweeping in from the northwest, dry Canadian air, as the weather forecasters liked to say.

Roxanne had heated up some homemade tomato soup, the early tomatoes from the Varneys' garden. Sophie was having lunch and had crushed most of a stack of saltines into the bowl and jabbed her spoon into the mound. Crackers and soup had spilled onto the table. I had just walked into the kitchen when I saw the mess, heard Sophie say "Oops."

And then she jabbed the soggy glop again, spilled more. Looked up at me, unrepentant.

"Sophie," I said. "What are you doing?"

"Making a mess," she said. "Why? Just eat your lunch. Where's—"

I looked for Roxanne, saw her standing on the deck. She was hunched over her phone, her thumbs twitching as she wrote a text. I grabbed a sponge, wet it at the sink, and went and wiped up crackers and pasta and carrots from the table.

Roxanne turned, grim-faced, turned back.

"What is it?" I said.

"She's flipping out," Roxanne said.

"Beth?"

"Yes."

"How?"

She shook her head, kept typing her message.

"Well, what is it?" I snapped.

I went to her side, looked down at the phone. I could see bits of the message: YOU KNOW THAT'S NOT GOING TO SOLVE . . . WE'VE TALKED ABOUT . . . DON'T MAKE THINGS WORSE FOR . . .

Roxanne pressed the SEND button and looked up.

"She's threatening to kill herself," she said.

"Where is she?"

"I don't know."

"Did you call the police?"

"Yes. But they can't find her, either."

"A rough idea?"

"Somewhere between here and Augusta."

"Here," I said. "You've got to be kidding me. How long has this been going on?"

"I got the first message at 10:33 this morning."

"Why the hell didn't you call me?"

"You were busy, Jack," Roxanne said. "I didn't want to interrupt you."

The words were carefully and precisely pronounced, the tone icy.

"Who did you call? Does Clair know?"

"Yes," Roxanne said. "He's been here."

"Where is he now?"

She turned toward the woods. "Out there, somewhere. He said he'd take a look around."

"What about the office? Have you told them?"

"Robert and Sandy know. So do the reporters, Caitlyn what's-her-name from the TV station, Sam whatever from Bangor Daily."

"You called them?" I said.

"No, Jack," Roxanne said. "She's been texting them, too. She's texting all of us. Robert said the TV station is putting the texts up on its website. They put them on Facebook. They're tweeting them. It's unbelievable."

Roxanne started to cry, a dribble of tears that cascaded into sobs. I held her, took her phone from her hand. Over her shoulder, I read the messages.

> NOBODY CARES ABT ME, JUST LIKE THEY DIDNT CARE ABT MY BABY. ITS JUST A F**N JOB FOR THEM. ROXANNE AND SANDY. KILL MY BABY + F**N WALK. OMFG WHAT A WORLD. I WANNA DIE NOW.

"God," I said. "This is going public?"

> I WISH I NVR GOT BORN. I WISH I NVR HAD RATCHET, SQUEEZIN HIM OUTTA ME FOR 19 F**N HOURS, HURT LIKE A BASTARD SO HE COULD LIVE ON THIS GD EARTH FOR 2 YRS BFOR THEY TOOK HIM AND KILLD HIM. IF I WAZ A RICH BI*** I WOULDA BEEN FINE, RATCHET WOULDA LIVED. BUT CUZ I WAZ POOR THEY CLD DO WHAT THEY WANT.

> EVEN WHEN I GOT CLEAN IT DINT MAKE NO DIFFERNC. SANDY WAS MAKIN HER MONEY, SHE WSNT GONNA GIVE HIM BACK. AND THEY R ALL IN IT TOGETHER, SANDY SH**HEAD AND ROXANNE HARD-ASS AND THE REST OF THE DHHS MAFIA. STEALN KIDS AND MAKING MONEY. PIMP THM KIDS OUT.

"Unbelievable," I said.

> NOBODY CARES, NOT EVN THE NEWS MEDIA. WHERES THE STORY ABOUT ME N RATCHET, MY BABY KILLED BY DHHS??? WHERES THE STORY ABOUT MY LIFE BEING STOLE AWAY BY MASTERSON AND THE REST OF EM? I GET THE DEATH PENALTY, BUT WORSE CUZ I GET TO SEE MY BABY DIE FIRST. WELL NOW YOU CAN WATCH ME DIE. SEE WHAT YOU ALL DID.

"She's drunk," I said.

"Or high on something," Roxanne said.

"Or she's just lost it," I said.

Roxanne eased away from me, her face drawn and streaked with dried tears. She looked toward Sophie, who was sitting at the table, eating saltines.

"Where's her soup?"

"I took it from her. She was just playing with it, making a big mess."

"Well, she can't just—"

"Which cops did you call?" I said.

"Foley. The state trooper. He called and said they were looking for her."

"Can't trace the phone?"

"She's moving," Roxanne said. "Driving around. They're looking for her car."

"What if she's in another car?"

"I don't know."

"What if she's got a gun? How's she going to kill herself?"

"I don't know, Jack," Roxanne said. "All I know is what I've told you. And Robert, he called the TV station, asked them to take the messages down, but they say they have that right because they were sent to them directly."

"They're right. They're like any other whacked-out letters to the editor."

The phone buzzed. Roxanne took it from me. I moved close beside her to read.

> WHEN I GO YOUR GONNA KNOW IT. GONNA GO OUT IN A BLAZE OF FIRE. LOOK OUT YOU DONT GET BURNED UP. WRITE THAT FIRE STORY, JACK MCMORROW, WRITE THIS. GO 2 HELL YOU MOFO BABYKILLR BITCHES.

Roxanne spun away from me, went inside. I followed, and while Roxanne was cleaning up around Sophie, saying "Honey, let me get you some new soup," I went to the study, flipped my laptop open, went to the Channel 11 website, the column headed:

BREAKING NEWS:
Distraught Woman Threatens Suicide over DHHS Child Death
By Caitlyn Carpenter

A Gardiner woman whose toddler son died in state custody was threatening suicide Wednesday over what she said was callous treatment by the Department of Health and Human Services.

In a series of profanity-laced text messages sent to this station, Beth Leserve, 22, pledged to kill herself over the death of her son, Ratchet.

The child died while in foster care after being removed from Leserve's home last year. A state investigation is under way, looking into the circumstances of the child's death in the home of DHHS foster parent Sandy St. John. Leserve has also criticized the actions of then-DHHS child protective worker Roxanne Masterson. Masterson, 38, of Prosperity, left the agency shortly after removing the child from the home.

In her messages, Leserve criticizes both women and blames them for her child's death, from blunt force trauma. St. John claims the child fell from a chair. Leserve charges that he died due to physical abuse. She also charges that the DHHS has not been responsive since her son's death.

A State Police spokesperson on Wednesday said authorities were aware of Leserve's threats and were attempting to locate her. Those attempts were made more difficult by the fact that the Gardiner woman was apparently texting from her car, the whereabouts of which were unknown.

"We're looking for her," said spokesperson Jeanne Dunlap. "It's only a matter of time before she turns up."

The child's father, Alphonse Celine, was released from prison to attend his son's funeral. He escaped during the service and remains at large.

Anthony Shea said DHHS officials were concerned about Leserve's well-being and hoped she could be located soon so she could receive appropriate assistance.

St. John and Masterson could not be reached for comment Wednesday morning.

The article was followed by Beth Leserve's text messages, like an online chat with a distraught, drunken, emotionally disturbed young woman.

I glanced across the screen, saw that the Leserve story was the most read and shared on the Channel 11 website.

"God," I said. "Is this what we've come to?"

I got up and walked to the kitchen.

Roxanne had gotten out flour, butter, and chocolate chips. Sophie was standing on a chair at the counter, wearing her apron.

"We're making cookies, Daddy," Sophie said.

"And no eating—" Roxanne said.

"—the dough," Sophie said.

"Gotcha," I said. "I'll wait for the real thing."

To Roxanne I said, "When did they call?"

"Starting at eleven. Every ten minutes after that."

"Mommy said not to answer the phone," Sophie said. "Somebody was selling something."

"And we're not buying," I said.

"No," Roxanne said. "We're not buying."

"Talk to Clair?"

"Not yet. I feel like every time something happens—"

"We call him? He'd be upset if we didn't," I said.

He was there in ten minutes. Sophie got a special treat, a DVD of The Jungle Book and a bowl of Cheez-Its. She watched the movie on my laptop on the couch while the three of us stood on the deck, under the canvas awning. It had started to rain, a soft but heavy mist, and the drips came off the edge of the awning and splashed against our legs.

Roxanne backed up closer to me and I put my arm around her. Clair stood with his back to the house, facing the woods, like Wyatt Earp with his chair against the saloon wall.

"I'm sure they'll find her," I said. "If she's driving around drunk or high, or whatever she is."

"I don't want her to hurt herself," Roxanne said. "I don't want that on my head, too."

"Why she's doing this . . . ," Clair said. "She's decided to hurt you in any way she can. A public suicide, even the threat of it—"

"She's all talk," I said.

"I don't know," Clair said. "Filled with drugs?"

"When I pulled Ratchet, she was really into meth," Roxanne said.

"Then she could go for days," I said.

"You can come to our house," Clair said.

"No," Roxanne said. "We can't keep doing that."

"Then you stay here," Clair said. "I'll keep an eye on things."

"But you won't get any sleep," Roxanne said.

"Wouldn't get any sleep anyway," Clair said.

We spent the rest of the rainy afternoon trying to pretend everything was normal. Roxanne did laundry, put dishes away, listened to a news show on NPR, and kept the phone off the hook. I sat at my study chair and went over notes for the story, began a rough outline. Sophie said she wanted to do a campout, so I made a tent with blankets in her room, putting her stuffed animals into sleeping bags made of towels.

I came back downstairs.

"Goddamn it," Roxanne said. "This is just nuts."

Her cell phone buzzed at 2:48 and 3:19. Each time she stared at it, walked away, then walked back and picked it up. Each time it was a text message from Beth.

> MAYBE I'LL DO IT ON THE STATEHOUSE STEPS . . . I HOPE SANDY
> DIES SLOW . . . ROXANNE, EVERY TIME YOU HOLD YOUR DAUGHTR,
> KNOW THATS A FEELING I'LL NEVER HAVE AGAIN . . .

At 3:30, Sophie came downstairs, a stuffed animal under each arm. Roxanne gathered her up and they snuggled on the couch and Roxanne told her a story about when Sophie was little.

"I couldn't talk at all?" Sophie asked.

More messages, 4:05 and 5:19.

> HOW CAN YOU FUCKEN PEOPLE SLEEP AT NIGHT? . . . WHY SHOULD
> I DIE ALONE, SANDY? I WANT YOU WITH ME . . .

Roxanne got up, made coffee.

"I want to call Sandy," she said.

"You can't," I said.

"I want to ask her what happened. Again."

"You don't believe her?"

"I don't know what to believe anymore," Roxanne said. "About this, or about anything."

She turned away from me, went back to the couch.

At 5:45 p.m. the three of us went to the barn to see Pokey. I called Clair on his cell and told him we were coming. He met us on the path, materializing out of the trees.

Clair had the pony tethered in the small pasture outside of the paddock, next to the barn. Pokey looked up when he saw us, then lowered his head and continued grazing. Sophie helped Roxanne fill his grain bucket and gave him water and raked the stall, which Clair had already mucked out. He and I stood in the shop door and watched them, listened to Sophie's chatter.

"No music?" I said.

"Sometimes you need to hear what's going on around you," he said.

"You think she might do something?"

"To herself? Fifty-fifty. To you guys? Twenty-eighty."

"But still."

"Hope for the best, plan for the worst," Clair said.

"Yes."

"She's enjoying the melodrama."

"Definitely getting her fifteen minutes," I said.

"Wonderful world we live in," he said.

Mary appeared at the back door of the house, called, "You're staying for dinner," and then closed the door and went back inside.

"They can stay," I said. "I might go back to the house."

Clair nodded, turned and stepped into the barn and the shop. There was a bulge at his waist, under his T-shirt. I followed him to the workbench, where he reached to a shelf above his head, the butt of a pistol showing above his belt. He took down another, a handgun in a small black fiber holster.

"You want this, just in case?"

I took it from him.

"Waist holster," he said. "Glock twenty-three. Light but very reliable. Forty-caliber, good punch."

He handed me an extra clip. "Thirteen rounds."

I slipped the gun out of the holster, popped the clip out, and jammed it back in. It felt cold and lethal, like I was handling a poisonous snake. I slipped the second clip into the pocket of my jeans.

"If I have it, I won't need it?" I said.

"Like when you bring an umbrella," Clair said.

"And it never rains," I said.

"Almost never," he said.

Roxanne and Sophie came out of the barn, walked around the paddock to the pony. Roxanne undid the tether from its stake and Sophie led Pokey to the barn door, Roxanne alongside. She looked at me, pointed to the house. I shook my head. She nodded.

"I'll walk them back," Clair said.

"I don't think she'd come through the woods," I said.

"No. More likely try to crash her car into your house."

"Or blow her brains out on the front lawn."

What was the good news?

I turned and headed for home. The path wound through a glade of birches, then dense thickets of blackberries, high as my head. Halfway there I took the gun from the holster, snapped the clip in and out. There was something reassuring about the metallic clack. I holstered the gun, the holster clipped to the back of my jeans. I walked on, scanning the thickets, then the clumps of sumac, the patches of spruce.

When I reached the house, I circled it once, checked the front and side doors. I walked to the end of the driveway and looked up and down. It was quiet, robins clucking in the trees, a phalanx of goldfinches flushing themselves from the brush on the far side of the road. I looked up, saw a pair of turkey vultures circling high above. I glanced once more up and down the road. As I walked back to the house, I adjusted the gun at my waist.

They came home at 7:30, Clair watching from the lawn as they came in through the sliding door. I waved and he did, too, and was gone.

Sophie was telling me they'd brought me a package and she ran to the table with a brown paper bag and stood on the chair as she opened it. She named the items as she pulled them out.

"Potato salad. Coleslaw. Salmon. Mary said you can heat it up 'cause it's cold now. She said she couldn't give you ice cream because it would melt, even if I ran."

I said it all looked great and I was starved.

Roxanne smiled, helped Sophie pull the lid off a plastic container.

"Pickles," Sophie said. "Mary knows you like her pickles."

"Yes, I do," I said. And I turned away, listened.

A car was crunching the gravel on the road, slowing. I looked at Roxanne. She glanced toward the road.

I went to the mudroom door, opened it. I heard a motor idling, adjusted the gun, and stepped out.

The cruiser was in the driveway. Trooper Foley got out, reached back into the car and got his hat, put it on. He turned to me, nodded.

I met him by the front of the cruiser.

"Evening, sir," he said.

"What is it?"

"Beth Leserve."

"Yes."

"I just want to let you know, we found her car."

Roxanne appeared in the doorway, stepped out. She was carrying her phone.

"Where?" she said.

"About ten miles from here. In Palermo."

"Was she in it?" I said.

"No," he said. "She was not."

"Well, was she beside it? What?" Roxanne said.

"Her car was in the driveway of a home. There's an indication—"

He hesitated.

"Of what?" I said.

"It appears Ms. Leserve broke into the house and got keys and took a car or truck from the residence. She also took other items, we believe."

"Such as?"

"At least two firearms," the trooper said.

"Jesus," Roxanne said.

"A two-seventy deer rifle and a nine-millimeter handgun."

"Ammunition?"

Another small hesitation.

"We believe she also took ammunition for both firearms."

"You're looking for the car?" Roxanne said.

"Well, we're checking that. The owners of the house live out of state. They own multiple vehicles. There's some confusion as to which vehicle was at the house."

We stood there as it sank in. I touched the gun at my waist, under my shirt.

"So where the hell is she?" I said.

Roxanne's phone chimed. A real call.

28

She looked at the number, pressed a button, and held the phone out. Speaker.

"Yes," Roxanne said.

"He's dead," Beth said. "I'll never hold my baby again."

Roxanne looked at the trooper.

"I know that, Beth," she said.

"We're all dead," Beth said.

"What about Heaven, Beth?" Roxanne said. "Don't blow this. Don't blow your chance to see Ratchet."

There was a clatter, road noise, the dinging of a car with a door open or a seat belt unfastened.

"Changed my mind on that," Beth said. "I got to thinking. I'm thinking there's no God 'cause he wouldn't've let my baby die."

"Where are you, Beth? Let's talk."

A car door closing. The motor starting, the roar of a V8.

"Oh, 'Let's talk,' " Beth mimicked. "Sicka fucking talking. Is talking gonna bring my baby back? Huh? You tell me. What the fuck is there to talk about?"

And the phone went dead.

Silence hung like a cloud. And then Foley said, "Maybe you folks will want to move in with a friend or something. Until we locate her."

Roxanne looked at me. Gave her head a little shake.

"I think we'll be better off here," I said.

"Well, we'll have units in the area," the trooper said. "It's not like you'll be alone."

I thought of Clair.

"No," I said. "We won't be alone."

Sophie had a bath, with lots of soap, a rubber duck, and a squirt gun. Sophie floated the duck at one end of the tub and fired away from the other.

Join the club.

At nine, as they sloshed and chattered upstairs, I went outside, exiting onto the deck out back, circling the yard, pausing in the shadows at the east side of the house. I listened, watched the dusky woods. Birds flitted, looking for roosts. Bats were out and one passed near my head, so close I felt the wash of his passing, the flutter of bat wing. I stayed still for a minute more, than walked toward the woods. At the edge of the brush, I turned toward the road. At the edge of the ditch, I paused. Looked down the road toward Clair's, and jumped across.

"Seven-point two from the Russian judge," a voice said.

I turned. Clair was sitting in a camouflaged camp chair at the edge of the trees. He was dressed in olive and black. A black ball cap covered his silver hair. He was cradling a rifle, his favorite Mauser.

"Hey," I said.

"Nice night," he said. He looked up at the sky, the light dribbling away to the west.

"Been here long?"

"About an hour. Have another chair out back, northwest side by the woods. Has a sight line three directions—east, southeast, and south."

I glanced at the rifle.

"See you brought the heavy artillery," I said.

"Your State Police friend said she took a handgun and a deer rifle."

"I doubt she knows how to use it," I said. "She's a city girl."

"You never want to be outgunned. Range is everything in open terrain."

We stood, looked up the road. The strip of gray gravel was light against the dark woods.

"Why snipers were so effective in the hill country," Clair said. "Set up, shoot across a valley. Knowing you're out of enemy range is a damn good feeling."

Another pause. The bats had found us, the bugs we'd attracted. They swooped and fluttered. Clair said, "I could watch them for hours."

"Yes," I said.

We did, and then I said, "I think they'll find her passed out in a car someplace, once she reaches the end of this jag."

"Maybe so," Clair said.

"Call me when you're ready to head home," I said.

"Oh, I will," he said. He was looking up at the sky. His expression was calm, peaceful, nearly beatific.

"A gift to see these sorts of things," Clair said. "You know I saw a bobcat cross the road a little while ago. Big male."

"Did it see you?" I said.

"No," Clair said. A pause, and he added, "Woods are full of things that are invisible to most people. Foxes, coyotes, weasels, martens."

"Creatures that are at home in the woods at night. Like you, and whoever is burning the town down."

"Yes," he said. "At least this Beth, you see her coming."

"Count my blessings," I said, and I walked back toward the house, cut across the front lawn, and looked back. Clair was gone.

Sophie was in bed, waiting for me to say good night. Roxanne kissed her forehead, gave the blanket another tug, and left the room. I sat on the edge of the bed and held Sophie's hand, small in my palm, little fingers gripping mine.

"You're up late," I said.

"I can't sleep," she said.

"You haven't tried yet."

"I'm worried," Sophie said. "About Pokey."

"Why?"

"He's all alone," she said. "And it's dark in the barn."

"Horses are used to the dark."

"Not Pokey. He likes it when it's light out. And when we're with him."

"We can go see him first thing in the morning."

Sophie looked doubtful, frowning with the sheet tucked her under chin. "That's a long time from now," she said.

"Don't you worry, darlin'," I said. "Pokey will be just fine."

"You promise?" Sophie said.

I thought of Clair out there in the dark, the Mauser locked and loaded. Beth out there in the dark, too. Someone in the dark in Sanctuary, with a gas can and a lighter. I hesitated and finally rolled the dice.

"Yes. I promise."

Roxanne was cleaning up in the kitchen, wiping the counters and wiping them again. She arranged the chairs at the table, wiped the table down, too. Then the outside of the refrigerator, the stove, the inside of the microwave. I moved to her, put a hand on her back, and she jumped.

"Easy," I said.

"Yeah, right," she said.

"It's going to be okay."

"If saying it made it true," Roxanne said.

"It's all right. Clair's outside. He's gonna call my cell when he's ready to head—"

"Jack," Roxanne said, scrubbing the gleaming counter some more. "Our friend is guarding our house with a rifle. A distraught crazy woman is driving around with a gun, saying she's going to make me pay. Some nut is burning houses in a town barely twenty miles from here. Two people there are dead. A kid I was responsible for is dead. The dad escaped from prison and nobody can find him. Sophie told me she wants Pokey to stay in our shed so nobody can burn him up. And tonight she asked me if we'll all live in the same house in Heaven."

"Honey," I said, putting a hand on her shoulder.

"And we're practically broke and I should go back to work, but I don't want to leave our daughter alone. Not for a minute."

"Hey," I said.

Roxanne turned, tears welling.

"So it's not all right, Jack," she said. "It's a lot of things, but all right isn't one of them."

I gave her a hug but she was stiff, her shoulders tense. I gave her a kiss on the cheekbone and she frowned and tossed the cloth into the sink.

"I'm going to bed," Roxanne said. "I just want this fucking day to be over."

She used the word once a year.

Roxanne moved past me and I heard her steps on the stairs, weighted and weary. I walked to the bottom of the staircase and listened. The water ran in the bathroom and then I heard her walk down the hall to Sophie's room. After a minute I heard her come out. I heard the click of the lamp next to the bed. And I heard Roxanne begin to cry.

In the study, the only light from the laptop screen, the loaded Glock on the desk by my notebooks, I started to write.

> *Sanctuary, Maine wasn't like a town in a magazine. It was one.*
> *Selected by* American Living *as one of twenty "hidden treasures," the quiet community along the Sanctuary River was said to have it all: lovely historic homes, a close-knit collection of longtime residents and contented newcomers "from away," a picturesque town common with a homespun general store that sells the* Wall Street Journal *and the* New York Times.
> *And then Sanctuary added another element to its hidden qualities. An arsonist who strikes in the dead of night, has set fire to barns, homes,*

*a Main Street business—and has shaken the community to its core. The
fires have residents eyeing each other as possible suspects, armed men
in pickup trucks patrolling the back roads at night. A 16-year-old boy
said by some to be a suspect died after he was beaten by an unknown
assailant or assailants, fueling the tension running through the town.*

*"So why us?" said Sanctuary real estate broker Rita Stevens, whose
business was one of the properties targeted. "The short answer? I just
don't know."*

A snap at the window screen. I put a hand on the Glock and turned.
Listened. Heard the low hum of bugs. Then a soft rattle, a June bug flutter-
ing on the deck. Another crash-landing on the screen and falling. I waited a
moment, reminded myself that Clair was out there somewhere, turned back
to the keyboard.

Tory. I looked back at my notes. We don't have enemies. We aren't the
target of lawsuits. We haven't kept anyone's deposit. We haven't even had an
argument, with anybody or with each other.

But how unusual was this? How many arson fires were there in Maine
each year? How many concentrated in a single town?

I searched for Maine crime statistics, found the Uniform Crime Reports.
Looked for arson. Found that the vast majority of arsonists arrested were male,
that they were roughly split fifty-fifty, adults and juveniles.

So burning stuff was a guy thing. But why?

I leaned into the keyboard, typed. Up came a story in the *Los Angeles
Times*. The hook: Someone deliberately set brush fires, the kind that burn
thousands of acres and hundreds of homes. The lead: He is an angry young
man—a loner with a troubled past and a bad self-image.

Woodrow. Louis. Maybe one of the guys in the fire department. Half the
other teenage boys in town.

The story went on to cite a Finnish study that found links between arsonists and low serotonin, a chemical in the brain. Great, I thought. I just have
to go around Sanctuary taking blood samples. Case closed.

But was this a case of a chemical imbalance? Blind anger?

No. There didn't seem to be anything blind about it.

Back to Maine.

The state had roughly 250 arson fires a year, trending up and down like the stock market. They had them listed by county. Sanctuary was in Sagadahoc. Most of the set fires were in more-populated counties: Androscoggin, Cumberland, Penobscot.

The beetles buzzed and banged at the screen. I turned. Listened. Turned back.

I wanted to know if there had been any arson in Sanctuary before—other than Harold's—but there was no breakdown by town or city that I could find. I reached for a pen, made a note to ask Davida Reynolds.

Then I tried a general search for ARSON, SANCTUARY MAINE. I got the Harold story, four inches based on a guilty plea. My first story for the *Times*, and a rewrite by AP. That was it. And then I tried the same search for Portland, got a bunch going back years, two fatal. I tried Lewiston, got a few. I tried Bangor. Scrolled down the list. A guy convicted of torching his own house so his ex wouldn't get it. A kid who burned a stolen truck.

A house that exploded, two people killed, August 12, 1992. Reported in the Bangor Daily in 2009 in a story about unsolved murders.

The victims were a twenty-six-year-old guy and a nineteen-year-old girl. They were ID'd through dental records. In other words, burned to a crisp. The house, on a dead-end street, went up in a fireball. Investigators at first suspected a malfunctioning propane stove. Then the fire marshal's office determined that all of the burners were on. Stuff was strewn around the place (just metal skeletons left, like there'd been a fight). The victims—Ross Lucas and Julie Barber—had been alive when the fire started. They were found with soot in their lungs, according to the investigator, Linwood Penney .

The reality of all these fires—a horrible way to go.

I leaned back. Bangor, in 1992. Wasn't Tory/Tommy there then? I wondered if he knew Russ Lucas. That would be another reason to be afraid of fire. I made a note to ask.

And then I quit the web browser, tried to write.

A description of the town, as depicted in the "Hidden Treasures" magazine story. Chief Frederick and Paulie and the boys, the town's normal state of fire preparedness. Then the first arson, the second, the third, the townspeople assembled at Don's barn—the fourth fire—a feeling that it was some strange fire-lit social event. A section on the investigation, Reynolds and Derosby. The fire at the Talbot house. The town turning on itself, Woodrow and Louis. Lasha guarding her studio with a shotgun.

Word count: 2,400. Damn, this was going to be long. It was 12:35 a.m.

I got up from the desk and went to the door. Maybe I'd sleep for a couple of hours, then spell Clair for a while. Prime crime time was between two and four a.m. I'd be rested and ready.

I slid the glass door closed and locked it. Closed the laptop. Was on my way to the bathroom when I heard it.

The boom of a deer rifle. I froze. Another shot.

The bedroom door rattled open.

"Jack," Roxanne called.

"Stay here," I said. "And call 911."

I ran for the door.

29

There were headlights in the road in front of Clair's house, the beams askew, aimed at the woods. I had the pistol out, held low, stayed close to the roadside as I ran.

As I approached I saw something in front of the truck. I slowed, raised the gun higher. It was a guy on the ground, face in the gravel, hands clasped behind his neck.

I moved around him, said, "Hey," and he turned his head toward me.

Ray-Ray, pebbles stuck to his cheek.

From the other side of the truck I heard, "Okay, okay," a young guy's voice.

And then, "I say when it's okay. Down there with your buddy in the dirt." Clair.

He had Paulie at gunpoint, was shoving him up from the ditch. Paulie, hands raised, stumbled. Clair, the rifle under the crook of his arm, caught him by his waistband and yanked him back up. When Paulie had passed into the headlight beam, Clair hooked his foot around Paulie's ankle and shoved. He fell forward onto the road.

"Hands behind your goddamn neck," Clair barked.

"Yessir," Paulie said, and complied.

We stood over them like we were guarding prisoners of war.

"Not Beth," I said.

"No," Clair said.

"Both shots yours?"

"One warning. One front left tire."

"Wouldn't stop?"

"Kept right on coming."

"Dumb," I said.

"Callow youth," Clair said, "as they say."

It was Trooper Foley who arrived on the scene first, the blue lights of his approaching cruiser visible for miles in the blackness of Knox Ridge. He slid the car to a halt, rolled out with his gun drawn. He saw me, then Clair, then the guys on the ground.

Clair held out the rifle and Foley took it, then my Glock.

"Until we can sort this out," Foley said.

"Good luck," I said.

Two more cruisers arrived, another trooper and a Waldo County deputy. The lights were blinding, like spaceships had landed. We could see Ray-Ray in the back of Foley's car, his face grim in the strobes. Foley was going through the truck, handing items to the other trooper, a rangy short-haired woman: empty beer cans and an opened thirty-rack. Bud Ice. A sawed-off baseball bat, Louisville Slugger. A gallon of coffee brandy, two-thirds gone. A three-foot length of pipe, with some sort of leather grip.

"What did I say about superior range?" Clair said.

"What'd you tell Foley?"

"That they saw me in the road, I held up my hands to stop them, and instead they accelerated like they were going to run me down."

"Warning shot was above and beyond."

"I've gone soft," Clair said.

The deputy transported Ray-Ray and Paulie to the Waldo County jail in Belfast, the two of them looking me in the eye as the cruiser passed. A wrecker arrived from Knox to haul the truck. Foley watched as the driver winched the truck up the ramp.

When the wrecker pulled away, Foley walked over to us. He said the DA would review the statements, determine who'd be charged with what.

"They said they came to even things out," he said.

"The best-laid plans," I said.

"The drunk-driving and alcohol charges will keep them overnight," he said.

"One down," I said.

"Yeah," Foley said. "How many does that leave?"

"I'm losing track," I said.

We stood, the three of us illuminated in the wigwag of the headlights, the blue glow.

"Ms. Leserve," Foley said.

He looked at Clair.

"It's okay," I said. "He knows everything I know."

"We've been told she's started using bath salts, the street drug," the trooper said.

"Which would explain the rekindled paranoia," I said.

"People go literally insane," he said.

"She was close already," I said.

"So where is she now?" Clair said.

"We don't know," Foley said. "We think we know what she's driving. A stolen dark blue Nissan Pathfinder."

A long pause.

"So you'll be nearby?" Clair said.

"Yes."

"Because there's a little girl who's caught in the middle of this," Clair said.

"I understand, Mr. Varney," the trooper said.

"And if there's a real threat to her . . ." Clair said.

"Just call 911. We'll be here in a matter of a few minutes."

"Are you going to return our firearms?" Clair said.

"What if I don't?" Foley said.

"I'll have to go back to the house and get some more," Clair said.

The trooper looked at him. For a long moment we stood in the road in silence. And then Foley said, "Heck of a shot, taking that tire right out, in the dark, truck moving fast."

Clair shrugged. Foley went to the trunk of his cruiser and returned with the Mauser and Glock. I thanked him and he walked back to the cruiser. He wheeled the car around and started to ease past us, then stopped, his arm out the window. He reached over and turned the radio down, the laptop open.

"Mr. McMorrow, you're writing about these arson cases down in Sanctuary, right?"

"Yeah."

"A fatal tonight."

"Car accident?"

"Pickup," Foley said. "Off the road and into a pond. Lady drowned before she could get out."

"Jesus," I said. "Who was it?"

He turned to his laptop, scrolled up.

"Driver was Eve C. Johnson, DOB June 13, 1984."

"My God. I know her, her kids."

"From what I hear she was alone in the vehicle. Looks like she swerved to avoid an oncoming vehicle, lost control."

"Other car stop?" I said.

He shook his head.

"It wouldn't," I said. "Not in that town."

Foley nodded. The cruiser pulled away. Clair looked at me.

"You okay?"

"Yeah, but I just saw her. In the store. I interviewed her for the story. Husband's a trucker, in the fire department. Two little kids. Really, really nice person."

"Sorry," he said.

"I know. It's awful. I can't believe—"

My words trailed off. We stood in the road and I looked at the sky, the lights on in the houses, Clair's and mine. Above us the stars were glittering, cold and distant and unfeeling. Eve, her sweet kids, just like mine. Erased by some random act, a family without a mother, a dad suddenly weighted with grief and responsibility and crushing loneliness. All because somebody was on the phone. Or texting. Or reaching for the radio.

"What is it with that place?" I said. "It's like it's cursed."

Like that article—only the Hidden Treasure was really the kiss of death.

Roxanne was in bed with Sophie, the door ajar. I pushed it open wider, stepped in. At the side of the bed, I crouched down and whispered.

"Kids from Sanctuary Fire Department," I said. "No big deal."

"Nothing on Beth?"

"No. They're looking for her."

I told her about her new drug of choice.

"That would explain the crazy texts," Roxanne said.

"Explain, but not excuse," I said.

No reply.

"Another thing," I said, and I told her about the accident and Eve Johnson, her nice kids, a family shattered.

"Oh, my God," Roxanne whispered. "It's so sad." And she teared up, turned and looked at Sophie. We could hear Sophie's breathing, her shallow, rapid breaths, fragile as life.

"She woke up," Roxanne said.

"I figured."

"She's worried about Pokey."

"If she wakes up again, tell her I went to visit him," I said, and I kissed her cheek and stepped softly out of the room. In the hallway, I slipped my phone out, called Clair on my way down the stairs. He was walking the road, from his house to ours. I met him out front, where he slipped out of the darkness, rifle in hand.

"Aren't you going to sleep?" Clair said.

"I was going to ask you that."

"No need," he said. "Comes with advancing age."

"I can spell you."

We walked. I stepped on a branch and it cracked like a gunshot.

"I think you might be better suited to daylight patrol," Clair said.

"You're stuck with me," I said.

"Then maybe all the racket will scare her away."

We crossed the east side of our property at the tree line, followed it to the northeast corner, then turned west. Clair didn't walk so much as glide. Every five or six steps we stopped and he would listen.

At the northwest corner near the path through the woods to his barn, he put his hand out and stopped. We froze. There was a skittering noise, then a faint bump, like a cat had jumped onto a table. Clair slipped a flashlight from his vest, flicked it on. A flying squirrel skittered up the trunk of an ash tree.

"Look at that," Clair said. "That's why we live here."

"Beth won't come through the woods," I said.

"Maybe she knows that's what you think. Maybe the drugs make her see in the dark. Maybe she'll bring a friend who knows the woods."

"Prepare for the worst?" I said.

We walked. My eyes were adjusted to the dark and I could see the blue-black shadows, the shades of gray where there had been only a thick blackness.

I told Clair about Julie Barber, the girl who had died in the Bangor fire. I told him about the gas stove, the explosion.

"If this Tommy fella knew her, could make him extra jumpy, somebody setting houses on fire," he said.

"Troubling," I said. "I'm not sure why."

"I think it's because you're realizing you don't know any of these people. The artist lady who drinks. The Marine in the woods. The fake CIA guy and these real estate people."

"Don't forget Don, our guy out of a pickup truck commercial who landed here from Georgia."

"When it comes right down to it," Clair said, "we give people occasional glimpses through whatever windows we care or need to open. Other than that, we're strangers shaping other strangers to fit our needs."

He glanced at me. "Present company excepted."

"Likewise," I said. "You and me, we're a couple of open books."

We walked as far as the paddock and the barn, turned toward the road, and made our way out to Clair's house. Then we reversed course, did half the loop, and turned back. Did a quarter of the loop and turned again.

"Never want to let the enemy see a pattern," Clair said. "If you set one, break it. You want to be unpredictable."

The next hour passed in silence. The next. And then it was 4:15 and the sky was brightening to the east. On the road in front of our house, Clair said he was ready to turn in, sleep two or three hours until breakfast.

"Unless Mary's had the locks changed," he said, smiling.

He walked up the road, his usual pace. I turned to our house, the night-light glowing in the bathroom. I walked east again, went through the back half of the loop. I was thinking that I should get my deer rifle next time—that the Glock seemed small against the wall of trees and tangle.

I crossed the back lawn and went up onto the deck, unlocked the padlock on the mudroom door, and let myself in. The house was quiet, the kitchen clock ticking, the refrigerator humming.

I went to the closet, got the rifle out, the box of thirty-aught cartridges. I unlocked the trigger lock, loaded the rifle, then went back outside to the deck. I sat in an Adirondack chair, the rifle across my lap, and listened to the building crescendo of songbirds. Their world had none of this mayhem, I thought, then caught myself. They could be killed or eaten at any moment, not necessarily in that order.

I mulled it over. What sort of world was Sophie living in, sheltered as much as humanly possible? In two or three years, she'd be aware of all of it. The world of my stories and Roxanne's work. I wrote about people who were flawed, weak, struggling. Roxanne tried to minimize the damage in those lives. In the process, did we bring those people into Sophie's life? Did we expose her to the underbelly of country life? And maybe the reality of Clair's years as a commando would be revealed—that the grandfatherly man who had bought her a pony was trained to kill, and was very good at it.

But for now, it was a fairy tale she lived in Prosperity, Maine. Mom and Dad. Clair and Mary. Pokey, the wonder pony. Her outfit for the first day of school. A false idyll.

I watched the sky turn pink to the east, like it was a sponge sucking up a rose-colored sea. Heard crows hectoring a hawk or an owl.

Smelled smoke.

30

I walked to the door, poked my head inside, and sniffed. Nothing.

I turned back outside, head raised to the wind. I leapt off the stairs, rifle still in my hand. Crossed the grass. The smell was stronger to the west, toward Clair's. I looked to the woods, the brush, the path.

Started to run.

Down the path, sprinting until the barn came into sight, nothing showing. I slowed, trotted through the dooryard, the smell stronger now. A brush fire? A woodstove fire? I rounded the barn, ran around the paddock, heard Pokey kicking in his stall. Turned the corner, saw flames. Screamed to Clair, "Fire! The barn!" Pointed the Glock to the sky and pulled the trigger.

The flames were at the base of the building, the door that led to the open area below Pokey. Clair burst out of the house as I ran for the workshop and shouted, "Back doors—flames showing!"

I slammed the door open, saw the workshop dim with smoke. I ran across the shop, grabbed an extinguisher off the bench, another from the wall. Slamming the shop doors open, I ran deeper into the barn, the smoke dense and acrid.

At Pokey's stall, I wrestled the door open, found him circling and snorting. I dropped the extinguishers, grabbed his mane and yanked him, but he fought and bit and lashed out with his front hooves, scraping my shin. I got beside him and held him and ran him toward the door and he twisted to get free, whinnied, and dug in. I ran him again, like a football tackle and this time he went partway through the door, started to run toward the light. I was behind him as he hit the half-door to the paddock, kicked at it. I backed into him, felt hooves slash at my legs, a bite at my back. Got the latch free, threw the door open. Pokey knocked me aside and ran into the paddock, circling and shaking his head.

Clair was running for the back of the barn, pulling a hose, so I turned, and ran back into the stall and out, grabbing the extinguishers. At the last stall, I moved across the floor, yanked the trap door open, and saw flames. I aimed one extinguisher in, fired it off. The flames turned to smoke and I heard hissing as Clair trained the water on the fire from outside. I emptied the second extinguisher, fell back from the smoke.

Coughing, I ran in a crouch to the paddock door, plunged out into the clean air, climbed the fence, and half fell off the other side. I stumbled to the back corner of the building, turned, and saw the hose leading into the open double doors. I slid around the corner in the muck.

Clair had turned the hose off and was standing in the dim light, water dripping from the ceiling onto his head and shoulders. He pointed to hay bales that had been dragged to the corner of the dirt-floored room.

And lit on fire.

"Meant to be a warning," Clair said. "He could've torched the wall. Hay was burning, but it was going to take a while."

"Tell Pokey that," I said.

"Somebody's liking this. Showing you they can walk right into your backyard. Could have killed your daughter's pony."

"Got past both of us."

"When the guard changes, the most vulnerable point."

"He's not stupid," I said.

"No," Clair said. "But not as smart as he thinks he is."

I looked at him, his silver hair plastered to his head, his face smudged.

"Torched a man's property," he said. "Coulda killed that pony."

He trained the hose on the bales, squeezed the nozzle. Water came out in a steady stream, beating on the hay.

"Gonna run this guy to ground," Clair said, not to me but to himself.

"Or she," I said.

It was getting to be a regular thing, standing in a huddle of cops, staring at some burned stuff. The usual cast: Reynolds, Derosby, Foley, the trooper bending low to ease under the beams. Reynolds was squatting, eyeing the hay bales. She shone a flashlight on the bales, the manure and mud.

"Always this soft?" she said.

Clair nodded.

"Here we go. Footprints, back toward the field." Reynolds bent close to the sodden and charred hay. She sniffed. "Charcoal lighter," Reynolds said. "He was rubbing your nose in it. Smoky fire like that."

She looked at Clair.

"Where was the hay?"

"Out back. I put a few bales out for the deer in the fall. Had some stacked by the door."

Reynolds rose and turned and we all went with her, moving out from under the barn and toward the woods, fifty feet back. She stepped into the burdocks, scuffed around with her boot, then bent and parted the bushes. There was a red-and-white plastic bottle standing upright, a Bic gas charcoal lighter sticking out of the spout.

"Didn't want to carry those too far," she said. "We'll process them, but I'll bet they're clean."

She stood.

"So what the hell, Mr. McMorrow. Why drive all the way up here to light a fire that's barely a fire? I mean, he can do houses and whole barns, have fire trucks and sirens and crowds watching. Why burn a soggy hay bale?"

"To show that next time it might not be just hay," Clair said.

"Make me sweat a little," I said.

"But why?" Reynolds said. "What's the fun in that? People who do this, they like to see the towering inferno, you know? They want fire, baby. Flames shooting into the sky."

"Doesn't fit," Derosby said.

"Not a classic serial arsonist?" I said.

"This is somebody with something else going on," Clair said.

"Right," Reynolds said with unabashed relish. "This sort of psychological game, toying with people's heads. That goes beyond a typical thrill arsonist. They get off on the fire, the power. And sure, there's the excitement of getting away with it."

"But this person doesn't seem to always need the fire," I said.

"Right," Reynolds said. "It's like the fire is part of it, but there's something bigger in the background."

"Never worked on a case where it seemed like the idea was more to jerk people around," Derosby said.

"Killing a kid," I said. "That's serious jerking."

Clair took off his Stihl hat, put it back on and adjusted it. We looked at him and waited.

"Vietcong," he said. "They'd mix it up. Burn a village. Disappear the leaders. Poison the well. People wake up, the head of the village leader is on a stake outside his house. You never knew what was coming. That's what kept people terrorized."

"But who does he want to frighten?" I said.

"Maybe he has an ax to grind with the whole town," Reynolds said.

"Or," Clair said, "maybe there's one target."

"Lasha. Dr. Talbot. Don Barbier," I said.

"Arson to cover up another crime?" Derosby said.

"Then a lot of people are in the wrong place at the wrong time," I said.

We told Sophie that Pokey didn't feel good and needed to have a quiet day in the paddock, a break from being ridden. She and Roxanne filled a small bag with apples and carrots. Roxanne said she could bring Pokey's special treat—sugar cubes. When the bag was full, we started out the door onto the deck but then we steered Sophie toward the driveway and the road. The brush along the path offered too much cover.

When we got to the house, Mary was standing at the paddock fence, rubbing Pokey's muzzle. Clair came out of the barn, said, "Hey, pumpkin. Pokey was just asking where you've been."

"He can't talk human being," Sophie said.

"But I can talk pony," Clair said, and he snorted and whinnied and Sophie laughed and ran to Pokey. Mary lifted her to the top of the fence and she held out a carrot and Pokey, recovered from his morning, started to munch.

We stood, the three of us.

Clair said to Roxanne, "How you doing, honey?" and she said she was doing okay.

"We'll get him," he said.

"State Police dog tracked him all the way back to the ridge, then along there to a logging road, and then back to where he parked," I said.

"How'd he find his way right to that spot?" Roxanne said.

"GPS, probably," Clair said.

"Don Barbier said he scouted out his house on Google Earth," I said. "Knew the terrain on his property right down to the bush before he set foot in Maine."

Nobody answered.

Sophie jumped down from the fence and scurried toward Roxanne, who had the bag of carrots.

"Daddy, you need a haircut," Sophie said. "Go to the barber."

I looked at her. She said it again.

Barbier. Julie Barber. Dead in a fire, Julie Barber.

"What does 'Barbier' mean? In French?"

"Barber," Roxanne said.

"Listen," I said. "Can you guys stay here with Sophie and Pokey? For a couple of hours?"

Nods from Clair and Roxanne.

"I'll be back," I said.

I took the path. Out of their sight, I broke into a trot. Sparrows flushed and dove back into the brambles ahead of me. A red squirrel flashed into the woods, chirred as I passed. And then I was crossing the yard, unlocking the door to the mudroom. I closed it behind me, stood in the dim coolness and listened. Nothing. I moved to the inside door, unlocked that, too. Eased the door open and stepped into the still of the house.

Into the kitchen, the study. Went to the laptop and flipped it open. Searched for DONALD BARBIER, BANGOR, MAINE.

One hit. A lawyer. Palmer, Cloutier, and Barbier. I searched for the JULIE BARBER OBITUARY, clicked through.

She was survived by her mother, Nancy M. Barber, one brother, Terrence J. Barber.

I went on to the State Police website, scrolled down to the Bangor arson. Deceased: Julie Barber and Ross Lucas. Status: Open. Investigator: Davida Reynolds.

I leaned back in my chair, slipped my phone from my pocket, and called her.

"Hey," I said. "Where are you?"

"Driving," Reynolds said. "Route 17, near Jefferson. Headed for Augusta."

"Turn around and head back this way," I said.

I watched Reynolds back the Suburban in next to the propane tanks behind the Quik-Mart. She walked over and got into my truck, saying, "You don't mind meeting here? Saves me from having to go back to my office." She eased into the seat as I pulled a notebook out from under her butt.

"Sorry. Hey, you know your hay burner raked the gravel behind his car after he pulled onto the pavement? Didn't want tire impressions."

"No dope," I said. "Ex-cop?"

"Or watches a lot of CSI. Either way, I'm liking this."

The ex-jock, the challenge.

"You're assigned to an old arson fatality in Bangor," I said.

"Yeah," she said. "Cold case. We divide 'em up."

"Dead girl was Julie Barber, from Bucksport."

"Right."

"Any idea who did it?"

"I don't know."

"No theories?"

"I think the file says the guy killed with her was some sort of low-level drug dealer. I don't remember his name."

"Ross Lucas," I said.

"Right. Investigators at the time thought it was retribution."

"For what?"

Reynolds paused, that long hesitation while a cop decides whether to trust a reporter.

"Skimmed some of the product?" I prodded. "Faked a robbery?"

"You missed one," she said.

"Ratting somebody out?"

"Maybe you should've been a cop, Mr. McMorrow."

"I have trouble picking sides," I said. "Even if it is the good guys. So if the drug dealers knocked Lucas and Barber off—"

"Why didn't we catch them?" Reynolds said. "Maybe they hadn't been quite ratted out yet."

"So you had the informants on the line but hadn't yet set the hook?"

"Not me. I was in kindergarten. Investigator who worked it for us was in his last year before retirement."

"You ever talk to him?"

"Once. As I recall, they had names, three or four guys, possible suspects. But nothing close to concrete, and they scattered."

"This investigator still around?"

"Yeah, but he may not be very helpful. He has some sort of dementia."

"Too bad," I said.

"Yeah, must be hard on the family."

"For the case, I meant. Can I see the file?"

She gave me her bemused look, like she was impressed by my chutzpah.

"It's an ongoing investigation."

"Sounds pretty closed to me," I said. "Twenty years old, investigator has Alzheimer's, you're assigned to it, and you haven't thought about it in—"

"I've thought about it."

"Lately?"

"No."

"Come on. Just a peek."

"No can do, Mr. McMorrow."

"Who's the investigator?"

"Linwood Penney."

"Where is he?"

"Assisted living."

"Where?"

"Jeesh, Mr. McMorrow. Why so interested in a cold case when you've got hot ones popping up all around you?"

It was my turn to hesitate. Would Reynolds think I was nuts, playing a hunch from a five-year-old's chatter? She leaned forward in her seat so she could fix her eyes on mine. And she smiled.

"Come on, Mr. McMorrow," Reynolds said. "Spit it out."

I took a breath, then told her about Barbier, the French, Sophie's suggestion that I get a haircut.

"Bit of a reach," she said.

"She had a brother," I said. "Terrence."

"So you start with Barber, change it to Barbier?" she said. "Why?"

"I don't know."

"And if our Don's sister died in an arson fire, don't you think he'd be a lot more upset? I've talked to the guy. He seems to take it all in stride."

"Seems," I said.

"Why hide it, if he's this Terrence Barber?"

"I don't know."

"So what are you thinking?"

"I'm not sure," I said. "I just think it's an odd coincidence."

Reynolds looked at me, cocked an eyebrow.

"You're not putting this in your story, are you?"

"No, I'm just curious."

"Hey, I'm curious, too, Mr. McMorrow. But I'm more curious about what's going on today, in the here and now. Like who set your friend's barn on fire."

"I appreciate that," I said. "But there's something eating me about this town."

"Yes, there is," she said. "Somebody's trying to burn it down."

She shifted in the seat, readying to go. "Always good to chat with you, Mr. McMorrow," she said. "And I mean that." She reached for the latch, popped the door, and climbed out.

"Hey," I said, "where's this assisted-living place?"

Reynolds was standing by the open door. She turned back over her shoulder. "Bucksport," she said.

"Like the girl who died?"

"Coincidence. Penney lived in Brewer. They stick these people anywhere they can find a room."

"I'm sure," I said.

"Don't get your hopes up, Mr. McMorrow. Last time I went to visit, he thought I was his daughter."

Bucksport was thirty miles up the coast, where the Penobscot River flowed on its way to the bay. As I watched Reynolds's Suburban pull away, I looked at my watch; it was 3:35 p.m. Forty-five minutes to get there, call on the way and find out which of the assisted-living places had a Mr. Linwood Penney. Find Mr. Penney and sit with him long enough to figure out whether he remembered anything about the Julie Barber murder. I had a couple of hours before I needed to be back to relieve Clair, settle in for the night.

I drove fast, pounding the truck down the back roads. I flew through Hope, took the back road to Belfast. The truck motor whined as I whipped over potholes, skimmed the bumps, tapped the brakes for the occasional four-corners, the flashing yellow caution lights blinking.

At Belfast I crossed the bridge, then swung north, off of tourist-clogged Route 1, put the pedal to the floor. I passed trucks, old couples in sagging cars, went airborne on an unexpected rise. The tires chirped, the truck started to swing right, then left. I backed off, made Swanville, a smattering of houses and trailers at a crossroads, then swung east. Tacking left and right, I ran the back roads, past corners bearing the names of people who were dead and forgotten.

And then I was back on Route 1, the tourists continuing their slow procession, like traders in a caravan bound for some desert market. In traffic, I searched on my phone for "assisted living" and Bucksport. Came up with five possibilities and started calling.

"Hi, this is Jack McMorrow. I'm a friend of Linwood Penney's. Could you tell me if he's up to having a visitor?"

The first three had no one there by that name. The phone at the fourth was answered by a cheery-sounding young woman who said she'd check. I drove off Route 1 and headed for the Penobscot Narrows Bridge.

"Mr. Penney is awake," the young woman said, like I'd won the lottery.

"Great," I said. "Be there in ten minutes."

This was the River View Home, and the GPS put it among the old stately houses that were clustered above Bucksport's Main Street, overlooking the Penobscot River and the paper mill.

It was an optimistic sort of town, a little tired but still trying, with coffee shops and a bookstore and orange signs that told motorists to stop for pedestrians. There weren't any when I cruised through, took a right, a left, another right, and saw the sign for the River View Home, hanging outside a white Victorian house that might have been built by a sea captain or a mill manager. Now it had wheelchair ramps built of pea-green treated wood, blue signs that designated handicapped parking.

I parked on the street, a half block up, and walked back. There was another sign that said VISITORS and pointed toward a side door. I walked up the ramp, opened the door, and walked in.

It had been a parlor, but now was like a dentist's office waiting room. I walked to the window and a woman reached from her chair and slid it open. I said I was there to see Linwood Penney.

She said, "Oh, yeah. He's expecting you." As she closed the window she called to someone, "Is Mr. Penney ready for his visitor?"

He apparently was, because the same cheery woman on the phone came through a door and greeted me like I was her long-lost English teacher.

"Mr. McMorrow. How lovely to see you."

She was short and wide but with a broad, gum-revealing smile that said her cheeriness could not be deterred by any magnitude of tragedy. She introduced herself as Vanda, pronounced like veranda.

"Mr. Penney is going to be thrilled to have an old friend visit," Vanda said, taking me by the arm, like I might fall down. Habit. And then she led me from the waiting room, through a door that led to a hallway. The room was the last one on the left.

"Now, Mr. McMorrow," Vanda said, drawing me closer. "You know that Mr. Penney isn't quite as sharp as he was years ago."

"I've been told."

"Are you a policeman?" she said.

"Sort of an investigator," I said.

"Really," Vanda said. "How exciting."

"It can be," I said.

"Sometimes Mr. Penney tries to tell us about his work."

"Tries?"

"He gets frustrated," Vanda said. "It's common in the early to middle stages of his illness. Where you know that the information is in there, if you could only get to it."

She smiled, like memory loss was a pleasant sort of game.

Vanda opened the door. It was a small room: single bed, dresser, table, an easy chair with a folding chair beside it. Linwood Penney was in the easy chair, facing us. A thin, sunken sort of figure, he had combed-over salt-and-pepper hair and gold-rimmed glasses. He was wearing blue jeans and a long-sleeved T-shirt, the kind with a dark middle and white sleeves, like a coach would wear. His hands were folded on his lap.

"Mr. Penney," Vanda said loudly, as though volume could cut through his mental confusion. "This is your friend, Mr. McMorrow. He's come to visit. Isn't that nice?"

"Yes," he said, his voice a little croaky.

I crossed the room, held out my hand. He took it, gave me a hearty handshake, all the while peering at my face for a clue, like acquaintances at a high school reunion.

"How you doing?" I said.

"Good," Penney said. "Fine. They're very nice here."

Vanda beamed.

"Yes," I said. "They seem to be."

"Well, I'll leave you two guys to talk about old times," Vanda said.

She left. I pulled the folding chair around so I could see Mr. Penney's face. He smiled, gave me the searching look again.

"Did we work together?" he said.

"Not really," I said. "I was a reporter."

"Ah," Penney said, grinning. A clue.

"I don't read the newspaper anymore," Penney said.

"Doesn't interest you?"

He shook his head, but seemed perplexed.

"You know I don't remember things," he said.

"I know. That's okay."

"You sure we didn't work together?"

He examined me, his eyes squinting in concentration.

"Maybe our paths crossed years ago," I said. "Twenty years."

"Oh, yeah. What'd you say your name was—Jimmy, right?"

I didn't answer.

"I liked it, working the fires. Like a puzzle. Some of the people here, they do puzzles. A million little pieces. I don't care for that."

"Right," I said.

He sat, his hands folded on his lap again. He was wearing black shiny tie shoes, and he looked down as if surprised to see them.

"You caught a lot of bad guys," I said.

"Oh, yeah. There were some real bad apples."

"Murderers, even," I said.

"Yes, some of them were murderers."

"Shame about the people who died."

"My wife died, I think," Penney said. "She doesn't come here."

"Julie Barber, too," I said. "She died."

"Julie," he said.

"Died in the fire," I said. "The gas-stove explosion. In Bangor."

He looked away.

"Bound her up," he said. "With duct tape. Wrists. Ankles. Mouth. Lucas too."

"Ross Lucas."

"That sounds right. Bartender. And the girl."

"They'd just started dating?"

"Yeah. Bad luck. Remember? We told her mother she died of smoke but she didn't."

"A white lie," I said.

"Yeah," he said. "The lie was bad enough."

He was sorting mentally, face screwed up at the effort. Then the lightbulb.

"Extension cords, too, but the whatchamacallit, the stuff on the outside," he said, holding his hands out like he was handcuffed.

"Plastic," I said.

"Yeah. It burned off."

He rubbed his chin, the gray stubble.

"Julie," he repeated, pronouncing the word carefully, like he was learning a new language.

"She was only nineteen," I said. "Very young."

"Yes," he said. "She was alive, you know."

"Alive when?" I said.

"Alive when they burned the house. I remember that. Awful."

He looked at me.

"What did you say your name was?"

"Jack," I said. "Now, Julie. In the fire. You didn't catch those bad guys?"

He looked away.

"Bound her up. With duct tape. Wrists, ankles, mouth. The guy with her, too."

"Lucas," he said.

"Ross Lucas," I said.

"That sounds right. Bartender. And the girl."

"They'd just started dating?"

"Yeah. Bad luck. Remember? We told her mother she died of smoke, but she didn't."

"The white lie," I said.

Penney scowled, pale face wrinkling. I could see a whiskery patch on his cheek that he'd missed when he shaved.

"Told the father the truth. The boyfriend, too. Said they'd kill the guys. I remember that."

"Did they?"

"No. The druggies, they ran. I went to California, almost caught up with them. Awful traffic out there."

"Yes," I said.

Penney was quiet for a minute, rummaging through his memories, rubbing his lips with his forefinger.

"Pretty girl," he said. "In her picture."

"Yes."

"Boyfriend was lucky, have a girl like that. You remember him? Big handsome kid. Played something. Basketball? Baseball?"

"Right."

"Mark. No, Erik. No, Derek," Penney said.

I looked at him. Smiled.

"That's right," I said. "Derek. What was his last name?"

Penney shook his head. "Oh, jeez. It was . . . like the baseball player."

"Mickey Mantle?"

He scowled.

"Oh, I hate this."

"It's okay," I said.

He turned away and stared at the wall. I couldn't tell if he was thinking or if he'd checked out, but then he turned back to me.

"Say, hey," Penney said.

"What?"

"Say hey. The Say Hey Kid?"

"Willie Mays," I said.

He grinned, held his hand up for a high five.

"It's Derek Mays?"

"I got it," he said.

"You have a good memory," I said.

"Isn't what it used to be," Penney said.

"Mine isn't either," I said, and then we were quiet for a couple of minutes.

There were women's voices in the hallway, the rattle of a cart going down the hall. He pulled his legs up and set his black-shoed feet side by side.

"The drug dealers," I said. "The ones who killed Julie. Who were they?"

"Bad, bad people. To do something like that. For what? For nothing."

"You remember their names?"

He thought. "I used to know that. Went to California. Traffic was hellacious."

"Right. You don't recall the names now?"

"No," Penney said. "I can picture them. Old and young and one in between."

"Still out there somewhere," I said.

"I think they're dead," Penney said.

"Why?" I said.

"I don't know. I think somebody told me. Somebody said—"

Vanda pushed the door open and stepped in.

"—the goddamn head motherfucker is dead," Penney said.

"Mr. Penney," Vanda said, putting her hand to her mouth. "My goodness."

"When?" I said.

"I don't know," he said.

"Where?"

He shook his head, looked up at Vanda, standing there with her smile on. "What's your name again?" he asked her.

"Oh, you know my name, Mr. Penney," she said. "I'm Vanda."

He eyed her. "No," he said. "You're not."

I was walking down the hallway, the antiseptic smell layered over the stale odor of moldering humanity. A heavy woman in light blue slacks, a red printed top, squeezed by me. I was someone's visiting friend, brother, son—not a reporter faking his way in, talking the dementia patient out of information.

And then another woman—small and trim, short white hair, jeans and clogs. I bent to tie my shoe, turned and followed her after she passed. As she approached Penney's room, I called out.

"Excuse me."

She turned. There was a weariness in the set of her eyes, a woman who had been left on her own way too soon.

"Yes."

"You're Mrs. Penney?"

"That's right."

"I'm Jack McMorrow. I was just talking with your husband."

She turned warily, searching for a clue.

"Are you a detective?"

"A reporter."

She took a step back.

"Oh, but my husband has been retired for several years now. He's disabled."

"I know, Mrs. Penney," I said. "But I'm writing about one of his cases. Julie Barber."

A wave of sadness passed over her.

"The girl in the fire."

"Yes."

"That one stayed with me. With both of us. But why now?"

"Something's come up that may be connected to it."

Mrs. Penney waited, not quite convinced.

"I've been talking to the investigator on the case now. Davida Reynolds."

She shook her head. "I don't know the new people."

"No, and they don't know that case the way your husband does."

"Did," she said. "You know he has dementia?"

"Yes," I said.

"He may not remember any of it. Or he may remember it like it was yesterday. It's impossible to predict."

"We talked," I said.

"And?"

"He remembered a lot."

She looked proud.

"Well, that's good. That one really bothered him. The girl. The way . . . the way it happened."

"Yes," I said. "Horrible."

"He went to California. He really wanted to catch them."

"But he didn't find them?"

"Oh, California. You can imagine. All those millions of people. Easy to get lost, not like Maine."

"Yes," I said. "Mrs. Penney, I was wondering . . ."

The wariness again, like a veil.

"Did Mr. Penney keep files of his own? I know a lot of investigators do, if they're really into a particular case. The file that they have in Augusta now doesn't have much in it at all."

She considered it. I waited, trying to exude trustworthiness.

"There are boxes in the basement," she said. "I never touch them."

"Might I look sometime? See if the Julie Barber case is in there?"

Mrs. Penney hesitated.

"Do you have an ID?"

I showed her my Times ID, gave her my card.

"New York?" she said.

"I write for them here in Maine," I said. "I live in Prosperity. Over near Knox."

She looked at the card, turned it over and back again.

"Why don't you call me," she said. "We live in Lincolnville Center now."

We, not I.

"You can look. I haven't thrown anything out. Just in case—"

She paused.

"He gets better?" I said.

"I know the odds are a million to one. Maybe a million to zero. But Linwood—did you know him? When he was working?"

"No," I said. "But I've heard good things about him. He was very well respected."

Mrs. Penney beamed. Another white lie, worth every word.

"Sometimes I feel like just whacking him upside the head. Like smacking the side of the television, you know? Maybe get the picture to come back clear again."

I smiled. Handed her my pen and notebook.

"Your number. Could you write it there?"

She hesitated but then did it. Handed the pen and notebook back.

"I'll call you," I said.

"Okay," she said. "But you'll have to sort through the stuff yourself. I never go down there. It makes me too sad."

She turned toward the room, squared her shoulders. "Are you married?"

"Yes," I said.

"Well, you can just imagine."

"No," I said. "I can't."

I drove down the hill to the little downtown area of Bucksport, sat at the red light and waited. Some teenagers were standing on the corner, leggy girls with eyeliner, gangly boys on clacketing skateboards.

I called Roxanne. The phone rang and she answered.

"Hey," I said.

"Hi there," she said.

"Anything from the cops?"

"Not a peep."

"What are you doing?"

"Playing checkers with Clair and Sophie," she said. "The three of us. It's a round robin."

"Who's dominating?"

"Your daughter, but she bends the rules."

"Takes after her father," I said.

"Yes," Roxanne said. "She does."

I said I was on my way home, and told her about my visit with Mr. Penney. I left out the details about Julie Barber being tied up, the electrical cord, that she was burned alive.

The light turned green. The kids on the corner had sauntered into the street. They stood in the road in front of my truck as one of the boys bent to tie his shoe. The light changed to yellow and then red. They looked at me defiantly and walked on.

"Little bastards," I said.

"What?" Roxanne said.

"Nothing," I said. "Give Sophie a hug."

I pulled onto the main street and parked, got out of the truck, and walked down the block. There was a laundry, a five-and-ten, a thrift store, and a hair salon called Clip 'n' Snip. I stopped to look in the window. It was a bunch of women, most in their thirties and forties. One guy fiddling with a woman's hair.

I opened the door and a chime rang. There was a woman at a front desk, made up and well-coiffed. Looked like a mannequin until she moved.

"Hi there," I said.

"Hi there, yourself," she said.

"I'm hoping you can help me."

"Trim? A little highlighting?"

The women giggled, someone said, "Have a seat."

"Another time, thanks. Today I just have a question."

I took out my phone, scrolled through the photos. Then I held it up to the woman and said, "I need to ID a guy in a picture. Somebody said his name was Derek Mays, but I don't know. I think he went to school here; he'd be about forty now."

"What are you? A cop?" the front-desk woman said.

"A reporter," I said. "Jack McMorrow. You know Derek?"

"Do I look forty?" she said. She looked over at one of the older stylists and said, "Sorry."

Then she said to me, "Why don't you just ask him?"

"He left. I won't be able to find him again if I don't get his name right."

It sounded lame. I kept going.

"The guy was at the scene of something I was covering. It was kind of hectic."

"What was it? A murder?" the receptionist said.

"Karen," a woman protested. "Please."

"Something like that," I said. "Will you look?"

Karen took the phone, looked at the photo, said, "I'd like to talk to him, too. Kinda cute."

"How cute?" one of the stylists said.

Another said, "Let me see."

Karen got up from behind the desk and passed my phone over. It made the rounds, the women peering at the screen. I moved between the chairs, following the phone down the line, like the collection plate in a church. And then we were at the last chair. The hair stylist, fit and slim in jeans and cowboy boots and an undersized black T-shirt, was tying little ribbon sort of things in the woman's hair. He paused, looked at the phone, then held it up for the woman in the chair.

"My goodness," she said. "Look at Derek Mays, all grown up."

31

Her name was Susan, and Derek had been a friend of her older brother's. She'd had a crush on Derek but he'd never noticed her. He wasn't available anyway because he'd been dating Julie Barber since ninth grade, her sophomore year. Then Julie had gone to the University of Maine, and after a while they'd split up, so they could date other people. Derek had gone to the prom with another girl and Julie was seeing some guy she'd met waitressing in Orono.

"And then they got back together," Susan said. "Like, a week before she died."

"Oh, that's so sad," Karen said, and then Susan leaned toward me and confided, so that the whole room could hear: "I heard she got into drugs."

"Did the fire have to do with drugs?" I said.

"That was what people were saying. That Julie got in with the wrong crowd."

"Did Derek?"

"Oh, no. He was Mr. Clean. In high school he didn't party at all. I mean, he could've, but he kinda kept to himself. When he wasn't with Julie, I mean. One of those high school couples—it's like the rest of the world doesn't exist."

"You know the guy who died with her?" I said.

"No," Susan said. "He was older. Wasn't from here."

"Where'd Derek go afterwards?"

"Moved away, I guess," Susan said. "His parents split up just before all of it happened. I mean, he was an only child, too. So everything kind of fell apart for him. I thought he must have joined the service or something."

I held out the phone again.

"You're sure that's him?"

She took the phone and looked at the photo of Don Barbier at the fire scene, the crowd behind him. Karen and Jason leaned over and looked, too.

"Yeah, well, pretty sure. He's older and heavier and his hair is different and he has the beard. But I'm pretty sure that's Derek. You don't forget your first crush, right?"

"I guess not," I said, as she handed the phone back.

"So what are they all looking at in the picture?" she said.

"A fire," I said. "A house was burning."

"Another one?" Jason said. "I mean, really. What are the chances of that?"

I waited in the truck, small-town life flowing by me like I was a rock in the middle of a stream. Old people driving slow. A teenage girl on the phone, pushing a baby in a stroller.

After twenty minutes Susan came out, hair done up, and started for the parking lot. I pulled ahead and behind her SUV. Got out and walked to the driver's door.

Susan looked up, buzzed the window down.

"Hey," she said.

"Hi," I said.

"More questions?"

"Just one," I said. "Anything else you remember about Derek? Maybe didn't want to say in there?"

Susan stared for a moment, said, "You don't miss much."

I shrugged and smiled. She reached the key in, started the motor. I thought I'd lost her, but then she said, "He had his whole life figured out."

"How so?"

"Eighteen years old. I mean, this friend of mine, she was at a party. This was after he'd split up with Julie. My friend, she decides she's gonna hook up with him. Good-looking girl, too. I mean, wicked cute. Knockout figure. She comes on to him."

"And he says no?" I said.

"Not just that. He said he was gonna marry Julie after they got back together. And he got all pissed off. Like she was trying to wreck his world or something. I mean, it was way extreme. Like he didn't want anybody pushing him off this path. Had the blinders on. Marry the cheerleader, have kids, live in a nice house—the whole picket-fence thing."

"Interesting," I said.

"Yeah. I figured it was some reaction to his parents splitting up," Susan said, pulling at the bow at the back of her head. "And I remember thinking, well, it better work out. Because you're burning all your other bridges."

I called Davida Reynolds from the truck as I left Bucksport. She called me back as I reached the end of Main Street, turned with the Bar Harbor tourists to cross the small branch of the Penobscot. I told my story all the way to the Verona bridge, the cars slowing as everyone craned to see the view.

"I don't know, Mr. McMorrow," Reynolds said. "Maybe Barbier just looks like this guy."

"The woman was pretty sure."

"Twenty years is a long time."

"Sure, but if it is him, don't you think it's odd? His girlfriend dies in an arson fire, and now there are all these arson fires happening around him?"

"I don't remember the details, but I don't recall that Derek was a suspect."

"Who were the suspects?"

"DEA had a couple of names," she said. "Bad guys from Lawrence, Mass., I think. One from New York City, maybe. The Bronx? I'd have to look."

"But Ross Lucas, the guy Julie had been dating, died with her. Maybe Derek didn't want to lose her," I said. "This woman at the hair salon said she thought that Derek and Julie had decided to get back together just before she died."

I paused.

"See," Reynolds said, "that doesn't make sense."

"Maybe she changed her mind," I said, coming off the bridge, sliding into the shadows left by the sinking sun.

"So he ties up the love of his life and her new beau and burns them alive?"

"Crime of passion."

"One that took expert planning and preparation," Reynolds said. "The perp would have to be absolutely cold-blooded, and Barbier seems like a perfectly normal guy."

"Don't they all," I said.

"As a matter of fact, no," she said. "Spend enough time with these people and you begin to see through the cracks."

"Not if he's a true sociopath."

"Who's burning down his own property?"

We were quiet for a minute, still on the phone. I drove, the river somewhere to my left, the sun behind the ledges to my right, tourists driving at a stately pace. I heard Reynolds start the Suburban.

"Where are you?" I said.

"Leaving the Sanctuary General Store," she said. "Off the record?"

"Yes," I said.

"We're going to interview a person of interest. And search his house and vehicles."

"Really. Who is it?"

"Still off?

"Yes."

"Louis."

"The vet? Why?"

"We have this town totally saturated with law enforcement, especially if you count the citizen patrol. And this person can still navigate at will, set fires, disappear into thin air."

"Uh-huh," I said.

"You know where Louis went when he was in the military, for training?"

"No."

"Sapper school. And you know what they teach them there?"

"Tell me."

"Navigation. You know, like in the woods at night. Mountaineering. Reconnaissance. Raid and ambush operations. And, last but not least, demolition."

"Huh."

"And if you can blow stuff up, you can sure as heck set it on fire," Reynolds said.

"Sounds pretty circumstantial," I said. "What rubber stamp gave you that search warrant?"

"And your theory is based on rock-solid evidence?"

"No, it's based on the fact that I don't believe in coincidences."

"Go to the judge with that," Reynolds said.

"No, but I may go to Don Barbier with it," I said.

"And if you're right, he'll confess?"

"No, but it's like you said. You spend enough time with somebody, you see through the cracks."

"Huh," Reynolds said.

"Back on the record," I said.

"Yes."

"Are you close to an arrest?"

"No comment."

"Is your investigation progressing?"

"Yes."

"Mind if I call you later tonight?"

"No, I don't mind. Maybe I'll have something new to report."

"What if you can't find Louis?" I said.

"Oh, we know where he is," Reynolds said. "Off the record, since yesterday, we've had somebody on him every minute."

"He's a little touchy," I said. Be careful."

"You, too, Mr. McMorrow," she said. "You, too."

I was still in the driveway when Sophie hit me at a full run, leaping into my arms and wrapping her little legs around me. She clung there, telling me about her day—that she'd beaten Roxanne and Clair in checkers six times; that they'd made cupcakes and decorated them, and there were two just for me; that Pokey'd had a rest, but Clair said he'd be better in the morning; that she had macaroni and cheese out of the box for dinner as a special treat, and they were going to save me some but they forgot.

Sophie waggled her legs happily as I carried her into the house. Clair, at the kitchen table, said hello. Roxanne, scrubbing a pan in the sink, said nothing.

I put Sophie down and she ran to the refrigerator, yanked the big door open, and reached in for a can of Ballantine. She brought it to me and I took it and then she went to the counter, climbed her stepstool, and took a cupcake from the plate. She climbed down and brought it to me.

Drawn on the cupcake in frosting was a rough facsimile of a pony's head.

"It has a picture of Pokey on it," Sophie said. "Mommy helped me. You can have it with your beer."

"Thanks, honey," I said. "You have a nice mommy."

Roxanne put the pan on the counter, kept her back to me.

Sophie said, "Go ahead."

"Go ahead and what?" I said.

"Eat it."

"Oh. I am hungry."

I removed the paper and took a bite. Sophie bounced up and down and waited for my reaction. I chewed, then smiled.

"Aren't they delicious?" she said.

"Hmmm," I said.

"Clair needs another one," she said.

She went to the counter again. I stepped to Roxanne, put a hand on her shoulder.

"How are you?" I said.

"Okay, considering," she said.

Sophie bounced back, skipping across the kitchen.

"Honey, you know the pictures you did? Why don't you get them and show them to Daddy," Roxanne said.

Sophie whirled and dashed for the stairs.

"Considering what?" I said. "Did they find Beth?"

Roxanne turned to me.

"They found the car. An hour ago in Searsmont. But they think she took another one."

"Great," I said.

"But they don't know what kind of car it is. Or truck." Clair said. "Can't find the owners of the house to ask them."

We paused. Roxanne folded a towel and put it on the counter.

"So she's still out there," I said.

"That much is certain," Roxanne said, her voice cool but at the same time on edge.

"You'd think they'd be able to find her."

"Erratic folks," Clair said. "Sometimes they're the hardest to find because there's no pattern. You can't predict what they'll do next."

"No more texts to the TV station?"

They both shrugged.

"I just know that I feel like a prisoner in my own home," Roxanne said.

"I'm sorry, honey," I said.

"I'll head back out," Clair said, finishing his cupcake in two bites. Roxanne walked to him and handed him a napkin. He wiped his mouth, took a sip of coffee, and put the mug on the counter. I put the beer down beside it, unopened.

"Thank you, Clair," Roxanne said, squeezing his arm. "Thanks for everything."

"No thanks necessary," he said, and turned to the sliding glass door, open to the screen. Froze for a millisecond, and then had his Glock out, raised, ready.

I looked. Beth stood on the deck, six feet from the door.

32

She had a revolver in her right hand, hanging down along her thigh. She started to raise it and Clair barked, "Drop it."

Roxanne backpedaled into the kitchen.

"No, Beth," Clair shouted.

"Daddy," Sophie called from the hallway. "Wait 'til you see."

I lunged, ran into the hall, scooped her up, the papers flying. Roxanne had circled through the dining room, met us at the bottom of the stairs. I handed Sophie to her and she bolted up the steps, saying, "I'll call 911."

Sophie said "Mommy," and started to cry.

I turned, moved down the hallway until I could see them, Clair's back to me, two hands on the gun. Beth stood beyond him, wearing a black sweatshirt. The revolver was pressed to her temple through the hood.

"No, honey," Clair was saying. "Don't do that. I can help you. Come in and have a cup of coffee and we'll talk."

Beth smiled, shook her head.

"No, I'm really sorry," she said, her voice slurred and vague. "It's just that it's, like, time for somebody to pay, even if it's me."

She lowered the gun from her head, held it in front of her, pointed sideways.

"That's right," Clair said. "Now just toss it."

But Beth put it back to her head.

"I'll talk," she said. "Where's Roxanne? I'll talk to her."

I backed down the hallway, out the front door. I ran to the truck, yanked the passenger door open, the glove box. I took out the Glock, the clip. Jammed the clip in and ran along the side of the garage. At the end of the building, I stopped. Listened.

"Honey, we can sort this out," Clair was saying. "But the first thing you have to do is get rid of the gun so I can get rid of mine. Can't talk with all these guns around."

I stepped around the corner. There were dead lilacs, and I eased past them, the withered blossoms sprinkling down like snow.

I heard Beth saying, "Talk, talk, talk. All we ever fucking *do* is talk."

I moved closer, alongside the last bush.

"Then we can just sit," Clair said. "Sit and have a beer and figure out what to do next."

"What to do, what to do," Beth said, her voice singsong now, like Sophie humming to herself. "The important thing is to fucking do something, right? If we don't, it's just more of the same bullshit. I'm drowning in bullshit."

"No," Clair said. "Please don't."

I could see her now. The gun against her head. She was wavering on her feet, drunk or drugged, or both.

"Where is she?" Beth said. "Where's Roxanne? I want to talk to her. I want to talk to her so she can tell me all the things I'm doing wrong."

"You're fine, honey," Clair said. "Nothing's wrong."

"I'm not fine," Beth said. "I fucked up. You ask Roxanne. She'll tell you."

I was crouched at the corner, the gun low, my finger on the trigger. And then I heard Roxanne's voice from inside, saying, "Beth. This isn't the way. You know that. I know you do."

I heard Clair say something unintelligible, maybe warning Roxanne to stay back. And then Beth lowered the gun from her head, looked at it, raised it again, pointed it at the door.

"No, Beth," Roxanne said. "Do the right thing. Drop the gun. You can do it. Do it for Ratchet. Do it for him."

Beth took a step toward the house. I eased out, raised the gun. Beth took another step and I followed, keeping her in sight. And then I heard the screen slide open, Clair saying, "No, don't." And then he stepped through the door and onto the deck, the Glock in front of him, ready.

Beth raised the revolver, pointed it at his face. She was trembling, the barrel making small circles. From the distance came the sound of a siren.

"Go ahead," she said, beginning to cry. "Finish it. Go ahead."

And Clair lowered his gun. I could see that he was smiling.

"I'll do it," Beth screamed, stepping toward him, the gun leveled at his face. I stepped out, the Glock raised. Started to squeeze the trigger.

"No, Jack," Clair said. "Don't."

I eased off, barely. He slipped the Glock into the holster at the back of his waist. And then he stepped to Beth, took the gun from her hands, and put it down on the table.

Just like that.

She wobbled for a moment, like a tree about to fall. And then she collapsed into him, sobbing. He held her and I walked toward them, the Glock down. Roxanne stepped through the door.

Clair said softly, "It's okay, honey. It's really going to be okay."

Roxanne went to them, put her arm around Beth, and eased her to a chair. I went to the table, picked up the revolver, a heavy .38 with a six-inch barrel. I started to open the cylinder.

"It's not loaded," Clair said. "I could see the empty cylinder."

"You couldn't see behind the hammer," I said.

"Sometimes you go with your gut," Clair said.

I flipped the cylinder open and tipped it up. A single cartridge fell into my hand.

It was a sheriff's deputy who arrived first, but it was Trooper Foley who put Beth in the back of his cruiser. She rocked forward and back, her hands cuffed in front of her, her hood up. He sat beside her for five minutes, talking and taking notes, then got out and walked over to Clair and me, standing by the house.

"Is your wife—"

"She's with my daughter," I said. "Do you need to speak to her?"

Foley shook his head.

"Not now. Beth just said she wanted to tell her she's sorry. She was trying to die."

"Suicide by cop," I said. "Except it was Clair."

"Very troubled young lady," Clair said.

We looked over toward Beth, who had started to cry again, her sobs muffled from inside the car.

Foley said he was going to take her to the county jail in Belfast, that there were multiple charges, she wouldn't make bail. He had our statements, and Roxanne's; he'd be in touch with us if he had any questions. We said okay, and he walked to the cruiser, got in, and backed it out into the road. Beth stared at us through the rear window, forlorn and alone, like a stray dog collected from the street.

As the cruiser started to pull away she mouthed the words "I'm sorry."

"Lost soul," Clair said.

"Could have put a thirty-eight slug through your head," I said.

"But she didn't," he said.

"I was a hair away from shooting her."

"But you didn't."

He took a deep breath and looked up at the sky, rose-colored above the trees to the west, darkening to the east.

"This, my friend," Clair said, "is our lucky day."

He smiled, and there was bone-deep weariness in his eyes.

"I'm going to go home and have dinner with Mary, if she'll reheat it. You go tend to your girls."

I touched his shoulder and he said, "No man hugs," and walked down the driveway and up the road.

I went into the house, making my way up the stairs toward the sound of their voices. They were in Sophie's room with the door closed. I knocked and pushed it open, saw Roxanne on the bed with Sophie tucked in the crook of her arm. Sophie's face was blotchy and her eyes were red.

"Hi, Daddy," Sophie said.

"Hey, honey," I said, moving to her and sitting on the bed. "How's my girl?"

"I was scared," she said. "Because everybody was yelling and I was all by myself."

"That's a scary thing," I said.

"Is she gone?" Roxanne said.

"Yes," I said.

"Where did they take her?" Sophie said.

"To the jail," I said. "They'll help her to calm down, maybe give her some medicine. She can sleep. I think she was very tired."

"I could hear her crying," Sophie said.

"She's been upset," Roxanne said. "About her little boy."

"She should have another baby to make her happy," Sophie said.

"Maybe she will," I said, putting my arm around her shoulder. "Maybe she will."

Sophie was quiet, one of us on either side of her. She seemed small and delicate, precious and vulnerable. I held one of her hands in mine and she squeezed, her fingers barely covering my palm. I held it up and kissed it.

"Is Beth coming back?" she whispered.

"No, honey," I said. "She's not coming back."

Sophie fell asleep in our arms. We waited until she'd gone limp and I stood and held her while Roxanne pulled off her shorts and tucked her under the covers in her bed. There were two chairs by the window, and we sat. I took Roxanne's hand, bigger than Sophie's but still soft, and I looked out, saw the sun fall behind the trees, the flaming clouds billowing above it.

"It's over," I said softly. "Next they'll pick up Alphonse."

"I prayed to God," Roxanne said.

"Did you?"

"Yes. When she was standing there, I was praying."

"It worked," I said.

"Yes," Roxanne said. "I guess it did."

We were quiet, and then she said, "Will they let her out?"

"Not soon."

"Weeks?"

"At least. With the gun thing."

"There's good in her," Roxanne said.

"Hard to find it," I said.

"She's just all scrambled up."

"All the king's horses," I said.

"But I tried," Roxanne said, a tear spilling down her cheek.

"Yes," I said. "You did."

We were quiet again. A wood thrush was calling from the trees. I squeezed Roxanne's hand and she said, "Are we safe now, Jack?"

"One step closer," I said.

"Alphonse. The arsonist," she said. "Maybe we should move."

"This is our home."

"Maybe there's too much baggage. Maybe we need to start clean."

"Here," I said. "Right now."

"We were happy before," Roxanne said.

"We're still happy," I said. "We're very, very lucky."

"Sometimes I think we want this fairy-tale life and it doesn't exist. I mean, all around us. People hurting each other, in this beautiful place."

"It's still beautiful," I said.

"I want Sophie to believe in our fairy-tale life," Roxanne said. "But I don't want her to think we lied to her."

"She won't," I said. "We don't."

The thrush kept calling, another thrush answering from deeper in the woods. The sunset was deepening, from rose to red.

"I'm going to have her sleep with us again tonight," Roxanne said. "I don't want her to wake up alone."

A pause as Roxanne looked over at Sophie, her head cradled on a stuffed lamb.

"You wouldn't lie to me, would you? About our fairy-tale life?"

I put her hand to my mouth and kissed it.

"No," I said. "I wouldn't lie to you about anything."

Roxanne put on a flannel nightgown, an extra layer of protection. Then she went to go get Sophie and bring her into our room.

I had two pints of Ballantine, sitting out on the deck. The sky darkened. Bats visited and I watched them, swooping back and forth like dolphins.

By nine o'clock the bugs were out so I went inside, sat on the couch with my notebooks. I went through my notes from the visits with Mr. Penney, the folks at the hair salon; Louis, now an official suspect.

I looked out at the new darkness, the thrushes still calling, and I put my head back on the couch. Closed my eyes. Dreamed that an alarm clock was ringing but I couldn't find it, awoke to see the lights on, realize the alarm clock was my cell phone.

I staggered to my feet, moved to the counter, picked up the phone. It was 4:37 a.m.

I said hello.

"Jack," Lasha said. "Did I wake you?"

"No."

"You're sure?"

"Yes. But it can't be."

"It is."

"Where?"

"Tory and Rita's," she said.

"Their house?"

"And it's really burning," Lasha said. "I can see it from here, the glow in the sky."

33

I looked in on them. They were asleep, Sophie's head back and mouth open, wrapped up in Roxanne's arms. I watched them for a minute, then went back downstairs.

I left the note on the kitchen counter: WENT TO A FIRE. BACK SOON. XOXO

I hesitated, then collected my stuff, locked the door behind me.

It was a fast ride in the dewy dawn, the truck tires slapping the wet road. I passed a milk truck, pickups, and then I was in Sanctuary and I could see it, from the Ridge Road, the orange glow and glimpses of the popping strobes, red, white, and blue.

The driveway in was gravel, single lane, and there were firefighters' pickups parked at the entrance, a deputy doing guard duty. I parked at the end of the line and walked toward the house, notebook and recorder in hand. It was the same buzz-cut cop from Don Barbier's fire and he recognized me, held up his hand.

"Sorry," he said. "We're keeping the public away from the—"

"I'm not the public," I said, and I strode by him, didn't look back.

The smoke smell was all through the woods, the sound of radios, too. When I was closer I could see the orange glow, hear the crackle. As I came out of the woods and into the grassy field in front of the house, there was an explosion, shouting, sparks and embers shooting into the air and floating down like glowing confetti. The firefighters, silhouetted against the flames, staggered backwards with their hoses like the winners in a tug-of-war.

The public had beaten the deputy to the scene, and there was a sizable group watching the blaze. I moved into a clump that included Tory and Rita, Russell, the purported ex-spook, Don Barbier. They stared into the flames, squinting when a billow of smoke washed over us.

Rita was sobbing quietly, a balled-up tissue over her mouth.

"I'm sorry," I said.

"Our pictures. My wedding dress. All my clothes. My shoes."

Tory stared, didn't speak.

"All that work," Rita said.

"Insurance?"

"For the purchase price, not the replacement or the actual value."

"I thought the banks—"

"We paid cash," she said. "Just did the bare minimum, figured we'd up it later."

"It's okay," Don said. "You can replace a house. You guys are safe; that's what matters."

He reached past me and gave Tory a pat on the shoulder.

Ray-Ray ran by, pulling a hose. Chief Frederick was shouting into his radio from close to the fire, his face flushed in the glow. Derosby strolled by with a video camera, filming the bystanders. He was followed by the dog, sniffing for accelerants. I looked to the other group, didn't see any unfamiliar faces; they were all regulars at the Sanctuary General Store. The dog came up empty. There was a roar as flames shot from the roof.

Rita cried out, "Oh, my God." She moved close to Tory, put her arm around his shoulders and led him away, somewhere behind us.

"So it was—"

"Set?" Don said. "Yes. Roaring when they got here. Somebody called it in from a mile away."

"Unbelievable," I said.

"Yup," Don said. "That it just keeps happening."

"With all these cops, the fire marshal's people. You guys on your patrol."

"We were out," he said.

"Where was Rita?"

"At the firehouse. They had coffee, doughnuts. Some of the guys were headed that way when the call came in—"

"Tory must have freaked," I said.

"I guess. More like paralyzed, you know? Like he just couldn't take any more. I was getting the truck gassed up, ready to do the second shift. Heard it on the radio. I said, 'You have got to be shitting me.' I mean, how many times . . ."

There was a pause, the sound of the fire, Chief Frederick on the PA, the radios amplified from one of the trucks. Rita sobbing.

"You've been through this before," I said. Not a question.

He glanced at me, his eyes glittery black in the firelight.

"Sure. My place. Their office. The Talbot house."

"No," I said. "I mean, years ago."

He was staring at me, then looked away.

"Not sure I follow."

"When you were in high school," I said. I watched him, but there was no reaction, then a shake of his head.

"Still not sure I—"

"When you were Derek," I said. "Derek Mays."

He didn't look at me, just watched the fire. I could feel his boot tapping the grass.

And then I felt someone behind me, at my right shoulder. I turned and saw Tory. He was back, looking at Don strangely, almost angrily. And then he turned and hurried away.

"I don't know what you're talking about, Jack," Don said.

An awkward silence, the crackling of the fire and radios in the background. And then Don turned and looked back toward the driveway, where

Rita was being hugged by a woman while another waited her turn. I didn't see Tory. I moved closer to Don and we both watched the flames. When the wind shifted and the smoke crawled over us, neither of us moved.

"I talked to Penney, from the Fire Marshal's Office," I said. "He told me the whole story."

He didn't answer.

"I'm sorry for your loss."

He stared.

"Penney's still around," I said. "I talked to him for a long time. He remembers it. Julie. The duct tape. The explosion."

I paused as the firefighters trained water on the garage. There was a hiss and a billow of steam and smoke.

"A nice lady at the hair salon in Bucksport—she knew you from your picture. Twenty years and a beard and a few pounds, but still."

He watched the fire like he was studying a painting.

"This must be hard for you," I said. "Not just this one; all of them. It must bring it back."

I waited. Waited some more. Still nothing.

"I can't call you Don Barbier in the story if I know that's not who you are," I said. "Would be dishonest."

"And you're never dishonest?" he said, his first words.

"I try not to be."

"Good for you," he said. "What if I don't want to be in your story at all?"

"Too late," I said.

He mulled that over for a bit. The smoke swept over us again but we stayed—like our conversation had to take place on this very spot.

"When does it run?"

"I'm not sure. I'm writing it in the next couple of days."

He waited to answer and then said, "Don't you want to know why?"

"Yes."

"I had a nervous breakdown, or whatever they call it now. I loved her completely. I mean, not like a high school thing. I was going to spend my life with her."

"But you broke up," I said.

"She wanted to make sure I was the one. Spend a little time on her own."

"And what did she decide?"

"That I was the one."

"Who was the guy who died with her, then?"

"Bartender in the restaurant where she worked. She dated him for a while, but was gonna tell him it wasn't working out. She was coming back to me."

"But she was with him that night?"

"I think he was giving her a ride. Her car wouldn't start."

Fate, I thought. Very bad luck.

"Why the new identity?"

"After she died, I ran. Like, if I could run far enough, fast enough, it wouldn't have happened. When I stopped running I was in Indiana. Ended up in a psych hospital. There for a couple of months, them trying to get me back on my feet. Finally it was this doctor who suggested it. Try being somebody else for a day. I picked a name. Barbier. It was my way of remembering her."

He paused. I waited.

"But it wasn't for a day. It was for years. Many years. Until just now."

"Sorry," I said.

"It's okay," he said. "But it's weird. I don't even know Derek anymore. It was like he died, too."

We stood. The firefighters were knocking the fire down, the diminishing flames popping up here and there, guys starting to hack at the edge of the rubble.

"Did you ever think you'd see one more arson fire, let alone this many? I mean, up this close?"

He shook his head.

"No," he said. "It's so weird. I mean, what are the chances?"

We watched as the water cascaded onto the blackened rubble. I wasn't sure what the fire department had saved—whether it was worth the effort.

"Penney said the suspects in that Bangor fire were drug dealers," I said. "That the guy who died with Julie was dealing, too."

"Cocaine," he said. "It was everywhere back then. I mean, not me. I was in high school, a total jock. But I heard about it."

"Was Julie mixed up in it, too?"

A flicker of anger, then nothing.

"She wouldn't even take aspirin," he said. "No, it was just wrong time, wrong place."

"Horrible," I said. "Kill an innocent bystander like that."

"They were animals."

"And they never caught them."

"No, but they're probably dead by now. People like that don't live long."

"Live by the gun," I said.

"You got it," he said.

"Small consolation, I'm sure."

The fire was all smoke now, steam from the embers. The chatter on the radio had subsided, leaving the sound of idling trucks.

"So what are we going to do, Jack?" he said.

"I think we should talk," I said. "On the record. Have a real conversation about all of this."

"Or else?"

"Or else I write it anyway, with what I have now."

He considered that.

"I could call your bluff," he said.

"Sure you could," I said. "But you'd lose."

He looked at me.

"For a nice guy, you're pretty much a hard-ass, aren't you?" he said.

I didn't answer. He looked away, his jawline hard and lean.

"Okay, Jack," he said. "We'll talk. But not today. Give me a day or two, to gather my thoughts. It's been a long time since I've been Derek Mays. I'm gonna have to get to know myself again."

I held out my hand and he shook it, a strong, long grasp.

"Musta been meant to be," he said, looking to the fire. "All this was digging him up anyway."

He started to walk away and I stayed with him.

"If you don't mind my asking," I said, "what made you come back? To Maine, I mean? You're only twenty-five miles from Bucksport. Eventually somebody was going to recognize you."

"You know, that's a good question, Jack," he said. "A very good question."

But he didn't answer it, just said, "Should find my partners."

I walked with him, both of us searching the dwindling crowd. The cops were conferring by Derosby's Suburban.

Tory was nowhere to be seen.

"Must've left," I said. "Hard to watch, I'm sure."

"I'll just have to catch up with him later," Don said.

We turned to the women, Rita red-eyed, the women holding her on both sides. She clenched a tissue, looked at Don.

"Hang in there, Rita," he said. "We'll build it back like new."

She nodded, pursed her lips, then said, "Oh, Don, it's so awful."

She hugged him and he patted her back.

"It's just a house. You still have each other, right?" Don said.

She nodded. He stepped away and I moved in.

I told Rita I was sorry, gave her arm a squeeze, guided her a few feet away from the other women. She sniffed and took a deep breath and I asked her if I could talk to her for my story. She looked back at the charred rubble that had been her home. Blackened beams, broken windows, furniture burned down to metal frames.

"I don't know what there is to say."

"What will you do next?" I said.

"I don't know. We haven't talked. Do you know where Tory went?"

"No. Will you rebuild?"

"Sure. I mean, I think so. We like it here, and even if we didn't, we've got so much invested. I mean, my God, we're in so deep."

She shook her head, fought back tears. I waited, pen and notebook ready.

"We put everything we had into this town, the business. I mean, the Hidden Treasure angle and everything."

"But someone is doing this, Rita. One house you had listed. One you owned. Your office. Are you beginning to think—"

"That someone's out to get us? But why? No. I mean, what have we done? We're good people. Everybody likes us. I mean, Tory's the president of the Sanctuary Business Alliance; I'm secretary. We're putting this place on the map, for God's sake."

"Maybe some people don't want to be on the map," I said.

"We haven't even told people how we were working on the magazine angle—I don't know how many phone calls we've made, e-mails sent—so they would connect it with us, with this town. And anyway, we like everybody. There's no reason."

"Do you like everybody still? How do you feel about the Hidden Treasure thing now?"

"Well, Jack, I don't know. Maybe it's somebody from outside of town. Maybe it's just one crazy person, somebody who's sick. In the head, I mean. Why else . . ."

The words trailed off. Rita looked thin, and worn, and haggard.

"Are you afraid?" I said.

She looked at me, started to answer. Stopped. Started again.

"Should I be? I don't know. I mean, what can he do now? Our house is gone."

Rita paused. Looked at the house and said, her voice lowered, "I feel like I don't know anyone. I don't know who people really are."

And you don't, I thought. Not even good old Don.

I wished her luck. She thanked me, gave me a washed-out version of the Rita smile, a reflex she couldn't control. I turned away and left her standing alone, until the women closed ranks and, like bridesmaids surrounding a reluctant bride, propped her up again.

I was in the truck, headed back to the center of town, when the maroon Suburban pulled up behind me, flashed blue grille lights. I eased over, saw Davida Reynolds, grim-faced at the wheel, as the truck passed.

And then an Impala, State Police unmarked, on the Suburban's bumper. I glanced left, saw a detective driving, Louis hunched in the backseat. He was staring straight ahead.

I swung back onto the road, reached for the phone. Punched in the number as I shifted through the gears.

"It's me," I said.

"McMorrow," Reynolds said.

"What's going on?"

"No comment."

"What's with Louis Longfellow?"

"No comment."

"Off the record."

No reply. The Impala was gaining on me.

"Way off the record, then."

"You don't write anything until there's a disposition?"

"Until there's a conviction? No way."

"No," she said. "A decision. Charged or not charged."

"Deal," I said.

"Louis Longfellow is a person of interest."

"Enough interest to take him in?"

"He was uncooperative."

"That doesn't make him an arsonist. Or a murderer."

"I can't tell you what it makes him," Reynolds said. "It's just another variable in the problem set. We'll chat with him today and probably end up driving him home. If it's him, he'll at least slow down."

"Want another one?"

She said she did. I gave it to her. Linwood. Don Barbier. Julie Barber. Derek Mays.

"I don't remember him. From the file," Reynolds said, over the sound of the truck accelerating.

"Ex-boyfriend," I said. "A year younger. Split up when she went off to college. May be pretty far down in the weeds."

"Huh," Reynolds said.

"That's all you got? Huh?"

"Weird coincidence. Weird that he changed his name. But it was a long time ago, Mr. McMorrow."

"Disappeared for twenty years, too."

"You're right," Reynolds said. "Three weird things. But I've got a disturbed military vet with explosives and reconnaissance training and gasoline on his boots. Who, when he was asked about his whereabouts on the nights of any of the arson fires, pulled a loaded Beretta M9 handgun from under his shirt and told us to get off his land."

"Huh," I said.

"Right."

"Looks bad, but I don't think he's the one," I said.

"He's trained to kill," she said. "Strong as an ox. Could have taken Woodrow out with a couple of swings. The kid comes along, sees him about to torch that truck. Reflex. Boom, boom, and done. Moves through the woods like a Navy SEAL."

"I still don't buy it," I said.

"Do you have a reason, or is it just reflex for you to disagree?" Reynolds said. She was testy, amped up after having a gun stuck in her face.

"Because Louis doesn't really know Tory Stevens. Or Rita. He just doesn't like outsiders in general. Or people, for that matter."

"So?"

"So he'd be more random." I said. "Fires all over the place."

"After the first three abandoned buildings, we've had a barn and a house."

"And an office door," I said. "And the hay in Clair Varney's barn."

"Right."

"Three out of those four had some connection to Don, aka Derek, or to Tory and Rita."

"Meaning what?"

"I'm not sure."

"It's a small town," I said. "There's gonna be some overlap."

"I know, but still."

I paused, plunged ahead.

"You know what Louis told me?"

"Nope."

"He said he watches people in town. At night. And this was really interesting: He said he watches people watching people."

Reynolds said "Huh."

"So he's not the only one out there," I said.

"Christ," she said. "Somebody could be following him."

I thought of Louis, the way he moved through the woods like a shadow, appeared like a ghost.

"I don't think so," I said.

Lasha's Jeep was parked by her house. I sat for a minute, waited. Finally I got out of the truck and, mindful of Lasha's shotgun, called out. "Hey. You home?"

I waited for a reply, some sign of life.

Nothing.

I walked to the side door, the one in the ell that led to the kitchen. I listened for a moment—for the sound of bacon frying, NPR. Nothing.

I knocked. Waited. Knocked again. I turned the knob and the door opened. I stepped inside.

The kitchen was still. "Hey, Lasha," I said.

I walked into the kitchen, called, "It's Jack. You home?"

Nothing.

I went to the door to the dining room, looked in. The table was covered with magazines and newspapers, empty beer bottles. I turned back to the kitchen, crossed to the door that led to the studio. I lifted the latch, called again. Looked for a trip wire, a crossbow—this being Lasha.

Nothing.

I walked down the short passageway, knocked on the next door, opened it and called, "Lasha. You out here?"

I heard a sound.

A woman's moan.

I crossed the studio, past the menagerie of wooden animals and their keepers. Looked to the right, the corner, the big easy chair. Saw Lasha's bare foot. Her leg. She moaned again.

I came around the corner of the cabinet. Lasha was in the chair, her head splayed back. She opened her eyes and looked at me, tried to focus. I moved to her, took the shotgun off her lap. I placed it carefully on the table, facing away. Screwed the top back on the nearly empty bottle of Glenlivet.

"Jack," Lasha said.

"Morning," I said.

She pulled herself up, tugged her shorts down where they'd hiked up.

"So much for your security plan," I said.

She looked at me blankly, then said, "Oh, that. I decided that was no way to live."

"An army could have marched in here," I said.

Lasha ran a hand over her hair. Smiled blearily.

"But they didn't," she said. "You did. Change your mind, McMorrow? Succumb to my feminine charms?"

I smiled back.

"Almost," I said.

"Well, forget it," Lasha said. "I'm not a home wrecker. May be a lot of things . . ."

"I went to the fire."

Another blank look.

"Tory and Rita's. You called me."

"Really."

"You're drinking way too much, Lasha," I said.

"Spare me the lecture, Jack. It's all coming back to me now. I could see the flames."

"Right."

"Burned flat?"

"Will be after they bulldoze it."

"Arson?"

"What else?"

"This town is screwed-up," Lasha said.

"They think it's Louis Longfellow."

"Huh. The nut-case army guy? Too easy. Life's not easy, Jack. If you think it is, you're kidding yourself."

She looked at the bottle.

"If we can't have morning sex, how 'bout a drink."

"I'm driving," I said. "And I have a question for you."

"You're no fun at all, McMorrow."

"So I've been told," I said. "Don Barbier."

She looked at me, made a sour face.

"What's this, a contest? Name all the guys who refuse to sleep with me. You forming a club, or what?"

I smiled.

"Hey, did I tell you he called me? Said he wants to try again. I said I'd think about it. He said he'd stop by. Said he isn't used to alcohol, sorry he got so drunk. He even wanted to know what he said. I said, Oh, you just told me your whole life story. For his sake, I hope he doesn't remember wee little winky."

I waited, said, "I found out some things about him. I'm wondering if he is what he seems."

"You and me both," she said.

"Tell me about your date."

She reached for the bottle, opened it and sniffed. Her head jerked back like it was smelling salts.

"Let's just say, guys like you and him, they could do a number on a woman's self-esteem."

"You're very attractive," I said. "But I'm happily married."

"Total non sequitur, in some circles. But thanks."

"Tell me about when you were with Don—"

"Don the Monk? Let me see, we were—how should I put this for your delicate ears, Jack?—on our second date, me having asked him out both times. And we're, how to put this, getting ready to do the deed."

The animals and wizards were poised to listen.

"And he says he can't. I say, 'Were you injured in the war or something?' He says no. I mean, just my luck, you know? Big macho carpenter guy and he's gay, or he's saving himself for marriage."

I waited.

"So he says he isn't ready for love. I'm thinking, love? Who said anything about love? I'm looking for a roll in the hay."

"He wasn't?"

"Not that night. He'd had a few drinks. I mean, I do have a tendency to drink guys under the table. But anyway, he starts going on about the love of his life. I'm like, 'What am I? Chopped liver?' But he's off down Memory Lane, you know? He found the perfect woman, they met in high school. Sweet, huh? By the way, as he's telling this story, I'm not entirely clothed."

"Huh."

"And get this. I had his jeans down. I know this is too much information, but when I start to get his boxers off, I see this tattoo."

"Okay."

"On his thigh. 'Julie and Derek. Forever.' "

"Huh," I said.

"I said to him, 'Who the hell is Derek?' He says it's his middle name. Used to go by it."

She paused.

"You don't seem surprised," she said.

"He changed his name," I said. "Entirely. What did he say about Julie?"

"All this stuff about how she died when they were young and he's been grieving ever since."

"Twenty years?"

"Right," Lasha said. "I mean, ever heard of counseling?"

"Huh."

"She was perfect. She was an angel. They were so in love, blah, blah, blah. As soon as she finished that year at college, they were gonna elope."

"Really."

"Oh, yeah. I got the whole long story. I mean, talk about a buzz kill. I had time to put all of my clothes back on, tie my shoes, tighten up my corset."

She reached for the bottle, took another sniff. A small sip. She grimaced.

"And then?"

"And then she up and died."

"He say how?" I said.

"No. I figure it was some sort of sickness, you know. A rare form of cancer. Like in a movie you see on a plane."

"Huh. Anything else?"

"No, just that he kind of cracked up, left Maine, wherever it was, just traveled around the country. Had to keep moving or else she got back into his head."

"Really."

"I'm gonna go online, see if I can find out about her. I mean, who would've thought he was a total head case?"

"So where'd he go?" I said.

Lasha looked at me.

"Tell me again why you want to know all this?"

"Just need to know that I really know him. For my story."

"Derek, huh," she said. "Derek what?"

"I don't know if I can—"

"Gotta give to receive, Jack," Lasha said. She looked at the ceiling. The beasts and wizards waited.

"Okay. Mays. Derek Mays," I said. "So where did he say he went? Georgia, right?" I said.

"Yeah. That was most recent. Let's see. Talked about Massachusetts. He did work on condos down there, in one of the mills. I don't remember all the details. I was half listening as I looked for my underwear."

"And anywhere else?"

"Oh, let me think. Texas. He said he liked Austin. And Arizona; he said he had business there, but I don't think he stayed long. And California. Not LA. I asked him if he'd been to the Getty. He'd never been south. Said he lived in Humboldt County. Said everybody there was in the marijuana business."

"Was he?" I said.

"No, he's a straight arrow," she said. "At least, I think he's straight." Lasha raised an eyebrow.

"Where was he in California?" I asked.

"Oh, jeez. Eureka, maybe. I think they called it that because of the gold rush. You know, 'Eureka!' I remember him talking about a place called McKinleyville, named for Mr. McKinley. I said, Who? Sometimes we were on different wavelengths."

"You'll see him again?" I said.

"Sure. But he's gotta come to me. Like on his knees. In the meantime, I'll check him out."

I smiled. Lasha got herself up out of the chair and stretched, her hands behind her head, her back arched, breasts pointed toward me.

If Don wasn't gay he was crazy, I thought, and Lasha caught it, smiled.

"We could be having a hell of a time, Jack," she said, brushing against me as she passed. "While Rome burns."

34

I called from the parking lot of the general store, sitting in the truck, facing the door.

"Yeah," Roxanne said, her voice flat and cold.

Hi," I said. "How goes it?"

"It goes," she said, then away from the phone, "Honey, I think he's had enough carrots. We'll save the rest for tomorrow."

"I'm in Sanctuary," I said. "You at the barn?"

"She had to see the pony."

"I'm sure. How is he?"

"Pokey? He's full."

"How's Sophie?"

"Okay. I'm trying to keep her busy."

"Anything from the cops about Beth?"

"Nope."

"You sound tired," I said.

"Well," Roxanne said, "it's been a tough stretch."

She paused.

"Not for you, apparently," she said. "You sound pretty chipper."

An edge in her voice.

"I went to the fire. Tory and Rita's house. Someone torched it."

"That's one messed-up town," Roxanne said.

"Somebody else was just saying that."

"Who's that? Your artist friend?"

"Well, yeah."

"Glad you're having these heart-to-hearts with her."

"It's not like that, honey," I said. "She's just a source."

"I'm sure," she said. "When are you coming home?"

"Soon," I said.

"Soon, as in you're on your way? Or soon, as in don't wait up?"

"In between. If you're okay, I think I want to check on a couple of things. Is Clair there?"

"He took Mary to breakfast at the restaurant at Knox Ridge."

"What? He left?"

"I told him we were going shopping in Bangor. There was nobody around at all. So we left and then we got a mile down the road and Sophie felt car sick. So we came back home."

"Did you call him to come back?"

"He'll be back soon, I'm sure. We're fine." Away from the phone she said, "I think that's enough brushing, honey. I think Pokey's getting crabby."

"I gotta go," she said.

"You all right?" I said.

"Me and Pokey," she said. "We're getting close to the end of our rope."

"They took Louis into custody," I said.

"Good," Roxanne said. "The fire department can get a rest. You can come home to your family."

"I hope so."

"So where are you going now?"

"Lincolnville."

She didn't answer.

"If you don't mind," I said.

"Doesn't matter if I mind," Roxanne said. "I can tell by your voice that's you're going. You're like a dog on a scent or something. Your nose takes over."

"No, I can come home."

"Go, Jack. Talk to your people. They got the guy, so you're near the end, right?"

I hesitated. Roxanne said, "Oh, honey, no." Then to me, "I've got to go. She slipped and there's horse poop—honey, don't touch it."

And they were gone.

I leaned back. A log truck roared by, its load swaying precariously. I waited, tossed the phone on the seat, and pulled out. Home was north. I drove east. I was ten miles out when the phone buzzed. I picked it up and glanced at it. Lasha.

The voice-mail beep.

"Jack. I'm in town. Something happened that I think you'll find very interesting. Call me. I'm gonna go do some more digging."

I put the phone down, thought of Roxanne, and drove.

The house was gleaming white, with a screened-in porch on the front. Mrs. Penney's Toyota sedan was parked loyally beside what I assumed was her husband's pickup. I was out of the car, Mrs. Penney standing expectantly at the side door, when my phone buzzed. I looked at it: Lasha again.

Mrs. Penney was dressed in khaki slacks and a white cotton blouse that matched her hair. Her lipstick was fresh, and she had rosy makeup on her cheeks. Gussied up for company. She held the screen door open and I followed her into an immaculate kitchen, scoured for surgery. There were photos on the refrigerator door. Cats—two of them, one gray and one white—were eating out of a bowl on the floor.

"Company for me," she said, then turned and looked at me hard. "My husband thinks you worked with him back in the old days. He said you might need help with an investigation."

"To write a story. But the same result, if I get the story right. Somebody gets locked up, maybe."

She looked at me. "You won't make him look bad, because he never caught them?"

"I think he's a hero for trying," I said.

Mrs. Penney took a deep breath, pursed her lips. Her lipstick smudged. And then she reached for a door, opened it, and turned on a light showing stairs going down.

"He was very organized," she said. "If her name is Barber, it's probably in the left-side file cabinet, under B." She turned away and left me to descend.

The basement was cool and damp, like the cabin of a boat. The dark green metal file cabinet stood by a dark green metal desk. The desk was against a wall. On the wall were a couple of plaques and a couple more framed certificates. FBI investigator's school. The Institute of Fire Science. Scant recognition for a long career.

The bottom drawer was A through H. Kneeling on the clammy carpet, I flipped to B. Inside was a folder that was thicker than most, the tab well worn. It said J. BARBER in careful printing. I opened it, saw transcribed interviews, some typed on a typewriter, some from a dot matrix printer, the pages torn from the continuous feed. I pulled a paper out, started reading: JOSHUA M. COE. DOB 6/5/68. INTERVIEW: BANGOR, MAINE, 10/18/93.

> *I met the subject, Joshua "Josh" Coe, at his place of employment, Johnny B's, a restaurant and tavern in Bangor, Maine. Mr. Coe consented to the interview being recorded.*
>
> *DP: How well did you know Julie Barber?*
>
> *JC: Pretty well, for, you know, someone you work with. Not like I hung out with her, like, outside of the restaurant. She was a little out of my league that way, you know what I'm saying?*

The phone rang upstairs, a harsh jangle. Mrs. Penney crossed the kitchen, said, "Hi, dear. No, it's okay. Someone's here. A reporter, looking at Dad's files. . . . The Barber case . . . You know how hard Daddy worked on that one."

I tucked the file under my arm and slid the file drawer shut. When I stepped into the kitchen Mrs. Penney was saying, "I love you, too. I'll call you right back." She hung up, held the phone against her chest.

"Thank you, Mrs. Penney," I said. "I'll be sure to return it."

"No, that's okay. I trust you."

"I'm flattered."

"I think I have pretty good people judgment. Linwood did, too. Well, for his job, he had to know who was telling the truth."

"But he never found the truth in this case?"

"Oh, I think he knew the truth. He just ran out of time. His work was everything to him, you know. He used to say, 'What else would I do? I don't make birdhouses, and I suck at golf.' "

I took a step toward the door.

"But I can tell you, Mr. McMorrow, he wanted those people. The ones who killed that girl. Our oldest—that was her on the phone—was about the same age, so it hit him very hard. He'd say, 'The world's not big enough for them to hide.' Then one of them died, actually. In a fire, too. Linwood felt cheated, I think."

"Really."

"He said he wanted to use one to get to the others. He said, 'He's no good to me dead.' "

"What sort of fire?" I said. "Accidental?"

"I'm not sure. Burned up in a car, maybe?"

"Did he say anything else when the one guy burned up in the car?"

"Gee, I don't know. It was a while ago. So much has happened. I just remember he said he had to hurry. He had no idea he was the one running out of time."

And then the phone rang and I said good-bye, hurried to the truck, got out of there before the daughter told her not to give Daddy's files away.

The road went past hayfields, a dairy farm, a smattering of mobile homes. I drove three miles, took a right, and headed down a gravel road that cut through grown-over farmland, small poplars and birches threaded with flat-tened stone walls. There was a muddy slash into the brush and I stopped, backed the truck in, and parked facing the road, like a dog protecting a bone.

I shut the motor off. Picked the folder up and propped it against the steering wheel. Opened it and started reading, from the beginning. There were reports from the scene, description of the house. The oven open. The evidence of melted wax. The two deceased found together, remnants of what appeared to be duct tape on their ankles and wrists, and the same adhesive in the area of their mouths.

I flipped the pages.

Report of neighbors hearing a loud explosion, then seeing flames from the house. A sketch of the room, the location of the bodies marked by X's. Tran-scriptions of interviews. A neighbor seeing a truck leave the area at high speed; he wasn't able to ascertain the make or model, but said it had loud exhaust.

It was chronological, the investigation unfolding: Julie Barber, a part-time waitress and student at the University of Maine at Orono. Ross Lucas, a university dropout and bartender at Johnny B's; had attended the university but dropped out. They were believed to have dated but she had broken it off a month before. Reported to have remained friends, Penney had written.

More pages, a lot of repetition. And then, probably days or weeks into the investigation, the interview with Coe, then another and another.

Penney was persistent.

Weeks went by. Penney interviewed Julie's friends at the college. They said she had been dating Lucas but had decided to break up with him. They said he was a bad influence. Julie stated to the subject, Lori Kay Poulin, that Lucas was doing bad things that scared her, and she was afraid she'd get in trouble.

Then the first mention of Derek Mays, interviewed at his parents' resi-dence in Bucksport, Maine. Mays said he had dated Julie for several years, starting in ninth grade. They had split up when Julie had gone to college, so they could date other people, but were getting back together at the time of the fire. Mays hadn't met Lucas, but understood Julie had dated him a few times, after they'd met at the restaurant. Mays stated that Julie had told him Lucas was a drug user and was also known to sell drugs, and this scared her. She had told Mays that she did not want to be involved in his drug activities, and thus had ended the relationship.

A truck passed, a dilapidated pickup. The guy slowed and stared but kept going. I read on.

Penney had a confidential informant. I guessed it was Coe, the waiter. The CI, identified as No. 2, said Lucas had been selling cocaine out of the bar, "usually grams, but a few ounces too." He said most of his customers were students, but there were also some townies. The CI stated he did not know where Lucas obtained the cocaine.

In a subsequent interview, his memory got better. I figured Penney was squeezing him harder. CI No. 2 reported that three subjects had come into the bar and talked to Lucas on multiple occasions. They were in their late twenties and early thirties. One had a teardrop tattoo on his face and Lucas referred to him as "Cheech." The other two subjects were known as as "Kiko" and "Bear."

Street names.

I flipped the pages, as I sat there in the brush. Affidavits. CI Nos. 3, 4, and 5. Penney working it hard. An informant saying he knew Kiko and Bear from the Mad Dog, a biker bar in Lewiston. Kiko's real first name was Lester. Bear's was Alfred. More pages. More interviews. Then real names. When shown photographs of Kiko and Bear, another subject stated that she knew them as Lester Pope and Alfred Potvin.

I looked up, surprised to see the woods still there, the empty road. Plunged back in.

Pope's mother, Lucinda, interviewed at her home in Leeds, Maine, outside of Lewiston. She knew Bear. He and Lester had dropped out of high school together. She said she knew her son used drugs, "but denied he was violent or capable of hurting anyone."

Alfred Potvin's brother, James "J-Man" Potvin, interviewed at the Maine State Prison in Warren, where he was currently incarcerated. J-Man was four months into five to eight years for aggravated assault and probation violation.

J-Man admitted that he knew Bear. And Cheech.

A car passed. This time I didn't look up. I flipped the pages. I began to see question marks, scrawled hard in pen. Frustration with his forgetfulness?

It took Penney six separate visits, probably working a deal that didn't make the notes, but J-Man came through. He ID'd Cheech as Laney Watts. Watts was the next link on the supply chain, from Lawrence, Massachusetts. Cheech was the brains, Kiko and Bear, the muscle.

"Here we go," I said.

They all worked with Lucas. Lucas knew college kids. He lined up a couple of them to bring in the other college kids, for a small percentage. Find a buyer for an ounce, get 10 percent. A few grams for a frat party, get a few bucks. Like a finder's fee.

"It was business, very smooth," James Potvin stated. Asked if he could identify the university students who were working with the aforementioned drug suppliers, subject James Potvin said he only knew one by a real name. Tommy Stevens.

I fell back in my seat. "Oh, my God."

I read it again.

Then a third time.

Then the next paragraph.

Asked if he was aware of the whereabouts of Pope, Potvin, Watts, or Stevens, James Potvin said his brother and Pope and Watts all scattered after the fire. He said he believed they moved out of state, maybe out west. He said he didn't hear from his brother or the other subjects after the fire. He said he didn't know if they were connected to the murders. "I have no friggin' idea," James Potvin stated.

I went back.

Tommy Stevens.

A student. That would make him the right age. The right town.

Tommy. Tory.

I looked out at the woods, my mind racing. Tommy was Tory. Tommy was connected to the guys thought to have killed Lucas the bartender and Julie Barber, who were said to have been dating. Don was Julie's high school boyfriend. But Don/Derek couldn't have known Tory/Tommy, could he? Don/Derek was in high school. Tory/Tommy had only a tangential connection to Coe, the guy who worked at the same bar as Julie. Another guy who was dealing drugs; like Tommy, a low man in the supply chain. But if Tory and Don were both connected in some way to Julie, then how had they come together after all these years? Did they even know? If so, did they commiserate? Were they accomplices in the Bangor arson case?

And if that were the case, what about the arson fires happening now?

I looked through the papers again, but they came to an end with a flight reservation to LAX. No notes in the file about what Penney had found there, if anything. Was it in a separate file? Would Penney even know? His wife?

I reached for my phone, searched. Lester Pope.

Waited.

Hundreds came back. A professional skateboarder. An engineering firm. A guy who died in 1907.

I tried again, pounding the keys. Lester Pope . . . Maine . . . drugs.

A pharmaceutical company. A kid blogging about rehab. He was nineteen in 2010. Pope Francis.

A third time. Lester Pope . . . fire . . . arson.

I looked at the screen and froze.

Typed Alfred Potvin . . . arson. Hit return. Waited. The results came up. I opened one.

"My God," I said.

And then Laney Watts and arson. Same result.

I fell back in the seat. Arson fires. All fatal.

"He's killing them," I said. "Knocking them off, one by one."

35

The stories said Watts died in Milner, Georgia, in 2008; Potvin in Camp Verde, Arizona, in 2002, just south of Jerome. Pope died in Ranchos De Taos, New Mexico, in 1995. All of them died in arson fires.

Pope was found in the backseat of a torched car. He was identified by dental records. Potvin died in a trailer fire, the doors nailed shut. Watts had been shot in the leg, then burned alive.

Don Barbier had been in Milner; I'd seen the electric bill. He'd lived close to where each of the three had died.

But why all the fires in Sanctuary? Why not just go after Tory directly, I thought—but not for long. Barbier was playing with him, like a cat with a mouse. "This," I said aloud to myself, "is his way of making Tory sweat." The only question now was, why?

I looked out at the road, the woods, the raspberry brambles on both sides of the truck. Phone still in my hand, I started the motor and pulled out of the brush, weeds raking the bottom of the truck. I turned right, headed up a long upgrade.

The phone buzzed. I answered.

"Jack."

"Yeah."

"Tory."

I hesitated, all of it still running through my mind.

"How you doing, Tory?"

"Okay. How are you?"

His tone was slightly breathless, like he was nervous, working his way up to something.

"Jack," he said. "We have to talk."

"We are," I said.

"In person, I mean."

I hesitated. My turf or his.

"Sure. I'm not near Sanctuary, though."

"Where are you?"

"Forty minutes north."

"Split the difference?"

"I can come to your office," I said.

"No," Tory blurted.

So he didn't want Rita around.

"The Quik-Mart on Route 17," I said. "We can get a coffee."

"Awesome," Tory said. "I'll buy."

He did, two large coffees with milk. We sat down in a booth by the front window. Tory looked a little flushed, his skin pink against the blue Sanctuary Brokers shirt. His hand was shaking.

"So," I said.

"Yeah, so thanks, Jack. I mean, for taking the time. I know you're a hell of a busy guy."

"Sometimes," I said.

"How's the story coming?"

He looked at me expectantly, like my answer might reveal something.

"It's coming," I said. And I waited. He sipped his coffee, the cup trembling as it touched his lips.

I waited some more. An old guy came in, green Dickies and a trucker's hat. He nodded to us, went to the counter, and started choosing scratch tickets from the rack. The woman behind the counter waited, one eye on a game show on the TV on the wall. Tory glanced at the TV, took a swallow of coffee.

"Spit it out," I said.

Tory smiled, looked at me with his full-eye-contact stare.

"I've got something to tell you," he said.

"I gathered that."

"It's big, Jack."

"I guessed that, too."

"It's just hard to know where to begin."

"Just plunge in," I said.

"Off the record," he said.

I didn't answer. Tory took a deep breath, clenched his paper coffee cup.

"I've worked hard to build the business. Both of us have."

"No doubt."

"I mean, I started with nothing. No dad in the picture. My mom worked in a store like this place. Four bucks an hour. I started working when I was fourteen. Had to pull my weight, you know? If I didn't nobody else would."

I waited. He hadn't come here to tell me his Horatio Alger story.

"When I was in college—I got a scholarship to go to the University of Maine—I got a job in a bar."

Here we go, I thought.

"With Julie Barber," I said.

He stared.

"How did you know that? Jesus Christ, I'm glad we're having this talk."

"Likewise," I said.

"Yeah, so I worked with Julie. Washing dishes, making sandwiches, scrubbing the floors. Didn't make much. My spending money, you know? But then—"

I waited.

"But then, there was this guy who was sort of the assistant manager. Used to be a student. Got kicked out or something, and he—"

Tory paused, took a breath.

"Was selling drugs," I said. "Ross Lucas."

He looked at me, startled.

"Who have you been talking to?"

"Just people. Keep going."

"Wow. Okay. Well, you can probably guess the rest."

"Not all of it," I said.

"Right. Well, I got involved in drugs. I mean, I was just a kid. I'd worked so much in high school, never had time for that sort of thing. But there it was, you know. So I started in. At first it was free, we were just partying. A few lines, you know, after the bar closed."

"Uh-huh." "And then this guy, he said he needed some money, couldn't give the stuff away anymore. I'd give him half my check. And then that wasn't enough. He said his suppliers were squeezing him, jacking up the price. I mean, a hundred a gram adds up."

"I'm sure."

"So I started selling a little. In the dorm, nothing major. But I'm a good salesman."

He looked at me for confirmation.

"Yes, you are," I said. The old guy walked by with a fist full of tickets, went out to his truck. Tory waited, looked to make sure the woman behind the counter was still there. He leaned forward.

"It got kind of out of control. I mean, I was making, like, five hundred a week. Clear. More money than I'd ever seen."

"Living the dream," I said.

"Right. Me and Julie dated a few times, but she was pretty straight and was going back to her boyfriend anyway. This guy Derek Mays, still in high school. I never met the guy, but I could tell she was still really into him. So it never went anywhere. But then," he began. Stopped.

"And then, what?"

"These guys showed up in Orono. They were the suppliers' suppliers. I mean, real hard-asses. Had been in prison, connected to some biker gang. I mean, scary."

"Cheech, Bear, and Kiko," I said.

Tory looked stunned.

"Keep going," I said.

He looked around, down at his coffee, over to the woman behind the counter. Anywhere but at me.

"One night," Tory said.

Another pause.

"One night we were closing up. Me, Julie, Lucas. Those three guys came in. They said they were through fooling around. I mean, they kind of pushed us up against the bar. Lucas was saying, 'I can get it, I can get it.' I'm saying, 'This isn't my fight.' Julie is crying."

A long breath. A sip of coffee.

"One of them has a gun and they herd us out of there, into a van. Lucas is freaking now, Julie is hysterical. I'm thinking of diving through the window or something. But then we go a few miles, on the edge of town, toward Bangor. They pull into this driveway. Looks like nobody's been at the house for a long time. Take us in, the two of them crying now, I'm thinking, I'm gonna die. I'm gonna die. They take tape and do Lucas and Julie, hands and feet. Two of the guys want to, you know, molest Julie, but the boss guy with the gun, he says no. I'm thinking. maybe there's hope."

I waited.

"And then he tells me to just stand there. They sit Julie and Lucas on the chairs. In the kitchen, I mean. And one of them goes to the stove and opens the oven door and reaches in and jiggles something and then turns on the propane. And it comes billowing out. The smell, I mean. And then the other of the two guys, without the gun, he takes out a candle and he puts it on the table. And he lights it. I'm thinking, are you crazy? And then they push me out of the house and leave Julie and Lucas in there. They say to me, 'You're the witness.'

"So we drive in the van down the street and stop. And we wait. I don't know how long. Five minutes? Ten? It seemed like forever. I'm saying, 'Let's go back. They get the message. We all do.' They hit me in the face, tell me to shut up and watch."

He paused, shook his head.

"And then it just—it just blew up. The whole house. This huge boom, flames blowing out of the windows."

"And then what?"

"They said something like, 'Now you get the message. Go get the money.' "

"How much?" I said.

"Seventy-three hundred dollars."

"For that they incinerate two people."

"I know. It was surreal. Like a movie, except it didn't end."

"Did you get the money?"

"You kidding? I took off. I didn't look back until I was in Utah."

Tory paused.

"In a way, I've been running ever since."

I'll bet you have, I thought. I looked at him. Stared hard. He smiled, a reflex he couldn't control.

"Why stop now?"

"Because, Jack. Because something happened."

"A lot's been happening."

"Something else. Yesterday we got a call. Buyer wanted to look at a property. Woman said she was an artist, lived on Deer Isle. Getting inconvenient, wanted to be closer to Portland. The restaurants and all that."

"Yeah?"

"We showed her three properties. Probably a little high for her price range, it turns out. She's thinking low threes. These were all mid-three and up, though one you could probably get—"

"Tory."

"Right. So we're doing this, late morning, stop at the store, a little community ambiance. She meets Harold, he gives her the shtick. She says, 'People are so nice here. I thought with all these fires it was gonna be weird.'

"And then it gets better. She meets Lasha. Turns out they know each other from artist stuff, galleries or whatever. So they're talking. And then we're standing in the parking lot of the store, just chatting, and Don drives by, waves."

"Don Barbier."

"Right. Don. And she says—her name is Constance, not Connie, Constance—and she says, 'Wow. Small world. I think I know him, too.' I say, 'You know Don?' She says, 'Oh, I thought it was somebody else. A guy named Derek.' "

"Derek Mays," I said.

"Right. The boyfriend. Julie's boyfriend. Talk about a blast from the past."

"And he's here," I said.

"Yes," Tory said. "And it's no coincidence."

"I know," I said. "No coincidence at all."

I thought for a second.

"Who did she say this to?"

"Me, Lasha, Rita."

"Did Don see her?"

"Oh, yeah. Slowed down, gave us a big wave, a smile. Constance waved back."

"Did he recognize her?"

"They kind of locked in. I mean, she said she knew him from high school. He was a big jock, and he used to flirt with her in study hall or something. She said he looked different, but it was still him. I'm guessing she was secretly obsessed with him or something."

"And Don kept going?"

"The rest of us, too."

"Did you tell Rita any of this?"

Tory shook his head.

"Where is she?"

"Closing at a bank in Augusta. This retired three-star general from Maryland, he's buying—"

"What did Lasha say?"

"At the store? She sort of listened, said something like, 'Nobody here is what they seem.' I'm like, 'That's no way to sell our town, Lasha,' and I'm laughing. But not on the inside."

"No," I said. "On the inside you were—"

"Scared, to be honest."

I thought for a moment, took out my phone and tapped down the list, dialed a number.

Lasha didn't answer.

"Tory," I said. "Why are you telling me all of this?"

"Because ever since then, the thing at the store, Don's been sort of—I don't know. Stalking me. Wherever I go, there's his truck."

"Did he follow you here? Does he know we're talking?"

"No. I mean, I don't think so. I took the Ridge Road, made a couple of turns."

I looked out of the store window at the silver Mercedes, the Sanctuary Brokers sign on the door. Way to go incognito.

"Maybe I'm losing it," Tory said. "I mean, all these fires, the Woodrow kid—it gets to you. And Louis, the army guy?"

"Marines."

"Right. I swear he's been following me, too. Drives this Jeep, big tires. So with all of that, you think to yourself, maybe I'm just cracking up. The stress. Carrying all this debt. And Don, I mean, I worked with the guy. Maybe it's some bizarre coincidence. Or he's just this Derek guy's look-alike, or—"

"Tory," I said, "No more bullshit."

He looked at me.

"Cheech and Bear and Kiko," I said. "They're all dead, aren't they."

"Yeah, well, drug dealers, not like they have a long shelf life. You know that. Eventually they run into somebody tougher than—"

"You know they died in fires. Arson fires. Somebody torched them, Tory. I know the whole story, so cut the crap."

He went pale. Swallowed hard. The glad-hander mask melted away and he looked wan and small.

"I've been running for years, Jack. I'm so tired. Keeping it all inside. I mean, I couldn't tell Rita anything. So it's just all on me, all the time. It's like I haven't slept, I mean, really slept, in forever."

"For good reason," I said, thinking of the way Julie died. She never got the choice to run. "Three down, one to go."

Tory looked at me, his mind grasping for the next move. Even then he managed a half-smile. "Yeah, but now that I'm telling you, I'm safer, right?" he said, clinging to the power of positive thinking.

"No," I said. "Just makes for a better story after you're gone."

36

Tory insisted he ride along with me as I drove into Sanctuary to Lasha's. We left the store, crossed Route 17, and followed the Sanctuary River south. The sun was moving from cloud to cloud overhead and the shadowed woods on both sides seemed not lush and green, but dark and dangerous. Even Tory, sitting beside me with his legs crossed and boat shoe dangling, seemed oddly lethal, the smiling real estate guy who had watched two people—one innocent—burn to death.

I glanced at him, quiet for once. Was he worried about Rita? And what did the deaths of the three drug dealers mean to him? It was in his best interest that the last three witnesses to the Julie Barber killing had been eliminated. His word against—nobody's.

We were approaching Lasha's drive, the mailbox tilting from the raspberry brambles at the roadside. I swung in, bounced up the rutted drive, and emerged in the grassy clearing. Lasha's Jeep was parked by the open studio door and I pulled in beside it and shut off the motor. Reaching down beside the seat, I took out Clair's Glock.

Tory looked at me, said "Jesus."

We got out and I slipped the gun in my waistband, went to the studio door, and peered in. The lights were on. The menagerie was still.

"Lasha," I called. "You home?"

No reply. Then a rustle as the cat slipped around the back corner of the shed and hurried toward us. I walked that way, waiting for Tory to catch up, keeping him in my view. He was wary, the salesman's smile vanished. We rounded the corner of the shed. Crossed the grass. I called again. "Lasha."

Nothing. Lasha's lookout chair was empty, the only movement yellow goldfinches twittering in the burdocks at the edge of the woods. I stopped, started to turn back, saying, "She must be inside."

And stopped.

A bit of something, in the undergrowth beyond the chair. Something that didn't look right.

I slipped the gun out, pulled the slide back. "You stay with me," I said, and let Tory get a half-step ahead. We crossed the grass and the something turned into skin. Then a bare foot, the leg leading into the grass.

We approached, slowing. The foot was pointed upward.

The leg, a skirt.

Lasha.

"Oh, my God," Tory said.

She was on her back, arms thrown up, the shotgun beside her. There were bruises on her throat and her eyes were open, frozen in an unblinking stare, just like her creatures.

I bent to her, dropped to my knees. Touched her cheek. It was cold and gray, the life drained.

"Oh, Lasha," I said, then eased to my feet.

Tory was already backing away. I scanned the woods once, then followed, the gun raised. At the corner of the shed my phone buzzed.

I took it out. Looked.

Roxanne.

"Hey," I said.

"Jack," Roxanne said.

Her voice, something wrong.

"What is it?" I said.

"There's somebody here," she said.

Alphonse. The bastard.

"Who is it? Alphonse? Call Clair. What is he—"

A clatter, the phone being passed.

"Jack."

"Who's this?"

"Don. Don Barbier. We need to talk."

37

I had the gun in one hand, the phone in the other. Tory watched me from the other side of the truck and listened.

"I'm looking for Tory," Don said.

I looked at him.

"I'm sure he's around," I said.

"I asked the girl at the Quik-Mart if she'd seen him today. She said he was in there with the reporter guy. The one with the blue Toyota pickup. She said Tory and the reporter had coffee. Talked for a long time."

"Is that right?"

"I'm figuring you had lots to talk about."

"I suppose," I said. "Where exactly are you?"

"Standing in your kitchen," Barbier said. "Just met your lovely daughter. And your beautiful wife."

I didn't reply. Waited.

"So Jack, I'm thinking you have something I want. And you know I definitely have something you want. So I propose that we just trade. For you it's a hell of a deal. Two for one."

I looked at Tory, who was listening intently. I made the decision.

"Okay. I'll be there in a half-hour or so."

"Great, Jack," Don said. "Call when you're five miles out. The three of us, we'll be waiting."

"Right."

"And Jack. Anybody else shows, I'm done and they're going with me. No cops. Nobody."

"Okay," I said.

I lowered the phone.

"What?" Tory said.

"I'm gonna head home."

"What about the cops? Aren't you gonna call them?"

"I'll call them on the way."

"Shouldn't we wait for them or something?"

"Nothing we can do here. Lasha's gone."

"I know, but shouldn't we just—"

I raised the gun and pointed it at him.

"We're going," I said. "You drive."

I called Clair, both numbers. Got voice mail.

We were on Route 17, headed west, Tory driving the speed limit. Hills rose to the north, pastures shorn from the woods. There were decaying businesses, sagging barns, trailers flanked by broken-down trucks. I saw none of it, just Tory at the wheel, the Glock heavy in my hand. He started to slow and I said, "Faster. If you try to bail out, I'll shoot you."

He sped up, eyes fixed on the road. I told him to take a right and he did, onto the back road we'd follow all the way to Prosperity. More woods, a farm. He got the truck up to speed, rattling over potholes. I switched gun hands, my right going numb.

"You're trading me, aren't you," Tory said. "Me for your family."

I didn't reply.

"He's nuts, you know. Have to be, hold a grudge this long."

"If someone tied Rita up and burned her to death, what would you do?"

He was quiet, hands massaging the steering wheel.

"I guess he couldn't find Rita," Tory said. "That would have been the simplest thing." He swallowed hard. "I was afraid it was coming. Sometime. I just didn't know who it would be. I kept checking, once I found out their real names. I'd Google them. Then I just put them on my Google alerts. And up they came, one by one. Like you said: Dead in fires. Burned."

Another swallow, his hands twisting on the steering wheel. "But then I thought, well, who knows how many enemies these guys have. Live by the gun, die by the gun, and all that. Hey, these cartel types. They'll torture you, cut your head off, whatever. Burning somebody. That would be nothing."

"Faster," I said.

"So after one, I thought, probably has nothing to do with me. Then two, I'm thinking, this is not good. After the third guy was killed, we sold everything and moved. I told Rita we were on the bubble in Chesapeake, time to cash in before it burst."

So here we are, I thought. The end of the line, Don desperate to keep his cover from being blown before he finishes the job.

"There's gotta be some way to deal with this," Tory said. "I mean, maybe if you go talk to him alone—"

"Just shut up and drive," I said.

From a ridgetop near Lake St. George, I called Clair. Voice mail again.

Tried Roxanne, straight to voice mail.

Tory drove on, his face tense and pallid. Miles passed as we descended into a valley and I called Roxanne from the next ridge, juggling phone and gun. Voice mail.

In Knox we slowed and stopped. I switched the gun back.

"Left," I said, and we pulled out and climbed and saw the valley laid out below, pasture in rectangles, cows ambling, stone walls creeping up the hillsides.

Five miles.

Tory sensed something, said, "We could team up, take him together."

"Shut up," I said, and I fingered the phone, one eye on him, the gun wavering. Tapped Roxanne's number. It buzzed.

"Yessir."

Don's voice, menacingly cheerful.

"Five miles," I said. "Top of Knox Ridge, Route 137."

"You got him?"

"Yes."

"Have him say something."

I held the phone up, said, "Talk."

Tory hesitated, then said, "This is nuts, Don. Are you crazy? I never killed that girl. Those three guys did it. So it's all over. You're taking this too far, man. Really, just get a grip. We can talk. We can talk this out."

He was still going when I put the phone to my ear.

"How's that?" I said.

"Pathetic," Don said. "He's a piece of shit. Call from the end of your road."

He was gone. I told Tory to keep driving west. Tapped Clair's number again. He answered.

"Where are you?" I said.

"On the way back. The girls went shopping. Followed them out. Nobody in sight up to the main road. Stayed with them for a couple of miles beyond that."

"They went back home. Sophie felt sick. Now Don's there. He has them. He's the arsonist."

"Shit," Clair said. "Twenty minutes."

"He's calling the shots," I said. "No cops."

"Gotcha. You armed?"

I heard the roar of the big Ford.

"Your Glock. One clip."

"Torso," Clair said. "Bursts of three."

Tory looked at me, his eyes starting to fill.

"You know you're bringing me to my own execution," he said.

"If you run, I'll do it myself," I said. "I'll shoot you in the back. Don't think I won't."

We drove the last miles in silence, then I motioned with the gun for Tory to go right. He pulled off the main road, onto the gravel, and we continued a mile in. At the end of the Dump Road, we slowed and stopped.

I called. He answered.

"Yup."

"We're here," I said.

Tory's left hand dropped from the wheel to his lap, started to move toward the door handle. I put the muzzle of the gun hard against his cheekbone. He moved his hand back.

"Drive up in front of your house," Don said. "Call when you're there."

He was gone.

"Drive," I said, and Tory slowly reached for the gearshift, then swung his arm right, caught me under the chin. I gasped and he was rolling out, the door half open. I got him by the neck of his shirt, yanked him back. The shirt tore, and he spun and started to pull it over his head, falling out the door. On my knees I crawled after him. He backed away and I fell headfirst out of the truck, caught his knee, tripped him up, and as he fell, the shirt over his face, I slammed him across the head with the gun.

He grunted and I hit him again and he swayed on his hands and knees, blood seeping through the Sanctuary Brokers blue.

"Up," I said, and I yanked the shirt down and him to his feet. I reached into the truck cab and got my phone, then grabbed him by the shirt collar again, and pushed him along. Blood ran from his hair down his neck. He stumbled and I held him up, said, "I don't care if I have to carry you, I'm getting you there."

It was a long quarter-mile. Tory walked in front of me, weaving his way, his shirt balled up in my fist at the back of his neck. He dabbed at his head, looked at his hand covered with blood.

"Oh, my God," he said.

When he slowed, I prodded him with the gun and he lurched forward. I looked at my watch, counting down the time until Clair would get back. Seventeen minutes to go.

We marched like Tory was a prisoner of war, which he was. Barbier's war. Roxanne and Sophie caught in the crossfire. God, they'd be terrified. If he'd hurt them . . .

Even if he hadn't.

We walked in the shade of the woods, birds flittering in the undergrowth, chipmunks skittering into the stone walls. Tory stumbled, put his hands to his knees, said, "I'm gonna be sick." I pulled him back upright and he retched but kept walking. And then the house showed through the trees. We trudged past the end of the stone wall, out from under the trees, stood in the road in front of the house.

Eleven minutes.

I called.

"Yeah," Barbier said.

"We're here. Out front."

"I see you."

I looked at the windows, couldn't see anyone. Looked to the woods; nothing.

"So you can send them out," I said. "We'll do the swap."

"Not here," Barbier said. "Come down to the big barn. We'll do it there. Two minutes. You're not here, I have to start hurting people."

I heard Sophie crying and then he was gone.

"What?" Tory said.

"Move," I said, and we did.

I pushed him up the driveway, into the backyard, down the garden path toward Clair's. As I approached the barn, I saw movement in the loft window. Barbier's vantage point, a clear sight line to the road.

We walked through the trees, up to the front of the building.

I called Clair, said, "Upstairs in your barn. Don't come up the road from the east side."

"Ten minutes," Clair said over the roar of the motor, then hung up.

My phone buzzed.

"Up the stairs, then up the ladder," Don said. "Keep him in front of you. One minute."

We stepped through the barn door into the shadows. I had the gun out, Tory in front of me. We crossed the workshop to the wooden stairs. Tory hesitated and I put the gun to his head. He started up, his boat shoes scuffing on the treads, his khakis smeared with blood. The stairs led to the main loft, hay bales and hand tools, empty chicken cages. At the far end of the loft, a ladder led to the third floor. We paused at the base and Tory looked up.

I checked my watch. Eight minutes.

"Up," I said.

He climbed slowly, like it was the gallows. I was two rungs below him, the gun pointed up. When he poked his head through the floor he said, "Oh, God."

And let go.

He fell against me, almost knocked me off the ladder. I hung by one leg, one arm, strained to hold him up. I pressed him against the ladder in front of me, jammed the gun into his spine, and said, "Climb, damn it. Climb."

Tory gathered himself up, put a boat shoe on the rung, and heaved himself upward. Four rungs to the top. I pushed him up and onto the floor, tucked the Glock in the back of my jeans, and pulled my T-shirt over it.

And there they were.

Roxanne was sitting on a hay bale, Sophie on her lap. Barbier was standing ten feet away from them, a sawed-off shotgun in his arms, red plastic gasoline can at his feet. He smiled, like it was a picnic and we were late.

"You son of a bitch," I said.

"Easy, Jack. Everything's going according to plan."

Roxanne was drawn and pale. Sophie's face was pressed to her mother's shoulder. Roxanne looked at me, at Tory, the blood. She clenched her lips to keep from crying. Sophie turned to me, her face red and streaked with tears. "Daddy," she said. "I want to go home."

"We're going home now, honey," Roxanne said, pressing Sophie close. Tory, sprawled on the floor, looked up and said, "I didn't kill her. I swear."

Barbier looked at him, said, "This is a special day."

And then he looked at me. "A deal is a deal. And nobody can ever say that Derek Mays isn't a man of his word. I promised Julie I'd finish this, and I will. I promised we'd trade, and we'll do that, too."

He looked at Roxanne and said, "You can go now. I'm very sorry I upset your daughter. It really was the only way."

Roxanne got up from the bale, walked quickly to the ladder. She handed Sophie to me and turned and started down. I bent and lowered Sophie to Roxanne, felt my shirt ride up.

They started down. I watched them until they were on the loft floor, heard their footsteps on the floorboards, then on the stairs. I turned back.

Barbier had the shotgun pointed at me.

"Drop the gun onto the floor with two fingers and kick it away. Just a little extra precaution. We've come this far—don't want to trip up at the finish line. It's been too long, man, too hard."

"So you killed Lasha?"

"Hey, I had no choice. She was figuring things out too quick. That woman with Tory at the store—I suppose it was only a matter of time. Then Lasha jumps on freakin' Google, you know? And she got me off track a couple of times, talking too much. I said to her, 'Just give me a couple of days and then I'll be long gone.' But no. She was gonna run right to you, McMorrow. 'I gotta talk to Jack.' "

I sagged inside, then pushed it away. Not the time.

"And Eve Johnson? The woman in the car?"

"Oh, jeez," Don said. "That was unfortunate. Really. Wrong place, wrong time, you know? Once she knew, I couldn't let her go. Not then. Not now."

He raised the shotgun.

"The gun," he said.

I slipped the Glock out with my thumb and forefinger, crouched to put it on the floor. Gave it a scuff and it slid away.

Don moved and stood over Tory, who was still on his hands and knees.

"How's it feel, Tommy boy?" he said. "I'd tape your mouth, but I want to hear you scream."

He lifted the gun, slammed the butt down on Tory's back. Tory grunted, dropped to his belly. His face was against the floor and he started to sob.

Don moved to the gas can and, still watching me, bent and picked it up. The gun in one hand, the can in the other, he moved to Tory and began to pour.

Tory screamed, said, "No. Please, no." Barbier circled him, then sloshed gas over his back. Tory screamed again. The barn filled with fumes.

"This is nuts," I said.

"No," Don said. "It's justice. That's all. You don't understand because you didn't know her. Her smile. I mean, the way she looked at you. Her eyes. The most beautiful eyes. Just the way she was, this gift to the world. Julie was the most—"

"I didn't kill her," Tory bellowed.

I got a glimpse of my watch. Two minutes.

"We have a pony downstairs," I said.

"You'll have time to get it out. Fire moves upward. I should know. It'll take a long time to get all the way down there."

"It's an awful nice old building. Belongs to a friend of mine."

"I heard. Some retired guy, your wife said. I'm sorry about this, but it's a little risky doing it in plain view. Be glad I didn't burn your house down. Or his. Barn's insured, right?"

"Jesus, Don," Tory said, raising himself to his hands and knees. "Please don't do this."

"You killed her," Don said.

"I had nothing to do with it. I was a victim, too, for God's sake. Those guys, they were fucking crazy."

"Oh, I know that," Don said. "Though it was funny to see one of them going through his prayers at the end. 'Our Father, who art in heaven.' Well, God may be up there, I said, but you'll never see him, you piece of shit."

He put the gas can down. Reached to his back pocket and took out a lighter.

"No," Tory screamed. "Jack, don't let him do this."

I heard the faintest sound, a scrape below me. The ladder.

Clair.

"You sure you can't just do this outside, Don," I said. "I mean, I have no sympathy, none, for this guy. But this barn. And what if the smoke gets to the pony. Hay fires, they're really smoky."

"Jack, no," Tory screamed.

"Oh, don't I know it," Barbier said. "Wet hay? Smokes like hell. Learned a few things about fire over the years. Had to, get the job done. Really wanted to do this right, not just go around shooting people. That wouldn't do at all, not at—"

Tory lunged, got halfway to his feet. The shotgun boomed and Tory fell, his foot mangled, boat shoe shredded into bits of bloody leather and flesh. He fell back in the circle of gasoline, shrieking. Don lowered the gun, flicked the lighter. The click was loud, the flame bright in the dim light.

He moved around the circle toward me and the ladder, readying for his exit.

"Take it easy, Don," I said. "What if he's telling the truth? What if he was just a witness?"

"He sold them out," Don said. "Julie died. The coward traded her life for his."

He bent to the floor, held the lighter out to the puddle of gas. There was movement on the ladder and I said, "I don't know, Don. Seems like you've become just like them. Cheech and Bear and Kiko. They probably thought they had some justification for what they were doing, too. Business, sending a message, some twisted drug-dealer creed. You killed an innocent old man. A troubled kid. A woman with little kids. Lasha."

"Collateral damage," Barbier said, flicking the lighter again. It was the kind that stayed lit until you snapped the lid on it. "Like drone strikes in Afghanistan, as Russell used to say. Sometimes people are in the wrong place."

He leaned back down.

And Louis Longfellow came up out of the ladder hole, snapped four quick shots from a rifle. Barbier was still standing when the last shot hit him in the buttocks. He tried to get the lighter down but fell forward instead.

There was a whoosh and the flames shot sideways and I started to move, then stopped. Tory was screaming, his khakis starting to burn. Barbier's hands and arms were in the fire. I stood and watched as Louis popped out of the ladder way, the rifle in one hand, the .22. He started to move to the fire but I put my arm in front of him.

"Wait," I said.

They were both screaming now, swatting at the flames. The smoke was acrid, cloth burning, Tory's hair smoking. He was writhing now, rolling right into Don, who was trying to get up but couldn't. I watched, stood stock still. Their skin was blistering, hands slapping at the flames like they were swarms of biting bugs. As I watched I thought of Woodrow and Lasha. Eve and the old doctor. I thought of Julie, too.

I stood. Don was grunting. Tory shrieked. They both writhed.

"This is wrong," Louis said, and tried to move by me. I blocked him again, said, "No."

"Come on, McMorrow."

We were chest to chest, face-to-face, Louis moving right and left. I held his arms, pushed him back. Screams filled the loft, the smoke thick, curling to the peak of the roof.

"Enough, McMorrow," Louis shouted. "Enough."

He tried to shove me aside but I held him back, saw the panic in his wild eyes, heard the screams.

I held on.

I still held him.

Longer. Longer. Longer.

And then I let go.

We stomped the fire with our boots, snuffed the fire out, the blue flames flickering around our feet.

When there were no more flames, just the smell of gasoline and singed hair and burned flesh, we stopped.

I picked up the shotgun, its wooden stock charred, and tossed it to the side. Tory and Don were side by side on the plank floor, gasping and moaning. Don took a feeble swing at Tory and Tory held his arm up to block him. Both arms were blistered, hair burned off.

They fell back, Tory saying, "Oh, God help me—God help me."

Don said, "I'll still get you. I'll find you and kill you, I swear to God."

We stood, Louis was trembling. I reached for my phone just as Clair's head popped through the opening. He clambered up, surveyed the scene, said, "Log truck flipped; stanchion let go and spilled the load in the road. Had to take the long way around."

"It's okay," I said. "The Marines showed up."

We put the fire out with fire extinguishers from the shop, the gas burning but only singing the floorboards. And then a clamor of people, up and down the ladder.

The Prosperity Volunteer Fire Department in their boots and helmets, spraying the floor with extinguishers where the fire had been. Cops, state and county. Ambulances. Paramedics going up and down the ladder, IV bottles and tubes, stretchers hefted down the stairs. A helicopter to transport Don to the hospital in Portland, the gunshot wound and the burns a bad combination. Tory kept on screaming all the way out. Don was silent, staring straight ahead as they hoisted him aboard.

Scalabrini was there. Davida Reynolds. Even Trooper Foley.

Jack McMorrow: This is your life.

We sat in police cruisers and told the story. Me and Roxanne. Louis and Clair. Mary had Sophie in the house, making cookies, as Mary put it, "for all the nice policemen." Pokey got a bucket of oats for his troubles and calmly munched as the helicopter landed outside his paddock.

Skittish he was not.

Cops took notes, asked a lot of questions. Then they left, one by one.

Four murders solved, a bunch of arson cases. In that way, and only that way, it was a good day.

After my formal interviews, Davida Reynolds still wanted to talk.

We moved away from the group and stopped and leaned on the paddock fence. Pokey looked up from his stall at us, then bent back to his feed. On the far side of the paddock, Clair and Louis leaned and talked.

"It was clear Louis hadn't done anything," Reynolds said. "He said he never wanted to see fire again. After twenty minutes I brought him home."

"He told me he'd been watching Don because he knew Don had been watching Tory. At night," I said. "Then today he saw Don leave his house with the shotgun wrapped in a towel. He thought Don was gonna kill Tory someplace."

"He was right," Reynolds said.

"He'd killed Lasha. He was going down fast. Had to get it done before it was too late, before it all unraveled."

"I know you cared about her."

"I did," I said. "She was a special person."

"I'm sorry."

"Yes," I said. "I am, too."

Reynolds was quiet for a moment and then said, "Tory says you stood and watched and let him burn. Both of them."

"I'm not a firefighter," I said. "I guess I froze."

"He says you prevented Louis from coming to their aid."

I shrugged.

"So, a revenge arsonist. Multiple times. Fire for a fire, eye for an eye," she said.

"One for the books, huh?"

"I'm taking this as a learning moment," Reynolds said. "What could I have done differently?"

"Penney," I said.

She looked at me.

"Yeah. I should have considered that maybe he'd come up with something before he really started to lose it."

"On his good days, in his lucid moments, he probably was still a decent cop."

"But nobody took him seriously," she said. "It wasn't just me. I mean, he couldn't find his way back to the hotel in California. Lost the rental car. I mean, you couldn't put him on the witness stand."

Pokey chewed, swished his tail. Behind us the cop radios murmured.

"My other mistake," Reynolds said. "When the fires were all directed at Tory and Rita and Don, places they were connected to, and they were clearly being hurt by that, I figured somebody was targeting them. My hunch was that Louis was singling them out for some reason, some slight. I didn't think they could be targeting themselves."

"Or that they weren't a single unit. That one was targeting the others. And the fire at Don's was a smokescreen. Probably was going to raze the barn anyway."

She mulled it over, shook her head.

"Not sure where I went wrong there. The most basic question with an arson fire is always who stands to benefit."

"Hard to find the answer to that one unless you know who the players really are," I said.

Pokey lifted his head and eyed us, started to amble over. Reynolds bent down and picked a clump of clover and held it out. Pokey gummed it from her hand.

She said, "What did you learn from all of this, Mr. McMorrow?"

I thought for a minute.

"That people are weak. And troubled. Even the ones who seem to have it together. We just see the veneer, the public face. That innocent people die all around us. In fact, it's the innocent ones who die most."

Reynolds looked at me. Smiled. "I am what I seem, if that makes you feel any better."

Reynolds went back to the other cops. I walked around the paddock. Clair and Louis were leaning, silent now. I took a place beside Louis and put my arms up over the fence. Pokey headed over, ready for a handout.

"Thanks," I said.

Louis shrugged, stared straight ahead. We were quiet, and then Louis said, "The anger, the things you see—it just takes over you like a demon. Thing about evil is that it doesn't just destroy you or kill you. It can do that, but most of the time it just absorbs you. Sucks you in. And then you've gone over. If you do that, there's no going back. There are some black marks you can't erase."

I hesitated, then said, "But you've tried?"

He turned to me, smiled sadly.

"I'll die trying," Louis said, and he shoved himself back from the fence and turned away. He touched Clair on the shoulder on the way past, said, "Stay in touch, Recon."

Same fence, two hours later. Mary was leading Sophie around the paddock on Pokey. Sophie was holding the reins loosely, letting them drape in front of her.

"That's right, honey," Mary said. "Now that's a horsewoman."

I stood with Roxanne on my left, Clair on my right. Roxanne leaned against me. We watched Sophie, and Roxanne said, "I'm sorry. About your friend."

"Me, too," I said.

"It's so sad. Senseless."

"Yeah," I said. "Both those things."

"You liked her," Roxanne said.

"Yes, I did. She was an interesting person. Talented. Funny. She didn't deserve any of this."

"I'm sorry I was jealous."

I started to say there was no reason. I stopped.

Clair said, "Guy must have loved that girl, in a weird way, to track them all down over all these years."

"That's not love," Roxanne said. "That's obsession."

"A fine line," I said.

"No," Roxanne said. "This was all about Don, not about Julie. All this vengeance. Horrible."

I caught Clair's shrug. I waited.

"I don't know," he said. "Sometimes I think vengeance, reprisal—it's the only thing that maintains order. You hurt my family, I hurt yours. Otherwise there are no consequences."

"But then you're just repeating the same offense over and over," Roxanne said.

We were quiet for a minute, no way to resolve it. Roxanne shook her head.

"I've got to believe in the power of forgiveness," she said. "I'm thinking, once they find Alphonse, I'm going to meet with Beth. Help her get on track, if I can. See if we can get back to where she was before Ratchet died. She was doing okay then."

Alphonse. I felt a tremor. Anger. Fear. An urge to finish this once and for all. Me and Clair. Maybe Louis.

After all of this death and destruction, still a very loose end.

"Fine," I said. "Just make it a very public place."

That night Sophie fell asleep on our laps. I carried her upstairs and laid her in her bed and we tucked the blanket in around her. Then we walked down the hall to our room. We undressed and slid under the sheets and Roxanne rested her head on my shoulder. Outside the window a mourning dove played its ocarina song. We listened, and then it flew off into the dusk, its wings whistling.

"Do you ever think it's all going to hell, Jack?" Roxanne said. "I mean, all of the violence, the sadness?"

"Sure," I said. "And sometimes I feel like some sort of angel of death, people dying all around me. Maybe it's my fault, and there's nothing good anywhere. I mean, this was one little town, in one week. It's madness, and you can multiply it by the thousands."

I paused.

"But then I look around me, at you and Sophie, at Clair and Mary. And I know better."

"But Beth and Ratchet, and the fires. That poor boy and Lasha and the doctor, that mother with her young kids. And what about Alphonse? Where is he?"

"They'll find him," I said. "Don't despair."

"I know," Roxanne said.

"We're in this together, you know."

"I know that, too," she said.

"Fighting the good fight," I said.

"Always," she said.

I felt her smile, and I leaned down and kissed her forehead. She looked up at me and I kissed her lips. Gently, just a touch. She moved up and we embraced, and when our cheeks touched they were wet.

POSTSCRIPT

The *Times* sent a freelance photographer named Tilar Huntington up from Portland to shoot the Sanctuary story. Huntington was a go-to for the *Times*. She was persuasive, charming, beguiling, known for portraits that seemed to get inside the subject's head.

The people of Sanctuary shut her down.

No one in town wanted to be photographed for the story. Not Harold at the store, not the remaining members of the citizen's patrol, not Chief Frederick or Paulie or Ray-Ray, or Davida Reynolds or any of the cops.

My story ran with a single photo: a wide-angle shot of the square with the general store in the background. The photo was taken from across the green. The flag was at half-staff. A handwritten sign had been placed at the base of the flag pole. The sign said, PRAY FOR THEM.

HAUNTED BY WOMAN'S MURDER, VICTIM'S BOYFRIEND REPEATS THE CRIME
By Jack McMorrow

SANCTUARY, MAINE—A crime spree that left four people dead and a small town terrified ended here when a local man tried to kill a man he said was the last of the perpetrators of a double murder—a crime he had sworn to avenge.

Police say Derek Mays, 38, aka Don Barbier, tracked four men he contends burned his girlfriend to death in a drug-related execution twenty years ago. The young woman, Julie Barber, was said to have been a bystander when she died near Bangor, bound and gagged and left to die in a burning house. Mays, also from the Bangor area, tracked the men he believed responsible for the crime and killed three of them in separate arson fires in Arizona, California, and Georgia in recent years, he admitted to investigators.

Mays came to the small central Maine town of Sanctuary last spring in search of the fourth man, Tommy Stevens. Police say Tommy Stevens was known as Tory Stevens, a local real estate broker. The vendetta came to an end Thursday when Mays abducted Stevens and attempted to burn him alive in a barn in the nearby town of Prosperity. Stevens survived the incident, but both men suffered serious burns.

The murder of Julie Barber remains an open case, said Davida Reynolds, lead investigator for the Maine Fire Marshal's Office. Mays, who remains in a Boston burn center this week, along with Stevens, will be charged with multiple counts of arson and murder, Reynolds said.

"We hope this will bring closure and let this town start to heal," Reynolds said.

Four people died in Sanctuary: Lasha Cabral, 46, an artist who was strangled outside her home; Bertrand Talbot, 69, a retired physician who died in his summer home when it was set ablaze; Woodrow Harvey, 16, a high school student who was beaten when he came upon Mays starting a fire; and Eve Johnson, 28, a mother and housewife who died when her truck was deliberately run off the road. Police say Mays will be charged with at least one of the deaths, and possibly all four. He was said to be cooperating with investigators, although his injuries had delayed a full accounting for his actions.

Investigation of the Julie Barber killing is ongoing, Reynolds said.

She said she believed the Mays arrest "broke the chain," but acknowledged that this provides little consolation for the families of the deceased. "Evil begets evil," she said. "These were all good people who didn't deserve to be dragged into this."

Asked if Mays's motive was love or obsession, Reynolds said, "In this case it appears that one turned into the other."

She paused and added, "It happens, doesn't it?"